Lady of the Glen

Lady *of the* & *Glen*

a novel of 17th-century Scotland and the Massacre of Glencoe

Jennifer Roberson

Kensington Books

http://www.kensingtonbooks.com

KENSINGTON BOOKS are published by

Kensington Publishing Corp.
850 Third Avenue
New York, NY 10022

ISBN 1-57566-129-2

First Kensington Hardcover Printing: April, 1996
First Kensington Trade Paperback Printing: January, 1997

10   9   8   7   6   5   4   3   2   1

Printed in the United States of America

Acknowledgments

To the true professionals:
Russell Galen, agent; Ann LaFarge, editor
Deepest thanks for unflagging faith, support, and tenacity.
∽
And especially to the friends and family:
Debby Burnett; Mike Stackpole and Liz Danforth; Sam Stubbs;
Shera Roberson and S.J. Hardy; Georgana Wolff Meiner;
Arzelle Drew; Clare and Dick Witcomb;
Phil and Greta Murnane; Jay Dunkleberger; Tom Quaid;
Simon Hawke; Robyn Carr; Melanie Rawn; Alis Rasmussen;
Sam Hardy; New Years'/40th Birthday Gang;
Thursday Morning Corgi Club; GEnie "Runcibles;"
the household menagerie.
All of whom were there when I most needed them.

Preface

By the seventeenth century Scottish politics could not be divorced from English politics, and were directed from London at the behest of English monarchs. Yet despite the incompatibilities of language, dress, and customs, and despite England's numerous campaigns to subjugate the Scots, Scotland enjoyed in 1603 a perverse revenge: it was to Scotland unmarried Elizabeth I was forced to look for an heir, and on her death James VI of Scotland became James I of England.

Decades later, Oliver Cromwell subverted the monarchy, but his regime was of short duration; eventually Charles II, a Stuart, assumed the throne in place of his executed father. But the Queen was barren, and on Charles's death the throne passed to his brother, James—a man who provided both the English and the Scots new ground over which to battle. For James II was Catholic, and England Protestant.

In the midst of political turmoil, strong men came forward to demand the throne from James, an ineffectual and politically dangerous king. One of these men was Archibald Campbell, the ninth Earl of Argyll, a Scot who supported Charles II's illegitimate son, styled the Duke of Monmouth. This bid to wrest the throne from James and place his bastard nephew on it failed; Monmouth and Argyll both were executed.

Thus besieged, Catholic James II fled England for France, leaving the throne to his Protestant sister, Mary, who had married William of Orange, by blood half a Stuart, by upbringing thoroughly Dutch.

With James in exile, with William and Mary as joint monarchs, England settled into a measure of civil stability. But there was the war with France William was determined to win at all costs, and thus Scotland became vital to his success. William needed men. He wanted Scots. Primarily Highlanders, fierce and loyal fighting men who would serve ably as cannon fodder.

The Highlanders themselves were divded as usual by clan rivalry and feuding. It would take a very strong man to unite them, to persuade them to give up their oath to the exiled King James—a Stuart, a Scot—to swear allegiance to William and Mary. The Earl of Argyll, a Campbell, was dead. But another rose to the forefront, Grey John Campbell, the Earl of Breadalbane. And he, working closely with a Lowland Scot, Sir John Dalrymple, the Master of Stair, concocted a plan that would, by example, unify the Highlanders in the name of William and Mary.

But old oaths forgiven, and new oaths made, require peace. And peace in the Highlands was dearly bought with the blood of Glencoe.

Listen, then, to my pibroch,
it tells the news and tells it well
of slaughtered men
and forayed glen,
Campbell's banners and the victor's joy!

—Breadalbane bagpipe rant, 1692

Glen Lyon

Summer
1682

—so bonnie was he . . . bonnie, bonnie prince—bonnie lad, bonnie lad—

She made up the tune as she went, singing it in her head where no one could hear, neither her father the laird, called Glenlyon, nor her brothers, any of them, Robbie or Jamie, Dougal or Colin, who would surely laugh, or worse. She would offer them no *sgian dhu,* to stick its blade in her heart.

—with silver in his hair, and white teeth a'gleaming—

With grave deliberation, Catriona Campbell walked the wall. It was a pile of tumbled fieldstone, all ash and slate and pewter . . . was the drawbridge over the moat leading into the magical castle, where surely she would find her prince languishing in captivity, the bonnie prince, bonnie lad, with silver in his hair and white teeth a'gleaming.

—bonnie, so bonnie was he . . . Cat sucked at her lip, reconsidering. Not stone, but a serpent, a silver serpent; a silver serpent-bridge stretched from bank to bank across the moat full of kelpies bespelled by a witch. She would walk the magicked serpent to rescue her bonnie prince.

—silver in his hair, and white teeth a'gleaming . . . Traversing the serpent-bridge required such sacrifice as the shedding of shoes, which she undertook readily; immense concentration, with bony elbows out-thrust like the wings of a hissing greylag; and lastly, most importantly, the insertion of tender tongue between teeth. But the tongue was uninhibited by a portcullis of teeth. Ten-year-old Cat had shed her front teeth the week before.

"Hag!" her brothers had gleefully chorused immediately upon sighting her lack. "Toothless auld crone!"

To which Cat had replied, with grandiose derision, that at least *hers* would grow back in; fifteen-year-old Robbie, who had lost a dogtooth in a fistfight with a Campbell cousin, would lack his forever.

The argument but ten days before in the doorway of Chesthill, in the laird's own house, might have escalated into a pitched battle save for the intervention of her oldest brother, Robbie, who had led the chorus himself. He merely picked his sister up, lugged her out of doors to the barrel put out to collect rainwater, and stuffed her headfirst into it.

Bubbling outrage, Cat banged and scraped her elbows, thrashed her legs frenziedly, and eventually realized she might do better to husband her breath rather than spend it on curses. She stilled, holding the remnants of air, hoarding her last reserve, aware of pressure stuffing her ears, dimness crowding her eyes, and the taste of whiskied water.

Sturdy Robbie slapped her on the rump as if she were a weanling calf, then dragged her forth. "There now, Cat, ye'll learn your manners better."

In silence, courting patience, Cat allowed him to set her on her feet. Inside her head sounded a voice, *her* voice, the one she kept secret from others. —*wait you . . . wait you, Cat*—

Robbie grinned, displaying the gap in his teeth. "There, now, Cat—"

—*now*— She loosed the mouthful of water in a deliberate, vigorous spray that soaked Robbie's face. Astonished, he let her go; Cat tore loose and ran away before Robbie or the others, equally astonished, could catch her again.

Heading toward the front door of her father's house, Cat twisted her head to cast a glance at her brothers. Robbie, Dougal, Colin, and Jamie were, as she fully expected, in demented pursuit.

—*I'll beat you*— A vicious, malignant joy welled up in Cat's chest as she thought quickly ahead to escape.

She snatched open the door, darted through, delayed three ticks of a clock, then slammed it shut in their faces.

Silence. There were no shouts, no threats, no flinging open of the door. Poised to flee, Cat waited for the rattle of the latch, the adolescent curses, the cacophony of brothers bent on punishing the youngest of them all, and a lass at that. They made a practice of it.

Surely they would come. They always had before.

Wet from her hips up, Cat dripped onto the polished oak of her father's floor. Foreboding knotted her belly. She scowled at the nearest glazing, wondering if her foolish brothers would have the temerity to break it. Glass windows cost dearly; likely there'd just be a shutter nailed over it again, and they'd lack for daylight in the gray gloom of a Scottish winter, still months away.

And then the door at last was flung open. Cat twitched, preparing to run, and felt the welling up in her chest of the great shout she meant to make, fierce as a clansman slicing the air with a deadly claymore.

But the shout withered to breathy exhalation; shock grew roots from bare feet into the hardwood floor.

—*not Robbie*— Nor Jamie, nor Colin, nor Dougal, but a man she did not know. Cat gaped. —*giant*—

In fact, the largest man she had ever seen, *ever*, even in her dreams. His height was such that he was required to stoop to enter her father's house, so he wouldn't knock his white-maned head on the lintel . . .

after he jerked open the heavy wooden door and bellowed rudely for attention. —*like one of Father's bulls*—

"I am MacIain," he shouted, "come to speak to a Campbell, aye?— and wi'out a dirk in my hand, or a sword, but soft words and fine courtesy in my mouth, instead." He paused just inside the door, now filled with other men, and none of them her father's. "I am Glencoe," he roared, "come to speak with Glenlyon!"

Transfixed by his hugeness, his thunder, his overwhelming *presence,* Cat stood before him, dripping, staring, because she could not believe any man would shout so in her father's house, or make such outrageous statements.

The giant eventually looked down at her. She saw the great white mane curling around broad shoulders; a thicket of brows hedging blue eyes; backswept, elegant moustaches, and thick, snowy beard.

Zeus! she decided instantly, well taken by the tales her brothers had told her of Olympian lairds. But this Zeus was plainly a Scot: she saw the sett of his plaid; the great circle-shaped penannular brooch pinning the cloth crosswise to the shoulder of his buff-dyed jacket; the silver clan badge and accompanying plant crest affixed to his dark blue bonnet, clinging slantwise, Highland-style, to his massive head.

The badge glinted in wan light, transfixing her gaze. She saw the crest more clearly than the rest: a sprig of purple heather. And so she knew who he was, this giant, and what the giant wanted, and of what treatment he was deserving, he and his clansmen, his tacksmen, all gathered behind in the doorway.

She did not see her brothers. Had they run, then, knowing whom they faced? Had MacIain chased them away?

Cat was humiliated. Carefully, she spat onto the floor before his feet, clad in leather brogues glinting of silver buckles. "Dinna you knock on doors in Glencoe?" she asked with a ten-year-old's eloquent derision born of a lifetime of bloody feuding. "Dinna you behave yourselves like true men do, and come wi' manners as well as shouting?"

Blue eyes in deep sockets caught fire. He bent down, put out large hands, caught her by the upper arms. The growl arose from deep in his plaid-swathed chest. "Dinna ye ken who I am?"

She did. They all knew him, and cursed him over whisky. "I do! MacDonalds, from Glencoe: the Gallows Herd itself, come to steal more cows from Glen Lyon!"

Huge fingers clamped more tightly upon soaked linen and the fragile arms beneath. He plucked her from the ground as easily as he might a sprig of heather. He lifted her and left her hanging in midair, wholly dependent upon his temper as to whether she would be set down again, or dropped.

—dinna drop me— She thought he might; he was that angry. But he didn't. He drew her close, still hanging, and thrust his big, bearded face into her own considerably smaller one. "Dinna the Campbells teach *you* manners, then?"

He was hurting her, though she doubted he knew it. He was so huge and she so thin; undoubtedly he'd forgotten how solid his grasp on her arms. And scrawny arms they were, too, like all the rest of her.

"I *am* a Campbell!" she cried. "And Glenlyon has taught me all the manners I must have, dealing with MacDonalds!"

"Has he, now? And why?—what would the laird want with a tart-tongued scullion like you?"

She gaped. Scullion, indeed! Her father would be furious.

But for the moment, her father wasn't present. "Put me down," she said. "Put me *down,* MacDonald, and take your hands from the flesh of a trueborn Campbell!"

He laughed. The giant *laughed,* throwing back the large head with its tangled swath of snowy curls. And then he set her down, firmly, and took his hands from her arms. She forebore to rub them. "Trueborn Campbell, are ye? Well, then, fetch your master, lass, and tell him Mac-Iain is here to speak words wi' him."

"I'm certain he knows," she said coldly, "you with all your shouting."

And indeed her father did know, shouting or not, and was abruptly *there:* startled, puzzled, frowning, yet saying nothing that might cause dirks to be drawn, or swords. Her brothers, brave now in his presence, gathered behind him, slanting her startled, disbelieving glances.

Have they naught to say to him? Campbells to a MacDonald? Well, if they did not, she did; and would say it, wouldn't she, no matter what others thought!

Men came into the house behind the MacIain, Highlanders all, like him, in kilts and breeks and bonnets, all wearing bright sprigs of heather and showing hard MacDonald faces. She liked none of them, not knowing what they wanted, and particularly misliking the way they brushed her aside, this way and that, until she stood at the open door, alone, behind the sea of tall MacDonalds.

Whom her father was welcoming in.

MacDonalds, in the house.

Surely the world had ended. Or surely the world would; likely the MacDonalds intended to murder them all.

Where are OUR men—? Where were the Campbell men sworn to the laird of Glenlyon?

The only men in her father's house was the laird himself, called Glenlyon for his holdings; her brothers, who were boys; and a hard-faced clutch of Glencoe MacDonalds, whom she knew, and had always known —*and likely will always know!*— as the Enemy.

Catriona Campbell, like her brothers before her, had suckled on bedtime tales of MacDonald enmity; of the raids to lift Glenlyon's cattle, to plunder Glenlyon's holdings, to injure Glenlyon's men. In her turbulent, angry dreams, Glenlyon's only daughter courted a perfect revenge.

Now she moved to slam shut the door, hoping its noise would remind MacIain of his neglectfulness; what manner of man left open doors to houses? But a hand was there before her, preventing the closure, purposely holding the door open.

She looked up at once, thrusting out her chin. The voice in her head rang loudly. *Dinna stop ME!*

She tugged at the door rudely, challenging his grasp; he did not permit it, which infuriated her. She glared at him all the harder, wishing she could kick him in the shin so he'd turn his attention elsewhere. But something about his posture stopped her.

He wasn't a giant, like MacIain, being of a size with other men, if tall as opposed to short. And he was smiling at her, a little, but with no dirk in it, as if he understood her feelings of anger, resentment, hurt.

Cat didn't smile back. *MacDonald!*

The man looked down on her, but his expression lacked the ridicule of MacIain's. Gravely he studied her, marking her expression, the set of her chin, the tears of humiliation in her eyes.

"Come out the house," he said gently. "Leave the others to their business."

"Cat," Robbie warned; he was the eldest, and knew MacDonalds best.

For that, then, she went out the house, to poke a stick at Robbie.

The day was bright, dusted with dew. It glistened against the ground except where the MacDonalds had trampled it into the dirt. In deference to summer and Highland custom Cat's feet were bare, making their own prints. She studied her muddied toes a long moment, wondering what he thought of a barefoot, dripping, hot-faced Campbell; then fired up again as she reminded herself it made no difference at all *what* he thought of her, she being bred of Glen Lyon and he of Glencoe.

He linked his hands behind his back as if to indicate he offered no hostility, no hand with a dirk in it, but she knew better. —*dirks come from beHIND backs as well as from in front!* She scowled fiercely, clenching her teeth, daring him to try.

He said nothing of her damp state, though plainly he saw it. He smiled. "Little Campbell," he said, with no derision in it, "my father's a harsh-speaking man. But he means nothing hostile by it, being more intent on the reason for coming to Glen Lyon, and to the house of his enemy."

"*His* choice," she stressed, raising her chin defiantly. "Tell him to no' send his men out to steal our cows."

His smile widened. "Well, I will, then, for you—though I doubt 'twill do much good. We've been at it for years and years, ye ken . . . and Campbells returning the favor."

She knew it to be true, no matter what she felt. Her kin and his had traded black-coated cattle for years, albeit unwillingly, and in the dark of countless Highland nights with only the moon to see.

He sat down on the bench beside the door, linking hands over one bent knee. She lingered, irresolute—this man was a *MacDonald;* after a moment, discarding the opportunity to leave, she sat down beside him, pointedly keeping her distance. She ignored soaked braids exuding rivulets of water. "You're MacIain's son?"

"Second son," he elaborated. "Alasdair *Og,* as I'm younger, but you should call me Dair. I much prefer it to Sandy. Too many men are Sandys."

She nodded emphatic understanding. "Too many girls are Catriona, and so my father calls me Cat."

"Cat Campbell." He grinned. "Aye, a cat, not kitten; I've seen your claws unsheathed."

"There was need for them," she told him plainly. "He was rude—and shouting, besides."

He nodded, unperturbed by the bluntness that disturbed so many others. "MacIain rarely whispers. Even to his sons." White teeth glinted briefly. "Though he's more quiet with his grandson."

"You have a wife?" She thought him young for it. Then again, not; he was at the very least sixteen. He was man, not lad.

He grinned again, unhindered by his knowledge of who he was, or what *she* was: Glenlyon's daughter. The flesh crinkled at the corners of his eyes. "Not I; my brother, John. There's no woman in my house." He looked down at her. "And have they promised you yet?"

The curl of humiliation twisted in her chest, dug deeply into her belly. But her tone gave him nothing save scorn for ignorant people. "Not *me* . . . who'd be wanting—" But she broke it off; she would no more put a *sgian dhu* into his hand than into the hands of her brothers, who would happily prick her with it. After all, she knew very well what she was; those same brothers had made it plain.

Weary of dripping braids, Cat squeezed out excess water. The fingers that worked the hair were long, large, bony, and the thin pale flesh, where it wasn't scabbed over, displayed blue veins. The braids themselves, when dry, were a vivid, flamboyant red; wet, a bloody auburn. Her father once had said there was nothing subtle about her, in spirit or coloring. She had asked him what he meant by the word *subtle*, not knowing what it was, but he had laughed and merely said she'd know it herself, one day.

Cat did not know it, yet. She wondered if MacIain's son did, weighing her with inner words she could not comprehend.

Suspicious, she slanted him a glance. His expression was free of beguilement as he looked straight back at her, offering no answer, neither disagreement nor confirmation.

For all he was a MacDonald, he had sense. He offered no falsehoods by naming her beautiful, or promising a handsome husband. But he was, after all, a MacDonald; perhaps it was intended as a different kind of torment. Perversely she appreciated it, for truth was important to her. She hated idle falsehoods, no matter how well intended.

He studied her as critically but not unkindly, unlike her father once a year on her birthday, when he despaired aloud of ever finding a husband for Glenlyon's plain-faced lass; unlike her brothers, who did it happily out of spite.

Alasdair Og—*Dair*—MacDonald smiled faintly, as if he understood what was in her mind. "Not a beauty, no," he said quietly at last, "not now. But you'll grow, Cat Campbell, and what you hate about yourself now may well be different when you're older."

She scoffed, mimicking the rude sounds of her brothers, who mimicked the tacksmen, which widened his smile.

He exchanged one paramount knee for the other and leaned nonchalantly against the wall. Sunlight glinted wanly on a silver clan badge. "It happened to me."

"To you?"

"I was early in my birth, and a wee bairn for so long they despaired of my life." He shrugged elegantly. "I stayed small for fourteen years, Cat—so small for so long men began to say amongst themselves perhaps I was a changeling, and not MacIain's son at all."

"Changeling!"

He grinned, slanting a bright glance her way. "You've seen MacIain. Nigh on seven feet, he is . . . and John is three fingers over six."

She eyed his folded body up and down, calculating its length. "You're not so small now."

"I grew. 'Tis respectable I am, six feet even." The corners of his eyes crinkled again. "But it came late, verra late, long after I feared to be a runtling all my life."

She caught a bedraggled braid and shut it up in one hand. "You're saying I might do the same?"

"I'm saying you will." Brown eyes were warm. They were cider-bright, and whisky-dark, and something else her father called brandy-wine, glowing rich amber-gold. He had showed the drink to her once, before gulping all of it down. "But the truth of it is, they'll be finding someone for you no matter what happens. Glenlyon's lass is worth something."

Glenlyon's lass isna. But she didn't voice it to him. "Why have you come to this house?"

"MacIain wants a truce."

She was a deflating bagpipe, expelling it abruptly. "With *Glenlyon?*"

He nodded ruefully. "We've a problem with MacGregors."

Cat was only ten years old, but in the Highlands ten was not so young to know the business of adults. She had been raised on Campbell history, and the histories of others. The MacGregors as a clan had been broken years and years before by Letters of Fire and Sword, proscribed by the Crown, which took everything from the MacGregors: houses, cattle, crops, clan holdings, even their very name. Those remaining lived like bandits where and as they could, in secret, little more than animals. Many of them lived on Rannoch Moor, the bog-strewn barrier between Glencoe and Glen Lyon. But some of them lived very near Glencoe, stealing MacDonald cattle.

Cat almost laughed. The MacDonalds, who stole Campbell cows, wanted to enlist Campbell aid against MacGregors who stole *Mac-Donald* cattle.

MacIain's son, seeing her amusement, nearly laughed as well. But it was a wry, crooked, bonnie smile, white teeth a'gleaming, that bespoke his awareness of irony; almost at once, despite her inclination, despite his name, and *hers,* Cat was vanquished by that smile, the face, and the eyes kindling in it.

But he was still Enemy; she daren't give in to him.

Red-faced, Cat frowned, seeking words to remind him of who they were and where he was, speaking to Glenlyon's daughter. "Your hair has *speckles* in it."

At once he put up his hand, fingering the faint silver hoarfrost amidst the near-black beneath his bonnet. "Eighteen and near to gray," he said ruefully. " 'Tis a family trait."

"Not so much," she assured him, enmity melting away in the face of his resignation; she well knew what it was to hate one's appearance. "Most 'tis nearly black."

"But I'll be white-headed before I'm forty." His smile was back, full-fledged, working its magic on her. "Especially treating wi' Campbells."

His lilting Scots came and went, sometimes very strong, sometimes suppressed by nuances of another accent she didn't know. She studied him more closely. A Scotsman, aye, and Highland-born, in the shadow of the Devil's Staircase west of Rannoch Moor. He wore tartan breeks like the tacksmen, forgoing a kilt, pinned plaid thrown over one shoulder, and a bonnet with badge and heather crest; no different from anyone else. But there was something more to him. *He's no' like the others.* "Have you been in England?"

He shook his head, smiling. "In the land of the Sassenachs? Och, no—*France,* last year, and I'm due to go again." The wry twist of his mouth showed itself. "MacIain has a surpassing fondness for refinement, when he can get it; he sent John before me to Paris, and now Alasdair Og." He shrugged. "I'll be back soon enough."

"If you survive the MacGregors."

He grinned engagingly; he lacked none of *his* teeth. "Oh, I think I will. We're bonnie fighters, lass . . . and I've a mind to live forever."

Something cold touched her spine. "No one lives forever."

"Scotland will, my lass. Have ye no' heard it on the pipes?"

Cat grimaced. "My father plays the pipes. Whenever he's *fou.*"

Dair MacDonald laughed. "Sober, the pipes are difficult—*drunk,* impossible!"

"A bag of hooting, honking wind, like the geese gone over the lochs." Cat sighed forlornly. "Auld Robbie the Red died last year—he was our clan piper—and since then we've had naught but my father's noise."

Alasdair Og nodded his sympathies, though his mouth twitched. "Then come to Glencoe, my lass, and hear our Big Henderson. He'll wrench the tears from your eyes." He leaned down toward her, brushing her shoulder with his, speaking warmly and very softly. "You've bonnie eyes, my lass . . . all bluey-green and bright. The sort of eyes a Highlander likes to come home to."

Cat smiled sweetly. *"After* a cattle raid?"

He threw back his head and laughed out loud, much as his father had done. But the thick locks beneath his heather-sprigged bonnet were black instead of white, with only a frosting of gray.

The door was opened then and a tall MacDonald showed his face, framed by dark hair more generously salted with silver. "Alasdair," he said, "you're wanted. What are you doing out here?"

"Passing the time wi' a sharp-tongued Campbell lass." With a secret smile for Cat, Dair rose with indolent grace. "She was right to take him to task, John; 'tis no' our father's house."

Cat barely glanced at MacIain's heir. Instead she looked at Dair standing before her door, wanting to say something to him, to thank him for his kindness and understanding. But what she meant to say fell away; something entirely different slipped out between her teeth. "Dinna steal our cows no more."

John, astonished, stared. But Dair, understanding, laughed aloud again, setting brown eyes alight in a face dark as a Spaniard's. And then he told her good-bye and with his brother went into the house, *her* house, and shut the door behind them, leaving her alone.

Wishing he'd come back out.

Even if he were a MacDonald, and she Glenlyon's daughter.

Memory was vivid. Cat sighed atop the wall that was bridge over the moat, recalling the introduction with exquisite clarity; she had dreamed of him every night since.

—a bonnie, bonnie prince, wi' silver in his hair . . . The serpent-bridge was quiescent as Cat negotiated its treacheries. Not so many steps left to her now. *—bonnie, bonnie lad* . . . He lay beyond, in the castle. She had only to cross the moat, to break the bonds, and spells—

"*Cat!*" Robbie bawled, from just behind.

The serpent-bridge was banished, as was her balance. Cat wavered atop the wall. Jamie, Dougal, and Colin, seeing her state, jeered and hooted, grasping her ankles to shake them.

Dignity, too, was dismissed, coordination utterly vanquished. Cat fell, landing awkwardly in dirt and turf and manure square on elbows and buttocks, which only gave her brothers more fodder for their gibes.

She blinked back tears of embarrassment and glared at them all. Robbie grinned, baring the gap in his teeth. "No more MacDonalds," he said. "Or shall I dunk you in the barrel again to wash them out of your head?"

She scrambled up, prepared to flee. "They've more manners than you!" She thought of Alasdair Og; of the bonnie, bonnie prince with silver in his hair.

"Oh, have they?" Robbie, at fifteen, was the eldest of them all. They were all of them red-haired, though Cat's the most vivid; the boys took after their father, with more yellow in the red. "We've heard naught from you but MacDonalds, MacDonalds, MacDonalds since MacIain was here last week!"

"What of it?" Cat swatted dirt from the seat of her trews, hoping they would not notice the flush that burned her cheeks. "We've sworn an alliance, now—we're no more enemies!"

"No more?" Jamie jeered. "Then what of the cattle they lifted last night?"

"Last night?" Cat stared. "Last night?"

Dougal nodded. "They came across in the moonlight and lifted fourteen cows."

"They didna!"

"They did!" Four faces scowled back at her. Robbie's was the blackest. "Go ask Father, then, ye bizzem; he'll tell you the truth of it."

"They swore a truce, Father and MacIain!"

Robbie scoffed. "Shows you what their oaths are worth, then. Go ask him, Cat." His expression altered, fading from belligerence to momentary disgust. "If he'll take his mouth from the whisky glass long enow to tell you."

I'll no' listen to their muckle-mouthed jabbering. Cat turned her back on them. *They're naught but moudiworts.*

"He was *with* them!" Robbie shouted as she stalked toward the house. "One of the tacksmen saw him!"

She did not ask. She would not give them the satisfaction. Nor did she need to ask. She knew whom he meant. She knew all too well.

It infuriated her, that they could use it to hurt her; that she had invented the weapon. But far worse was the pain, the regret, the grief in the knowledge that Glenlyon's own daughter was foolish enough to permit herself the conviction that a MacDonald spoke the truth.

The voice in her head was conspicuously silent. No chiding, no chastisement; nor a wail of disbelief. Perhaps it had known all along, even if she had not.

They were hot, the tears, and quick, like the stabbing humiliation. Her grime-smeared face was wet as Cat snatched open the door. She slammed it closed once through, shutting away the memories of kind words and kinder eyes.

Trying to shut them away.

The voice in her head gave way to the one in her throat. "No better," she choked. "No better than anyone else!"

The latch rattles. She takes a step toward it, reaches out a hand, and then the door is thrown open to admit riotous images:

—blowing snow become blizzard—

—men clustered in her dooryard—

—red-coated soldiers with muskets and swords—

Their mouths and noses are masked by cloth. The man in the doorway raises his musket. "Campbell?" he asks sharply.

There are questions in her mind but her mouth forms only one. "What are you doing here?"

He levels the gun and fires.

Part I

1685

One

Cat Campbell, flattened behind the bug-ridden peat pile to hide herself from Robbie and the lass but a stone's throw down the hill, was at first aghast that her brother would dare such thing, this forcing a kiss from a woman— —*no, a lass still is Mairi Campbell, not so much older than me*— —but Robbie had always been a lad who took, be it from his sister or younger brothers, and now, at eighteen, was counted a man. He was eldest, he was heir, he was Glen Lyon's future; they had no choice but to give to the one what he wanted, who would one day be laird.

Cat grimaced. *Robbie would take it today, given the moment!*

But he wouldn't be given the moment. His father, for all Glenlyon drank, still held authority. Robbie would have to wait.

But not just at this moment, with Mairi Campbell.

Cat scowled. The pungent odor of drying peat cut out of the hillside filled her nostrils, left its taste in her mouth. But it was not *her* mouth which claimed her attention, now; the mouths glued together below, seeking, sucking, smacking—

" 'Tis her," Cat muttered. *"Her* as much as Robbie." And as bad, she decided, as a ram with a ewe, or a dog with a bitch, if somewhat more polite; Mairi, at least, seemed to *want* the attention.

Cat's lip curled. The movements were confusing, and without dignity. How could Mairi expose herself so? How could she let Robbie dictate what she would do?

"Not me," she declared to the peat. "I'll no' give up so much of myself like—like . . . *that*—"

And likely a bairn would come of it; often the ewes and bitches settled after consorting with the male. Which put in her mind her father, and the mother she barely recalled.

Cat grimaced. Disgusting indeed, that her mother would permit such liberties, such indignities of person. Five children of it, not counting the bairns who died. And Robbie, born first of them all, seemed wholly intent on starting a string of bairns even as his father before him.

Mairi Campbell, Cat decided, was a fool. Unless she *wanted* a bairn; or possibly wanted Robbie.

That was a thought worth considering. Cat scowled over it and turned her back on them, leaning instead against the pile of peat squares while she contemplated the unexpected and alien idea of having a sister.

The crowd in Inchinnan, a hungry hound, was fed on anticipation. Alasdair Og MacDonald, in its midst, was less a hound than others, but nonetheless sensed it, smelled it, tasted it. If the captive were not brought out soon, the Marquis of Atholl—the victor conducting the execution—would soon find himself struggling to control the very men who had supported him against the man he meant to die.

Dair chewed absently at his bottom lip. *A hound starved for too long*— And wanting blood for blood, to pay back the loser for his temerity in trying to replace one king with another. *They hate him as much for his title* . . . And for his name, his heritage; for the blood of their kin spilled during decades of his power, and the decades before his birth: he was the ninth Earl of Argyll, Archibald Campbell, once the most powerful man in Scotland. *Now naught but a traitor condemned to die.*

The square was filled with Jacobites, Highlanders sworn to King James despite his Popery; he was, after all, a Stuart, and therefore Scottish—and they had not fought for James so much as *against* Argyll and Clan Campbell, and cared little enough for the political vagaries of England. What concerned these men, lairds and chiefs and tacksmen, was the ending of Campbell power.

It was mid-May and warm; warmer yet because of so many wool-swathed men packed together. Dair was aware, as always, of his father's huge body overshadowing his own. They had named him for his father, then called him *Og* so as not to confuse others in reference, but by adolescence Dair knew very well the distinction was unnecessary.

A stirring ran through the crowd. The hound shifted stance, hackles rising, then moved aside sullenly as the master brought out the miscreant who would die for his heritage and clan affiliation as much as for his belief in a king other than James.

Caught in the shuffle as the crowd was parted, Dair saw nothing of Argyll as the man was led out. He saw only his own father's fierce face, nearly buried in beard and moustaches, and the glitter in hard eyes. "Campbell," MacIain muttered, "your cattle will be in my glen before the month is done."

Dair looked beyond to the center of Inchinnan's square. Beside the Mercat Cross stood the Maiden, the woman whom no man desired. The guillotine machine was lashed to a wooden platform with wheels at each corner, so it might more easily be taken from place to place. The steel blade, raised high, was as yet unblemished by the gore of

Argyll's death. It glinted in clean Highland sunlight. *How many necks will she kiss—?*

But the thought was broken off as MacIain's callused hand came down on his second son's plaid-swathed shoulder and closed so tightly Dair nearly grimaced. "Count your cows," the laird rumbled. "With each drop of his Campbell blood, count it a cow for Glencoe!"

The warping of the crowd left a channel between oceans of kilts and plaids and gave Dair a clear view. Surrounded by the enemy, the ninth Earl of Argyll walked steadily to meet the Maiden.

"Traitor begets traitor," MacIain muttered. Then, in a lion's roar: *"Traitor begets traitor!"*

Argyll's step faltered as he heard the shout and the response it prompted; the eighth earl, his father, had also been charged a traitor. Dair knew this day was the genesis of legend: because father and son were executed, they would say the loins were tainted.

He glanced at his brother. It was John, not he, who was heir; John, not Alasdair Og, who would be judged by his predecessor. He was himself entirely free to act in whatever manner he chose —*with my loins left out of it!*

Argyll stopped altogether as he reached the enemy from whom the shout had issued, the white-haired Glencoe giant known to all as MacIain. There Argyll held his ground, if briefly, to match fixed, unwavering gazes; to witness an enmity and spite that were yet mutual but would be, very shortly, a one-sided affair, because only a man with a head on his shoulders could nurse a Highland feud.

Nostrils pinched in Argyll's aristocratic face, as if he smelled a foul odor. Unlike MacIain's it was not a warrior's face, not the face of a man who wielded a sword but who wielded the words that would set men against men, Scot against Scot, Highlander against Highlander.

The Earl of Argyll disdained his soiled kilt and torn coat, the spatters of flung mud, the ruffling of his hair by an impudent wind uncognizant of his rank. His bare head, naked of bonnet, struck Dair as oddly vulnerable: a thistle on too slender a stalk. Would the executioner, once his task was completed, catch a fistful of the graying hair and hoist the grisly prize?

Argyll's face was stubbled and grimy. The bruised mouth, so tautly compressed, loosened to emit a curiously flat voice. "There were Campbells before me. There will be Campbells after me. But what will they say of Glencoe when all the MacDonalds are dead?"

It silenced those near enough to hear. In the mass of shorter men, MacIain had no need to raise his voice, to lift a hand, or rely on artifice in stance or gesture to hold the attention of his kin, or the others in the square. He smiled. He jerked his head toward the guillotine. Teeth gleamed briefly in the mass of curling white hair. "Dinna keep her waiting, your woman. She despises a cold cock, aye?"

In the male roar of approbation for the vulgar sally, Argyll was escorted to the Maiden. He offered no statement, no declaration of innocence; he had backed the wrong man and now would die for it, as his father before him, the powerful marquis, had been executed for his beliefs.

But as the Maiden's blade descended, Argyll, leader of Clan Campbell, locked eyes with MacIain. The gaze was broken only as the blade dropped and the neck was severed, and the wind-ruffled head toppled onto stained wood in a gout of arcing blood.

MacIain's eyes narrowed. His head rose a fraction, lifting his bearded chin. Nostrils flared once above the grandiose sweep of dual moustaches. Even as his mouth tightened the flesh by his eyes hardened.

This hunt, then, was finished, but there would be another. Dair, like his father, like his brother, knew too much of Campbells to dismiss the great clan's power with the death of a single man. There would be another.

Uneasily Dair muttered, "There is always another man."

The Earl of Breadalbane, Grey John Campbell, had never been a man who forsook opportunity when it behooved his plans. In his expensive Edinburgh town house near Holyrood Palace, Breadalbane received the news of the Earl of Argyll's execution with the grave concern and deep regret due the bereaved; Argyll had been his nephew. He closeted himself in his private quarters, poured himself whisky, then walked deliberately to the mullioned window overlooking Canongate.

All was darkness, save for a winking necklace of palace lamps, and the diffused glow of distant torches atop the massive rock hosting Edinburgh Castle. Breadalbane stared fixedly at the black bulk of castle. He was a robust man not dissimilar to his dead nephew: clear gray eyes; a narrow, prominent nose; thin, compressed lips; and the fair skin and reddish hair, now graying, not uncommon to Highlanders. He was no longer young, at fifty, but neither was he too old to comprehend or appreciate the politics of the situation.

Breadalbane drank most of his whisky, savoring the pungent, peat-flavored taste. He envisioned the execution; the report said Argyll had coupled with the Maiden in a brief, deadly embrace.

Argyll is dead.

A tremor of unexpected emotion caused the tide of whisky to slop against costly glass. The earl stilled it instantly, squeezing the glass with thin, well-groomed fingers; he was not a man given to physical display, lest it hand claymore to the enemy.

Argyll's death was significant. The enemies of Clan Campbell would move to replace the traditional strength of Argyll's clan—and Breadalbane's—with another, possibly even the tumultuous, thieving Mac-Donalds, that most despised of all clans, though particularly by Campbells; specifically by Breadalbane. MacDonald holdings were wide-ranging, their numbers vast.

Taut lips parted in a brief rictus of enmity. "Their women are rabbits," Breadalbane murmured, "and their men rut upon them like boars. 'Tis why they steal the Campbell cows, to fill their gawping mouths!"

Argyll is dead.

Breadalbane stood transfixed a moment, staring blindly into darkness. Clan Campbell was in one fell slice of the guillotine blade rendered leaderless.

Argyll is DEAD—

Abruptly he barked a brief, satisfied laugh and raised a mute toast to the executed. He in his nephew's place now commanded Clan Campbell. And he in his *own* place would find a way to destroy the MacDonalds.

The Laird of Glenlyon let the reeds slip from his mouth. No more keening wail of pipe-song; he was left now with nothing but a clutch of raddled leather hugged against his ribs.

Christ Jesus . . . He exhaled heavily, emptying his lungs as the bagpipes had emptied, wishing he might give way to a belly-deep moan as evocative as the instrument's wail and wheeze. But there was no one to fill him again, to set lips to his reeds and breathe new life into his spirit, that he might once again fill the air with a rousing pibroch, a battle rant so stirring that he would go down against the enemy knowing himself invincible.

He was not invincible. The battle he fought was personal, and the enemy himself.

He looked around his room, marking sparse furnishings, an interior as naked as his own. Chesthill was not a huge, imposing manor such as the English had, or rich Lowlanders. It wasn't even a castle, and certainly not a palace. It was, simply, a stone-built Highland house, large enough for Glenlyon, his daughter, his sons, and a handful of loyal Campbell servants. He was laird over all of Glen Lyon, but he wasn't a rich one. He wasn't a poor one. What he was, was bankrupt.

It was dark, save for smoky light exuded from the oil lamp on the table next to his elbow, beside the decanter and brimming silver cup. It cast but piecemeal illumination; the lamp glass was caked black with the soot of oily smoke, so that only the smudged blots made by finger-marks let the light shine through cleanly.

If there were another way . . . Glenlyon stirred sharply in the chair: an awkward, involuntary spasm of denial, of acceptance, of an abiding despair impinging on desperation. His movement brought forth a final brief wheeze from the bagpipes. He did not take up the reeds again or set aside the pipes; forgotten, he allowed the instrument to fall slackly between his ribs and the chair as he reached for the cup of whisky.

As he drank, taking solace in the harsh seduction of the liquor, he heard the scratching at the door. *No, no—not now—*But wishing away solved nothing. If such things as that had power, he'd be a man of honor again, a man with dignity, with all his debts paid off and his heritage unencumbered.

The scratch sounded again, more importunately. He was tempted to ignore it altogether; a servant, receiving no answer, would go away. But he knew the sound. It was Cat, not a gillie; wearily, falling back against his chair, the fifth Laird of Glen Lyon called for his daughter to enter.

She was dressed for bed, as she should be at such a late hour: a tattered tartan plaid doubling as shawl was pulled haphazardly across thin shoulders clad in dingy nightclothes. Her hair was braided carelessly, one loose strand hanging beside her face. It was, like the braid itself, a brilliant, unmistakable *red,* even in wan light; he had not bequeathed his daughter the yellowed strawberry of his own now-graying hair, nor the watery gray-blue eyes through which he watched the world.

Acknowledgment pinched; he had sired handsome boys, and one unhandsome daughter. *What will I do with this lass? What man will have her?*

Barefoot, Cat came into the room and stopped but two paces from the open door, as if wary of his mood. She left herself escape; Glenlyon's smile was warped as he recognized the foresight, the care with which she approached the man who had sired her.

He was not so *fou,* so drunk as to be blind to her resolution. He saw it in her eyes, in her jutting chin, in the stubborn set of her mouth. "Tomorrow," she said.

"Tomorrow," he agreed; there was no need to elaborate.

Blue-green eyes held steady. "Can I come?"

"You canna."

The wide mouth—too wide for her face, he thought absently—tightened fractionally. "You promised me I could go to Edinburgh."

"You will go—but not tomorrow."

She raised her chin. "I'm thirteen, now."

He smiled. As he lifted the cup to his mouth the welcome tang of whisky filled his nostrils, begging to be swallowed. Saliva flowed into his mouth. He savored the peat smell, anticipating the bite, the taste, the warmth, the empowerment—and the escape. "So old?"

It was challenge, not question. "No longer a wee bairn."

He swirled liquor in his cup. The pungency of the whisky, reinforced by the motion, made his eyes water.

"Why can I not go tomorrow?" The plaid slipped off a shoulder; she dragged it up again. In the brief, impatient motion he saw the texture of prominent knuckles newly scraped raw, glistening wetly in lamplight. "You'll be taking Robbie—"

"I willna."

It stopped her in full spate. Straight but eloquent eyebrows slid closer to her hairline. "You *willna* be taking Robbie . . ."

"I said so." The waiting was done. He drank, gulping steadily. He saw the sharpness of her attention center briefly on the cup, as if she blamed whisky for his intransigence, and then her gaze slid aside. "I'm taking no one, Cat. No one but me was summoned."

"Summoned!" Astonishment was plain. *"Who* can summon you? You're Laird of Glenlyon!"

His hand shook. Whisky slopped over the rim of the cup, trickled between clenched fingers, dripped to his kilted thigh where it beaded briefly on wool, then soaked in slowly. The addition of his other hand temporarily stilled the trembling, but Glenlyon was aware of it nonetheless. The tremors, he knew, were merely outward manifestations of the soul shriveling within.

"Who?" she repeated.

"Breadalbane himself."

The mutinous set of her mouth slackened. "Oh."

She knew. They all knew. With Argyll's recent execution, the Earl of Breadalbane—and half a dozen other lesser titles—had stepped into the void. Clan Campbell was his now, because he had assumed control before anyone else could suggest another man. In disarray, it was far simpler to let the earl assume control. Until—and *if*—he disproved his ability, they would answer to him.

As for Glenlyon of Glen Lyon, such answering was required. He and Breadalbane were cousins, but there was more. Far more linked them than the natural fealty owed to an earl, or kinsman. There was also the small matter of *comhairl'taigh,* the oath Glenlyon had sworn—and signed—giving over to Argyll and Breadalbane jointly the guidance of his house.

Because he could not guide it himself.

"Why?" Cat asked sharply. "Why does he summon you?"

He drank. She asked out of wariness, of anticipation; out of a desire to protect him, not to accuse. But he could not tell her. He could tell no one. He could not form the words that would adequately explain what he had done.

"Why?" she repeated.

Harshly he said, "Go to bed."

It shocked her. *"Father—"*

Protest, or plea for an answer. He did not know which. He had never struck her, to cause her to flinch; he rarely shouted at her, though her brothers were more deserving. He tolerated her with something akin to bemused if distant affection, though he was not a demonstrative man, because she was so unlike other girls, and he was not a man who understood women of any age. He dealt with his daughter as he dealt with his sons; it was far less taxing than to recall there were manners a woman should be trained to. His wife would be appalled, but Helen was dead. It was his task to do; he had raised all five of them in his offhand, wary manner, finding it far simpler to let Cat mimic her brothers than to look for another wife.

There were women to sleep with. He need not marry them. No more than his heir would wed with Mairi Campbell.

Steadily he said, "There will be Robbie to answer to. He's a man grown." Cat's mouth twisted. He cut her off before she could frame a retort. "And the others, as well."

Cat set her teeth. "I'll answer to myself."

He took his mouth from the cup. "Whose blood is that on your chin? Yours?"

Startled by the incongruity, Cat touched her chin and found the crusted smear. Her mouth twisted briefly. "Colin's." She saw his expression and fired up in abrupt defiance. Her Scots broadened perceptibly. "He said I'd a face like a moudiwort, then called me a muckle-headed, pawkie bizzem—so I skelped *his* for him!" She picked the crust away, satisfied. "I mashed his nose."

Abrupt depression commingled with disgust. He thumped down his cup with a crack. "Go to bed, Cat—and wash your face. I've enough of this foolishness. You prove you're no' but a child with behavior such as this."

It cut her, he saw, but she did not permit herself to bleed. She flashed him a glance of purest scorn, then turned sharply and marched out of the room, jerking the door shut behind her. It rattled on its hinges.

Glenlyon waited. A moment later he heard the echoing thump as her own door was closed, and the click of its latch. She did not cry easily, except from anger or frustration; if she meant to now, if the cause were enough, she would take precautions so no one could see it, least of all her brothers.

Glenlyon's mouth twisted. "Least of all her father."

The room was cool, but he sweated, staining the linen shirt beneath his plaid. Robert Campbell ignored his physical discomfort and stared at the door. Cat was gone, but he saw her. He saw her face before him, the rigid body beneath as she asked, but did not beg.

A thin, plain, awkward girl too tall for her age, with prominent knees and elbows, feet and hands nigh as large as a boy's "—and an unfettered, unmannered, overbusy tongue!—" and an unwavering predeliction for acquiring layers of blood, scabs, and grime—some her own, some not—that did her no other service but to hide the corpse pallor of her flesh, where the blood surfaced like bruised grapes in eyelids and elbows, in wrists, and the backs of her knees.

He was Glenlyon. A man *might* marry her—if the dowry were enough. But he had gambled away her dowry. He had gambled away everything. He had even gambled away the coin paid him by Breadalbane to make good on his debts. *And now I owe more . . .*

And Breadalbane summoning him.

Despair engulfed him. A shaking hand recaptured the cup and carried it to his mouth. He gulped down the rest of the whisky in hopes it would dull the fire, but the coals burned steadily in the wreckage of his spirit. They would reduce him completely to ash, leaving him vulnerable to the cold winter's blast of Breadalbane's wrath.

Comhairl'taigh.

He had signed away his oath. He would sign away his daughter was there a man who might accept her, dowry or no.

But Cat, being *Cat,* was safe.

Two

Cat lay belly down in the streamside turf, transfixed by water. That the earth was damp and her clothing soiled because of it did not discomfit her; she trailed one sleeve of her threadbare shirt into the water itself, soaked now to her elbow, and attempted to sing the speckled trout into her hand.

Such blandishments did not impress the trout. Cat thought of tickling it, but she had neither the patience nor the skill; a hook worked best of all, but she had lost her only one in a stubborn snag. Now she used her body as the pole and her song as the bait.

Shadow stirred, blocking out the sun. "There's naught to catch, in there."

Cat ceased singing and clamped her teeth together. "There is."

"Och, no—you've scairt them all away with your noise, aye?" Robbie, the eldest, threw himself down beside her, stretching out full length to examine the stream, and her arm in it. "You've done naught but soak yourself."

The speckled trout darted away beneath an outcrop of sedge-sheltered granite. Cat cast a black scowl at Robbie, who seemed disinclined to explain his presence. Pointedly she asked, "Has Mairi run off wi' a man in place of the lad?"

Unprovoked, Robbie laughed and displayed his missing eyetooth, then rubbed a rough-knuckled hand through his red hair. "Och, no—not from me, aye? She'd do no better than the laird's own son. And I've no complaint of her that I am lad in place of man."

Still Cat sought provocation; better to sting him before he stung her. "And have you told her you'd handfast with her?"

Level brows twitched; he, of them all, shared more of Cat's features, though on him, a male, they were more comfortable. "I dinna mean to handfast with her. Why would I tell her so?" He paused. "And what do *you* ken of Mairi and me?"

Cat held her tongue. She would not admit she had spied upon them.

Robbie did not seem perturbed that she knew. " 'Tis her time now," he said briefly, explaining away Mairi's absence. "She isna a woman who wants a man when her courses are upon her."

Cat felt the blush engulf her face until she burned with it. She was not a fool, nor blind; she knew what courses were, and she knew how bairns were made. But she did not know how to discuss either with her brother, who had teased her all too often about such things as breasts unbudded.

Robbie rolled over in extravagant abandon onto his spine, settling shoulder blades into the turf. He flung an arm across his eyes to block the sun. "So, he is gone, and I am left to be laird in our father's place."

Cat, out of habit, was moved to protest. "Not *yet*. He isna dead, aye?"

"Gone," he repeated succinctly. Then, thoughtfully, "D'ye think Breadalbane will give him silver again?"

She stared into the water until her eyes burned. "He isna a fool, the earl. He must ken Glenlyon would only wager and lose it again."

"Aye, well—he is head of the clan, aye? He will do what he will do." Robbie's tone hardened. "But 'twill be my misfortune Father leaves naught to me to spend by the time he is in the ground, and pastures empty of cattle.''

"Dinna count the silver and cows beforehand,'' she said sharply. "You are not Glenlyon yet.''

Robbie dug his buttocks more snuggly into turf. "He said so, Cat: while our father is gone, I am laird in his place.''

She made a rude sound. "And what d'ye get of it?''

Robbie's soft laughter was muffled by his shirtsleeve. "The chance to be a man.''

"Mairi would say you are, aye?''

"No, not just because of Mairi. Because of—other things.''

It was highly suspicious. "Other things?''

"Things that dinna concern you, as you're naught but a lass. Men's things, Cat.''

"You mean to drink his whisky.''

Robbie grinned. "Och, we've done that, already.''

"Then what? You've bedded Mairi, drunk the laird's whisky— though that he left any for you is a shock, aye?—so what is there left to do?''

"Men's things,'' he answered, still grinning.

Cat sat up. The day now was ruined. Robbie had come to tease her after all, to remind her yet again she could do nothing they, as males, would do. " 'Tisn't fair,'' she muttered.

"What?'' Robbie rolled over yet again, this time shifting onto a hip and elbow. He peered at her out of brilliant blue-green eyes. Her own eyes. "That you're naught but a lass?''

And a plain-faced one, at that. She waited for him to say it. But this time, unaccountably, Robbie did not.

"Och, Cat . . .'' He grinned and slapped one of her knobby knees with the flat of a callused hand. A man's hand, broad and strong, but the slap was not so heavy as to harm her. " 'Tis the way of the world, lassie—men do what men do, and women—well . . .'' Robbie laughed. "Women please their men.''

"As Mairi pleases you.''

He lay back again and shut his eyes. "For now, aye?''

For now. And then he would turn to another. He was the laird's son; would be laird himself, one day. There were lasses aplenty for Robbie. *Who for me?* she wondered, and then was shamed by the question. And even more shamed by the male face manifesting before her eyes, hiding within her head: with white teeth a'gleaming and silver in his hair.

"D'ye mean to catch us supper, then?'' Robbie asked idly.

Cat hitched a shoulder, though he could not see it. "Canna.''

Robbie laughed softly. "Not singing to fish, no. I dinna think they have ears."

She stared hard at the ground, hating to admit it. "I lost my hook."

"*Again?*"

She made no answer. Hooks were dear in the Highlands.

After a moment Robbie sat up, eyed her, marked her shame, her sullenness, then smiled crookedly. "Aye, well—come along, then." He rose, bent down and caught her hand and pulled her to her feet. "I'll fetch you one of mine."

This once, this first time, he was not teasing. Cat could tell the difference. It astonished her.

She decided perhaps Mairi Campbell was good for her brother after all, if she softened his temperament.

MacIain of Glencoe gathered his sons together at a tiny table in the common room of a prosperous Inveraray tavern. Tonight they would sleep on the beaten floor, wrapped in their plaids, because there were no rooms to be had. Quarters had run out, rented or usurped in robust fashion by thousands of jubilant Highlanders heading home from victory.

Dair squatted on his low stool, guarding his wine cup from spillage by establishing an elbow as ward on either side, then wrapping his hands around the dented pewter. He leaned forward, shoulders hunched, and inspected the common room with a single sweeping glance as he raised the cup to his mouth. The wine was sweeter than he preferred, but the ale casks were empty. His father and brother drank whisky.

Inveraray was much larger than Inchinnan. The army amassed by the Marquis of Atholl to defeat Argyll and subdue other malcontents who might support someone other than King James—though now it appeared potential pretenders were dead—no longer was required to take the field of a battle already won, its leader executed, but to reap the rewards. Atholl had promised that clans joining his own men would be paid in more than coin, but in plunder.

Dair glanced at his father. Atholl in fact promised Argyllshire, which would please MacIain.

Scattered throughout the tavern were clutches of men Dair recognized, tacksmen and gillies clustered as chicks around the hens who were their lairds: MacDonalds from Keppoch and Glencoe, Stewarts from nearby Appin. He knew none of the Stewarts personally, though his father did; MacIain knew everyone. Dair met bright, laughing glances, nodded at shouted greetings, smiled and raised his cup to answer or initiate repeated salutes to victory over the Campbells, and to

MacIain via his son. They were most of them *fou,* drunk on liquor and sheer elation, which promised fast friendships and a fight or two.

"Alasdair!" He was never Dair to his father. "I'll have your ears, if ye please—have ye no' heard a word I said?"

The MacDonald clansmen clustered behind his father fell silent one by one. Dair, abruptly the focus of MacIain's fierce attention, was preternaturally aware of their movements: they elbowed one another carefully, arched anticipatory eyebrows, doffed or resettled bonnets, scratched heads and beards, rearranged plaid folds, smiled sideways into smothering hands, into mugs and cups.

"Well?" MacIain thundered.

"D'ye want them?" Dair was not in the least embarrassed; in fact, his spirits sang with the same elation that infected others. Archibald Campbell was dead. His power was ended. The greatest threat to such men as MacDonalds, Macleans, and Stewarts was disarmed. This night, he could meet his father on common ground.

The hedgerow of white eyebrows lowered over piercing eyes. "Want what?"

"My ears." Dair swept off his bonnet, ruffling tangled hair. "You bred them, aye?—they're yours."

The hedgerow swept up in astonishment. "By God, I should snatch them off your head, you whelp!"

Dair tugged an earlobe in elaborate acknowledgment. "I heard *that.* A good pair of ears, then; d'ye want them, or no?"

MacIain clapped a huge hand across one of the offending ears, though he took care not to break the eardrum. "You deserve a skelping for that! Aye, I bred them—I bred more than *ears,* ye glaikit boy!" MacIain caught Dair's bonnet out of slack fingers and threw it back at him. "Did ye hear naught o' it?"

"Enough." Dair grinned and let the bonnet fall free; his ears, for the moment, were safe. "We're reivers to go a'raiding."

"And where is that?"

"Campbell lands. Argyllshire." Dair could not help himself; his attention was snared by a distracting glint of lamplight off a piece of metal in a far corner. A man was moving, taking a seat given up by another clansman, and the badge on his bonnet sparkled silver. "As for where *specifically—*"

The huge hand swung again. Dair ducked part of the blow, but the remainder of it was nonetheless powerful; MacIain clouted him hard enough across the side of his head to rock him on his stool. "I did say so, you ken! Specifically!"

"Christ—" Wine looped out of Dair's carefully warded cup and splashed in an arc across his shirtfront. His plaid shed most of it; beneath the wool, the saffron-dyed shirt took on the color of old blood.

John MacDonald, nursing whisky, laughed. "Aye, you appear to have worked a day after all. A man too clean after battle has no' done his share!" He plucked at a stained sleeve. His own small wounds were healing cleanly, but the shirt needed washing.

Dair reached down and scooped his bonnet off the floor. "I am clean because I bathe . . . and because I'm quicker than you"—laughing, he ducked John's swooping hand—"but if ye want honest blood, I'll let you bloody my nose—providing you can reach it!"

John shoved aside his cup and leaned to rise, but MacIain's huge hand imprisoned his nearest wrist. "Not now. Leave his nose be; he needs it for the women, who like a pretty lad." A glint in the giant's eye belied the harsh derision in his tone. "Argyllshire," he said heavily. "I've portioned it out. D'ye care which you get?"

"*I* get?" Dair was startled. "You're giving Argyllshire to me?"

" '*Specifically*' "—MacIain's eyes were bright—"Kilbride. D'ye ken where it is?"

Dair grinned briefly. "I ken."

"Go home, then," MacIain ordered. "Through Kilbride. And bring its cows to Glencoe."

Dair considered it as he drained what remained of his wine. "Who is with me? John?"

MacIain hawked and leaned to spit, barely missing the leather brogan of a clansman. "John is bound across Loch Fyne to Cowal, then to Ardintennie. He says he's heard John Campbell has some new books."

Dair laughed, glancing at his brother. "*And* cows?"

John shrugged indifferently over his cup. "I shall bring the cows for MacIain. I want the books for myself."

MacIain's toothy grin was brief and ferocious. "There is plenty for us all, aye?"

Dair glanced at the others, marking this man and that, the eager eyes bright with anticipation and usquabae, called whisky. "Who is with me?"

His father was matter-of-fact. "Some o' the Appin men." MacIain waved a huge hand across a shoulder weighted with a massive brooch. "That lad there, in back. The sandy-haired lad—d'ye see him?"

Dair looked. The man his father indicated was the one whose badge had caught his eye before. The Appin Stewart was fully aware of the abrupt and pointed scrutiny by a cluster of armed MacDonalds and answered in kind, displaying even teeth in a broad, overfriendly smile below the glint of shrewd blue eyes.

Dair turned back. "I see him."

MacIain nodded. "Robert Stewart. He's laird in all but name; his father's an old man, and dying. They look to the son."

Dair's brows arched. "Robbie Stewart of Appin?"

"He holds Castle Stalker. A wee bairn yet"—MacIain bared big teeth in a ferocious grin—"but he's killed his share of men."

"And lifted his share of cows?" Grinning back, Dair nodded. "Let John bring home the books. The Stewart lad and I will bring home the cattle . . . and whatever else we find." He rose slightly, leaned across to steal John's whisky, then raised the cup in Stewart of Appin's direction. "A near-laird, and a laird's son—we'll do ye honor, MacIain."

MacIain grunted. "You'd best. Or I'll have those ears skelped off and presented to the flames."

John reached across and recovered his whisky. "And then the lasses will look to *me!*"

"You're married," Dair said dryly. "Eiblin would skelp *your* ears."

John fingered a lobe half-hidden in hoarfrosted hair, sighing ruefully. "Aye, so she would. But depending on the lass, it might be worth it."

Dair knew better. John loved his wife and she returned the favor. His brother would no more think of bedding another woman than Eiblin would consider removing his ears.

He cast a sidelong glance at his father, then looked across to Robert Stewart. The heir of Appin, smiling faintly, stared back with a hard, speculative look in clear blue eyes. Then slowly, with measured movements, the new-named compatriot lifted his cup to Dair and tipped his bonneted head in a quiet, respectful salute that was nonetheless as much a challenge as acknowledgment.

The Glen Lyon Campbells, despite their name, despite their father's title, were not a wealthy clan. Well-worn wool trews were passed down from Robbie to a succession of brothers: first to Jamie, then to Dougal, lastly to Colin. To Cat he left nothing; she was a lass, and he a lad.

Therefore Cat stole an old pair of threadbare trews nearly worn through in the seat, cut off the ragged hems, and snugged a belt around her waist to keep them up. She was taller than Dougal and Colin, respectively sixteen and fifteen, and exactly the same as Jamie at seventeen, who was himself nearly as tall as eighteen-year-old Robbie. She added soiled shirt, mud-stained plaid, a bonnet to hide her hair, and one of her father's old nicked dirks tucked through the leather belt wrapped twice around her waist.

"Go without me, will you?" She stuffed tightly plaited braids into the bonnet, from which she had removed the badge. She knew enough for that; in the moonlight the silver would glint and betray her presence. "Plan all you like, aye?—but you willna leave *me* behind!"

The laird was gone but three days, and already they planned a raid. Cat approved of that well enough "—'tis time Glen Lyon cows are retrieved from MacDonald lands!—" but she *dis*approved of her brothers leaving her out. She was a Campbell, too.

The lone candle in its clay cup guttered, shedding wan and fitful light in the tiny room that was not much more than a closet, containing a narrow bed, a chest with hasps and hinges verdigrised with age, a three-legged table (once there had been a fourth) wedged into a corner, and a single rickety stool.

It was nearly time to go. Cat studied her face critically in the small mirror she retrieved from the chest. The glass was cracked through the middle, but its grime-etched ivory frame held the halves together. Helen Campbell had bequeathed few things Cat wanted, since she preferred her father's pipes, dirks, and claymores, but the mirror occasionally came in handy.

Cat laughed softly. "Even though 'twas was meant for a lady, and not a cattle-lifter!"

She stilled abruptly, twisting her head to listen. From downstairs she heard a sound she could not identify, then muffled conversation. She could decipher none of the words, but recognized two of her brothers by the breaking of their voices. Jamie and Dougal would sound like men in a matter of weeks, but for now they were caught somewhere between boyhood and adulthood.

She scowled, knowing full well what they were about. They believed her innocent of their intent, but only a deaf man could miss their whisperings, and a blind fool the furtive, excited glances Dougal and Colin had exchanged all day. Robbie and Jamie were better at it, but she could read them also.

She heard the rattle of the latch on the front door, the throttled exclamation of someone who had, apparently, put a foot where he shouldn't, and the brief cuff of remonstration undoubtedly from Robbie, who knew better than any of them what risks they undertook. For all she detested her eldest brother—usually—Robbie was not completely witless.

Usually.

Cat grinned fiercely at her distorted reflection and hissed the ancient battle cry of her clan. *"Chruachan!"* She was above all a Campbell. "With brothers or no, I'll bring home to Glen Lyon a cow!"

In Edinburgh, Robert Campbell of Glen Lyon sat rigidly in the chair, waiting for the Earl of Breadalbane. The room was small, dark, sparsely furnished. *Much like my cousin's soul!*

No whisky. No pipes. No dice. Nothing with which to content himself, to occupy his thoughts, his restless hands and spirit, while he waited on the man who had assumed Clan Campbell in the executed Earl of Argyll's permanent absence.

He pressed fingertips deeply into his fleshy sockets. The eyes beneath wrinkled lids were overweary, protesting the journey from Glen Lyon; the hours without sleep; the smutty atmosphere of the earl's room illuminated by a single sooted lamp.

"Christ Jesus, will he keep me all night?" Glenlyon slid more deeply into the chair and chewed obsessively at a ragged fingernail until the nail itself was vanquished, and the flesh around it bled. When that finger grew too painful he began on another. It was not the nail or cuticle he desired so much to destroy, but the tension in his soul that so blatantly defied the calmness of demeanor he wished to display before the man, before this man of all men, to whom he had, in his desperation, in despair and helplessness, sworn the oath of *comhairl'taigh.*

The latch clicked. Hastily Glenlyon roused, wiped bloodied, damp fingers on the journey-soiled kilt, and pulled his coat into order. *Should have taken more time—* A hand passed quickly across his head restored haphazard neatness to his hair; with effort he summoned decorum and dignity to match that of Grey John Campbell, Earl of Breadalbane.

The earl came in and shut the door. He carried under one arm a leather-wrapped casket hinged with beaten bronze. The high arch of his nose displayed the shape of the bone beneath, and the rectitude of a man who trusts himself to be profoundly correct in all things.

Glenlyon rose, thrust out his jaw, and turned handily so that his plaid swung. In a perfect courtesy he inclined his head to acknowledge the earldom if not the man who held it. "Cousin."

The latch rattled again as Breadalbane released it. "We shall be undisturbed," he said evenly, "so you may speak out honestly with no worry of being overheard. 'Tis family business, this, as well as a clan concern."

Glenlyon waited tensely as the earl moved to his desk and sat down. A deft gesture indicated he was to take his seat; after a pause Glenlyon did so. He pointedly eyed the decanter on the sideboard.

Clearly Breadalbane saw it, yet he extended no offer, no hospitality beyond a chair, his roof—and the honor of his presence. *Good Christ— he denies hospitality to a kinsman?* Glenlyon clenched his teeth. *Or just to me?*

The earl set forth the casket between them, then folded slender fingers atop the wooden desk. His gray eyes were steady, belying no intent beyond a quiet conversation. "Have you spent it all, Robin?"

Glenlyon began to perspire, though the room was cool. Breadalbane, when he fell back on familiarity, was at his most dangerous. "I paid my debts."

The earl registered the belligerence. His answering smile was slight. "Of course. You're an honorable man, aye?"

For all it was couched in gentleness, the blade struck keenly. Campbell's armpits tingled. *He knows the silver's gone—all five thousand—* And none of it spent on debts.

Glenlyon tensed as the earl's water-colored eyes took on a wholly unanticipated sparkle. "I was thinking of Jean Campbell just before I came in. A redoubtable woman, your mother—and well worth the wake ye hosted for her."

Wary of kindness, Glenlyon picked his way with care. "I willna deny it."

"And they still tell the tale of the stone." Breadalbane's smile broadened. "How you wouldna let the MacGregors or Appin Stewarts beat a Campbell and sent for that herdsman to defeat them."

The remnants of tension vanished. Glenlyon laughed in relief. "Good Christ, no! That pawkie MacGregor thought no one could match his throw!"

"Through the tree . . ."

"Through the *farthest* tree; through the crotch . . . but I sent for MacArthur."

"Who came at a run—"

"—wi'out doffing bonnet or plaid—"

"—and hurled the stone farther yet."

"A brawlie man, MacArthur!"

Breadalbane laughed. "And in celebration you didna bury your mother that day after all, but broached more whisky and bade them celebrate again."

"The feat deserved it!"

"And so she wasna buried until the day after that." The earl nodded as the flesh by his eyes creased. "No one went home speaking poorly of your hospitality."

"They wouldna." Pride inflated Glenlyon's chest. "No wake ever was like it before or since, nor any woman the like of Jean Campbell."

"Well mourned by sixteen children." Breadalbane's narrow mouth below the prominent nose stretched a fraction more. "A fine woman—a *brawlie* woman—my aunt. She would have been proud of you then, Robin . . . but no' so proud now."

Tension flooded back. *His knife cuts sideways, snooving through my ribs!* Glenlyon swallowed down the dry lump in his whiskyless throat and sat more rigidly in his chair. Mutilated fingers pressed new folds into his kilt. "Say your words, John. You ken I've come all this way to hear them, aye?"

"I ken." Breadalbane undid the hasp on the casket and lifted back the lid. From the interior he took a folded paper. "Not my words. *Your* words, Robin. The oath you swore yourself."

He had anticipated discussion, a hint of sternness, but not abject humiliation. It stung. "Good *Christ,* John, I'm no bairn to be treated this way—"

"*Comhairl'taigh.*"Breadalbane's tone was gentle, his precise enunciation lacking in hostility. His Highland dialect faded into more precise speech. "You did confess before the Provosts of Perth and Edinburgh, Robin, that your way of life had brought your estates and family into ruin. And that you alone were incapable of saving them."

Pressure built up in Glenlyon's chest. *I'll burst with it* . . . like a bagpipe overfilled, spilling out his anger, his shame, his bitterness in a cry that would shake the rafters of Breadalbane's fine town house.

Breadalbane said, "You did confess so, aye?"

On a hissing breath Glenlyon admitted, "I did so confess."

Breadalbane observed him in something akin to grave sympathy. He stroked his narrow top lip, then proceeded to read aloud the words which now burned away the last vestiges of his kinsman's dignity.

Glenlyon stared straight ahead. His neck was a cairn of granite mortared into place around the iron of his spine.

Lengthy moments of the facile reading, condemning stupidity. At last, silence. And then Glenlyon barked a sharp, ironic laugh. "He is dead, is Argyll, and well beyond such oaths be they his own *or* mine!"

The earl did not immediately answer. In the rift between them Glenlyon heard the rattle of unexpected rain against mullioned windows. It would be a wet walk back to the tavern.

Breadalbane's posture did not alter, nor did his expression. "I am not dead."

"Good Christ, John—"

"Campbell or no, I will pay no more debts."

Glenlyon thrust himself from the chair. "Then I'll see to them myself! D'ye think I want your silver? I'll tend my own business—"

Breadalbane, quoting, cut him off. " '—*how easy I may be circumvented and deceived in the management of my affairs*—' "

"Then I'll sell all I own in the glen, you pawkie bastard, so that henceforth not a single blade of grass will belong to a Campbell—"

" '—*whose counsel and advice I now resolve to use and by whom I am here-after to be governed in all my affairs and business.' *"

Tears threatened to wrest away what small portion of dignity remained to him. "Christ, John, you leave me no choice!"

Breadalbane put down the paper. It crackled in underscore to the pressure of decisive fingers. "Whisky leaves you no choice. Dice leave you no choice. *Weakness of character* leaves you no choice."

"I once led an army for you—"

"I ken it well, Robin. But you've indebted your family since. Getting no satisfaction of you, the men who hold your bonds have come to me. To the head of Clan Campbell. To the man who holds your oath of *comhairl'taigh.*" For the first time a trace of contempt edged the earl's tone. "I've paid them so many times, ye ken, with none of it paid back. Well, I will not pay them this time."

The redoubled effort to stop tears of bitter frustration made it difficult to breathe. "Then I'll do as you make me do; blame yourself, John! I'll sell all but what Helen brought me." Glenlyon snatched from the chair his fallen bonnet. He yanked it onto his head. "And you've no hospitality to deny a man whisky!"

Breadalbane did not rise. "And you've no honor, to deny your family the legacy of Glenlyon. But there may be, there may yet be, a way to restore it . . . if what I work toward comes to fruition." Then his voice cracked in the room. "Sit down, Robin!"

Glenlyon's legs collapsed. His buttocks thumped into the chair. He had always been a man who answered another's thunder; he claimed none of his own. And whisky, despite his longing, despite his dedication, offered little also.

It was farther to MacDonald lands than Cat had anticipated. She rode her shaggy garron—hers more pony than horse—in increasingly tense silence, giving away nothing of her presence to the brothers who rode some distance ahead, praying the pony would keep his footing on the narrow track and make no noise, nor greet his kin ahead. But the excitement had begun to pall some time ago, edging from sharp awareness to a wholly unexpected fatigue.

The moon was halved, but nonetheless shed enough illumination for her to see the countryside, to mark the distant upthrustings of hills and crags. The track she followed in the wake of her brothers skirted the bogs of Rannoch Moor, and would eventually wind through the gorse, heather, and stony outcroppings of the upper slopes. Spring-and rain-fed burns ran full with water, carving wet convolutions of veins through hummocky turf to the black soil beneath.

Cat tipped her head to stare up at the moon. The adventure had palled, the resolution now wavered; part of her wanted very badly to turn back—her brothers would never know she came, so her desertion could not be thrown in her face—but the other portion of her would not permit such cowardice. She had come to steal —*"recover!"*—a cow, and recover a cow she would.

It was summer, but Highland nights were cool. She tasted mist, felt its kiss on her cheeks and nose. She was thankful for the plaid, grateful for the bonnet.

The garron stumbled. Cat reined its head up; then, as it slowed, planted heels again firmly to urge it onward before she might seriously contemplate turning back. *"Chruachan,"* she murmured, relying on the magic contained in a single word to reconfirm her intent, reestablish confidence. *"Chrua—"*

She broke off, hissing a startled inhalation. Through the darkness, burning brighter than the moon, blazed a small, steady flame.

Cat shivered convulsively. Where were her brothers? Still ahead—? Or had they turned off the track? *—do they see the fire—?* Surely they had; *she* had. Which meant if they claimed any wits at all they would get off their mounts, snoove down through darkness, huddle up in rocks, and brush and peer downslope at the fire to discover who had laid it.

"MacDonalds." A frisson of fear and trepidation twisted her belly inside out. She knew, as her brothers did, that most of the Glencoe men had gone to fight Argyll, leaving behind but a smattering of male protection. But even a single MacDonald provided a threat to Campbell cows.

She licked dry lips, then rolled the bottom one between her teeth. She need not face MacDonalds, nor did her brothers. They had only to find the nearest herd, gather up what they could, and without excess commotion drive them back to Glen Lyon.

It could not be difficult. Men did it all the time. And if she and her brothers knew where MacDonalds were, keeping warm by the fire, they could avoid them easily.

Cat nodded vehemently to herself, finding renewed courage. There was no danger. Only stealth was necessary, and cleverness. She thought neither required a man.

From ahead a garron whinnied: one of her brothers'. Her own immediately answered it.

Panic seized her body. She bent down across the garron's neck, hugging it rigidly. In broad Scots she pleaded for silence. "Och, houd your gab—"

But it was too late. The fire flared up as wood was added, and she saw man-shapes against it; heard hated MacDonald voices. Dirks and swords glinted.

Her whole body trembled violently; this was worse, far worse, than anything she had expected. Cat thought instantly of fleeing, of yanking her garron around and going back the way she had come, beating a tattoo against the ribs of her mount. But that was predictable, and instinct insisted that in predictability lay the truest danger.

—they'll likely circle around— She heard the scrabble of hooves from up the track, between her mount and the fire. She wanted badly to wait for her brothers, or to ride up to join them, but something beyond fear drove her to serve herself.

Humming a pibroch in her head to drown out the upsurge of fear, Cat swung her garron from the deer track they had followed and sought shelter among the scree, behind tangled heather and the scrubby oaks huddled against mounded hilltops clustered with time- and rain-broken stone. There she climbed off her garron and flopped belly-down on the ground, scraping herself to the lip of the slope to peer down toward the fire—

—and scrambled back, flattened in panic, as bodies backlighted by flames tumbled over the slope. Her garron whinnied again.

"Cat!" The voice broke; it was Dougal throwing himself over the slope. "Cat—is that *you?*" With him was Colin, big-eyed in the darkness as they came scrabbling over the scree, dragging ponies at the end of taut reins.

Her heart surely would burst as it hammered within her chest. Cat lifted her face from the ground. "Where's Jamie?" It was little more than a wheeze. She spat grit. "Where's Robbie?" She wanted Robbie. They *needed* Robbie. He would know what to do. He was always telling them so.

Dougal stuffed his reins into Colin's rigid hand and motioned for the youngest boy to get the garrons down behind the slope. He jerked his head over his shoulder, indicating the fire. "Back there. He sent us away when the garrons whinnied—Cat, they're *MacDonalds.*"

Fear made her blurt of laughter harsh. "They should be, aye? We're on MacDonald land!"

"No." It was Colin, smallest of them all, hunkering down rigidly against the slope with two garrons pulling at reins. "No, Robbie said we're not—"

Dougal took it over. "—We're no' to Glencoe yet, or even near it—we're still on Rannoch. They've come *here*—"

Cat was outraged as the full meaning sank in. "They've come for *our* cows!" Fear dissipated abruptly into insulted pride. "Where are Robbie and Jamie?"

From below they heard a triumphant shout. Silhouettes converged;

a body held between two others was escorted toward the fire. Struggles were futile.

Appalled, Dougal murmured a prayer. Colin dragged the ponies closer; Cat's garron had wandered off a pace or two to forage.

She dug her nails into the earth as she watched the captive avidly, trying to identify him. *—let it be Jamie . . . let Robbie be free . . . Robbie'll ken what to do—* And felt guilty for it, and shamed, that she should wish upon Jamie that which terrified her.

Dougal shut a hand around Cat's upper arm. "Why have you come? What are you doing here? Robbie said naught of *you* coming!"

It was easier to be angry. "Would he? Not Robbie! He thinks I'm worthless." Cat glared downslope, hoping they would not see her tears; was it Robbie they had caught?

Another thought snooved in. *Is Alasdair Og with them?*

It infuriated her that she should think of MacDonalds as anything but enemy, even for an instant. To dilute the guilt, Cat turned an accusing glare on Dougal. "You shouldna come away. You should have stayed wi' Robbie and Jamie!"

Dougal scraped a forearm across his face. He was white with apprehension, eyes little more than black sockets in the shadows. After her, his hair was reddest, a yellowish, bloody tangle extruded beneath his bonnet. "Robbie sent us. When they heard the garrons."

"You could have *stayed*—"

"He *sent* us—"

Moonlight and fear leached Colin's face of angles, of hollows, of the spirit that made him human. "We're to go home. He said so. He sent us back."

"And leave Robbie and Jamie behind?" Cat doubled up a fist and smacked him on the shoulder. "You muckle-mouthed coward, we're *Campbells*—" She looked beyond Dougal, beyond the scree, to the fire beyond, where she saw man-shaped shadows and the glint of a bared blade. "Campbells, ye ken—" She let loose the Campbell war cry in her deepest voice. *"Chruachan!"*

"Cat—Cat, *no* . . . dinna let them ken—" Dougal clutched her shoulder, pressing her toward her garron. "Go—"

"Let them ken!" she spat, twisting away. "Let them think we've more men than they . . ." Cat frowned. "How many? How many *are* they?"

Colin sucked a scraped thumb. "Ten," he said flatly, around the battered thumb.

"Four," Dougal declared.

"Ten, or four?" Scowling, Cat stared toward the fire again. Her scalp prickled annoyingly beneath the bonnet; a grue coursed down her spine. She marked several shapes, but none of them stood still long enough to make her count accurate.

"*Chruachan!*" came the hoarse cry from the MacDonald fire, stilling them all in shock.

She saw a man-shape fall, struck down by another, and then a taunting answer sang out in a deeper voice than she could manage, filling the moonlight and moor with the hated MacDonald slogan. *'Fraoch Eilean!"*

Cat was immobile. "Robbie—" she breathed. " 'Tis *Robbie* they've caught—"

"Run!" Dougal's undependable voice broke even as Colin scrambled to mount his garron.

"Come *down* from there—" Cat lunged up and caught fistfuls of Colin's carelessly pinned plaid. She jerked him away from his saddle. "If they've got Robbie and Jamie, 'tis for us to get them free!"

"Us?" Dougal shook his head as Colin, pulled awry by his sister, got up from the ground. Plaid torn free of its brooch fell in coils around his ankles. "We're but three, and you're not but a lass—"

Cat shut her hand over the handle of her father's dirk. "Even a *lass* is better than a coward, aye? All we have to do is distract them, make them think there are *more* of us. Jamie is still out there—will ye come? 'Tis for Robbie!"

Their faces were taut and white. Dougal and Colin exchanged frightened glances, then looked back at her.

"Have you broken your lug-holes?" she demanded. " 'Tis our brother they've got—*MacDonalds* have got!"

Dougal nodded reluctantly. His voice was a man's, for once. "We'll leave the garrons here. We're quieter on foot."

Cat grinned. She was impatient now. She rose to skyline herself against the deeper night; it was time to do the task.

"*Chruachan!*" she shouted again, loosing her garron, and turned sharply to pelt down the hill. "*Chru*—

She ran headlong into a plaid-swathed, bonneted man rising from the heather with a dirk a'glint in one fist. The other hand closed itself firmly around her upper arm and yanked her onto her toes. '*Fraoch Eilean,"* he said lightly, "has a better sound to't!"

Cat filled her lungs with air. "Run!"

Dougal with Colin deserted.

—*run—oh, run—* She grinned fiercely at the MacDonald whose face, against the flames, registered surprise; he had not realized how many Campbells were huddled behind the slope. She saw it in his eyes, in his mouth, in the tautening of the flesh over his cheekbones, bled dry of blood in the firelight.

The grin fell off her mouth. He was a MacDonald. She was a Campbell. *"Chruachan,"* she said hoarsely, and spat in the dirt at his feet.

He shook her. He *shook* her, as if she were merely a puppy guilty of misbehavior. "No more," he snapped, clutching her arm more fiercely.

Cat tested the MacDonald's grip once, then went with him without further physical protest as he led her downslope toward the fire. She slipped and slid in scree and loose gravel, but his grasp never relaxed. By the time they reached the fire her arm felt more like a piece of wood than a human limb.

There were five of them, not ten. And none of them all the way grown. They were, Cat realized in stabbing dismay, not so much older than Robbie himself, if any older at all; one or two perhaps younger.

She looked at them one by one, marking youthful faces, thin and pale; dilated, darting eyes; rigid, expectant expressions.

She could not help herself. She looked, stared hard, examined . . . *No Alasdair Og* . . . The response was immediate: overwhelming relief. Her bonnie prince with the speckled hair was not among the thieves.

She sought Robbie then, feeling the heat of guilt in her face, the shame for her thought on behalf of a MacDonald when MacDonalds had captured them. He stood with a dirk at his spine and another threatening his side. His own dirk and *sgian dhu* had been tossed aside, out of reach; Cat's borrowed dirk was yanked roughly from her belt and flung on top of Robbie's with a dull metallic clank. Firelight flashed on steel.

Robbie's expression was grim as he watched her brought close to the light. He was cut along a cheekbone, his mouth swollen and bloodied. His hands were free, but empty, and like to stay that way: two MacDonalds with naked dirks stood at either side reminding him what it felt like to have steel stuck into flesh.

She felt the prick of the same against a rib, digging through plaid and shirt; felt the numbness invading the fingers of her captive arm. She smelled whisky and ripe wool, the sharp pungency of stretched nerves.

"Naught but a lad," one of the MacDonalds murmured, staring hard at Cat, then grinned sidelong at Robbie. "D'ye bring the bairns along when you go cattle-lifting?"

Robbie put up his bloody chin. "You're no' so old yourselves, aye? Is there a beard among ye?"

There was not. Cat saw a tightening of mouths, a narrowing of eyes. Firelight sparked on steel as a dirk point niggled at Robbie.

She bit her tongue on a protest. To them she was a lad. She knew instinctively it was best they believed her so.

Wood popped in the fire, startling twitches in them all. Robbie grimaced as a dirk point cut flesh. Cat waited stiffly. No one said anything. There was no sound at all save for the crackle of the fire, and the grit of brogans on stone. She swallowed tightly, staring hard at Robbie. He would do something. He *would*.

She shivered involuntarily, then winced as the grip on her arm spasmed shut. She felt tension in the air, sensed a subtle, increasing anxiety, and realized with a twitch of surprise that none of their captors knew what to do. The men were off with Atholl, or raiding Argyll's lands; the young men left behind had gone reiving for cattle, not for people, and were none of them experienced at dealing with captured Campbells.

"Who are you?" one asked sharply. "Which Campbell are *you*?"

Cat stared wide-eyed at her brother, begging guidance; it came as a single raised shoulder: *'answer them as you will.'* She swallowed hard again, then made her voice gruff. "Colin."

"Colin? Colin? Colin and Robert?" One of the MacDonalds by Robbie grinned. "The drukken man has a son named Robbie, and a son named Colin. Have we caught Glenlyon's bairns?"

The 'drukken man.' Humiliation stung. She saw the same response in Robbie's face: a taut, angry mortification that MacDonalds should know Glenlyon's weakness and bait his children with it.

"Glenlyon's bairns?" another asked, and a third made a vulgar joke about the Laird of Glen Lyon and sheep.

The MacDonald who held Cat's arm dug the dirk point into her rib. It was a small pain, a petty taunt meant to force acknowledged submission; Cat squirmed off the point with her lip caught between her teeth and swore mutely to give him nothing.

"Are *you* a sheep, then? Have you wool on your head?" He pricked her again, giggling, then abruptly snatched off her bonnet. "Have ye—" But the taunt died out on hiss of shock as coiled braids fell down.

"—lass," someone blurted.

Another hooted. "—*ewe*—"

Robbie's anguish was eloquent, his helplessness exquisite. But acknowledgment was swift. *They'll no' be expecting a lass to fight—* Cat made a fist of her free hand and swung with all her might as she wheeled sharply toward her captor. The blow landed square on his nose. *"Chruachan!"* she shouted furiously as the blood burst forth in a torrent.

Crying out as Cat's fist struck his nose, the MacDonald fell back. Robbie lunged as the others moved. "Dinna *touch* her—" He tried to tear his arms free. "Cat—Cat *run*—"

Cat staggered away. "Robbie!"

"—Cat—*run*—" He struggled again, drawing their attention away from her.

It nearly was successful. Startled MacDonalds grabbed for him, shouting frantically at one another not to let the Campbell go.

"Cat—*run*—"

She stumbled, fell, scrabbled up again.

Robbie cried out furiously. Cat swung around . . . saw the struggle, the steel, the awkward scramble; saw the tangle of scrabbling limbs as they pulled her brother down. One of them sat on the upthrust rump, pressing Robbie's body flat; another lay athwart his shoulders with an elbow dug into an ear.

I canna leave him here . . . Cat could no longer see her brother's face. Beneath the cluster of kilted MacDonalds she could no longer see much at all of Glenlyon's heir, nor the scatter of dirks and *sgian dhu* tossed carelessly on the ground. They lay beneath her brother, beneath the pile of bodies.

Her captor nursed his nose, hawking and spitting blood. Cat snatched up rocks and began hurling them at MacDonalds.

Several of Cat's stones struck flesh. Then the MacDonald whose nose she had broken garbled something unintelligible and caught a flopping braid, roughly jerking her down. Screeching, Cat sprawled; he jerked again, then dragged her across rocky soil. One thick Mac-Donald wrist was pressed against his streaming nose.

She clamped a hand around the braid near her scalp to reduce the pain and tugging even as she scrabbled with her other hand, hunting rocks. The MacDonald saw it, jerked again, then began to wind the braid around his wrist. He would pull her in, she saw, until he owned more than her braid.

Someone shouted something. Cat understood none of it. But abruptly the MacDonald who restrained her released his grip.

Cat lay belly down against hard ground. She twisted her head toward the others and saw how they scrambled up; how they backed away; how, with faces blanched white, they stared at the body lying slack upon the ground.

At Robbie Campbell's body.

"Robbie—" Cat scrabbled to hands and knees. *"ROBBIE—"*

The MacDonald nearest turned on her sharply; before she could rise he planted a foot against her shoulder and shoved her down again.

"We didna *mean*—" someone began, while another MacDonald hushed him.

"Come away," another said to his bleeding kinsman.

"But we *didna* mean it!" another cried. "Not this—"

"Ewan—come *away!*"

As Cat scrambled to her brother the MacDonalds came away, fading out of firelight into the shadows beyond. She heard the sound of horses. Heard the sound of flight. Heard the sound of MacDonalds who had killed Glenlyon's heir.

At first she could not turn him. He was heavy, and slack. Finally she gripped the cloth of Robbie's shirt and plaid and pulled him over, grunting with the effort; one arm flopped across her rigid thigh. Cat hung there, staring at the bloodied shirtfront. At the dirk, *her* dirk, that Robbie had grabbed as the bodies came down upon him, the weight and force driving the blade meant to defend himself into his belly instead.

Her dirk. Her *father's* dirk, that she had stolen.

His mouth hung slackly, crusted with dirt. Blood smeared his chin. A welt ruined a cheek. His eyes were open, transfixed by shock and death. They stared at the darkness.

To Cat, they stared at her.

"Robbie!" she shrieked.

And shrieked, and shrieked, and shrieked, until the night rang loud with her grief.

Three

R obert Stewart of Appin hooted aloud and swept off his dusty bonnet. He ran a hasty hand through sandy hair, mussing it so thoroughly it stood up in tufts. "Christ's wounds, MacDonald, but there isna a bonnier place in Scotland, aye? Have ye no' seen such a brawlie castle?"

Indeed Dair had—in Edinburgh, Inveraray, Stirling; but he agreed amiably that indeed Castle Stalker was superior in all ways. *Best to let Robbie have it, or he will argue about it all day!*

But he felt a pang of guilt. To be fair, Stewart's beloved home *was* impressive: Castle Stalker was an upthrust, sharply rectangular explosion of perfectly quarried stone. It shook its peaks and angles free of the tiny islet of Loch Laich, offering but a few trees for character, and rose importunately from the waters of Loch Linnhe, where a man required a boat to cross from land to islet. Against the pewter blue of the loch and the viridescence of hills beyond, it loomed a rigid sentinel in defense of its inhabitants. A cocky rival chieftain who thought to throw out the present clan and replace it with his own would find cold welcome.

He knew better. He was MacIain's son, albeit second-born; nonetheless, Dair wanted little to do with the castle and nothing at all to do with lairdship.

Stewart stood up in his stirrups. "The brawliest castle in Scotland!"

Dair grinned as the Appin men shouted clamorous accord. He purposely did not glance at his MacDonalds for fear he would see in their faces what he felt in his soul: a deep love for the harsh grandeur of Glencoe's mountain fastness, the hard-running waters of its river, the looming mountain called the Pap, the array of falls cutting vertical cliffs out of jagged granite.

Appin's Loch Laich was very like a hundred other islets scattered as pearls from a broken necklace. Castle Stalker had a hard, sharp beauty, like cut diamonds; Dair preferred the rounded cabochon that was Glencoe.

He shifted in the saddle to ease weary buttocks. He was in no mood to visit here with Glencoe only miles away. But he and his MacDonalds had promised to aid the Stewarts in their quest to carry home vast amounts of plunder and their share of cattle. Once in Appin the ebullient young Stewart heir, oblivious to Dair's weariness and edgy restlessness, insisted MacIain's son come all the way home with him to Castle Stalker.

"You willna deny the hospitality of my house," he declared.

Dair, who had been suckled like all clansmen on the sacred Highland duty, thought of his father, of his father's insistence on proper manners, and most particularly of his father's wholly predictable reaction if *his* son were so benighted as to decline an invitation to sup with the heir of a clan traditionally friendly to MacDonalds.

And now the clouds had come down to mass across the land. Rain was imminent. "I'll come," Dair agreed.

Robert Stewart, leading the tail of gillies and tacksmen who tended the myriad livestock acquired from their raiding forays, nodded matter-of-fact acknowledgment; he had expected no other answer. "We'll butcher a stirk for meat, and I'll have the bard in to sing you the songs of Stewarts, and Appin." He grinned slyly. "Come get out of the rain and meet my sister, Jean, who will no doubt be much taken with all the Glencoe-men!"

Dair slanted him a sidelong glance, then squinted at the castle in elaborate skepticism. "And is she bonnie, your sister?"

Stewart's laughter rang loud, echoing against the castle perched on its rocky islet. "Good Christ, MacDonald, of *course* she's bonnie! She looks like me!"

Laughing in spite of himself, Dair clapped a hand to his heart in mock pain. "A brawlie blow, Stewart!"

Stewart nodded matter-of-fact agreement. "I'm verra good with dirk or *sgian dhu*—" He grinned. "And never cross me with a claymore in my hand!"

Dair grinned back. They were in that instant in perfect accord. *But if it should ever come to a battle*— He broke off the thought, looked again at the almost-laird of Appin, who seemed as sharply cognizant of the moment as he himself. *If it ever comes to a battle, I want Robert Stewart at my side.*

Of such men, of such ruthless, reckless, resolute men was a stronger Scotland born.

Cat's trews had come to be torn. She did not recall how, only that the threadbare seat had at some point surrendered its meager strength and abjured responsibility for guarding her dignity.

She had no dignity. She had no mind to care. She had only a wild grief that drove her ruthlessly through the darkness, stumbling and staggering her way along the narrow track in an effort to go home. *There is Robbie—Robbie to tend—* If she could reach Chesthill, or even a tacksman's dwelling, someone would help her do it. She would not fail him in this, albeit she failed him otherwise.

Guilt was merciless. *Without me, he wouldna be dead.*

She flogged herself with it. Perhaps that was how her breeks had come to be torn. *Without me, he wouldna be dead.*

She heard a sound, and stopped short. *MacDonalds . . .* Were they coming back? Did they mean to kill her, also? Cat hugged herself, shivering in the darkness.

Without me, he wouldna be dead. Without MacDonalds, also. But it was *her* dirk, the dirk her father had set aside because of all the nicks. She had lifted that dirk as she intended to lift a cow, and it had killed Robbie.

Without me . . . Cat heard the rattle of stones. A muffled, wuffling sound. Even as she prepared to flee, a shaggy calf wandered out of the darkness and stopped, blinking great eyes at her.

"—only a *cow*—" Cat clutched her plaid-swathed chest, breathing rapidly. She convulsed as fright bled away, replaced with a bone-deep trembling in the aftermath of panic.

A cow. A calf. A Campbell calf, or a MacDonald. She believed it more likely it belonged in Glen Lyon, as the MacDonalds had come raiding before *she* could.

Cat laughed a little, then bit it back before the noise escaped her control and she keened like an old woman. "—brawlie calf," she crooned, marking its plumpness. "A braw, sonsie calf—" It was significantly less painful to think of living calves in place of dead brothers.

She put her hand on its damp, flared muzzle. Its breath was warm, sweetly redolent of summer grass. She bent, blew her own breath into its nostrils. It whuffled back.

A little Campbell calf.

The thought was abrupt. *Robbie would want me to bring him home—*

Robbie would.

For Robbie.

Robbie's calf.

Behind her, away against the scree, the untended fire beside her brother's body died to ash and embers. It had been a small, unprepossessing fire, meant for men bent on cattle-lifting; was now lackluster tribute to Glenlyon's slain son, the impetuous young Campbell heir who one day would have been laird. The embers, Cat knew, would burn out before dawn. But by daylight she would be back, and the firelight wouldn't matter.

Robbie's calf whuffled again.

If she unwrapped her belt, she would lose her trews entirely. So Cat unpinned and shrugged out of her plaid, then twisted it into a rope. With it knotted around the calf's neck, she turned toward Glen Lyon. *We'll go home, brawlie lad.*

She thought briefly of Mairi Campbell, now bereft of her Robbie. And if there were a bairn, it would never know its father. Only its begetting, its heritage, and the name of a man long dead.

In Edinburgh, with the rain rattling glass, the Earl of Breadalbane looked upon Glenlyon. Nostrils flared slightly: Distaste. Distrust. But the earl had learned never to discard a single potential ally, despite apparent ineptness, lest he relinquish an advantage. *And there will be one—there will be a task for him. I will use him well, one day.* "Robin." He waited until Glenlyon's attention came back from its wandering. "You are not a political man."

Glenlyon shifted irritably. "What do I care for such things? Kings do as they will. Parliament does as it will. Politics have naught to do with the Highlands."

Breadalbane demurred politely. "It is no man's failure that he not be acquainted with the perambulations of the Privy Council and such men as Tories and Whigs—God knows there is intrigue aplenty both foul and formidable." He tapped a fingertip against the paper. "But there is the matter of the king."

Annoyed, Glenlyon frowned.

"There is opposition to James."

Glenlyon stirred. "Argyll's dead."

And replaced by his son, the tenth Earl of Argyll . . . Inwardly Breadalbane grimaced. Glenlyon was blind, unremittingly blind. "Other opposition. James is Catholic. He holds the throne though Catholics are barred from such things; Parliament, for now, looks the other way. But he is unpopular with those men who prefer to retain what power they carved out of the Commonwealth."

Glenlyon frowned incomprehension.

In brief digression, the earl wondered if it was a natural inclination for his kinsman to be ignorant of such matters, or if perhaps the whisky had rotted his brain. Patiently, he said, "James was permitted to inherit the throne despite his faith because his brother, Charles, sired no children on his barren queen . . . and after the turbulence of Cromwell's interregnum, no man desired political upheaval. Thus Protestant England inherited Catholic James and his equally Catholic wife . . . but there are those who now desire the sister in place of the brother. Mary."

He waited for comment. Glenlyon offered none. *It* has *rotted his brain!* With precise diction, he clarified further. "Mary is Protestant. Her brother *defies* the Church of England . . . but Mary is of the proper faith, and she had the foresight and good sense to marry a Protestant, albeit a Calvinist: the Dutchman, William of Orange." He waited again. "Do you understand?"

"What has this to do with Scotland?" Glenlyon asked peevishly.

It took immense patience not to shout. *"All* things have to do with Scotland. Mary is a Stuart, aye? Her husband is not. He is a Dutchman. His interests are different, his priorities otherwise."

"Good Christ—d'ye think this matters to me?" Glenlyon was clearly out of his depth, and frustrated by ignorance. "James. Mary. What is the difference?"

"The difference is *power,* Robin. Until Argyll's downfall, Clan Campbell was the most powerful in all Scotland. Our position is precarious, now . . . there are MacDonalds to contend with."

He paused. He wondered briefly if his ignorant, bankrupt cousin comprehended any measure of what the Earl of Breadalbane hinted. One man might call it treason.

I call it survival. "Folly, aye?" Breadalbane sipped whisky; smiled across the liquor at his befuddled kinsman as he spoke of treason. "To put all our faith in a king who may be removed within a year?"

Glenlyon was silent. Rain rattled the latch on mullioned windows. Outside, the glow from lamps in Holyrood were wan blots against the darkness. The earl did not know if Glenlyon contemplated the magnitude of what he suggested, or cared little enough about any of the repercussions that would alter the shape of his country. But then Highlanders, for the most part, cared more for cattle than politics.

Breadalbane took up the folded paper and replaced it in the leather casket. He closed the lid, fastened the hasp, then looked once more at his kinsman. Commitment was his to make, his sacrifice. Or Glenlyon would commit nothing to Breadalbane when the earl most needed it. "I supported Charles during and after the Restoration," he said. "I supported James against Argyll's folly by keeping half of Clan Campbell home from the most recent hostilities. But I am convinced the days of our present monarch are numbered, Robin—and I am not a man who desires to see his clan fall on hardship because of policies determined by the Sassenachs in London."

Two spots of color burned high in Glenlyon's face. "You willna support James now?"

"True power lies in supporting the man most likely to keep the throne. James will lose it, I think . . . and a woman shall inherit it from him. But William of Orange is no fool; he will make his own decisions. England will answer first, and Scotland shall follow." Breadalbane's gaze was unwavering. "I prefer to lead."

Glenlyon sat very still. Then he stirred, like a dog newly roused, and pulled himself upright. He looked at the casket on Breadalbane's desk. *"Comhairl'taigh."*

"Indeed." The earl spread his right hand over the domed lid. "If I am to succeed in maintaining Clan Campbell's preeminence, I will require the support of Breadalbane and Glenorchy, which are mine—and Glenlyon, which is yours." He paused. "For the time being."

Robert Campbell's lips pulled back from his teeth. "You've no respect for *me!*"

"You were a soldier, once; I do not forget it." Breadalbane smiled unctuously. "There is worth in you yet, Robin. One day, I shall require it—*and you*—in some other enterprise."

Glenlyon's waxen face congealed into something akin to a painted mask come to life. His voice, newly strengthened, boomed out harshly. "Until then?"

Breadalbane spread his hands. "Until then, go home to Glen Lyon. Keep your cattle close. Let no MacDonald set foot on Campbell land, lest there be tragedy of it." He rose, pushing back his chair. "Will you drink whisky with me, Robin? To the destruction of MacDonalds?"

Glenlyon, exalted by renewal, laughed too loudly as he lunged from the chair. "Christ, John, I thought you meant to put me out wi'out it!"

Breadalbane recoiled. "What kind of a Scot—a Highlander!—

would I be if I denied a man hospitality?'' He briefly touched his cousin's shoulder, then moved to the sideboard. He poured two glasses full, put one into trembling hands, and waited.

Glenlyon offered a too-hasty toast—*"Chruachan!"*—and gulped down the whisky.

Breadalbane, with less need, swallowed only a small amount. "And to the monarchy!"

Startled, Glenlyon lowered his glass. A sheen of liquor stood on his lip. "To—James?"

Breadalbane merely smiled and offered no answer.

To James. To Mary. To William. He would serve the strongest of them, in the name of his clan, his God, and himself.

Dair MacDonald, feasted within the walls of Castle Stalker, warded against the rain that now shrouded the loch, was not blind to Jean Stewart when she came into the hall. He, as the other Glencoe-men, marked her at once; no man could not. No man could not look at her and not want her. And he was no Papist priest or saint, sworn away from women.

Robbie Stewart, slouched in his chair, arched sandy brows. His was a mobile face with features made for movement, and he used it well. Just now he smiled benignly, blue eyes preternaturally bright.

His sister moved to stand just off Dair's right shoulder. He smelled her perfume as, with elegant aplomb, she bent over his arm and reached for his horn cup, taking it from him so she might refill it with the whisky in her flagon. She performed properly as chatelaine, mindful of her duties; but no man there was unaware of other such duties as they would take up willingly, did she give them leave.

With murmured thanks, Dair accepted the filled cup. He did not look at her. He looked instead at her brother, who grinned broadly and buried his face in his own horn cup as if he had nothing else on his mind save the taste of the liquor.

After brief hesitation, Jean moved away. He felt her go, intensely aware of her obvious interest as well as her allure. He ignored her no more than any other man, MacDonald or Stewart, because no man could. And she knew it. And he knew she knew it. It was withal a cunning game, if left unspoken, yet played nonetheless.

Robbie set down his cup. Like a cat he stretched, then leaned forward in studied nonchalance. Lamplight glistened in wiry hair, deepening it to purest gold. "Och, aye," he said quietly, "I see it. I ken it. And I willna interfere—she'll do as she chooses, my Jean . . . but a wise man kens I am a protective brother." He pushed his cup over to smack against Dair's in unstudied toast. "You will do as *you* choose, aye?—but a wise man kens I will kill the man who hurts her."

The rain infuriated Cat. But it also reinforced her determination; to give up the calf after bringing him so far, after falling so many times into burns both wide and narrow and the sticky edges of bog, was to admit defeat, and that she would not do.

Dampness was no burden; she was soaked already. And when the rain at last beat through thick hair to the pale scalp beneath, she turned her face to the heavens and laughed out loud. "Are you kin to MacDonalds, come up against me to steal my cow? Well, you willna. He's mine, the brawlie lad—he'll be home to Glen Lyon with me!"

Thunder answered lightning. The calf at the end of her twisted plaid skittered sideways.

Cat nearly lost her grip. "No, no—dinna fash yourself. Brawlie lad, sonsie lad—" She took a firmer grip on the sodden wool. "You're a Campbell cow, now; likely before, as well. Come along wi' me, then, brawlie lad, and forget the poor grass in Glencoe. We've better to offer in Glen Lyon!"

A burn cut through the track. Water ran hard in it, swollen by new rain; Cat slipped in, climbed out, and realized she had lost a battered brogue. Likely the shoe was gone before she got out; the water ran that fast.

She turned her face to the sky again. "A poor blow, that! Here— have the other one!" She stripped off the remaining brogue and tossed it into darkness. "I'm a *Campbell;* d'ye hear? Naught so pawkie as that can defeat a Campbell!"

The calf protested again, twisting his head against her makeshift rope. Cat inspected and repositioned the plaid, testing its strength. It was good wool, or had been, once, loomed in Glen Lyon. "Naught so puny as a tug or two will tear it . . ." She scratched the calf's knobby poll, grooming wet hair with a deft twisting of big-knuckled fingers. "There now, you'll see all is well—"

The skies lit up around them, illuminating the wasteland of Rannoch Moor with its treacherous bogs; blighted, twisted trees; the frenzied vegetation. In lightning's wake thunder crashed so loudly Cat thought her skull might split.

She cupped one hand over an ear. *Can thunder break my lug-holes?*

It broke the calf's courage. Panicked, it tore free of her grip and shed the tattered plaid.

Blinking rapidly in the aftermath of blinding glare, Cat saw the flick of the calf's tail as the shaggy beast scrabbled clumsily away from her, heading back into renewed darkness.

She lurched after it. "Wait . . . *wait—*" She stumbled three steps, still clutching her plaid, still meaning to catch the calf "—you canna go! *Wait—*" to put the twisted wool around him again, to lead him once more out of Rannoch Moor to the gentler lands of Glen Lyon . . . *where he can spend his days with good Campbell cattle—*

All at once she began to cry in great heaving gulps. She did not shout again for the calf to wait; did not offend the skies again with a Campbell challenge for fear the storm would consume her "—*MacDonald clouds—*" and take again, this night, the life of a Glen Lyon Campbell.

Cat collapsed onto buttocks naked of breeks, clad only in threadbare smallclothes, and dug brogueless heels into mud. She scraped fingers into her hair until the nails abraded scalp. The tattered, ruined plaid echoed her dishevelment as it dangled from rigid fists. *"Ochone,"* she wailed, in traditional Gaelic lament. *"Ochone, ochone—"*

Robbie was dead. Robbie was dead.

And I have lost the calf—

The brawlie, sonsie calf.

Robbie was dead.

—oh God, oh God—

What would her father say—

—what will he SAY?—

—to know the dirk he had cast off that she had later lifted was the means to his heir's death?

"O—O—" She buried her face in sodden wool and began to rock in the rain. *—o-chone—* Back and forth, back and forth, while the thunder crashed around her.

Ochone. Ochone.

Robbie. Dead.

She flinched away from it. Far easier to greet for the calf. In that, there was no guilt.

Thunder was muffled by the stone walls, forming only a dull, rumbling mutter inside Castle Stalker, like a hound displeased by his master. Jean Stewart stood near the doorway leading into the hall, counting up the men; counting *on* one man. Twin-born, Appin-born, bred of reckless Stewarts, Jean claimed her own tenfold measure of intransigence and volatile Highland pride. She was, as was her brother, overblessed of ambition, ruthless in implementation.

Alasdair Og MacDonald. Not blind to her—no man was blind to her—but seemingly indifferent, circumspect, careful. *Or warned away by Robbie* . . . Which irritated her intensely. Here was a man *she* wanted, who did not, apparently, want her badly enough to risk her brother; Jean took it as a personal affront as well as valid challenge. She would win his regard. She would win his worship. She would win his body, his soul.

She would take him prisoner as she had so many men, and turn him out of his dungeon on the day she wearied of him.

Thunder rumbled again. Jean Stewart smiled. *He will do, aye?*

For now. For the night, the day, the week. Until the next man with naught beneath his kilt but the all too transient bounty bestowed by God.

There is no shooting here, no shouts of fear and fury, no triumphant war cries. What has been done is done, and no one remains behind.

She runs until she trips over an obstacle just before the door. Pain steals her breath; until she finds it again she lies where she has fallen, unmindful of her sprawl.

It isn't until her senses, less startled than her thoughts, identify the obstacle as a body does she makes any attempt to get up and then it is in a lurching scramble that flings her back from the corpse.

Her fall has disturbed the snow. She sees the trews around his ankles, the bloodied nightshirt, the hair dyed crimson. Nothing remains of his face save the dull white splinter of jawbone.

Part II

1689

One

*A*t the edge of the gloaming, as the day faded to night, Dair saw the fire blossom. It was but a spark at first, a distant blot of flame dipping up and down the hilltops, but he knew what it was without seeing its shape. The wind had carried rumors, and a name as well: *James Graham, Viscount Dundee.*

His view was of water, and hills beyond, framed by a narrow window. He watched the fire blossom, then bloom, spilling over the hilltops. Up and down, up and down, across the weft of burn-broken braes, and at last to the lower slopes spilling down to the water's edge. It was an eloquent dance, an ancient dance, the dance of a thousand men; of thousands and thousands before them, Norse and Pict and Scot, sleeping now in barrows still swelling under turf.

Dair shut his eyes. Behind his lids he could see the flame yet; see in its passage a tangled skein of smoke fading into darkness. He could hear the pipes, the pibroch; the keening of fresh-honed blades, the battle cry of the men, his men, Glencoe-men: MacDonalds. The distant fire kindled in his blood until he burned alive with it; until his genitals tightened and the fine hairs stood up on his flesh.

He opened his eyes. The fire still burned, still smoked, still came on. Not a loosed fire, but a carried one, a *purposeful* flame; its message, though lacking in detail, was well known to every man of Appin, of Glencoe, of Argyllshire and Breadalbane. To every man Highland-born.

Dundee wants us.

Dair did not hear her, but he knew the instant she entered the chamber. He had memorized her scent, her step, the fit of her neck to shoulders, the slant of hip curving into waist, the husky catch in her voice. He knew all parts of her, all manner of her habits.

She came to stand behind him, but did not put her hands on his flesh. " 'Tis come, aye?"

He watched the flame carried nearer, lighting up the darkness. His voice belonged to another man, though it came from his throat, his mouth; he was more than Alasdair Og, MacIain's son, the second son, but a Highlander who knew the task before him. " 'Tis come."

"Robbie said it would."

Dair smiled faintly. "He's no' a liar, your brother. He merely—elaborates."

Her laugh was quiet, then faded, shut up inside her mouth. "You'll go." It was not question, but declaration; she knew him that well, now. She had taken pains.

He did not turn to her; did not reach for her; did not so much as tilt his head. The burning cross transfixed him. Its message fired his blood. "I am a man, Jean."

She moved beside him. He saw in her profile the clean purity of her nose, the arch of brow above it, the sweet sharpness of her chin, and the lushness of bottom lip. A strand of sandy hair fell down beside one eye, curving on her cheekbone. In the only eye he could see, blue as Robbie's own, burned the reflection of the cross calling him to war.

I am a man, Jean. What else does a man do?

"For James," she said; it bordered on contempt.

"He is king."

"In *France.*"

"But *of* Scotland, and England."

Jean Stewart laughed bitterly. "He was a fool to leave. 'Tis always harder to get back what one has lost, aye?" She turned to him then, and the blazing cross bloomed in her other eye. "I'll no' lose you, Dair. Come back to me from this. You'll go, and so will Robbie—good Christ, I *ken* you're men!—but I'll have you both come back!"

Outside, the gillie stopped on the edge of the shore. He raised the cross high. *"Robert Stewart, laird of Appin; Robert Stewart, his son; and all the gillies, clansmen, and tacksmen!"* he cried *"In the name of James, King of Scotland and England: loyal Scots are called to battle!"*

Jean's inhalation hissed. "Swear it! I will have you back!"

"In the name of James, King of Scotland and England—"

Her bared teeth glinted briefly in firelight. "Alasdair Og Mac-Donald—"

"—loyal Scots are called to battle!"

In the waters of Loch Laich, so shallow by the shore, flames reproduced on wavelets. From the threshold of the doorway below Dair's window a voice answered at last: young Robert Stewart of Appin, bellowing at the gillie. "Will you bring your news inside? Will you drink whisky in the name of the king?"

The man bent and doused the flames. His voice carried clearly. "I'll come. Will you?"

Robbie Stewart laughed. "Oh, aye, we'll come to fight for Jamie . . . we've naught else to do the summer!" He strode out of the castle toward the water. "Bide a wee, will you?—I'll have a boat to you."

"Naught else to do?" Jean Stewart laughed. "He's no' got a woman, then . . ." And she turned fiercely to Dair, catching up great handfuls of his shirt. "If you willna swear it in words, I'll have it another way . . . 'tis but pace or two to the bed—" She loosed a wad of cloth and grabbed in its place the hair on the back of his neck —"or will you have me here?"

Outside, the cross of war was extinguished in the waters of Loch Laich. In her bed they rekindled it in a battle of their own making.

"Dead?" Glenlyon cried. "Robbie is dead?"

Cat was aware of her clothing sticking to her. She was wet all over beneath, hot with fear and sickness and shame; she had lied to her father about the death of his son.

What else? The truth? That she had as much as MacDonalds killed the young man who would have been the sixth Laird of Glenlyon?

Coward. And she knew it.

But it was such an easy thing to blame the MacDonalds. Without them, without their interference, Glenlyon's heir would be alive.

Not so much a lie.

The knot lay deep in Cat's belly, as deep and painful as the memory. She massaged the flesh, hoping to ease the pain, but it did not aid her.

Beyond her flimsy door, behind his own, her father played the pipes.

"Robbie . . ." Glenlyon murmured, and his face collapsed.

Cat curled bare toes into the wooden flooring of the room. Her arms were stiff at her sides, fists pressed against thighs. She gripped captured cloth, digging broken nails into the crude weave.

She waited as her father sat hunched at his writing table, hands cupping his skull so fiercely she feared he might burst it.

"Go," he said.

Cat writhed in her bed. Robbie dead four years . . . and she was a woman now, according to Una, who had served Lady Glenlyon. By Una's lights, then, Cat had been a woman for two years, though she did not feel it herself; her courses were, Cat thought, naught but an inconvenience, setting greater distance yet again between her remaining brothers and herself. Men need not worry about such things as linen at the ready, nor the cramping deep in a belly.

Robbie need not worry about anything again.

Her breasts, too, were sore. Cat cupped one through the fabric of her nightclothes, gently squeezing the contours of flesh that had been, but a year before, as tight against her body as a kneecap.

Cat detested sewing. But she and Una had had to remake the bodices of her dresses so she could continue to wear them. They had no silver to spare for such things as cloth; they would make do with what Cat had until she matured enough to wear her mother's clothing.

She thought again of her brothers, those who survived: Jamie, Dougal, Colin. They did not know. They viewed her still as *Cat*, not as a woman; if they knew, they would tease. And that she could not bear.

Cat chewed her bottom lip. She supposed some lasses might be glad of womanhood, of the proof of their fertility, so they might marry or handfast and begin their own families. But she wanted none of it, yet. She preferred life the way it was, unencumbered by the responsibilities such as her father knew. Let all the other girls-become-women bear the children and tend the men; Cat wanted better. Cat wanted more.

She grimaced against renewed cramping. *I wish I were a lad.*

For more reasons than courses, or cramping, or breasts rearranging her chest. Perhaps, had she been a lad, she might have kept Robbie from dying.

Yet there was more to it than that. Cat knew she was meant for something far different than the tedium of a woman's life. *I would sooner steal a cow than tend a man's meal.*

A woman now. The world within her changed, as much as the world without. And she a hostage to both.

Bagpipes squawked into silence. In the blessed cessation of noise, Cat relaxed. The cramping had passed, as had the noise. She could sleep at last.

Her eyes flew open as she heard the sound of garrons outside in the dooryard. "Father—?" But she dismissed that at once; likely he slept in his chair. "—oh *CHRIST*—" She flung herself out of bed and went at once to the window, heaving back the shutters.

She saw what she feared to see: three bonneted, plaid-swathed brothers, already mounted, and a handful of gillies with them. The moon was full, flooding rumpled, summer-clad hills, but nothing metallic glinted, no badges, no buckles, no bared dirks, nothing to give them away.

"I willna let them—" Cat snatched up her shawl, yanked it on over her bedclothes, jerked the door open and ran down the stairs two at a time. "—willna *let* them—"

She was utterly heedless of bare feet. She had to stop her brothers before they left Chesthill, left Glen Lyon, went out on Rannoch Moor; before they went to Glencoe, to MacDonalds, to death.

The dogs commenced barking as Cat ran out of the house. She saw horses abruptly reined in and the pallor of Campbell faces turned sharply in her direction as the door, flung open in violence, smacked the wall behind it; she left it so, and ran.

"Jamie!" It was his horse she caught, clutching leather reins tautly. She jerked the garron to a decisive halt, ignoring its gaped-mouth protest. *"You willna,* Jamie! None of you!"

"Let be!" Jamie shouted. "Christ, Cat—"

"Dinna GO!" she cried.

It was Dougal's turn. "Cat, 'tis none of it your concern."

"None of *my* concern? Mine?" She clung to the reins, only vaguely aware of the garron's damp, noisy snort, its pinned ears and white-edged eyes. "Have you forgotten it, then? Forgotten Robbie?"

Colin pressed his own garron close to her. She felt the warmth of its shoulder, the pressure of Colin's brogue against her hip. "Cat—we've no' forgotten Robbie. But 'twas *four years* ago. We're men now, not lads!"

"Men die too!"

Jamie swore, yanking ineffectually at his captive reins. "Go be a woman elsewhere! We've no time for greeting!"

Dougal was less abrupt. "Cat, by God's eyes . . . 'tis over. 'Tis done. Robbie's dead four years."

"We've cattle enough." She clung to Jamie's reins, undaunted by human or horse. "Have you been out to the shielings? Have you counted? We've cattle *enough!*"

Jamie laughed. "We've never cattle enough! Christ, Cat, *let be*—" Then, angrily, "—have ye spilled your Highland blood and replaced it with Sassenach?"

"Then go to Appin!" she shouted. "Go there, and not to Glencoe."

"Jamie, hold." Colin put up a silencing hand. He was less impatient, less harsh; at eighteen no longer a boy, but not quite a man, either. "Cat—we canna hide ourselves forever. The MacDonalds are lifting our cows with no protest from Campbells . . . dinna you think 'tis time we got them back?"

She did not release the reins to Jamie's garron. He could cut himself free with his dirk, but she'd not let go. "I willna lose another brother."

"Then stay here!" Jamie snapped. " 'Twas *you* who got him killed. Had you no' come, Robbie'd be alive."

It was burnwater over her flesh. Cat shuddered violently. *—told them naught . . . told them NAUGHT of the dirk—*

"Let be," Dougal said. "Cat—they're gone, the MacDonalds. Dundee sent the burning cross around the lochs. They've answered. They've gone to Dalcomera, to fight the Sassenachs."

"Jacobite fools," Jamie muttered. "They'd do best to support William. If I'm to die in battle, it were better to die for a king in power than one beating his breast in France!"

"I'd go to fight against the Jacobites," Dougal said seriously, "but Breadalbane keeps us home."

"He's a woman," Jamie declared in disgust, "and so is our father. A letter from Breadalbane, and we're all of us unmanned!"

Cat did not care about who was king, who was not, and who kept whom from war. All she wanted was to keep *them* from raiding Glencoe. "The MacDonalds were gone before, aye?—and Robbie still died!"

Colin slid off his garron and gave his reins to Dougal. His hands on hers were gentle but firm as he peeled her fingers loose one by one from leather. She was not a small woman nor a weak one, but he was, at long last, taller and stronger than she. "Go to bed, Cat." He jerked his head at Jamie in a mute order to back away. "When you wake up in the morning we'll have more cows on the braes."

"Colin—" But protest died. Sickness rose up in her belly, tickling the back of her throat. She wanted to spew it out, to purge herself of the guilt. —*none of them ken it was MY dirk*— "Colin, dinna go," she gulped. "Promise me."

"I willna promise such a thing." He guided her back from the horses, turning her toward the house. "Go to bed."

Protest was futile; helplessness enraged. She thought her skull might split with the virulence of her frustration, the pain of powerlessness. "Then kill them all!" she shrieked. "Kill every MacDonald there and be *done* with it, and then they willna kill you!"

"Go inside," Jamie commanded. "Colin—mount your garron. We're away." He looked back at his sister. The moon leached his face of expression, but she heard the disgust in his tone. "Christ, Cat, go inside—you're no' fit for a man to look at!"

Her belly knotted again. Cat clutched awkwardly at her straggling shawl before it fell entirely from her body; one corner of the wool was soaked through. She was *not* fit, she realized: Jamie's horse had left a wide swath of turf slime across her nightclothes; her braid had come half-undone and tangled hair defied her attempts to push it from her face; the hem of her nightclothes had torn free of her ill-made stitches and dragged damp ground. Bare toes were muddy, peeping through the tatters.

But there was more, far more, to think of than her appearance; and they knew her anyway, the gillies who served her father. They none of them held illusions as to what the laird's daughter was.

Cat put up her chin, disdaining futile attempts to bring order to dishabille. "Dinna go, Jamie. You're the heir, now. Robbie's dead, and you're to be laird in his place."

But none of them listened, none of them. They were men, and she a woman. And as the shadows swallowed them she realized it was for naught, all of it, every bit of it: her protests, her fears, her anger; she was at best their sister, and worth very little in their reckoning of the world.

Cat turned abruptly and walked back to the bench beside the door. She shut the abused door, then sat down upon the bench with her feet tucked under shawl. She had no intention of going back to bed; she would wait for as long as she must to see the men come home.

Futility was painful. It was a boulder in her belly that swelled to fill her throat. "Kill them all—" she choked, angry that she cried. *Except Alasdair Og—*

Who once had been kind to her.

Dair had taken up residence on an outcropping of granite in the shadow of Craigh Eallaich. He perched there lost in thought with knees doubled up beneath his kilt; he would not wear breeks to battle. One hand absently and wholly ineffectively groomed dark hair now more thickly speckled with gray; the other dangled limp fingers from an arm hooked but lightly over a knee. He stared blindly into the distance, fixing his eyes on other clansmen who tended weapons and wit, laughing loudly at weak jests and friendly insults built up as a wall, brick by brick, to ward away apprehension, to spend a time quickly that would otherwise last forever.

His dusty blue bonnet lay across one thigh, silver clan badge garnished with a sprig of purple heather and the red feather of James Graham, Viscount Dundee. He wore *sgian dhu* strapped to one calf, a dirk in his belt; the round wooden targe, covered with brass-studded leather and boasting a central spike, was tilted against the pewter-green, knobbed granite beside his knee. Next to it, at his feet, lay steel claymore, the dreaded Scottish sword, supremely elegant in its unadorned, deadly simplicity.

In his mind he saw Jean's face, Jean's eyes, the avidity of her need; felt again the supple body as it writhed beneath his own—and the instant response of flesh that now prepared for war.

He grinned mirthlessly. *'Twill be a different sort of battle, aye?* But a battle nonetheless, waged warrior to warrior instead of warrior to woman; and the battlefield significantly less comfortable than Jean Stewart's bed.

Dair squinted. It was but an hour or two before sunset. The summer day cooled into evening, raising a breath of a breeze carrying with it the scent of grass and heather, soil, stone, water, and the tang of whisky. Mountains surrounded them. At his back was Craigh Eallaich, its rumpled face lurching upward from high soft braes and lower, lesser slopes. It neared the end of July, and the cattle were on the braes in Glencoe, fattening for winter near the summer shielings; here Dundee fattened men on the Jacobite cause.

Dair heard a step behind him. He knew his brother's shadow even without benefit of the voice. "Thinking of Jean Stewart?"

He smiled crookedly. "You are thinking of Eiblin, aye?"

With a sigh MacIain's heir dropped down onto his haunches beside his younger brother. Targe and claymore clattered as he set both aside. " 'Tis what most men do before battle: think of women, and bairns." His glance was speculative as he plucked a stalk of grass from the ground and pruned it free of soil before placing it in his mouth. "Will you handfast with her? Formally?"

Dair squinted again into the lowering sun. "Dinna ken, John."

John was grayer than ever, though the arching brows remained dark. "Dinna ken? After—how many years? Four?"

"Not altogether." Dair's wave gestured dismissive elaboration. "A week here, a month there . . ." He sighed and scratched at stubble; they had none of them shaved with battle in the offing.

John grinned. "Enough time to ken a woman!"

Annoyed as much by himself as his brother's persistence, Dair took up his bonnet and began to rearrange the fit of heather beneath the badge, and the scarlet feather. It consumed his concentration, as he intended it to. If he made no answer—

"Alasdair—"

Patience evaporated. "I dinna *ken,* John! Christ, I'm but twenty-six—there is time!"

Around the stalk John said mildly, "By twenty-six I had a wife and a bairn."

"It doesna matter," Dair declared. "I willna be chief, *you* will."

" 'Twould be a good match, Alasdair. The Appin Stewarts and Glencoe MacDonalds are near to blood kin . . . and according to the old ways, the Appin laird is our superior. Once we paid him life-rent."

"Dinna remind Robbie of *that.*"

John laughed softly. "Is it because of that, then? That she's Robbie's sister?"

Dair sighed and sloughed the bonnet to the grass beside him, stretching legs to pop taut knees as he leaned back upon rigid elbows. "Before you married Eiblin, did you ever bed a woman who pleased you at night—Christ, pleased you better than *any!*—but made the day difficult?" He curled forward again and scraped splayed hands through cropped hair, standing it up in peaks and clumps against his skull. "Christ, I canna say it . . . she's all a man dreams of, John—especially before a battle—but . . ." He ended in a growl of sheer frustration. "I canna *say* it! I dinna have the words!"

"Bonnie to sleep with—"

"—*Christ*—"

"—but no' so bonnie to live with." John pulled the grass from his mouth and frowned, waving the stalk. "They'll come there, MacIain says."

Another subject, praise God— Dair twisted his head to follow the line John indicated. "There?"

"Through the pass, and down. Killiecrankie." He reinserted the stalk. " 'Tis almost upon us. Mackay's coming up the other side even now."

The flesh squeezed his bones. "Where is Dundee?"

"There." John removed the stalk again and pointed with it. "And the pipers—"

Even as he spoke the low drone of a single bagpipe set the braes to humming. Another took it up, and another, and another, until every clan piper on Craigh Eallaich sounded the summoning.

"Holy Christ—" Dair bolted upright before his brother. "Dundee?"

"And MacIain, and Ewan Cameron of Lochiel, and Clanranald Mac-Donalds, MacDonalds of Sleat, Macleans, even the laird of Duart—and Robbie Stewart of Appin, in his father's place." John MacDonald grinned and stood up more slowly, gathering targe and claymore. "We'll send them back to William with their tails between their legs, and bring King Jamie home again!"

Craigh Eallaich quintupled the sound of the pipes until the world was filled with it. From all around men came up, carrying, axes, targes, claymores, a few muskets; with dirks and *sgian dhus,* and bonnets bearing crimson beneath the glint of silver.

A tremor shook Dair. He felt his belly clench, his genitals tighten; felt the taut tickle of hairs rising up on his flesh. It was an almost sexual tension, an overwhelming emotional and physical response that took him whole, and shook him, until his breath ran shallow and tight and the tears stood in his eyes.

—Dundee—

—on his horse, in crimson coat; a hat festooned with leaves; a flash of silver in his hand: the cup of wine for the toast. Around him gathered the chiefs: MacIain, Appin, Lochiel—

—and the sound of pipes everywhere, swallowing the world, skirling into sunset the pibroch of all pibrochs, the wailing rant set to the task of swelling Highlander hearts; of firming their wills, their convictions—

—Clanranald, Sleat, Maclean—

Light sprang up as a pox: here—and there . . . and there . . . here and there again . . . torches set afire and lifted to beat back the sunset.

—MacNeills, MacLeods, MacLachlans—

Dair laughed softly, joyously; beside him, John prayed fiercely for victory, Dundee, MacDonalds.

—*Grants, Frasers, MacMillans*—

Dundee drank with the chiefs, and then looked out upon the mass of tartan and steel. The pipes died abruptly, cut off into an expectant silence nearly as noisy. Dair did not draw breath, lest it drown out Dundee.

"They are Sassenachs," Dundee declared with eloquent derision. "They are Lowlanders, and Sassenachs, and they ken naught but what they are told by a Dutchman who calls himself king." A rising wind whipped the torches. No man spoke a word, but Dundee. "We are *Highlanders!*" he thundered. "Let us fight as Highlanders!"

Dair shuddered again. A terrible sweet joy filled his breast.

Dundee waited for the cheering to die down, then continued more quietly. "Let them come over the pass . . . let them come down . . . let them come into our dwelling here at Killiecrankie—and at the cry of '*Claymore!*' we shall fall upon them in the way of Gaeldom, so they may know what once Gaels were before they give up their souls!" He thrust his cup into the air. "Generals—raise your standards! In the name of God and King James, let us rout the enemy!"

As one, Dair and John MacDonald jerked dirks from their belts and thrust them into the air. '*Fraoch Eilean!*" burst from their throats even as from up the hill by Dundee himself came MacIain's thunderous roar: "MacDonalds for King James!"

Dair thrust his left arm through the leather strap on the underside of his round targe. Properly positioned, the small single-spiked shield rested near his elbow, warding upper arm and forearm; he would use it also to guard his head during the charge downslope.

First the targe. Then, when ordered, the long-bladed dirk clutched in his left hand; in his right the claymore. Mackay's troops, Dundee had told his chieftains, who passed it along to their men, were Lowland Scots mixed with recent conscripts who boasted little or no experience and training; while it was true Mackay's men had musketry and the vast majority of Dundee's Highlanders did not, they were also men unaccustomed to the old ways of Gaeldom. They would shoot a massive first volley and clansmen would die—but empty matchlocks required reloading, and it was *then,* in the first smoky, panicked moments immediately after, that the Highlanders would attack.

Dair grinned tautly as he tended the set of his targe. "Lowlanders dinna ken what true battle is."

"MacDonald!" A hand came down on Dair's shoulder, clutching familiarly. "By Christ, MacDonald, 'twill be a rout indeed!"

Dair arched one brow. "Have you deserted your Stewarts, Robbie?"

"Christ, no." Robert Stewart of Appin grinned as he squatted. His spiked targe was in place at his left elbow, his dirk yet sheathed; he set his claymore on the ground beside him. "I'm no fool to think Mac-Donalds are cannier fighters than Stewarts, ye ken . . . 'twas only I thought I'd invite you to fight alongside *real* men."

Dair scoffed. "You've never fought wi' MacIain, to disparage us so easily." He jutted his chin upslope. "Look on him, Robbie, and think again what you've said."

Stewart squinted up the hill toward Dundee, who was attended by a clutch of lairds. Above them all stood white-maned Alasdair Mac-Donald, the MacIain, plaid brooch glinting in the lowering sun.

Robbie hitched one shoulder. "He's a *man*, aye? MacIain."

"Then bring your Stewarts here to fight alongside *us;* you're no' but a pawkie lad, and not worth a whisker of that man's beard!"

Robbie laughed, crinkling the flesh beside his eyes. "Aye, well . . . one day I will be. After this battle, perhaps." He rummaged beneath his voluminous plaid. "I've a thing for you . . . she made me promise." He brought it out. Across his palm spilled a chain of gold, and a locket. "From Jean, of course; she swore me to an oath to see you got it before we met the enemy." His mouth jerked sideways. "She knew you'd no' take it from her, lest you think her too womanish."

Dair smiled. "She's prouder than you, sometimes; God forgive the man foolish enough to think Jean Stewart weak!"

But Robbie's expression was solemn. "Only one man matters."

"*And* her brother."

"And her brother, aye; but there's a bit o' difference between what she thinks of *me* and what she thinks of the man in her bed!" Robbie extended his hand. "Will you have it?"

Dair accepted the locket. He sprang the tiny latch and opened the oblong face; inside, against a scrap of blue velvet, was coiled a length of sandy hair.

" 'Twas our mother's locket," Robbie said diffidently. "You'll respect it, MacDonald."

Dair smiled; Robbie was not one for softness. "I will cherish it. 'Twill be my luck." He closed the face and tucked the locket into the leather binding on his *sgian dhu.*

Stewart nodded. "We had best both survive, or both die; if only one goes back to Castle Stalker, Jean will dirk him for it."

Dair laughed aloud. "She would."

"She made me swear to tend your welfare, MacDonald . . . I dinna see how I can do that whilst you're here and I'm there."

"Ask Jean to give up *her* clan, and see what she'd say."

"Aye, well—for a woman 'tis no' so hard, is it? She need only marry a man." Robbie grinned slyly, blue eyes alight. "But you didna hear that from me . . . she'd have both my ears for it!"

"Or your ballocks, knowing Jean." A distant glint caught Dair's eye. He stared hard, squinting, at Killiecrankie Pass. All his muscles tautened. "Christ . . . 'tis Mackay!"

Robbie snapped upright, poised as a hunting hound. He expelled a hissing sigh of joyous anticipation. "Aye, 'tis Mackay . . ."

As the general's Lowland troops poured down the pass toward the lower slopes of Craigh Eallaich, Dundee's voice was heard exhorting his Highlanders. *"Claymore! Gaels for Gaeldom!"*

Robbie's laughter skirled into the air as the bagpipes began to rant. "Gaels, is it? Christ, there are none better!"

'Tis here, then . . . at last. The flesh rose on Dair's bones as he stood upright. In concert with every other Highlander he deftly unclasped his brooch and stripped out of his plaid, unwinding heavy wool. His own words seemed to come from a great distance. "If you're to lead the Appin men, you'd best go. We've no time—"

Pipes wailed across the braes. Torch- and sunlight flashed from naked blades. "Christ, MacDonald—" Robbie clasped Dair's shoulder fiercely a moment. Fingers dug into flesh. "We'll give the bards something to sing about!"

"So we will," Dair said roughly, gripping Robbie's forearm. "Now *go!*"

Robbie went, stripping himself of plaid as he ran back toward the Appin men. Dair turned toward the pass, marking Mackay's men. His own plaid lay in a tangle at his bare feet. He unsheathed his dirk, then bent and took up his sword. *"Fraoch Eilean,"* he murmured, seeking his father's face in the cluster around Dundee.

He found it: the face of an eagle atop massive shoulders. MacIain also had shed his plaid. The proud, fierce laird bared his teeth briefly, then threw back his head and added his shout to Dundee's.

"Claymore!"

Heaps of wool, like tartan spoor, were left behind as Dundee's Highlanders, barefoot and bare-legged in the ancient tradition of Gaeldom, drew dirks and hoisted claymores, screaming for their king as they charged the enemy.

Two

Cat, who had agreed to practice her needlework only at Una's insistence, unhappily began to pull out every last stitch she had made in the threadbare, yellowed cambric—also at Una's insistence. Her temper was mutinous.

—*I am not made to be quiet*—

"Catriona."

—*I am not MADE to hem shirts*—

"Catriona."

Una never called her by anything but her Christian name. Since Lady Glenlyon's death a decade before, the woman had labored with excessive dedication to train her mistress's daughter to refinement; Cat knew better than any it had not been successful. She still preferred trews to skirts, despite little opportunity to wear them; on her seventeenth birthday the laird had declared she was a woman and he would no more tolerate a daughter clad in her brothers' breeks.

"Catriona, mind the thread . . . no, not like that! Dinna break it. 'Tis dear."

Cat gritted her teeth as she worked the stitches loose. The thread, once near-white, had darkened from the contortions of awkward, grimy fingers. " 'Tis *all* dear, aye? The coin for such things as thread is spent on dice, or whisky—"

"*Catriona!*"

" 'Tis true." She was heedless of snapping thread and Una's soft protest. "I'm not blind, aye?—he's *fou* most of the time, and he talks when in his cups—" Cat clamped her mouth shut as Una's face congested into two brilliant spots of color high in her face. *Dinna have a fit, Una!* She scowled. "You may beat me for lying, but not for the truth. He lost the sawmill and the river leases to a Lowlander—"

" 'Tis none of your concern," Una said tightly. Light sparked off the steel needle that was dearer yet than thread as she made tiny, meticulous stitches; her supple fingers were clean, and left no residue. " 'Tis for your father to tend."

"And he tends it gey well!" Cat glared down at the ruined needlework, marking broken thread and crumpled, sweat-soiled cambric. "You'll set me to stitching his hems as if 'twere all he needed, shirts with hems in them, when what he *needs* is his purse stitched shut so he willna spend all our silver!"

Una's mouth sprang open—like a gawping salmon, Cat decided—to make answer, but what she intended to say was lost in the crashing of the door.

Cat was glad of any excuse to cease hemming shirts, but as her eldest living brother crossed the threshold she forgot stitchery altogether and leaped to her feet. "Jamie—?"

His face was corpse white, stretched taut, too taut over the rigid contours of his skull. She thought at first he was ill, until she saw the hard glitter in his eyes, the shapeless line of his mouth, the balling of big-knuckled fists as he braced himself against either jamb.

"By Christ—" Jamie said thickly "—I should shoot the man, I should—had I the ballocks to do it—"

Behind him, pushing through with a snarled protest that Jamie should no' block the way, came Dougal, equally furious. Only Colin, entering last, appeared less angry; but Cat saw it was shock in fury's place as he methodically shut the door and set the latch. Even his lips were white.

She looked at the eldest again. Apprehension redoubled the pounding of her heart. —*never SEEN him so angry*— "What has happened?"

Jamie spun in place and smashed a fist through the glazing, shattering costly glass. Cat recoiled. Una's shocked outcry was lost in his furious shout. "By Christ, I'll see to it no Murray enjoys this house!"

"Jamie!" It was Dougal, markedly less angry now that his older brother had turned to violence, who reached for a taut shoulder. "He's not sold Chesthill. You'll be breaking your own house!"

"Or his hand," Cat declared; but one glance at Jamie's face kept her from going to him, to inspect his flesh for cuts —*too angry*— "What is it?"

Colin's voice was hoarse. "Murrays."

"Murrays?" It made no sense, none at all; they had naught to do with Murrays. "What Murrays?"

Jamie swung from the shattered pane, tearing down for a bandage the yellowing lacework curtain his mother had hung there the day after her wedding. Again Una blurted a protest; again he ignored her. "Murrays of Atholl," he said tightly, "who now own Glen Lyon." He glared at Una, thrusting bloodied lace before her face. "D'ye think this matters? 'Twill be Murray's, one day; see if the bastard doesna sell *this* house, too!"

The unhemmed shirt fell from Cat's hands. "He's not sold *Glen Lyon!*"

"Aye. For debts." Jamie's mouth was a rictus of rage. "He's no silver, he says, with creditors hounding him . . . *Christ*, the man will destroy us all—"

Dougal's tentative hand touched a rigid shoulder again. "We'll have something of him, Jamie. There's still Chesthill, and our mother's dower lands—''

Jamie spurned reason, shaking off his brother's hand. "Have you not thought? Any of you?" Tears stood in his eyes as he looked from Dougal to Colin, then glanced briefly at Cat. "There will be nothing left for us . . . we'll be no more than *tacksmen,* paying rent to Murray of Atholl on lands that have belonged to Campbells for centuries—'' Both large hands shut themselves into fists he raised to batter the air. "I'll be the sixth Laird of Glenlyon, and 'twill mean *naught!*''

Cat stared blindly at him, transfixed by shock as well as the magnitude of his anger. Then comprehension filtered through astonishment, lurid brushstrokes against brittle canvas, and at last she understood. She understood too well.

In the tense silence it was difficult to breathe. Cat's mouth was dry. Her lips were numb. *Tacksmen . . . to Atholl Murrays, on Campbell lands.* She looked from one to the other: from Colin, to Dougal, and lastly to Jamie, heir in dead Robbie's place. Her brothers, born to wealth and power, were in one heedless, selfish act impoverished by a father's folly, by his weakness, and summarily stripped of a future even as she was stripped of the dowry that might buy her a husband.

A man might have to wife a plain woman who came with a dowry. But a plain woman with naught was worth naught; and she would have no name, no family pride, because *he* had sold it away.

Dair MacDonald had said it long ago: *'Glenlyon's girl is worth something.'* Cat swallowed painfully. *But Glenlyon himself is worth naught . . . and his children less than that!*

She shivered once, then thrust aside such petty concerns as climate; as the response of her flesh to a thing so unimportant as a shattered window. None of it mattered. None of it mattered at all.

With meticulous deliberation, as her brothers stared incomprehension, Catriona Campbell retrieved from the floor her father's half-hemmed shirt. Before Una's startled gaze she tore the cloth in half. *"That* for your hems! I'll no' sew another for the man who sells Glen Lyon!''

The sound of battle was terrible. Dair, whose experience until Killiecrankie had been limited to skirmishes quickly ended, had not anticipated the cacophony of war: the wailing song of skirling pipes, the clashing of steel on steel, the exhortation of those in command, the cracking like bones of musketry, the hammer-beating of drums, the shouting of the living and the screaming of the dying.

"Claymore!" Dundee shouted.

"Claymore!" the lairds roared.

"Claymore!" echoed the Highlanders as they left behind Craigh Eal-laich and swarmed upon Mackay's forces.

The first volley thundered in the Pass of Killiecrankie. The Highlander immediately in front of Dair fell at once, gargling out his life in a spray of blood and throat flesh; but Dundee had made it clear the first volley would kill or wound hundreds, and it was only by immediately engaging Mackay's men that a second more lethal volley would be avoided.

Dair leaped the fallen Scot and continued his wild charge, wielding the wicked claymore. In that moment it was but a blade of grass, not steel; an extension of his arm, his hand, his heart, his soul. In his left fist he clutched the dirk, distributing the balance of steel and flesh; offering a two-pronged threat to the forces who found themselves un-weaponed in the aftermath of the volley, scrambling to fix the bayonet plugs that might yet ward off the bare-legged Gaels who poured down the mountain—

Dundee planned it gey well . . . But the thought was gone, banished by the powder-dusted face that fixed itself in Dair's vision. A man, a young man, a frightened young man whose gun, discharged, offered him no defense; the bayonet fell from trembling fingers as he dropped the gun and ran.

A second man offered himself: another face, more black powder grains embedded in fright-whited flesh; bulging eyes, a gaping mouth, then teeth bared as the lips writhed; and the musket, with steel attached, swinging up to implant itself in Dair's abdomen—

Dair twisted, offering a side in place of belly, warding himself with targe; then dirked the man high in the crimson-clad shoulder as he stumbled forward, caught off guard by the maneuver. The blade stuck briefly, trapped in flesh and bone and leather baldric; Dair wrenched it free even as the man, crying out, twisted and fell against the heather, banging his head on a scattered cluster of granite—

—another— Dair wheeled, dropping his dirk as he clamped both hands on the hilt of his claymore. He swung from hips, from shoulders, from elbows, from wrists; legs spread, bare feet heather-plan-ted— *"Fraoch Eilean!"* —and the man went down in an arc of blood, while silver steel ran red.

Dair was in that moment a man alone, a man completely apart: the skirl of pipes retreated, and the screech of steel on steel, the grunts, the cries, the screams; the crack of muskets as yet unsilenced by Highland dirk or sword. He heard only the noise of his own survival: the rasp of breath in his chest, the catch-gasp of a grunt in his throat, the throttled, almost-bestial growl as he stood his ground beside the dead man and warded off his *own* death as it snooved through the heather in the guise of Mackay's man.

Uphill, with the advantage of placement, Dair raised and brought over the claymore. Beneath the steel the skull split cleanly in half, spraying blood and brain as the blade sheared through neck to trunk, where it lodged high in the ribs. The body, in falling, wrenched itself free of claymore and collapsed slackly across Dair's feet; he stumbled, went briefly to one knee in bloodied, slippery grass, climbed up the braced, equally bloody claymore, and stood again. Breath roared in his chest.

"MacDonald!"

—*Robbie's voice*— and a blade was there beside him, and the black-pitted face of Robert Stewart as he blocked another blow, turning the bayonet-spiked rifle aside.

An acrid pall of powder rolled across the braes, clouding clarity. Dair heard Robbie's grunt of effort, a hissed curse, and then the manifest pleasure of a man who had succeeded in killing another before that one killed him. —*or killed a friend* . . . And then another man was there, another enemy . . . and Robbie already taken a pace away, shrouded in blackened smoke—

Dair swung, brought up the claymore nearly too late; the blade caught bayonet in a screech of metallic protest that offended his ears. He turned it aside, but footing was treacherous with blood-slick and fallen bodies; caught in a tangle of lifeless arms and legs sprawled against soaked ground, Dair staggered— —*too close now*— —the face was a rictus of rage as it swam into Dair's focus. He could not turn the claymore in time to offer blade; he offered instead the pommel, thrusting toward the powder-burned face to hammer it with steel.

—*beat him back . . . gain room*— The man fell away briefly, then surged forward again, emboldened by Dair's inability to swing the broadsword properly. The bayonet ran red, shining wetly in the sunset. —*has had a Highlander, then . . . now hungry for a MacDonald*— Dair flung himself across the sprawled bodies, rolled —*dinna stab yourself, Alasdair Og!*— and came up at once onto one knee, claymore levelled.

Mackay's man, unmindful of Dair's quickness, skewered himself. But in dying he sagged forward. Deadweight tore the sword from Dair's grasp; on one knee he grabbed for the blood-slicked hilt, wishing for his plaid to wipe it clean—

A shoe, and a foot in it. In the corner of his eye.

Dair flung himself headlong against the rock-encrusted turf. The blade followed him unerringly, cutting through the loose crumple of shirt at the juncture of upper arm and back. It snicked briefly on targe edge, then by. The flesh of Dair's side caught fire even as the rib beneath protested the grate of steel on bone. —*no' so bad* . . . He twisted, splayed hands against the ground, thrust himself up even as he snatched at his *sgian dhu*. Fabric tore; his shirt, pinned to the turf —*blade planted, then*—

With the sweep of his targe he knocked aside the empty musket now empty of threat as well, with its bayonet too firmly rooted, and caught a clutch of scarlet jacket. "For *James*—" He thrust the *sgian dhu* into the soldier's belly, driving home the blade, digging deeply; it was neither sword nor dirk, and its steel short. But wielded properly in the hand of a Highlander, the *sgian dhu* was nonetheless deadly.

Bagpipes were screaming. So were Sassenachs. As the dead man fell Dair hung on to *sgian dhu*. Blood thundered in his ears; he turned, squinted, saw the last glory of the sun as it slid beneath the ridge of mountains. In disbelief he marked the retreat: red-coated men deserting the field by the hundreds, leaving behind fallen comrades, muskets, swords, and William's cause as they ran toward the baggage near the river.

"—won—" Dair squinted again. The pipes on Craigh Eallaich shrilled a victory rant.

He sat down all at once. He trembled now, like a child, chilled and weak and weary; wanting to laugh, to cry, to sleep, to lie with Jean Stewart; to feast on beef and gulp down usquabae, until his head was full of it and he passed from among the living into something of less lurid reality, a state of less pain, less exhaustion, less overwhelming *weakness*—

"MacDonald." A man squatted down beside him. "Here. Let me bind it."

Dazedly he did not protest as someone helped strip from his arm the wedged targe and set it aside. Dair blinked. "Robbie—?"

Hands were on him. "Lift the arm—och, I ken . . . I've no whisky for it now; later—" Robbie Stewart bent his head to peer under Dair's lifted arm. "A flap of skin—here—"

Dair hissed an inhalation. "Christ, Robbie—hurts *less* wi'out fingers in it!"

The fingers retreated. "Ugly, but no' so deep. A sliver of bone gone, but 'tis whole underneath." Robbie pulled the remains of the bloodied shirt over the wound, then wrapped binding around Dair's ribs.

The rich and bloodied colors of the field were all at once watered into a pastel blur as Dair gritted his teeth. "A Stewart plaid—?"

Robbie's tone was brusque as he set the binding. " 'Twill do as a bandage until we find clean linen."

Dair shut his eyes. His body wanted to give itself over to trembling, to abject surrender, quivering in all his joints like a dollop of oatmeal porridge. Laughter bubbled up, inane and inappropriate; he wanted to rant like a bagpipe of the victory for James, knowing all the while that the enemy believed as firmly in William, and that the battle might have gone the other way so that instead of skirling of victory, the pipes would be droning of death.

Robbie worked methodically, doubling the plaid over Dair's left shoulder and tucking the end into the swath across his chest. He patted the wool. " 'Tis a thick man, MacDonald." His young face was grimy. A spatter of blood highlighted one cheekbone. Sandy hair was mussed, but he appeared whole. "The Stewart is dead, Dair. He won't miss his plaid. Nor you yours; here."

Dair accepted his own bundled plaid. Just now he could not bring himself to put it on. "I'd have died wi'out you, aye?"

Robbie hitched a shoulder. "You were entangled with the man whose skull you'd just split, aye?—the other would have had you."

Dair sat very straight against the ache beneath the Stewart plaid. "Jean will thank you."

"Oh, and you willna? Too proud to admit an Appin Stewart had the saving of a Glencoe MacDonald?"

"Not too proud." Dair smiled. "Too weary."

Robbie laughed. "Aye, well—I'll have your thanks in the morning, aye?" He glanced up. "Ah—here's John—"

Dair's brother squatted down. He had taken the time to kilt his plaid around his loins and the tails of his shirt, belting it into place. The shirt was torn and soiled, his face befilthed with blood and powder grime, but he was whole. "Alasdair?"

"A cut," Dair said briefly, "and worth it, aye? We won." He nodded toward the river. "Mackay is in retreat." He swallowed; his mouth tasted of metal. "What of MacIain?"

"Whole, as am I." For a moment John fixed him with a hard, assessive stare, as if weighing for himself the truth of his brother's condition, and then he relaxed. "But the victory is hollow—"

"What?" Stewart exploded. "Christ, man, we *won!* We've routed the Dutchman's forces!"

John's expression was solemn. "Dundee is wounded. The lairds have wrapped him in their plaids and mean to take him to Blair Castle, but 'tis unco' bad, Robbie. He is not expected to live."

"Dundee?" Dair's tongue felt thick. "But—without him—" He leaned his forehead into the heel of his hand, propping up his too-heavy skull. "We're too mettlesome, John. All of us. We need a Stuart, or a Graham . . ."

"The Stuart is in France, and not like to come again until we've secured his realm," John said. "And the only Graham left in Scotland who could bind us together in James's absence will not live to command again." He ran a crusted hand through disheveled hair, painting the gray red with blood. "At Blair the lairds will meet. Some alliance may yet come of this, even without Dundee. But . . ." He sighed. Lids drooped briefly; in the aftermath of victory exhaustion often usurped the place of exultation. "We've lost men. Not so many as Mackay has, but there are not so many men of Glencoe we can spare without hardship."

"Nor of Appin," Robbie agreed. "We'd do best to go home."

The day was gone. Torches whipped fitfully in the breeze, casting haphazard light across the dead, the dying, the living. "We're to go to Blair with MacIain," John said, "then to Perth. It was Dundee's plan, and his successor, Colonel Alexander Cannon, will carry out the order. But Dunkeld is in the way . . . there is a regiment of the Earl of Angus's Foot there, sworn to William and the teachings of the Covenanter preacher Richard Cameron. We must defeat them first."

"Cameronians," Robbie murmured. "Christ, I hate a man who puts God before a true Stuart king."

John laughed softly. "Dinna discount them—they are strong in the Lord, Robbie."

The Appin Stewart drew his bloodied dirk and uprooted grass to clean the blade. "And I am strong in this, aye?"

The Earl of Breadalbane knew himself a meticulous man of great self-control. He had labored to train himself so in the household of the weak man who had sired him—he would not mimic his father's fatuous follies—but such strictly held demeanor was banished in an instant as he strode into Glenlyon's Chesthill and faced his recalcitrant kinsman. "How could you be such a muckle-headed fool, Robin? 'Tis *Campbell* land, not Murray!"

Glenlyon's obvious shock at seeing the travel-stained earl appear in his front room was usurped by wounded pride. He drew himself up. " 'Tis my house," he declared with a pitiable dignity. "You willna shout in it."

"Your house! *Your* house?" Breadalbane slapped dust from one shoulder. "Didna ye sell it too?"

Glenlyon opened his mouth, then clamped it shut. He looked at his white-faced sons clustered near the door. "You'll go."

Breadalbane paid them little heed; they had come in not long behind him, tense and silent, lurking like wary wolfhounds with hackles only half-risen, uncertain of the moment. Three remaining sons . . . The eldest dead of MacDonalds, he recalled—*Devil take them all!*—but the others now were men well cognizant of men's concerns, and cer-

Lady of the Glen ❦ 77

tainly of more promise than their dissolute father. It was apparent they were no more pleased by Robert Campbell's folly than the earl; as clearly they wanted to protest the order to leave the house. He could see it in their eyes.

But they did not protest. With a grimace of contempt, the oldest—James, he thought, dredging up their names—yanked open the door so hard it rattled against the jamb and went out stiff-legged, followed by his brothers.

It left a girl, who did not go despite the laird's order; Glenlyon's get as well, the earl knew, though she did not resemble him.

Breadalbane said nothing as she stood resolutely in the room, chin thrust out in defiance. Insolent baggage . . . *and unmindful who sees it; does she think herself protected here before a guest—*?

She was a thin girl, tall as a man and awkward because of it. Haphazardly braided hair was a vivid red, as were the level eyebrows. The eyes beneath them were a peculiarly brilliant blue. He saw the sheen in them; her taut mouth jerked briefly. She was angry, he realized, that he saw her tears.

She did not look at her father. Her level stare challenged Breadalbane levelly, focused as any man. "Will you stop it?" she demanded. "Will you undo what this drukken fool has done?"

"Cat!" In two steps Glenlyon reached her; his hand flashed across one cheek. "You willna say such to the earl—you'll go *at once!*"

His splayed hand immediately raised a reddened blotch high on one cheekbone. She would bruise easily, Breadalbane knew; the blood ran too close to the skin. The blow had spilled the tears, but clearly she disdained them. *A plain girl of common looks* . . . And yet her fierce pride was tangible.

"Will you undo it?" she asked again.

Robin had spoiled his girl—or else she had grown wilfull in her father's absence and neglect. Which was but another sin; the girl should have been married off already and tending the household of a man better fit to give her orders. "If it is within my power, I will." Breadalbane felt the pride deserved an answer even if disobedience did not. "We canna have Campbell lands sworn over to Murrays."

"Good." She looked back at her father. Briefly her mouth twisted. "Then the skelping will be worth it, aye?"

"*Cat—*" But she went smartly out the door and jerked it closed behind.

Breadalbane looked on his cousin. He could not suppress his contempt. " 'Tis a relief to know that if I do have this sale overturned, someone in this family deserves the benefit."

Glenlyon's hands trembled. "I need whisky. Will you have—"

The earl cut him off, slapping again at dusted clothing. "I've no' come to drink whisky with you, Robin. You'll face me without it. 'Tis that, and other folly, that has led to this travesty."

Glenlyon's lips writhed. "You'll refuse my hospitality? What sort of Highlander are you?"

"One in sore fear of a foolish cousin who sells lands and leases without compunction . . . and all for debts incurred because of an overabundance of 'hospitality.' " Breadalbane's nostrils pinched. He was hungry and thirsty, but would not accept the suspect hospitality Glenlyon had bartered away. "You've robbed your sons of their patrimony, Robin; d'ye mean for them to work the land as tacksmen, then, owing rents to the Murray laird?"

Glenlyon's face was ashen. He wiped a hand over it, briefly stretching out of shape the soft, drink-sallowed flesh. "They'll have their lands back."

"When?"

"Before I've died. Before they're due to inherit."

"How?"

"I'll buy them back from Murray—"

"I say again: 'How?' With your winnings?" The earl did not trouble himself to adopt a diplomatic stance in tone or expression. "There will be no 'winnings,' only 'losings.' And when you *have* lost, what have you left to sell to make good *these* debts? Your sons' strong backs and straight limbs? Your daughter's maidenhead?"

The sound that burst from Glenlyon's throat was a garbled protest of outrage and torment. From another man it might prompt compassion, regret, a recanting of harsh words, but from Glenlyon, who knew what he was and what he had done, it prompted only Breadalbane's derision and a marked distaste that a man so close in kinship could be so great a fool.

"I swore to give you no more silver," the earl declared, "and I willna forswear myself. But for the sake of your children, and the children they will sire, I will go to Murray and do what must be done to overturn this sale."

Glenlyon pressed a trembling hand against his mouth. "He willna listen."

"D'ye owe him that much?"

"He's a greedy bastard," Glenlyon muttered. "If he smells silver in your pocket, he'll ask for that yet at home."

"Then if necessary, I will take this to the courts of law. I will do what must be done."

"How?"

"Comhairl'taigh," Breadalbane said curtly. "You turned over to the

Earl of Argyll and to me the administration of your estates. The old earl is dead, but his son stands in his place; therefore, only he and I are in position to sell such things as land and leases.''

Glenlyon's mouth slackened. "You would tell Murray of the oath? 'Twas a private thing!''

"There is no such thing as privacy in the household of a fool, lest he kill himself of his folly." Breadalbane looked beyond his cousin. "Drink your whisky, then—drown yourself in it, aye?—so you may forget what you've done. Just recall that when you've died and God weighs your worth, he will most assuredly find you lacking . . . and you'll have all the days in hell to repent of your doings.''

"But—*wait*—"

But the earl unlatched the door and departed the only shelter Robert Campbell still owned.

Dair roused to damp hands and hot water, and the rough tones of his father. "Will he live, John?''

"With rest, proper food, proper care—aye, he will live." It was his brother who tended him with firm gentleness, pressing Dair's left arm across his bare chest so the cloth could reach the wound. " 'Tis no' so bad as all that—a loose flap of skin, a sliver of rib gone—but the fever wracks him. Leave him here at Blair . . . we'll go on to Dunkeld wi'out him.''

Confusion held preeminence. But his father's words at last parted the clouds massed within his mind. Dair opened his mouth to protest that indeed he was well, not sick at all; his fever-chapped lips split and bled.

"Christ," MacIain growled. "He looks puny as an early calf.''

"—not—'' Dair managed, and cracked gummy eyelids. The room swam laggardly into blurry focus: stone walls, wooden beamwork, the smell of dampness and despair. Blair Castle, then, where Dundee had died— —*when*—? He could not remember. He could remember little save departing Killiecrankie for Blair. There was a journey in between, but none of it was in his mind. "—how long—?'' But he gave up; he sounded more goose than man, honking dispiritedly.

John soaked the cloth in a dented pewter bowl, then sponged the wound again carefully. "We came three days ago. You seemed well enough up to yesterday . . . but until you collapsed we weren't permitted to look at your wound. 'Twas healing, you insisted, causing no discomfort; you wouldna be so weak a man as to take much heed of it.'' His mouth jerked briefly in wry chastisement. "Unco' stubborn, Alasdair—and now you'll stay here while the rest of us go on.''

Dair chanced a glance at his father's malevolent face looming from a great distance over the rude pallet on the stone floor, like Moses from the Mount: white mane straggling over the furrowed brow, across massive shoulders; the thicket of snowy eyebrows clutched together above fierce, penetrating eyes.

—*I've disappointed him*— It chafed so painfully Dair stirred against the pallet despite John's protest, then wished he had not. But movement roused him fully; returning senses told Dair others in like circumstances also inhabited the chamber that had become an infirmary. It was rank with the thick fug of unwashed wounded and dying men: blood, urine, feces, the acrid tang of fever-sweat, and the decay of too-vulnerable flesh cut open by musket ball, sword, knife, bayonet—or the saw wielded by a man who meant to cut off the offending limb lest its corruption engulf the body.

He heard muttered prayers, keening moans, childlike sobbing and fever-ravings. But he did not care about the others just now; MacIain's expression was thunderous. "I'll go," Dair declared promptly, thinking no additional difficulty from the wound could be half so distressing as his father's disapproval. "I'll go with you . . . the fever's broken, and I'm back in my head again."

"You willna," MacIain growled. "Christ, Alasdair, you couldna hold up a *sgian dhu* in your state, let alone a claymore! You'll stay."

" 'Tis open now, and draining; it willna take so long before you've found your feet again." John carefully dried the wound; gentle fingers pressed the loose flap of flesh down again. "By the time we're back, you'll be well enough to travel."

Dair's laughter was weak, catching in his throat so that all he expelled was a faint breathy exhalation. "—so certain 'twill take no time at all . . ."

"And so it willna!" MacIain declared.

Desperation usurped weakness; he *would not* be judged as impotent in the ways of a warrior. "What about Perth?" he asked. "We're to take it after Dunkeld . . . if I canna come in time to Dunkeld, I'll go on and meet you there."

Ferocious white brows knitted themselves together. "I willna have my son riding about the glens before time! You'll fall off and break your heid and no' be found until next spring . . . will ye have me so shamed?"

Regret faded instantly, and the certainty of failure. He knew that gruffness. Dair wanted to laugh; there were times MacIain's bluff manner was belied by his true feelings, though neither of his sons dared to tell him so. Instead he smiled wryly, upholding his father's intent. "I'd no' shame MacIain so."

"Good." A bob of massive head. "You'll stay here while we go to

Dunkeld, and meet later at Perth—*if* you're able. And not before, aye? D'ye hear?"

"I hear."

"You'd better!" With a flaring of soiled plaid MacIain swung on bare heels and strode out of the chamber.

John displayed fresh linen. "We'll have you up, then, so I can bind you." One firm hand slid behind Dair's bare back, urging him upright. "You might send a messenger tomorrow; MacIain will worry with no word."

Dair struggled into a sitting position, gritting his teeth against nagging pain and an overwhelming weakness. "He'd no' welcome an interruption."

"He'd welcome word of his son. Here—lift your arm . . ." John began to wind the linen around Dair's chest, binding the wad of bandage against his wound. " 'Tis better for a father to know what's become of his son before going into battle."

"—Christ, John!—" Dair hissed as the binding jarred his wound. With teeth clamped together he muttered, "—he'll have you at his side . . ."

"He'll need to know, Alasdair." John tied off the linen. His eyes were steady. "And so will I."

"Aye." Perspiration ran down his temples. Dair was too weak to argue. "Aye, I'll send word."

"Good. Now here—lie back . . . I ken, lad—I ken." John's taut expression mirrored Dair's. "Rest. You're a brawlie lad—you'll be on your way to Perth in but a day or two." He held a cup of cool water to his brother's mouth. "After that 'tis home to Glencoe . . . unless you stop first in Appin."

Dair gulped until the water was gone, then frowned hazily. "Appin?"

"Loch Laich." John set the cup aside and pulled the blood-and soil-stained plaid across Dair's bandaged chest; there were no blankets. "To show Jean Stewart her MacDonald is whole, lest she geld her brother because he didna see to his health."

Dair managed a smile as he neared the precipice. "She would. First Robbie—then me . . ."

His brother laughed quietly. "I doubt she'd geld *you*, Alasdair . . . 'twould somewhat diminish the pleasure!"

"—locket . . ." Dair murmured, recalling Robbie's words prior to the battle.

" 'Tis here." John tucked the necklace into Dair's slack hand. "Dream of her, Alasdair . . . then ride to Perth as soon as you're able. We're needing every man."

Dair's smile was very faint. "Even a man puny as an early calf . . . ?"

" 'Tisn't what he called you when we carried you in here; 'twas plain you'd lasted longer than we had a right to expect." John pressed his shoulder briefly. "Sleep. I'll see you at Perth."

"John—" His brother turned back. "Dundee is dead. I've a recollection of that."

"Aye. And buried in the kirk."

"Then the lairds have met."

John's face was solemn. "They've met. They've sworn an oath to serve Colonel Cannon." He cast a quick glance around the chamber, then bent close. "He's no Dundee, is Cannon—'twill not last, this campaign, unless we can keep peace among ourselves. But for now there is a chance . . . Mackay has seen to that."

"Mackay survived the battle?"

"Oh, aye . . . and a furious man, is General Sir Hugh Mackay of Scourie." The flesh beside John's eyes creased as he smiled, robbing it of weariness and tension. "He sent word offering pardons and indemnities."

"But—he *lost!*" Dair was astounded. "What possessed him to offer such to the victor?"

"Pride? He is a Scot, a *Highlander,* though too long abroad in the Dutchman's service—and a Dutch wife!—has turned him from us; he serves the Sassenach cause. Anger?" John shrugged. "But 'twill serve a purpose, despite his intent . . . in doing so he infuriated the lairds who might otherwise have lost interest with Dundee dead. They sent him back a letter saying they would die with their sword in their hands before failing in their loyalty and sworn allegiance to our sovereign."

"MacIain's words."

"I dinna doubt he had much to do with the wording." John grinned. "But for now we're united. We'll no' go home before our task is done. First Dunkeld, then Perth, all before winter."

Dair stirred against the pallet. "I shouldna be lying here."

"But you will lie there. You told MacIain so." John rose. "Dinna forget to send word."

"No." Dair's eyes shut. *Look to MacIain . . . look to yourself . . .* But he realized, as the sound of John's footsteps receded, the words had been sounded only within his skull.

Three

Seated at his table near the leaded western window of his castle, the Earl of Breadalbane took up again the letter from the Master of Stair, Sir John Dalrymple, who was perhaps at the moment the most powerful Scot of all because he had King William's ear. It did not please Breadalbane that *he* did not know such grace, but at least Stair consulted him. At least Stair valued him. *If for no other reason than to use me; well, let it be so—I will use him as he uses me; I will use Glenlyon, I will use his daughter, I will use anyone I must!*

The letter had arrived a fortnight before; he read it several times each day. He scanned it again now, despite the fact he could repeat it word for word. *". . . wherefore it is suggested that perhaps a peace may be won by means outside of a sword, in that certain rebellious clans may well value personal safety as well as silver."*

The earl understood very well what Stair was declaring: that the Crown would bribe the clans to go home and forget all about James and his doomed cause.

Breadalbane stroked a fingertip along his bottom lip. Perhaps it was not doomed. Perhaps King William, more concerned with the Netherlands and France, might weaken his position in England through sheer neglect; he neither loved nor valued his wife's patrimony beyond what it offered him against France.

James was a stupid fool too much given to dismissing the true power of his subjects, but he was nonetheless a direct descendant of royalty. James had clear claim to the Crown; he had lost it through personal and political ineptness—and the question of religion.

Breadalbane quoted aloud. *". . . 'that perhaps a peace may be won by means outside of a sword . . .'"* Perhaps it might be; only a fool would rule it out. Occasionally alternatives proved sounder than the initial idea or intent. Perhaps a peace *could*—

A knock sounded at his door. When Breadalbane called for entry his gillie, Sandy, came into the room. He carried with him a sealed letter.

Murray again—? The earl accepted the letter. Or Glenlyon—? —*ah! Neither*— He tore it open, scanned it quickly, then rose abruptly to his feet. It took effort to keep his tone steady, divulging nothing of what he felt. "Pack my things and have my coach prepared . . . I am bound for Edinburgh."

The gillie departed at once. Breadalbane, standing, dropped the soiled, much-creased letter to the table, where it landed atop Stair's older correspondence. In view of the news just received, the earl saw no need to move on Stair's suggestion.

"Not yet," he said aloud. "Silver will not attract such fools as Mac-Donalds while there is blood running on the braes."

Unless that silver be robbed from Campbells such as himself, or his kinsman Robin, with Breadalbane, Glenorchy, and Glen Lyon lands lying in the path of the wolf.

"They will go home," he mused. "In a week, a month, six weeks . . . the Glencoe-men will go home through my lands, and steal for themselves every Campbell cow as well as Campbell silver."

Another man might stay at Achallader and fight them. But the Earl of Breadalbane was not known for his fierceness in anything but wits and thriftiness; he hired others to fight *for* him. It was his task, then, to flee to Edinburgh and wait for winter to halt the warfare.

For now the Highland Jacobites had won, but by spring William's forces would return. The clans were at their weakest after a harsh winter; it was then the promise of silver might mean more than the promise of blood.

There were things to do before rising, ways of making oneself presentable again as a true son of MacIain: Dair repinned the crusted plaid at one shoulder, settled the bonnet on hair too tousled for finger-combing, tucked Jean Stewart's locket near *sgian dhu,* sorted out targe and claymore, and stood up carefully from the pallet.

He had little about him save his weapons, his improving health, his bloodstained and sweat-soiled clothing. But he had survived the battle that had killed more than six hundred Highlanders at the first volley, and many others in subsequent hand-to-hand combat.

It was time now to ride for Perth. Surely the fighting at Dunkeld was finished. He would meet with his kin and clansmen and offer what aid he could in the Jacobite cause before fall set in, bringing with it the first early snow that would, in its bounty, lock in Glencoe against intrusion—or, for that matter, prevent its inhabitants from visiting such lands as belonged to Campbells in search of bovine wealth.

Clutching claymore and targe, Dair began the laborious journey from pallet to distant door. *There will be others bound for Perth . . . I willna be alone—*

Yet even as he made the door and rounded it Dair fell back, jamming spine against lintel. The brief burst of pain high in his side as the claymore pommel knocked against the stone was quickly forgotten. There was shouting in the corridor and from outside as well; a mass of filthy men in tattered, bloodstained plaids wound its way up narrow stairs with other men in their arms, wrapped in plaids equally tattered, equally bloodstained, save in most cases the blood was red and wet instead of brown and dry.

"Christ—" To give them room Dair scraped himself around the jamb, pressing himself against stone wall inside the chamber as clansmen carried into the makeshift infirmary a new host of wounded and dying. He saw his own pallet filled immediately by a man scarcely more than a lad, with the swollen flesh of his forearm cut away to expose shattered bone.

Dair had grown accustomed to the odor of sick and dying men, but the stink was fresh again with a new recipe: blood-soaked and smoky wool; singed hair; the effluvia of the dying, helpless to tend themselves; burned and rotting flesh.

He took a step from the wall, clutching targe and claymore yet feeling impotent. "What has happened?"

But no man answered him, too busy to spare even a single word. Still more wounded were carried into the chamber until all the pallets were filled. Plaids were spread, or bodies placed on bare stone. Clansmen squatted, murmuring to the wounded; others set about stripping limbs of makeshift bandages to inspect journey-plagued wounds.

Dair's throat was tight. Into the din of the dying he shouted but three words: *"Fraoch Eilean! MacIain!"*

Heads came up at the shout, answering the ancient slogan. A kneeling man near the door, a MacDonald of Keppoch by his clan badge, twisted his head to display a smoke-blackened face. His teeth flashed white in a grime-smeared mask. "Whole. I saw him as we left Dunkeld." A brief, humorless smile jerked the blistered corners of his mouth. " 'Tis hard to miss that man."

"And my brother? John MacDonald of Glencoe?"

"Didna see him with MacIain." The clansman hawked, spat out blackened phlegm, then shrugged. "Canna say. We left Dunkeld as we could."

"Then the others have gone on to Perth?"

The Keppoch MacDonald shook his head. "We willna go to Perth, so the lairds have said. The streets of Dunkeld are full of our dead . . . why waste more at Perth?"

Dair nodded his head in thanks, then went into the corridor, intent on finding his father.

"MacDonald!" A hand on Dair's arm jerked him to a painful halt. "Christ, Jean *will* skelp me; you're thin as a sapling, man!"

"Robbie?" Dair bent long enough to set aside targe and claymore in a clatter against the floor, then clutched Stewart's shoulders. "I heard my father fares well enough, but what of John?"

"A bit scorched around the edges, but—" Robbie's voice was

hoarse. His grin faded as he clasped Dair's rigid arms. "Dinna fash yourself—they are both of them whole and well."

Dair wobbled as nervous tension spilled away. He collapsed against the wall, unmindful of his sore rib. "Christ . . . *Christ*, Robbie—" The rush of relief was so powerful it set his limbs to trembling. *—early calf, again—* "What happened? Why have we turned back from Perth?"

Stewart stank of smoke and charred flesh, though it was not his own. "They fired the town."

"Dunkeld?"

"They burned it down." Robbie shook his head; blue eyes blazed like pockets of flame in the filth of his face. "Their own dwellings, they burned to the ground—"

"The Cameronians?" Dair nearly gaped. "I thought you meant *we* burned—"

Robbie shook his head. "We went into the town after three hours of hard fighting, but the Cameronians waited until we were inside the dwellings and put locks on the door, then set them afire. They meant us to perish in the flames of hell, they said. Covenanting fools; religion isna worth dying for." He raised a forearm and scrubbed his forehead against it, smearing soot and dirt down his nose and one cheek. "Dunkeld is naught but a smoking heap of split stone and charred wood." He paused. "And bodies."

"Ours?"

"Ours. Theirs. Too many." Robbie's face was grim, his blistered mouth set tautly. Sparks had left a scattering of black pockmarks high on one cheekbone. " 'Tis over, Alasdair Og. Too many dead all at once before winter . . . we need to go home and see to our holdings before the first snow." He licked swollen lips carefully. "The lairds are to sign a bond to come together again in the field should common safety or King James's cause require it, but for the time being we're done wi' fighting."

Stewart's eyes closed briefly. His news now had been passed, his fears laid to rest; Dair could see the exhaustion in Stewart's face and posture as his broken-nailed hands twitched from dissipated tension on the end of arms rigid as wood. "Robbie—"

But Stewart went on. The raggedness of slurred words had no birth in whisky or wine. "Colonel Cannon sends us home for the winter . . . on the way we're to see to it we take our pay out of Campbell lands . . . burn Achallader, he says, and plunder all of Breadalbane's holdings." His grin was swift and ferocious, heedless of blistered mouth. "As if we needed an *order* to do such to Campbells!"

———

Sunlight slanted through warped shutters, falling in a diagonal slash keen as a claymore blade across the lid of the leather-bound trunk. Cat knelt before it, hesitated, then deftly undid the hasp. Dust motes danced as she settled the lid quietly against the wall. Light glinted grimy green and dull gold off verdigrised brass studs.

Cat paused a moment, clutching the battered leather stripping with rigid fingers, then dug down through the clothing. She felt the hardness, fingered the shape, hesitated, then drew it forth hastily so she would not change her mind. But before looking into the cracked surface, or even *at* it, Cat pressed the mirror's face against her breast.

"A wee look, no more . . ." Yet she could not bring herself to it. No indication from anyone—father, brothers, tacksmen, gillies, clansmen or Una—led her to believe the mirror would display any single feature worth examining, merging together one by one to form a whole that someone, anyone —*even me!*— might find pleasing.

In the day she did not care. In the night she cared too much, dreaming of the enemy whose supple tongue, instead of praising in empty flattery a nonexistent beauty, had in its honesty offered her hope.

She had never lost sight of that hope. Wine, they said, improved with age; could not the same be said of people?

There was the water, of course, forming its own mirror, giving back a burnwater interpretation of Catriona Campbell, but this was a true mirror, brought by her father from Edinburgh to Lady Glenlyon years before, cracked now with age, its ivory yellowed and brittle, but nonetheless better than water. In a surface ever smooth, always unvaried, she would see the real Cat Campbell.

"A wee peek, no more—" She jumped as the door downstairs was flung open and crashed against the wall. *Jamie*—? Her eldest brother never opened a door quietly when a bang announced him better. The noise was Jamie's, but if it were, he had come home early. It was the edge of fall; Cat was alone at Chesthill, save for Una. The other women were yet on the summer shielings, preparing to come home, while the men tended the harvest.

"*Chruachan!*" cried the voice.

—*not Jamie*— Nor her father, nor Una. A lad. A lad she did not know.

Cat dropped the mirror, heedless of fragile glass, and ran for the stairs. She did not run away from the cry but *to* it, as a Campbell should, and by the time she was down the stairs she realized only one thing would bring a crofter lad into the laird's house unexpected or unannounced, save for shouting the Campbell war cry.

Barefoot, in breeks and saffron-dyed shirt, Cat stopped on the stairs but two steps from the bottom, brought up short by naked steel.

"MacDonalds—" the boy at the door croaked, but she had no need of him. She knew very well who they were and what they wanted, with the tip of a claymore blade dancing coyly at her throat.

"Some, forbye," the swordsman said, "but no' all." He put up a hand and beckoned Cat, waggling imperious fingers. "Come here to me, lass . . . come *here*"—more intently, as she stiffened to spin and run—"or I'll have a taste of your flesh."

He meant it; she felt the cold kiss of steel as it touched the thumb-sized hollow splitting her collarbones. If she so much as swallowed, she could be cut.

"To me," he said, and moved the blade minutely as she descended a single step. His grin was white-toothed in a grimy, spark-pocked face. "Aye, one by one, and slowly—have you a dirk behind your back?"

She did not. She wished she had. *Another step* . . . Careful inhalation; a fierce self-admonition not to tremble, lest the sword tip scratch her flesh, nor to show her fear lest he take pleasure from it. She stood on the stone floor now, cool against callused bare soles, and was supremely surprised to discover she was taller than he.

Clearly so was he; blue eyes blinked, sandy brows arched, and he laughed. His lips, she saw, had been burned enough to blister; minute peelings of dead skin curled up from newborn flesh. "Christ, lass—" He paused. "*Are* you a lass?" A broken-nailed hand caught at the folds of her shirt even as he shifted the blade aside. "Are there duckies beneath the cloth?"

Cat reacted instinctively, knocking aside his arm with her own in a sharp, sideways slash. She did not think of the sword, still gripped in his other hand; she thought of his fingers, of his broken nails, of his intimate, groping hand. "Dinna *touch* me, MacDonald!"

His surprise did not last long. He caught her wrist and crushed it cruelly, threatening the bones, then swung her toward the door. "A lad with breasts, is it? Or a boy-faced lass?" He glanced briefly beyond her, then jerked his head even as the croft-boy fell away, scrambling to escape. "Strip it," he ordered unseen men. "I'll have plates, rack-spits, candlesticks—anything of value! Spare Glenlyon nothing . . . he's naught but a drukken man; let him weep into his usquabae!"

"Leave it be!" Cat cried; they had so little left, now that her father had sold off anything that might bring a silver penny. "Dinna touch my house!"

"Your house? Yours?" His grip tightened. He was not, she realized, a MacDonald after all. His bonnet badge, though caked with soot, boasted another clan. "Are you Glenlyon's whelp, then?"

"Leave that!" she shouted as the first man beyond the threshold tore from the window her mother's lace curtains, painstakingly repaired after Jamie's recent fury by Una's careful work.

Her captor shook her. "I asked you: Are you Glenlyon's?"

Cat's head snapped on her neck, sending a sharp pain shooting into her skull. For all he was shorter than she, he was neither slight nor weak. His fingers on her wrist were rigid as wire.

"—daughter," she muttered, hating herself for the tears that sprang to her eyes.

"The laird's daughter? Then you're fit to serve the man outside. He's in need of a wet throat." He snatched a stolen cup from the clansman who had stolen it, then shoved it beneath her chin. "Usquabae."

Cat stared into his face. A young man; younger, she thought, than Jamie. *I should be afraid*— And so she was, but not *so* afraid that she could not think, could not consider and assess the result of this action, or that— *I am taller*— But she shut it off. He would hurt her. Any attempt at escape now, as he touched her, would fail, gaining her naught, and he would hurt her.

He laughed, as if he read her intent. A shiver coursed through her body. With the rim of the cup pressed cruelly against her chin, Cat nodded acquiescence as much as she was able.

They had plundered her father's whisky, but one man poured the cup full. The tang of liquor filled her head, stinging her eyes. As around her the MacDonalds stripped Chesthill bare of even such small riches as pewter spoons and platters, Cat made her way outside. It was no less frenzied there as men brought out their plunder from house and outbuildings. Iron clanked, and pewter, loaded onto garrons already bearing stolen wealth.

—they've robbed the croft-houses— From farther up the glen she heard the shouts of the clansmen who had already appropriated cattle, sheep, goats, and horses, gathering them for driving. *—they will leave us nothing . . . nothing at all . . .* Cat bit into her lip. If there was any consolation, it was that Lord Murray of Atholl would lose as much as her father; but winter would be hard, bitter hard, if not impossible. In their greed, in their ferocity, the MacDonalds would make certain nothing remained on which the Campbells might live. *Better to kill us outright, than starve us to death!*

Two garrons, one riderless, the other mounted, pawed idly at hoof-churned mud still puddled from morning rain. She refused to raise her head, to meet the eyes of the mounted man to whom she was to give her father's whisky in her father's cup. Through a haze of bitter tears Cat saw a foot thrust into the stirrup, a bare bruised knee pressed against horseflesh. The sett of the kilt was of the deep black-green and rich crimson colors often favored by MacDonalds.

Cat stared steadfastly at the mucky ground as she picked her way to the horse. *I willna look at him*— She stopped at the stirrup, clenching teeth so firmly her jaws ached. As the hand came down to grasp the cup, she deliberately turned it over. *"Chruachan,"* she murmured fiercely.

Whisky splashed bare feet, splattered mud on her ankles and soiled the ragged bottoms of her borrowed breeks, but she did not care. She exulted in it. *Chruachan. Chruachan. I'll say it till I die . . .for dead Robbie and for Glen Lyon—*

From behind someone grabbed a handful of hair. The grip twisted her head sideways, then a rough shove sent her sprawling to the ground. Cat landed on chin, hip, elbow, and shoulder, then dug the elbow into muck to lever herself up. She watched in numb comprehension as whisky and horse urine soaked her ill-plaited braid.

Inanely she thought, *Una will be angry.*

The man with the claymore stood beside her, setting the tip into mud so the sheen of steel was dulled. "Drink it, then. If you willna serve a MacDonald or Stewart, you'll serve yourself instead!"

Stewart. *Stewart,* not MacDonald; he had denied it at the beginning. Likely of Appin, then; they were nearly as close as Glencoe.

Glencoe.

Cat, still sprawled in muck, looked up sharply. She ignored the Stewart entirely and stared instead at the mounted man, the MacDonald, the laird's son to whom she had been ordered to serve Campbell whisky.

The man beside her stirred. "Christ, Dair, you're white as a corpse—" He forgot her abruptly, swinging toward the horse. "We'll have you down, aye? . . . we'll have you in the house—"

His eyes were the same whisky-gold, she saw, though sheltered in bruised sockets deeper than she recalled. The lean face was thinner, paler, nearly gaunt; a grimy smudge emphasized the hollows beneath sharp cheekbones, the stark contours of his skull. Near-black hair, curling this way and that beneath the fit of his bonnet, was grayer than Cat remembered, speckled more thickly. He had not shaved; dark stubble etched his jaw, proving only the hair on his head was graying to tarnished silver.

"I'll ride on to Glencoe," Alasdair Og said. "There will be warmer welcome there."

"Warmer yet in Castle Stalker, aye? Here—" The Stewart snatched something from a passing man, then thrust it toward Dair MacDonald. "Take something to Jean of the Campbells."

In sunlight, it glinted copper. Cat stared, outraged: *Even my mother's kettle!*

Dair handed down the reins of a riderless horse to the Appin Stewart. "Ride on. My garron's limping a wee bit—I'll catch up."

"But—"

"Ride on. The men are done here."

The voice was precisely as she recalled it, though a trifle frayed around the edges, as if he had spent its timbre on too much shouting.

Cat was aware of kilted clansmen departing the house with plunder stuffed into table linens, tied in bundles onto horses, or swung over plaid-swathed shoulders. One by one they mounted, laughing and jesting, shouting to one another of the booty they had acquired, and turned their garrons toward the track. Eventually even the Stewart, muttering of fools and madmen, departed Glenlyon's dooryard.

Dair MacDonald watched them go, then turned back. His expression was predominantly solemn, but Cat, sitting up in mud and puddles, marked a peculiar set to his mouth, as if there were other words he meant to say but dared say none of them.

Eventually he offered: "If I get down, I willna get up again."

From another man it might constitute apology. But not from a Mac-Donald, surely; a MacDonald would never dismount to pull a Campbell from the ground. Nor would a Campbell offer the service to a MacDonald. *I willna have his hands on me.*

Cat felt hollow and filled with light as she stood slowly. Wet breeks stuck to her thighs. Her muck-laden braid glued itself to her neck and shirt; she felt the damp weight of whisky-scented mud stubbling her chin, dribbling slimy wetness down her neck. She put up her dirty chin to ward away mockery, but into her mind leaped a wholly unexpected vision of Lady Glenlyon's French perfume packed neatly away by a girl who did not believe herself worthy of its scent.

A wild laugh bubbled up. —*usquabae and horse-piss*— She gulped a hiccup and bit into her lip, shutting off the impulse. "Go," she said tightly. "Have you no' done enough?"

He ignored her entirely, wholly focused on something else. "Catriona—? *Cat?*"

Humiliation gagged her. Seven years later he knew her, knew even her *name . . .* A wail of grief was briefly born, then died in her throat. It was worse, then, far worse. She had expected never to see him again; that he would never see her, all things she could bear, but to know he *remembered . . .* to know he saw her in such a state as this blunted anger entirely and robbed her even of pride. She bit again deeply into her lip, hoping pain would halt the helpless uprush of tears. Broken fingernails cut crooked crescents into the flesh of slimy palms.

"Cat—" But he broke it off. His mouth worked stiffly, then stilled into a rigid, taut-lipped line. With infinite care he climbed down from his garron.

He said if he got down, he couldna get up again. . . . But he *was* down, splashing into muck. It slopped across bare feet and ankles, but he did not heed it.

Cat shook back her sticky braid. She expected him to turn away from her, to inspect his mount's sore hoof; it was why he delayed as the others rode away.

But he did not. Instead he held out the kettle.

Cat gazed at him, uncomprehending. When he did not withdraw the kettle or speak again, she ventured to put trembling hands on the dented metal. As their fingertips brushed she jerked the kettle away. She stared hard at the callused male hands, now empty, because she could not look into his face, could not meet his eyes to see the pity there, the compassion, the comprehension of what she felt. He would know. He would understand. As he had years before.

Cat hugged the battered kettle, willing herself not to cry. She heard him turn away, saw the tarnished glint of silver. He moved stiffly, as if his joints ached. She remembered there had been a battle fought at Killiecrankie; that the Jacobites had won. He and others like him, fighting for King James, had defeated King William's men.

She wanted to ask it aloud: *How many men did you kill?* But she did not, knowing he would tell her only because she asked; he had proved his honesty seven years before in the name of a laird's boy-faced daughter. A battle was more important. Victory cried out for truth.

Yet he would tell her *because* she asked, and because it was the truth, not to rejoice in death. She prayed he would not rejoice, or become a lesser man than in the dreams she had created.

He mounted, muttering beneath his breath: *"Dinna be a puny calf, Alasdair Og—"* —and then he was in the saddle, gray-faced and sweating, gathering reins, settling kilt, plaid, claymore, and targe. His bonnet badge flashed argent in the gilt-and-rose light of fall.

Cat clutched the kettle. As he turned his garron after the others, she saw it did not limp after all.

Wind rustles trees. There is no peat-smoke upon the air, no smell of cooking meat, no odor of frying fish. No odor at all save of trees, of sap, of turf. Nothing at all of people.

The glen remains, girdled by cliffs and peaks, cut through by the river, but no one lives in it despite fertility. The valley is empty of habitation, save for its natural game. Empty of MacDonalds.

She rides unerringly to the house, ignoring the ruins of others. And there she finds identical destruction as well as similar methods: charred timber and broken stone shattered by the heat, collapsed roof slates. Wind has scoured the ruins free of ash, so that only the stark timbers remain thrusting impudently skyward, fallen into a tangle like a handful of dropped kindling.

Nothing remains to mark human habitation. No scrap of cloth, no pewter plate, no perfume brought from France. Only the detritus of massacre, of fire and plunder, and the flowers of late spring breaking up through blackened soil.

Part III

1691

One

*T*he road existed because of cows; there were ways held in common with other clans of driving cattle to and from pasturage, and later on to market. This road was one of them, a hoof-beaten, rock-strewn track wider than a deer trail but little better, and certainly no cobbled road like the Romans had built in the land of the Sassenach. But road it was nonetheless, hedged by granite, heather, and bracken, cutting across the mountain fastness warding the northern side of Glencoe.

Glencoe MacDonalds had come up the drove-road to see the English-speakers who, with their Lowland lapdogs, dared to come into the Highlands to set up housekeeping. There had been rumors of it since Killiecrankie, but now rumor was fact. At the behest of General Sir Hugh Mackay, who had lost Killiecrankie—and others who hated Highlanders—King William had given permission to build a fort near Inverlochy. Its placement clearly was deliberate: on a narrow spit of land beside the River Nevis, in the shadow of the mount, where once stood Gearasdan dubh nan Inbhir-Lochaidh, the Black Garrison. There were memories attached, and MacIain of Glencoe, accompanied by his sons and a small tail of men, said he should not doubt the recollections were stirred of a purpose.

The fort was as yet unfinished, though it neared completion. The ramparts of earth, stone, and timber stood firm, setting up a formidable barricade against the enemy. Inside stood crude-built buildings for the housing of ammunition, stores, and officers. Outside huddled a cluster of canvas tents, and the haphazard beginnings of peat huts far more crudely constructed than the shielings that housed the clans during summer. The common man gone for a soldier, wintering in hut instead of house, was less well off than the poorest Highlander.

The MacDonalds did not attempt to hide themselves from view. MacIain and his sons stood upon the crown of the hill looking down upon the fort, and let the men working there see who and where they were. There would be no fighting; there was at present no battle intended, nor even a skirmish, merely reconnaissance. They took the measure of one another.

MacIain's white hair blew in the breeze that crested the hill and set the bracken to waving. He had brought with him, by habit, an assortment of weapons, including claymore and blunderbuss, though he let those below at the fort see he had men to carry such arms for him, and a gillie to carry *him* across each stream so as to keep his brogues dry: he was a Highland chieftain.

Dair and John stood together, making independent count of the red-backed Sassenachs. It was early yet; there would be more men to come. Their task, then, was to make the coming dreaded by those men; to make the living so difficult—or even impossible—that no matter how many soldiers were garrisoned at the fort, they would find food less than plentiful and supplies such as clothing and other simple plenishings—pots, kettles, even spoons—nonexistent. It was a simple task: to fall upon supply trains wending from Atholl and Badenoch, taking such supplies as they could carry away. Glencoe would profit from it, while the Sassenachs did not.

MacIain's voice rumbled, though he spoke quietly. "They'll send out patrols to drive us away so they forage for food in peace. Thinking to be clever, they'll send out *Scots* levies . . . well, we're no' fools, are we, to let even another Scotsman take what belongs to Glencoe." His eyes burned like a banked peat-fire in withered, deep sockets. "We'll take the cows away."

Dair nodded, half-smiling. It was a simple and bloodless solution. Even with protection the soldiers dared not wander too far from the fort for fear of clan reprisal, and those who did would find there was little food to be had. A lack of cattle combined with diverted supply trains would soon combine to demoralize the hungry army. They would turn elsewhere, of course—likely to supply ships coming up Loch Linnhe—but those schemes would take time to implement. The Lowland government would initially delay turning to the sea out of pride and stubborn resolve, and by the time supplies were sent by ship the army garrison would be sick and half-starved.

Dair picked from his eye a windblown lock of hair. *Starving men dinna fight so well* . . . A movement from MacIain caught his attention. His father took from his jacket pocket a tarnished, battered spyglass brought home from France one year. MacIain raised it to an eye and peered down upon the fort.

When he took it away he was smiling sweet as a babe. " 'Tis as I thought," he said, tucking the glass away. "They've a graveyard begun already."

English-born Colonel John Hill, former Constable of Belfast and now Their Majesties' Governor of the fort near Inverlochy but newly named after its Dutch-born king, stood before the gates and stared up at the granite-crowned hills. Behind the rocky crest bloomed a lowering sun, but the silhouettes were eloquent enough for a man such as

Hill, who understood what a fort meant to the way of life most jeopardized by its presence. There were Highlanders up there, he knew, because he had been told so by a near-panicked English soldier; undoubtedly they were MacDonalds, and fully anticipated by anyone with wit enough to acknowledge the Highlanders would take a pointed and wholly natural interest in Fort William's construction.

Beside him, General Sir Hugh Mackay stirred. "I should take a patrol up there to send them scrambling back to their hovels."

Governor Hill did not acknowledge the comment, though he could not help a brief twitch at the corner of his mouth. He understood very well that Mackay's pride yet stung from his defeat at Killiecrankie, but Hill knew just such a patrol would win the king's general no sop to that pride; in fact, he would encounter an additional defeat. At home in their heather, hills, and crags, the clansmen would not be beaten by hungry, ill-clad soldiers more interested in food than in killing or catching a Scot.

"They've come to watch, no more," Hill said quietly. "We would do well to accustom ourselves to the glint of their steel and the sett of their tartan; we'll see them all through summer."

Mackay's sour mouth was grimly set. "We waste time. Breadalbane's scheming will accomplish naught; you should burn the houses, lift the cattle, and destroy all their crops."

Governor Hill did not answer. He had an entirely different opinion of the Campbell earl, whom he believed to be a man singularly dedicated to seizing the main chance for himself. For now Breadalbane spoke of treaties and peace; but Hill had heard rumors that from the other side of his mouth the earl, a Highlander himself, whispered of war to the chiefs.

"It will be left to you," Mackay said. " 'Twill be your task to bring the Highlanders to heel; the king has defeated the Irish at the River Boyne, but now there is another threat. A French fleet lies of Beachy Head and may invade . . . 'tis time I saw to soldiering instead of building forts."

Hill would not be sorry to see Mackay go, though he murmured his regrets. Mackay was a Scot, but his long years of service abroad in the Scottish Brigade had painted over his nationalism with a more lurid dedication to William of Orange. He held his fellow Scot in contempt, while Hill admired the Highlander's fiery pride and virulent traditionalist's culture.

"If it be within my power to persuade the government to send me the meat they promised, as well as other necessities such as beds, of which we yet have none, I shall be content to do as I may here," Hill said. "But leave me English in place of Scots, and all shall be well."

"No." Mackay shook his head. "You will have companies from Clan Grant and Clan Menzies—and four companies of Campbells from the Earl of Argyll's regiment."

Hill felt a twinge of uneasiness. "This is MacDonald country. To invite Campbells here—"

"This is land belonging to whoever is able to hold it," Mackay interrupted disagreeably. "Across the loch are Camerons and Macleans; to the east lie Murrays and Menzies, with the Hendersons closer yet. *And* Campbells." He glared up at the hill crowned with MacDonald tartan, sparking MacDonald steel. "They are cattle thieves, no more; let them all be hanged."

Hill, no longer young, was decidedly nearsighted; he could not see the steel. But he knew it was there. Mildly he said, "If you hang a man for lifting cattle, you will have to hang half of Scotland."

Mackay turned a congested face upon him. "I am a soldier! I know my duty!"

Hill did not dispute Mackay's choler; he did not blame the man for his frustrations. "Indeed, our duty is to the king . . . but just now a plan for peace prevails in place of force."

"Peace," Mackay muttered. " 'Twill delay the only means for subduing these savages."

"I have had some experience of men such as these," Hill began diffidently; he was not a man who sought confrontation or bombast. "A man keeping in his mind that these Highlanders are at once a proud and honorable people, but wholly reasonable when the way seems clear, can often persuade them to sheathe their claymores and set aside their targes."

"They are savages!"

"Savage in battle, savage in pride and honor; indeed, they are men apart from all, save the Irish, who are similar." The governor smiled; he had reason to know the Irish, after service in Belfast. "But there is kindness in them, given leave to show it." He squinted up at the man-shaped silhouettes clustered on the hilltop. "It is my task to present them with *presence;* with the promise of strength. They will respect that."

Mackay glared at him. "Is that what you will do? Promise them kindness?"

"Honor," Hill replied simply. "If you hold them in contempt, that is what you yourself shall reap."

General Sir Hugh Mackay of Scourie, defeated by the 'savages' now watching him from the hills, barked a derisive laugh. "And how will *honor* succeed where military strength has not?"

Hill smiled gently; he did not wish to offend the general, who remained in William's favor, but neither did he desire the man to consider the fort's governor incapable of grasping even rudimentary procedures. "I have promises of John Stewart of Ardshiel, close-linked to Appin's laird, that he and others like him will not protest my governorship with a show of arms. I have promises of Coll MacDonald of Keppoch that he and Ewan Cameron of Lochiel may yet be moved to persuade other clans not to rise, if—in his words—'they can be made to live.' "

" 'Made to live?' *Bribed,* you mean." Mackay's mouth knotted beneath his nose. "A dishonorable way of winning a war . . . and I'd trust no Highlander to respect his promise!"

Hill sighed inwardly, though he maintained an even tone. "If I can save the life of a single man, be he Sassenach or Highlander, I will praise God for the chance."

It brought hot color to Mackay's face again. He muttered imprecations beneath his breath as he swung away. "I have duties to attend!"

Hill felt a sense of relief as the general stomped off. He prayed nightly for peace, knowing its path was thick with human obstacles such as Hugh Mackay and John Dalrymple, Master of Stair—now also Secretary of Scotland—who advocated main force. But it was because of men like Mackay and Stair that an old campaigner such as John Hill was made governor, whom they believed could use his experience in the easing of Jacobites from freedom to subjugation.

"Ease it I will, in the true sense of the word, if they give me leave to do so." Hill shielded his eyes from the glare of the setting sun. There were men of the clans he trusted to hold their word if not shown another way as honorable. But a Highlander equated oaths and promises with a system of honor not wholly comprehended by Sassenachs. If one laird stood up to the rest and persuaded them that to tolerate William was to dishonor James, their rightful monarch, all of Hill's careful plans could collapse in disarray.

"One man," he murmured. "One old fox, such as MacIain of Glencoe, could bring down everything."

Breadalbane had lost Achhallader to the MacDonalds on their way home from Killiecrankie; therefore, the earl, possessor of many fine castles, took up residence in Kilchurn on the shore of Loch Awe and immediately set about repairing damages to his reputation.

A knock sounded at the door of his private study. Breadalbane sanded his signature at the bottom of the newly completed letter, then set it aside as he called for entrance.

It was not his gillie, Sandy, whom the earl expected, but his eldest son, Duncan, whom he did not like, had never liked, and did not desire to inherit; but short of petitioning the king to have Duncan set aside in favor of John, his second son, there was little he could do.

Breadalbane could not suppress a twinge of displeasure, though no guilt accompanied it. "Aye?"

Duncan Campbell was a thin, slight young man narrow through the shoulders, with long, ill-fleshed limbs. The neck separating head from shoulders was short, and the skull perched atop it a trifle too large, Breadalbane felt, for ordinary proportions. Duncan's coloring was sallow, his hair more brown than fair, but with no life in it to lift it from his scalp.

John should be in his place. "Aye?" he repeated.

Duncan Campbell shut the door behind him. He did not approach his father. "I've a thing to say."

"You've many things to say," his father observed, "but I've never known any of them to be worth my effort to hear them."

Dull color flushed the sallow, sensitive features. The eyes were brown, but so dark as to be indistinguishable between pupil and iris. "I wish to be married."

It was astounding news, though Breadalbane did not permit his surprise to alter the austerity of his expression. "Do you?"

"I do."

"And is this notion something that occurred last night over a dram of whisky, in some harlot's bed—or something someone else has put into your head?" There were men who would, the earl knew, seeking preferment through their daughters.

Duncan did not color up well. His sallow complexion darkened perceptibly, but in a complex network of splotches altogether displeasing. " 'Tis something I've been considering—"

"Considering!"

"—for some time," he finished stolidly.

"Ah." Trust Duncan to look to himself rather than to his father's counsel; John knew better. "And have you chosen a woman? Or have you no' got so far?"

"Far enough," Duncan countered, grimly implacable. "Her name is Marjorie."

"And is Marjorie a Campbell?"

Surprise flickered in Duncan's expression; he had not the imagination to entertain the idea that women of other clans might be potential wives. "Aye, Marjorie Campbell. Of Lawers."

Breadalbane snorted. " 'Twas her idea, was it?"

The overlarge head rose a fraction, stretching to its debatable length the overshort neck. " 'Twas mine."

"But she kens what you'll be when I am dead."

"Who doesna?" Duncan answered with a brief spark of asperity. "There isna a man in Scotland who doesna ken Breadalbane."

The earl smiled. "There isna, is there? So, Marjorie Campbell of Lawers has a notion to be a countess?"

"She's a notion to be my wife."

"One and the same, lad. Not now, but count the years; no man lives forever."

The dark eyes were opaque. "If it were one and the same, wouldna she set her cap for you? You've outlived three wives. You may be an old man, but you've more substance than 'wee Duncan,' aye? Aye, I ken what they say, and I ken how you answer: but for the order of our births, John would be your heir."

"I've never hidden it from you."

"You havena. You've done me the honor of being an honest man." Duncan's smile was slight and without levity in it. "Meanwhile, there is a Campbell lass I'd take to wife, but I need your permission. I am as yet your heir."

"Then 'tis a verra serious matter, this taking of a wife. I must think on it." The earl smiled thinly as he saw Duncan's dismay. "Tell the lass she'll have to wait. 'Twill give us the time we need to see if she is breeding." He gestured casually. "You've said the thing, then. Let me consider it without you in the room."

He did not doubt there was more Duncan desired to say, but he did not remain to say it. There were times the earl despaired of the lad's wits, and other times, though less often, he saw the vestiges.

A man with no wit was never a threat. A man with just enough was often too easily led.

He did not dare permit Duncan to have his way, lest he begin to exert himself in political matters. He was, after all, to inherit one of the most powerful and wealthy positions in all of Scotland. Men would listen to Duncan, even now. Some men, enemies, would seek to use him against a father for whom he professed no love.

"In that we remain in mutual agreement," the earl muttered to himself, then gave himself over to thought. "A Campbell lass for Breadalbane's heir . . ."

It did not require much thought, and even less time to initiate. He took up fresh paper, reinked his quill, and began in his careful hand to write with equal care the words he knew would elicit the response he required.

Cunning as a fox, they called him; slippery as an eel. Well, let it be true. When a man recognized power in another, he took it, controlled it, destroyed it.

Or married it.

Cat teetered on the brink of sleep as if she walked a sword. If she fell *this* way, she was awake . . . *that* way, she was asleep. It was a sensation she particularly relished, warm beneath the bedclothes on a still-cold, dark March night, and she wanted no one to interrupt it.

No one did. Some*thing* did: a harsh, hooting, honking drone that jerked her off the edge of the sword into wide-eyed wakefulness. *"Jesu,"* she whispered violently, "the man is at it *again!*"

She considered stopping up her ears with pillows, or fingers, or bed-clothes and burrowing back beneath the covers, but the sound of bag-pipes in distress was enough to disturb the bones in the barrows for a thousand years. Instead of stopping her ears she'd do better to stop her father. Certainly no one else would: the laird was in his cups.

Irritated, Cat threw back quilts and thrust herself out of bed, loath to leave the warmth, and swung her heavy braid behind one shoulder as she reached for a wool wrap. Quickly she yanked fabric around her shoulders and crossed the room to her door, nearly slamming it open in her haste. She caught it, cursed as she'd heard the tacksmen do— knowing her father abhorred it—and marched out of the room to the stairs that led down to the laird's quarters.

Cat snatched open the oak door. Weak light met her eyes, shed from an oil lamp blackened by spent smoke, for her father sat mostly in darkness, hugging the cloth-covered bag as if the pipes were a woman and he the woman's hungry son.

The reeds had fallen free of his mouth, fetching up against his cheek. She saw dampness there, and, ashamed of her twinge of disgust, believed it was saliva.

Then she realized the dampness was tears. The Laird of Glenlyon was crying.

Cat stood very still. The shutters were latched, the curtains dropped; the room was close and stuffy, redolent of whisky, of smoke, of a sour loneliness, and the acrid tang of a man less concerned by the scent of a body than the taste of his liquor.

She was ashamed of him, and *for* him: he was Glenlyon, *still* Glen-lyon, still laird despite the excesses that had nearly destroyed them, lurking yet in corners; still a Campbell and therefore worth the respect Campbell blood bought in Campbell-built Scotland if for no other rea-son; still a Highland Scot, though some said now his English sympa-thies made him over into a Sassenach.

He has no one else. If I turn from him, he is lost. Shame faded. He was not a man she admired because the whisky had robbed him of that, but he was nonetheless her father.

Cat moved forward in silence, though she knew he saw her well enough, even against the sienna wash of poor candlelight in the corridor beyond the open door. She went to him, and knelt, and put gentle hands upon his knee. "It canna be so bad."

The smoking oil lamp illuminated him from the side, throwing harshly patterned shadows across his ruined face and casting a nimbus around fading, yellow-red hair. Once he had been a glorious, handsome youth. Now he was nearly sixty, and looking years beyond that. The drink had stretched his skin, pulling it into bags at the eyes and jowls at his jaw, the once-fine, longish jaw his sons had inherited. He was puffy-faced, ill-kempt, smelling of whisky, sour linen, bad teeth.

Glenlyon blinked. Watery blue eyes peered at her from under sandy-lashed eyelids. His damp smile was tremulous as he wiped distractedly at the tears. " 'Twas only the pipes, lass. The wail and moan of the pipes . . ." It trailed off. He looked at her in silence, and put one hand over both of hers.

Cat's throat was tight. Painfully, she swallowed. "Leave the pipes to Hugh Mackenzie. He's as good as Auld Archibald the Red . . . and quieter about it, too."

Glenlyon stared back at her, still hugging the pipes against his chest. " 'Tis Breadalbane."

Cat's mouth curled. "That pawkie, useless man . . . what has he to do with you *now?*"

"He's offered to pay my debts."

She made a disrespectful noise. "He must want a service, then, aye? Now, or one day. He swore he would not give you silver again."

Glenlyon rubbed wearily at equally tired flesh. " 'Tis bad, Cat— unco' bad . . . 'twas all I could think to do. The creditors want their silver, and I have none to spare—"

She could not suppress the bitterness, the shame-bred hostility. "The MacDonalds left us little enough two years ago, after Killiecrankie, and you sold so much to Murray . . . now have you staked even Chesthill on a game?"

Color spilled out of his face. With an awkward, frenzied motion, he threw the bagpipes to the floor.

Cat nearly gaped. It wasn't the pipes that stilled her heart, but the look in her father's eyes. "Have you lost it?" she cried.

The sagging jaw tautened. Dulled eyes sparked briefly as he was roused to protest his daughter's temerity. "Breadalbane has agreed to pay the debts; Chesthill is still mine."

Cat was on her feet, clutching soft-combed wool around her shoulders. "But for how much longer?" she asked. "Until the next time? Until all the earls of Scotland say no to your crying and begging? What *then*, Glenlyon—will you even sell your clan?"

He looked at Cat. "I thought I might sell my daughter."

It silenced her instantly. She stood before him, shivering, digging nails into her arms. "You're *fou,*" she accused. "In your cups—you'd not say it, otherwise."

"Aye, in my cups," he agreed. "Could I sell my daughter sober?"

"You havena," she declared. "To whom would you? To whom *could* you?"

"Breadalbane."

Cat laughed harshly. "He's had three wives already, and sons aplenty, besides. What would he want with me?"

The pupils of his eyes, in dimness, in dunkenness, swallowed the blue of the irises. They were fixed on her face in a blind, empty stare Cat could not interpret. Then the gaze shifted, altering as he looked briefly lower than her face, to her breasts, her hips, her slippered feet. Glenlyon's eyes, before he shut them, filled with a too-bright, damp acknowledgment to which Cat was not privy.

He drew in a breath slowly, stentorously, and let it out again. "I've no' sold my daughter."

Relief nearly made Cat waver, but she was not the swooning sort. She swallowed the dryness out of her mouth and licked her lips to wet them.

"But I *could,*" he told her.

Panic had subsided; she knew how to handle this mood. Her mouth pulled into a sideways hook of wry disbelief. " 'Tis for the father to pay, not sell . . . 'tis what the dowry is. He'd be wanting silver *with* me, not giving it to you."

Glenlyon's mouth denied it; his eyes avoided hers.

"So," Cat said, "the earl will pay your debts. What I want to know is: *why?* He wouldna do it when you asked before; nor did he overturn the sale to Murray of Atholl. He's done little enough for us these past two years . . . why does he offer now?"

"We're cousins," he said softly.

" 'Twas *Argyll* who gave you a commission in his regiment. Breadalbane did naught."

"We're Campbells. The man looks after his house."

"It has been Argyll's house for years, since his father was executed—" Cat frowned. "Breadalbane and Argyll are both of them Campbells, but no' the friendly sort. Always rivals, the earls, always wanting the honor of cosseting Clan Campbell . . . 'tis a matter between them, aye?—to tend impoverished Glenlyon?" She considered. "If Breadalbane does make this offer, I ask: At what profit?"

Glenlyon shook his head. "He asked no collateral. He does it out of loyalty to the clan. He is Laird of Glenorchy, Cat, and a chief in his own right. Despite our troubles, he has Campbell welfare at heart.''

Cat's mouth twisted again. ''Grey John Campbell may have been born to Glenorchy, but he didna get to be the Earl of Breadalbane out of simple generosity . . . nor did he become as powerful as he is through kindness without intent.'' She wove fingers through her braid. ''Isna he a favorite of King William? Or is it Queen Mary?''

''No, of Sir John Dalrymple, Master of Stair; *he* is William's favorite.'' Glenlyon scratched the first trace of stubble on his chin, a thin, watery shadow of dulled silver-gilt. ''What does it matter, Cat? He is going to pay my debts.''

The retort came too quickly. ''So you can start over again.''

He did not protest, not even with a glance, though she believed— she hoped—he would. Glenlyon was too drink- and debt-wasted to mark the complexities of her tone, her posture, her expression.

Cat shook her head, aware of a great emptiness in her soul and a knot of grief that would not lessen. She pleaded now, hoping it might stir him to something more than the dull indifference bred of habitual despair. ''You have wasted so much. Waste no more, *lose* no more; let us hold up our heads again.''

''He has asked you to come to Kilchurn,'' he said abruptly, as if he had heard nothing of what she said; likely, he had not.

Cat stared. ''Who?''

''Breadalbane,'' he answered. ''His heir has yet to wed.''

In shock, Cat swung around and took two steps away from her father before she realized what she was doing. And then she did realize it, and stopped, and swung around to face him. ''Why does he choose me? I bring his heir no dowry, no honor . . .'' She would not speak of other things she could not offer; Breadalbane had seen her two years before. He knew.

''I havena asked his reasons.''

Because you need the silver too much. Cat gritted her teeth. ''Do you want me to marry him?''

He was not so drunk as she had thought. The tears had dried on his face. ''I want you to go to Kilchurn, to be a guest of the Earl of Breadalbane.''

''To marry his son,'' she said flatly, ''so you can pay off your debts— or begin new ones.''

''To enjoy his hospitality; he *is* a Highlander.''

''So am I,'' she said tightly. ''So am I, Glenlyon.''

Cat's father smiled. ''Dinna you think I ken that? Dinna you think I *see* it?''

She thought he could not; that he saw nothing but dice, debt, and lost silver. "Then why?"

"Because you may *like* the man!" Glenlyon shouted, coloring. "You know I canna do much for setting you up . . . and you're no' a lass anymore. You deserve the chance I canna give ye."

Two years before, in the echo of Stewart words and MacDonald perfidy, she had given up hoping, of dreaming. She was a laird's daughter and, therefore, above a common tacksman or gillie; she was an impoverished laird's boy-faced daughter, and therefore pitiable by another laird, or his son, though neither would admit it.

This was, indeed, her best and only chance. He could not give her another. But she was not prepared.

" 'Twould be a good match, aye," her father said wearily, "but I willna wed you to a man you canna like or respect. . . . I'm not so *fou* as that."

Cat almost laughed. But she couldn't, quite, because she didn't want to go to Kilchurn. Not under the circumstances.

She knelt, picked up the abused bagpipes, rose again, and put them into her father's lap. "And if I said I wouldna?"

He made a noise of disgust. "I willna force you, Cat. You're my daughter, not a cow."

This time she did laugh, but only a little, and the sound of it died as quickly as it was born.

She faced her father squarely. "He may not like me, aye?—Breadalbane's heir. I'm no' like other women."

Her father stared at her. And then he began to laugh.

The house was small, made of stone, smelling of peat-smoke, whisky, dampness, though it hadn't rained all day. There was little of wealth or refinement about the house, it being little more than a plain rectangular block of rough-cut drystone, hollow in the middle where Dair MacDonald lived beneath the roof slates. He was a man who required no trappings of luxury, though he had seen plenty in France. He left appointments to his father and his mother in MacIain's house at Carnoch, a short walk up the glen.

But neither was the house a byre; it showed a woman's touch. It was small but comfortable, and the company tolerable. He and Robbie Stewart sat together contentedly at the felted table over a game of backgammon.

Stewart leaned forward to catch Dair's line of vision. "Your face is as long as my cock!" he cried. "Did you think I'd never notice?"

The backgammon game, obviously, was no longer a diversion. Neither was the whisky; Dair pushed his horn cup aside. "Your sister," he said quietly, giving voice to what annoyed him, "has a tongue as sharp as yours."

Stewart grinned. It set his blue eyes alight and crinkled the flesh at the corners. The habitual hot temper, for now, was hidden. "Och, aye, she does, my Jean . . . but what should it matter to *you*, so long as she knows how to use it in bed?"

Dair grimaced. Robbie's tongue too often went unbridled, tending toward the vulgar. In its place the slyness was more than amusing, but Dair was not a man who liked it applied to himself. "Any sharper," he said pointedly, "and she could use it for a sword. And I dinna like to take a sword to bed."

Stewart laughed aloud. "Och, aye—'twould be more than painful wielded wi' my Jean's skill." He grinned, sandy gold hair curling crisply against his linen collar. "Where *is* Jean tonight? Have you put her out of your house?"

If I thought she would go, aye . . . Dair smiled a little, keeping the thought from his face; he and Jean spent more time arguing of late than trading gentle words. "Up the glen at Carnoch with my mother and MacIain."

"Well then, shall I say something to her? Shall I warn her your temper's fragile?"

But Dair shook his head; only rarely did he speak of Jean to Robbie, because they were so close. Twin-born, they'd defend one another to the death. Dair thought it unlikely Robbie would take his side when the conflict involved his sister.

"I'll tell her myself." If she did not know already. She should; they had spent much of the day before gibing at one another, though she tried to smooth his hackles in bed, as always. —*and I weary even of that* . . . But Dair shut off the thought. He did not choose to waste more time thinking of Jean Stewart.

Robbie sat back in his chair. "What you need is more cattle in your glen . . . and a fierce, bold raid to get them!"

Dair nodded sagely. "How far is it to Appin? How many shall we steal?"

Robbie laughed aloud. "No, no, not *my* cows. I was thinking Campbell cattle."

The lure was instantaneous. Dair was restless, as was Robbie, and feeling hemmed in by the fort near Inverlochy. But there were still concerns to be addressed. "They're not yet at the shielings," he said. "Still on winter fodder, close to Glenlyon's house."

"Which makes it all the bolder." Robbie shrugged. " 'Tis easier in the summer, when the shielings have people in them and the cows go

on the braes, but where is the risk in that? 'Tis greater if we go now
. . . and all the more irksome to Glenlyon.''

Irking Glenlyon was not necessarily what Dair wished to do, being
more interested in cattle than in spilling blood. But one could not go
cattle-lifting without irritating the laird who owned them. MacIain was
proof of that, whenever MacDonald cattle were stolen.

But then, it was Robbie's nature to revel in irking folk. Particularly
Campbell folk, though he had less reason than MacDonalds. The heir
of Appin, plain and simple, enjoyed stealing cattle no matter whose
they were. Highland wealth was measured in cows, but Robbie didn't
do it for wealth. He did it for the risk.

Dair did it for the cattle. "Well," he said at last, "MacIain will want
to know."

Robbie snorted. "MacIain will want to *come.*"

Dair, smiling, shook his head as he rose. "He has a new book from
France. He'll not be free for days."

Robbie rose as well, catching up Dair's unfinished whisky to swallow
it down himself. " 'Tis a waste of time, books. They canna lift a sword,
nor bed a bonnie lass."

Dair grinned. "Nor steal a Campbell cow."

Robbie, rounding the table, reached up to slap a shoulder. "Nor
drink good usquabae."

There were, Dair thought wryly, countless things books could not
do, yet also those they could. But he didn't say it to Robbie, who
wouldn't understand. *He will keep on counting the things they CANNA do
all the way to Glen Lyon!* "Rouse your tacksmen," he said. "I'll go up to
tell MacIain, then gather a few MacDonalds."

"Only a few," Robbie cautioned, "or we'll have no fun at all."

Two

Shouting awakened Cat. Peat motes filled the shieling, floating on
dawn light let in through cracks in the walls and the time-rent
leather door-curtain. She rolled over on beaten earth, half-tangled in
her plaid, and sat up rigidly, blinking bleariness out of her eyes even as
Una awoke.

—*I dinna ken those voices*— At first there was alarm; then a spurt of relief, the dissipation of shock. Cat tugged the twisted loop of plaid from under her hips as she looked at Una, whose face was gray as oatmeal porridge. "If 'tis trouble, Angus and the others will stop it."

Then she heard a muffled shout, a strangled outcry; a thump against the wall knocked crumbling peat to the beaten floor and relief was instantly banished.

Cat scrambled to her feet even as Una gasped a prayer, yanking wool aside to jerk *sgian dhu* from beneath heavy, still-damp skirts. She had carried one ever since the MacDonald raid on Glen Lyon following Killiecrankie two years before. No doubt Una would complain it wasn't a woman's task to go about with a knife gartered below her knee, but that did not disturb Cat unduly. Una wasn't a muckle-headed fool always. *She'll no' complain till the danger is passed.*

"Step away, Una." Cat motioned her back. "Give them naught to catch if they come through the door—"

Even as she spoke the curtain was jerked aside and men spilled into the shieling, men she didn't know, Highlanders all, in kilts and breeks and bonnets —*not Campbells, none of them!*— bent on some violence. Cat, recoiling even as Una did, was snatched abruptly back ten years to when MacIain of Glencoe had come to Chesthill demanding word with her father.

She was small suddenly, so small, infinitely insignificant to the huge Laird of Glencoe—

But the old memory faded, replaced by one more recent: MacDonalds in her house, tearing down her mother's curtains.

Even as she fetched up against the peat wall farthest from the interlopers, outrage kindled. It damped fear, gave her something else on which she could focus attention. As a child she had been spectacularly helpless in MacIain's grasp; seven years later a Stewart claymore tip teasing her throat had forced compliance. But she was no longer a child. Now she was full grown and angry, very angry, so angry she looked to it for courage, and found a cold, deliberate strength in place of helplessness.

The men clustered inside the door. That they were astonished was plain; they stared at her in amazement. *"Jesu,"* someone whispered. Another crossed himself, muttering of red-haired women and bad omens.

A wild, unbridled laugh bubbled up, was swallowed back only with effort. *They didna expect to find us here!* It was the cattle raid all over again, when young, inexperienced MacDonalds had caught Campbells in place of cows.

And then she thought of her oldest brother, of six-years-dead Robbie, long rotted in the ground like Norse bones in the barrows. Memory gave her a weapon. Recollection lent her strength. She shut her hand more tightly on the the *sgian dhu's* stag-horn handle. They'd not take her blade this time.

A sandy-haired man strode through the curtainless door, letting dawn come into the shieling. He was not tall—was shorter, in fact, than she—but what he lacked in height was made up for in width, in a compact, vital strength. There was an edge to his presence that made her unable to look away, like a mouse transfixed by cat.

Anger ebbed. She made a soft noise in her throat. Her hand on the *sgian dhu* was abruptly damp with sweat. She forgot dead brothers, forgot the raid that had won her a calf, then lost it, much as it lost her a brother. She recalled another time, another raid, and a Stewart in place of MacDonalds.

This time, there was no claymore. He was like other men, like all the men in the shieling, armed with dirk and *sgian dhu,* but this time there was no sword.

His smile was very broad, the glint in blue eyes pronounced. "A bonnie lass," he said, "trysting with her man."

Shocked, Cat was unable to answer. She had expected recollection, laughter, ridicule, the degradation such as she had suffered before, not the provocative overture of man to woman she had witnessed in her brothers when they soft-talked a Campbell woman. For this manner of battle she was wholly unprepared.

Cat felt a flicker of fear solidify, expand to fill her chest. She was experienced in derision both subtle and blatant, tuned like a harp peg to the song she believed he intended to play. But the notes this time were different, and the words she did not know.

He stopped before her. Smiling, he extended fingers to catch an errant lock of her hair—

Instantly Cat brought up her hand with the deadly, sharp *sgian dhu,* nicking impudent knuckles. She was distantly pleased to see his shock, to watch him snatch back his hand and press fingers to his mouth.

"You will not." She was relieved to hear the steadiness of her voice. In the face of his vulgarity some of her courage crept back to steady fragile pride. "These are Campbell lands—go home to your Glencoe hovels, to your Stewart castle keeps. Leave my woman and me in peace."

The man tilted his head, measuring her as he took away from his mouth the bloodied knuckles. *'Boy-faced lass,'* he had called her. A *'lad with breasts.'* Surely he would remember.

Cat could not forget.

Softly he said, "I am heir of Appin; no one, man or woman, tells *me* where I am to go or what I am not to do."

She hated him for that, for what and who he was, for what he had done and proposed to do; she did not doubt that, given leave, whatever it was he did would compromise self-confidence, erode self-esteem. *"I* do," she said clearly. "A Campbell tells you to go."

He laughed. "Appin does as he chooses!"

She wanted to put the knife to his throat so he felt the lick of its blade. He and men like him—men like Dair MacDonald—reduced in the name of arrogance the pride and spirit of other people. "Appin does as he chooses?" She matched him glare for glare. "Then he's no man at all, aye?—but a spoiled, selfish swankie wi'out the sense of the cows he's come to steal from men better than he."

She had struck well. The light in Stewart's eyes faded. Something of anger replaced it, tightening the line of his shoulders, robbing his posture of grace.

"Robbie."

Cat jumped. The voice rang out clearly, cutting through the cluster of men inside the door. They broke and made way, all the MacDonalds, though some of the Stewarts were slow. And then he was through them all, stepping into the room, and she saw him very clearly.

Something inside her leaped, then burned away into ash. *He is no better than Stewart.*

"Robbie," Dair MacDonald said quietly, "we've come for cows, not women."

Robbie. His name was *Robbie*. It made her bitterly angry. He besmirched her brother's memory by tainting his name.

"Look at her!" Stewart cried.

"I see her," Alasdair Og said steadily.

"Bluidy fool," Cat declared. "I am Glenlyon's daughter. Shall I cut out that tongue from your mouth to stop your foolish noise, or let him do it himself?"

For an instant she saw surprise in Dair's whisky-colored eyes; had he not known her at all? But he must have—how could a man forget whom he had humiliated?

Surprise faded from his eyes, replaced by intensity. "Cat," he said—overly familiar, she thought—"you'd do better to hold your own tongue."

Stewart's head jerked around. "D'ye know this lass, then? Is she waiting here for you?"

MacDonald's tone was unchanged, though his mouth twitched a little. " 'Twas your idea to come here; how could I have planned it?"

It cleared the blackness from Stewart's face, lending it merriment.

"Aye, so it was!" He grinned, good temper restored. "And you'd no' be looking to another woman wi' *Jean* in your house!"

Cat glared at Dair. Anger made it easy for her to speak so blatantly of a topic women avoided. "Hold my tongue? Well, I willna. Not if it puts me in his bed . . . I've better taste than that!"

Dair took a single noiseless step into the center of the shieling. He stood very close to Stewart, though he did not touch him. "This is not our way, Robbie—would you risk Letters of Fire and Sword?"

Stewart's head snapped around. "D'ye think *Glenlyon* would go so far as to involve the Crown? They've a bit to think about now, those Privy Council men . . . they wouldna involve themselves."

"What more would give them reason to put us to the horn?" Dair asked. "Ewan Cameron of Lochiel tells Colonel Hill at Fort William that he and his Camerons will no' raise arms, and you ken as well as I there are MacDonalds and Stewarts who have done the same. But we've not, have we, either of us?—'twill be the excuse they need to send Sassenachs against us!"

She could not keep quiet, not with a MacDonald standing surety for her. Campbell pride would not permit it. Cat seized the opening and inserted the blade with care. "I'm doubting the earls of Breadalbane and Argyll would ignore what was done here . . . likely they'd see to it the Appin Stewarts were made over into MacGregors!"

She might as well have slapped Stewart's face with a glove as tell him that. He turned burning eyes upon her and said something in Gaelic so distorted by fury she could not understand it. Cat doubted anyone did; his temper, now, was unchecked.

"Robbie." Again Dair MacDonald, who moved forward quietly, smoothly, casually inserting a shoulder between Cat and Robert Stewart as he swung slowly to face his friend. "I'm asking you to let her be."

"Why?" It was thrust out between Robbie's teeth, extruded like a blow. "What is it to you if I want a kiss of the lass? What is *she* to you? Your enemy, MacDonald—as much as Glenlyon himself! You've heard—had a taste of her tongue, aye?—sharp as an adder's bite!"

"Robbie," Dair said quietly, "no kisses of this lass."

Stewart challenged him immediately. "What will you do to stop me?"

"Knock you senseless where you stand and carry you home myself." Dair grinned. "You are outnumbered, aye?—we're ten men to your four."

She could not hold her tongue. She did not trust MacDonald's motives. "And what have you done with *mine*? Have you dirked them all in their sleep?"

Dair did not look at her; he was too intent on Stewart. "I'll take you to them, lass, as soon as we have Robbie's answer."

Stewart looked at Cat, at her *sgian dhu,* then back at MacDonald. A muscle leaped beside his mouth. "Christ, MacDonald—d'ye think I care so much? She's only a Campbell quean—there are others to be had, and more willing than the bizzem. She isna worth fighting over!" He slapped Dair on the arm in a gesture of restored goodwill, but Cat saw his eyes. He was not wholly reconciled, no matter what he said. "Dinna fash yerself, MacDonald . . . we've cattle to acquire!"

Dair glanced at Cat. She saw the twitch of his mouth, though the smile did not blossom. "We stopped because of the storm; we didna ken you were here. But then we saw your garrons, and the gillie before your door."

Cat thought of Angus, of the shouts outside the shieling. "Did you harm him?"

"A wee scratch on the neck," Dair explained, "when he tried to pull free of my men. He's with the others now, held in another shieling."

"I want to see them."

"And I told you I'd take you to them." Dair turned to stare directly at Stewart, as if challenging him to refuse.

Robbie swung away abruptly, plaid flaring from his shoulder.

Appeased, Dair turned to her. "Come out of the shieling, Cat . . . I'll take you to your men."

The Earl of Breadalbane, awaiting the arrival of his cousin Glen-lyon's daughter, drank fiery usquabae as the sun went down and re-read a portion of the Master of Stair's latest correspondence from Flanders regarding the recalcitrant Highlanders and his proposal to tame them. It pleased him that Stair put into writing his own confidence in Breadalbane's ability. It pleased him mightily.

The earl called his gillie to him. When Sandy Campbell came, his master smiled upon him. "Send word to the clans. *All* of them, aye?—no' just Campbells, Sandy. Have it said—have them reminded, aye?—that I am not merely an earl, but a chief even as they are, and that I am well cognizant of the demands upon the honor of his fellow chieftains."

He savored the peat-water flavor of his whisky, weighing words before he spoke them. "Tell them also they are right to distrust the words of a Sassenach, to distrust *that man Hill* at Fort William who even now plots against them, and should look to a fellow Highlander, a chief in his own right, to lead them out of war into a time of peace. There is honor to be satisfied in any such undertaking, and I willna have it overlooked by Lowland Scot, Sassenach, or Dutch king."

The gillie waited mutely.

Breadalbane finished the whisky and set the cup aside. "I value their words, Sandy, as I value their pride. Tell them to come to Achallader in late June, and we will each of us have something to say of the future of Stuart Scotland." When the gillie had gone Breadalbane poured more whisky and smiled at the closed door. "Achallader," he murmured, "so that no chief can but see for himself what I have lost to the Mac-Donalds. And when, in the ruins of my castle, I welcome even pawkie, thieving MacIain of Glencoe into our confederacy despite the evidence of his enmity, they will count me sincere!"

Dair pulled Cat out of the shieling, relieved her of *sgian dhu* before she could protest, and took her immediately to the closest shieling but twenty paces away. He pulled the leather curtain aside and escorted her inside where other MacDonalds waited, watching Glenlyon's men.

He saw the blossoming of relief in every Campbell face, followed almost instantly by humiliation that they'd failed to keep her safe.

Cat ignored him utterly and looked from one to the other. "They are cattle thieves," she said plainly. "What do you expect of them but to come in the night *like* thieves, aye?—and set the dirks against your throats!"

He looked sharply at the Campbells. As one they stared at her, startled as he by her vehemence. Then the one she had called Angus began to smile, though he had the grace —*or the wisdom, aye?*— to attempt to hide it from his captors.

"They canna keep us," she went on, with a scathing glance at the MacDonald clansmen, "and we'll no' be killed for the silence. I am Glenlyon's daughter; they know about MacGregors and what happens to proscribed clans."

The color was back in their faces and the brightness in their eyes. Now they were angry men hungry for redress. Dair sensed the renewed alertness of the captured Campbells and the accompanying tension in his own men. He grabbed an arm and yanked her back out of the shieling before she could say anything else that might stir them to revolt.

"Christ, MacDonald—will ye stop pulling me this way and that like a muckle-headed stirk—?"

He ignored the latter protest. "Fierce words, aye?—and likely to get them killed." He took her around the side. "We've no' harmed them save for a lump or two; d'ye want worse on your head?"

Cat stumbled over a stone, recovered stiffly, and turned to face him, ignoring the arm still clasped in his grip. "I willna let them be ashamed for being trapped by Glencoe men," she declared. "There's no honor in your clan. Why should they expect it?"

The virulence of her tone took him aback. Then the words settled themselves to pierce his pride. "Then perhaps I should let Robbie have his kiss and see what you say then, aye?"

Her expression was briefly anguished, then hardened into a commingling of frustration and bitter anger. "In God's name, MacDonald, what d'ye *expect* me to say?"

He opened his mouth to respond, but lost the train of his thought. He knew what he had *intended* to say, but it now lay tantalizingly out of reach, blown away on the rising breeze that lifted a lock of loose red hair and carried it forward to drape in unintentional coyness across one pronounced, oblique cheekbone.

"Well?" she prodded, and he recalled she had posed him a question.

He looked away from the strand of hair and the face from which she impatiently pulled it. "I would expect you to say—to *suggest* to them they make no attempt to fight."

"Why? Would you? Is that what you would say and do, in my place?"

It was irrefutable logic, especially from a Campbell, and he found it intensely annoying. Dair lost interest altogether in the hair and the cheek and scowled at her.

"Dinna show me that black look, MacDonald," she snapped. " 'Tis Glen Lyon we're in, not Glencoe."

"But we have the weapons."

"And we our tongues, aye?—" She was clearly unabashed by his perceived victory. "—which you well ken, being a Highlander, is as much a weapon as a dirk if wielded properly. D'ye expect us not to use them?"

He supposed not. He *knew* not; he himself would use whatever lay at hand. Dair's scowl deepened.

"Will you let us go?" she asked.

"I willna. Would you, in my place?" He arched ironic brows.

Her brows were level but equally eloquent; she wrenched them upward even as he had his own, matching his irony, but with a devastatingly effective grasp of condescension far superior to his. He had seen it in Jean as well. —*is it a woman's gift?*—

"As *we* havena gone lifting cattle in Glencoe for some time, I canna say," Cat declared. "For myself, I havena been in your place, and 'tis likely I'll never be."

He conceded that readily; he did not know a woman who went with men to steal cattle. —*though I dinna doubt this one would try!*

"Let go of my arm," she said coolly. "—And stop staring at me that way."

Until that moment Dair did not realize he *had* been staring at her.

Now that she had told him he could not look away from the face that had once been plain but now, as plainly, was not. Were it not for the color of her hair and her eyes— —*and her Campbell tongue!*— —he'd swear it was another lass entirely.

Her arm was still grasped in his hand. He did not release it yet, wanting something of her. "If you'll swear not to march back into that shieling and give them more words meant to rile them, I'll consider releasing you."

"I willna! Would you? Would any man? Why d'ye think *I* should?"

Dair felt a bubble of laughter break in his chest, suppressed from escaping his mouth only by an application of immense self-control. He had expected no other answer; she had not in girlhood been willing to do so, and now that she was a woman she proved even less inclined. "Then I'll keep your arm as surety."

The line of her mouth was mutinous. The mouth itself was a wide, proud slash beneath a nose lifted imperiously into the air, the vertical line of it dividing precisely in half the remarkable vitality of her features.

No languid lass, Cat Campbell— Dair scowled. He did not recall ever marking her mouth before, or her nose, or features singly or mutually beheld, but here they were before him and unavoidable. As was the rest of her.

"Cat Campbell," he murmured. "Good Christ, *Cat Campbell*—" Self-control vanished. The bubble broke free of its constraints and Dair began to laugh.

"You bluidy bastard," she said furiously, and swung her other arm to fetch him a clout on his ear.

He ducked enough to take the blow on the side of the jaw. "Christ, Cat—*wait* you—" It hurt, but not as much as his ear would have. He caught her arm so she dared not try again, with better result. "What I mean—"

She twisted in his grasp, jerking one arm free at last to scrape from her face the windblown lock of hair curling just beneath one furious, brilliant blue eye. "D'ye think I'll stand here and let you insult me? D'ye think I dinna ken what you're laughing at? Holy Mother, Mac-Donald, was it in your minds to come hunt up Glenlyon's daughter to see what has become of her now that she's grown?"

He met anger with quietude, knowing how self-control infuriated someone who lacked it; it was a subtle weapon he had learned early in life. "We came for cows." Which he knew *she* knew; why else would MacDonalds ride to Glen Lyon?

When her anguished scowl deepened he dismissed irony and replaced it with truth. "It wasna meant as an insult. Christ, Cat, how could it be?"

She swallowed visibly. Her voice was none too steady. "You came for cows—and everything else!—last time, aye?—"

"Cat—"

"—but still found the time to tell me what I am." Sudden tears stood in her eyes, prompting fresh anger and a twisted dignity that, despite its battered state, was rebuilt stone by stone out of its wreckage. "I ken what I am, MacDonald. I ken what that Stewart's told me, and what *you've* undoubtedly said: 'Glenlyon's boy-faced daughter'!"

He was not a man much given to having the speech knocked from his mouth by another's words. But at this moment, at this accusation, he found himself utterly bereft.

The tears spilled over. "Oh good *Christ,* here it is again—d'ye see?" She was disgusted, and clearly embarrassed; as furious with herself as with him. "There. 'Tis done, aye?—my weakness is uncovered. Put me in the shieling with the others, now, and tell yon swankie of Appin that you've reduced Glenlyon's daughter. *Again.*"

Dair knew then what had been done to her, knew the words that had been said over the long years of a harsh childhood with nothing of softness about it save what she made for herself, and that itself was difficult with so many to gibe at her for it. He could hear the words in her silence, in the anguish of her eyes, the words meant merely to goad, to poke a stick at her pride, but which she had taken seriously because there was little cause and less justification to break a lass's pride in the name of a lad's pranks.

He *knew;* he was a man who had once been a lad. A quiet, undersized boy often called a changeling by others, and whispered about behind MacIain's back when gossip ranged too far.

Dair looked into her eyes and saw the self-loathing there, the bitter recrimination that she should be made helpless before her direst enemies so that they, too, could hurt her.

He opened his mouth to tell her she was a fool, but shut it again. She would believe he lied no matter what he said.

And yet he could not let her believe it. "There is a pile of granite behind you. I'd have you sit on it." He guided her to it, waited as she sat down rigidly, then stood before her. He slid his hand down her arm until he clasped her wrist, then used his other hand to grasp and extend her fingers, easing the stiffened knuckles into suppleness. He had gentled garrons and puppies; he believed she would be no different. "You've long fingers," he said. "I remember a time there were scabs upon them; I saw so that day when we came wi' MacIain."

She tried to curl the captive hand into a knot; glared when he did not permit it. Her face briefly convulsed, as if his touch sickened her; but there was anguish there as well, and a bittersweet regret.

"But no more," he told her. "Oh, aye, 'twill happen now and again—just like it does to me—but what of it? The flesh beneath is pale and smooth, but for the work a woman does, and that isna something to greet about." He closed one hand more firmly around her wrist. "You've fine bones, *good* bones, well knit and well grown; they'll not break under the labor you must do, the bairns you must bear." Her elbow was stiff; he gentled it as well, then slowly set one knee against the turf to take his weight, while the other just touched the tented cloth of her tartan skirt. "And as for your face—"

Abruptly he stopped. He had intended a simple recitation of features meant to convince her she need not fear ridicule. But now suddenly he was close, too close, and the features that of themselves were nothing more than features merged to form a whole—

—Christ, what am I doing . . . is this for her, or for me—?

Dair released her at once and retreated on stiff legs, striding four long paces away before he could stop himself. There he halted on the lip of crumbling granite and stared fixedly into the distance.

Wind snatched at the loose folds of his kilt and teased bonnetless hair. He welcomed its cool breath, welcomed the promised summer, welcomed the chance to recover himself as he stood on heather-clad hills with an eagle in the sky and the glen below the wind-ruffled wings so lushly verdant and beautiful as to burst the heart in his chest.

"Why are you doing this?" she asked. "To humiliate me? There is no mud or spilled whisky or horse-piss, so you do it instead with words?"

He turned sharply. She had not yet retreated from her own outcrop, as if she understood he was no longer a physical threat.

"Have you used them up?" she persisted. "Are you thinking of new ones?"

It was difficult to speak. She was fierce and proud and bonnie, like the glint of steel in sunlight; like the blade of a deadly claymore, elegant in its simplicity. "I've never been a man for that."

"Oh, aye?" She was patently unimpressed by his avowal. "And will you say you didna laugh when the Appin Stewart called me a boy-faced lass?"

Wind buffeted him again, lifting the swoop of plaid draped from shoulder to hip. The weight of the brooch tamed it, tugging against his shoulder. "You've seen me but three times, and never once have I treated you with anything but honor. And aye, I'll say I didna laugh; he never said it to me."

"And now? What is this, MacDonald?"

"This?" He wanted to laugh, but she would misconstrue it. Even though the laughter was for his own undoing, with none of it hers. *"This* is a man reconciling himself to a woman's beauty."

She recoiled as if he had slapped her.

In another woman it would have been blatant prevarication and as unamusing; it smacked of Jean Stewart, who was beautiful and knew it, yet teased him for flattery. But this was not Jean . . . "Dinna tell me you've not looked in the glass."

" 'Tis broken," she retorted. "The day you came two years ago, I broke it then."

"Then I'll give you another." It was small compensation for the other things she had lost, but he had no more to offer.

She sat very straight upon the granite. The wind came from behind her now, working more hair from her loosened, slept-upon braid. It blew around her face, underscoring the clean line of jaw, the belligerence of her chin.

She wasn't truly beautiful . . . not as Jean was, or other women who had, briefly, attracted him; in fact, he knew of no *civilized* man who would, feature by feature, praise her in poetry, but the bards of Scotland would: she was Gaeldom come alive again upon the heathered braes where great-thewed heroes once strode; a human equivalent of the wild, barbaric Highlands, less a woman than a legacy of those who had gone before them all bearing shields and swords and axes.

He had a Highlander's expert nose; with the wind from behind, Dair could smell the scent of her. Nothing so elaborate as French perfume, which Jean favored and he provided, but peat and smoke and wood, soap and wool and damp turf, and inevitably of woman; of the things he loved most in a Highlander's harsh world.

She scowled. "What are you doing, MacDonald?"

His admission was more than he had intended to offer, but none he did not regret; it was the unadorned truth and therefore honorable. "Trying verra hard not to kiss a Campbell."

She scrambled to her feet and lurched two steps away. "Kiss me!"

"Trying *not* to kiss you." Dair grinned; the admission freed him from denial and brought relief to his soul. "There is a difference, ye ken."

Color slowly drained, leaving behind in its place a collection of brittle bones now starkly pronounced. "But—why?"

He laughed. "Why should I want to? Or why should I *no'* want to?" And then relief died, was replaced by immense regret. The lass deserved better . . . far better, he knew, than he could offer: MacDonald to a Campbell. *'Tisn't born in us, the hatred. . . . 'tis cherished through the years, sung about by bards, played upon the pipes—*

Abruptly Dair swore and looked away, squinting down the brae. "Good Christ, I am a fool . . . but a man for all that, aye?—and one with all his parts in good working order. And these parts dinna care *what* our names are!"

She made a small sound, a soft blurt of anguished discovery. Then she said, unevenly, "You're no' but a bluidy MacDonald, come to lift our cows."

He turned, grinning. "Well, aye, we did come for that, but—"

Her tone steadied; there was an edge to it freshly honed. "And whether you use dirk or tongue, you always find ways to hurt me."

He lost his patience at last. "In Christ's name, Cat, I havena come to hurt you!"

She glared at him. "You're a bluidy MacDonald."

"And you're a bluidy Campbell." He scowled. "There. We've explained it all gey well, aye?—pointing out to one another what we are. And has it answered anything? D'ye know me better for it?"

"You're naught but a cattle thief—"

"Christ, Cat!—have you forgotten the times Campbells came a'raiding to Glencoe? I could sing songs of it!"

She was abruptly and utterly white.

"What is it?" he asked sharply. "You'll no' swoon, will you?" It seemed entirely unlikely; she was not, he was certain, that kind of woman. She would break the rocks into dust before she showed such weakness to a MacDonald.

"I will not," she said distantly. "And no, I havena forgotten that Campbells raided Glencoe—or that Campbells *meant* to do so, but lost a man—a lad!—instead, and went back home."

Dair knew then there was more; that her answer was intended merely as purposely oblique diversion. "What happened, Cat?"

With skin so pale, she could not hide the rush of blood that set her cheeks afire. "You wouldna give it credence!"

"I've only to look at you to know something happened, something you regret. I'm asking you to tell me."

"I will not."

"Because 'tis easier to shout at me, a MacDonald, than speak to me of truth."

Cat glared at him. "I've naught to say to you."

He realized she was adamant, fixed on a single thought: that because he was a MacDonald nothing he said could be anything but insult, and certainly not truthful. And he knew if he did not offer redress, some recovery of her pride, she would curse him forever for being what she *thought* him to be, or had made him be in her memories, which was not at all the same as being what he was.

He held out the *sgian dhu*. "Take it."

Cat stared at him. She did not move.

"Take it. Have it back." He took the necessary steps and offered her the *sgian dhu* hilt first. He smiled. "Put it behind your skirts, Cat, or tuck it into your plaid. Dinna show it to Robbie unless you must, or he'll have it of you."

"He'd have more than *that* of me, the vulgar swankie!"

"Aye, well . . ." Dair sighed. "Robbie isna attracted to boy-faced lasses, Cat. Take that for your truth if you willna believe me."

"Why should I believe you?"

"Because we came to lift your cattle, and we hold four of your men in yonder shieling. Dinna you think I'd humiliate you, in such circumstances, instead of offering flattery?"

Irresolute, she stood her ground. He saw the doubt in her eyes, the confusion and the hope; she would hate herself if she realized he saw through the brittle shield of her pride to the uncertainty beneath, the need to believe he told her the truth not solely because she longed to be beautiful, though he supposed a woman yearned for that as a man did potency, but because she was far more after all than what everyone else had told her.

For myself. I told her she would grow up for the better. . . . Dair nearly laughed. *I am all at once both prophet and converted!* And then amusement dissipated, replaced by an intense emotion as abrupt as it was wholly unexpected, especially in a man who was not easily tempted. "Cat," he said curtly, "go back inside the shieling."

She took it as rude; and it was. It prompted like rebuttal. "Why?"

"Because if you stay out here a moment longer, I'll have that kiss of you after all."

She raised her chin like a targe. "I have a knife."

He managed to smile. "And it might be worth dying for."

She jabbed him, but lightly; was pleased to see him flinch. "That for your lying, MacDonald. No man would die for a kiss."

Softly he said, "Go inside."

Something moved in her eyes. The mouth loosened as if to open, then reset itself. And then she turned away.

He saw the swing of hair, a brilliant rope of braid dangling down a rigid spine swaddled in twisted plaid. Sun glinted off the blade as she put the knife away into the folds, and then she walked unsteadily to the shieling in which he had found her.

Dair sat down again, all at once and clumsily, upon the granite outcrop. He drew up his knees, planted his elbows upon them, then bent his head and scraped rigid fingers through his hair, murmuring imprecations against himself and his folly as he waited for the ache in his loins to subside.

"Christ," he murmured aloud, "isna Jean enough for you?"

No. She was not.

Indisputably not.

Three

*J*ean Stewart sat quietly in the chair in MacIain's house, near to Lady Glencoe, darning stockings. She wanted very much to say something but held her tongue; she was a woman, a Stewart, and they men, Mac-Donalds, save for the sole Campbell. *And of late I have wielded my tongue too frequently.*

She had seen Dair's eyes and knew she cut too deeply. It was not her intent to do so, but she had never been a woman who locked her words away when the man himself handed her the key.

She did not desire the key save to give it back, or to throw it into the deepest loch so it might never be found. But Dair kept finding it. Dair kept fashioning others.

If he would agree to handfast . . . But he had not, not formally. She had believed it unnecessary; they lived openly together according to hand-fast tradition when no kirk was near for a proper wedding, nor a proper minister, but there were bindings even upon such agreements. There were intentions to be declared. Irregular marriage was a marriage in fact, so long as the intent was there.

There were three circumstances of such marriage sanctioned by Scottish law: by mutual consent declared sincerely before two witnesses; by promise of marriage followed almost immediately by the bedding, subsequently proved by witnesses; and by living together openly a year and a day as husband and wife.

But they had consented to nothing save their own desires. Dair had made her no promise, nor had she made him one; and their cohabitation had been so intermittent that no one could claim with certainty they had reached a year and a day unless one stitched together all the parts of the years.

According to Scottish law, if they did not mutually consent to a continuation of the relationship after the year and a day, both were free to part. Even if only one of them desired to part.

Jean's stitches wavered until she steadied them, hoping Lady Glencoe did not see. *I gave him his freedom too long!* She had taken enjoyment of him as he had taken it of her. In the beginning there had been no need for more, no need for promises; he had come back to her always, despite separations, and she had found it enough. Jean knew *she* was enough; no man, sharing her bed, was left unsatisfied.

But Dair MacDonald was unlike other men. His soul was complicated, his needs more complex. He was not a man well contented by nothing beyond the bedding; he wanted more of a woman than Jean was prepared to give. She was not capable of surrendering more than she had, because she did not comprehend what it was he wanted. *What more is there for a man to have than the use of a woman's body?*

He had spoken of spirit, of ideals; of the hidden inner spaces that made a person whole, more than just a body. She had found it incomprehensible, and told him so in the only way she knew: by stopping his mouth with her own; by silencing his questions, his ponderings, turning his mind from such confusing things as these to the issues of the flesh.

One day he stopped asking. One day he stopped sharing. Jean found it both respite and relief; she understood intimately the needs of the human body and did not care to speak of spirit, of ideals, of the hidden inner spaces. Such things were beyond her ken. Such issues made her uneasy.

It was then, only then, that she saw Dair begin to make the keys and to hold them in his hands, demanding that she take them, to unlock and open the door to the multiplicity of incompatibilities she could not understand and dared not acknowledge.

Too often she took the keys. Too often she opened the door. Too often the door, thus opened, spilled out the small desperate fears that fashioned additional keys, until she slammed shut that door and opened instead the one that led to the room housing the well-used bed.

It was the only key *she* could make. But he used it much less often.

Her fingers worked deftly as she listened to the others in MacIain's house. It was men's talk, this, and none of it her business; she was Stewart, not MacDonald, with less enmity toward Campbells despite occasional dirkings over stolen cattle. The Appin Stewarts owed feudal fealty to the Earl of Argyll, himself a Campbell, and though time had weakened such bonds, there remained tradition in it, and Highlanders honored tradition. The Appin Stewarts had long been allies of the Glencoe MacDonalds, but there was knowledge between them of the ancient order of things.

As the men spoke she tied a knot in the yarn, then bit it off without taking her eyes from MacIain, his oldest son, and the man who visited them. A Campbell he was, but entering the MacDonald house under the surety of hospitality, a sacred bond no Highlander would dare break. He spoke diffidently, raising between them no spectre of bad blood, courteously accepting the offered whisky and MacIain's gruff wishes for his health.

Jean watched the eyes. MacIain's were sheltered in deep sockets beneath bushy ramparts of brows, indistinguishable in lamplight; John's were, as was his wont, quietly contemplative; while the Campbell messenger, knowing where he was, wore the expression of a man counting the minutes of his life, wondering when he might at last be walked to the door so he might escape the lair.

She wondered what Dair would say, to hear the Campbell speak. He was less constrained than John in saying what he thought, but he was a careful man; she knew he would offer no language that might be construed as offense, though his eyes, masked in their thoughts to all but those who knew him well, would declare without reservation what he thought.

He couldna hide his heart. Not from me. Jean threaded her needle again and began work on another stocking, while the Campbell man explained the Earl of Breadalbane desired MacIain of Glencoe to come to Achallader. He said nothing at all of how MacIain and his men, on their way home from Killiecrankie, had burned the castle to the ground, but the memory lay between them. Jean could see it clearly.

She expected MacIain to laugh; did the man truly believe he might fall for such a ruse?

But MacIain did not laugh. He listened thoughtfully, then asked the Campbell who else had agreed to come.

"Stewarts," the man answered promptly, and Jean thought of Robbie; he would be asked next. "And Macleans, and Camerons. Even MacDonald of Glengarry, hosting Major General Thomas Buchan and Sir George Barclay."

"They'll come?" John blurted. "They represent King James."

"They represent the Stuart cause," the Campbell said, "as does my master, the earl."

This week, Jean thought cynically. *What does Breadalbane want that he lies so glibly, and sends gillies out as well to spread the falsehoods?*

"So many clans," MacIain observed, "answering to a Campbell."

"This isna a Campbell summons," the earl's man insisted quietly. " 'Tis in the name of Scotland, and the future of King James."

"Well, then." MacIain's smile was measuring in the thicket of his beard. "We'll no' stay home, will we, when the realm's at stake. 'Twas MacDonalds that held it first . . . but you're no' to ken that, aye?—when the Campbells came so much later." As the Campbell bit his lip on a retort, the old man bared his teeth in a ferocious grin. "There's no man in all of Scotland who has more care for the realm than Alasdair MacDonald, himself a direct descendant of the Lords of the Isles, once kings of Gaeldom. 'Twould hardly be a proper gathering, would it, if *he* stayed home!"

Robert Campbell, called Glenlyon, stood upon a hillock not far from Chesthill and stared down the track. From its crown he could look upon part of the glen, marking his house, the outbuildings; the cluster of lesser dwellings nearby; the smoke-blackened huts of peat and wood scattered across undulant, rock-scarped land.

Glen Lyon.

Twenty-five miles of fertile valley, boundaried at either end by Loch Tay and Loch Lyon, called many things by many men made humble by its beauty, among them Glen of the Black Water, and the Glen of Crooked Stones. Rich in fir trees and salmon, it had been coveted by many clans throughout the centuries: MacDairmuids, MacArthurs, MacCallums and MacGregors, and lastly by Stewarts, from whom the first Campbell, Black Colin, took it by right of arms. Eventually that ownership had been ratified by Crown Charter, leaving neighboring clans to raid cattle as they would, but unable to steal back the lands on which the cattle roamed.

It was the current fifth Laird of Glenlyon's cross that he had sold away for debts what his ancestors had kept and cultivated for two hundred years.

He was summoned now to Stirling, to serve at last the commission given him by the latest Earl of Argyll, Breadalbane's rival as had been his father before him. At eight shillings a day Glenlyon felt himself poorly paid and his stature ill-used; had anticipated silver for his debts, not a captaincy. But it was done and he was called. There were duties to attend in Argyll's new regiment.

He said it aloud. " 'Captain Robert Campbell.' "

A plain, unmelodious sound. But if he were to be a proper laird again, a man of whom bards sang, he must prove himself worthy. He would serve as told to serve, in any enterprise, and let the world see that Robert Campbell, direct descendant of Black Colin Campbell who first took Glen Lyon for his own, was more than merely a drukken man owing silver to every soul.

Dair moved quietly, crossing rain-damped turf with no sound in his footsteps. He thought she might be gone, returning inside to her woman—but Cat, too, had lingered. She was unaware of his approach

and therefore was free of acrimony for such men as MacDonalds. He
found he desired very much to make the moment last, and the innocence of it, so he might look on her without such feud-born folly as
would corrupt them otherwise.

He wondered if she wished it; if the thought crossed her mind; or
was she too warped by ancient-bred enmity that she could not think for
herself? *For that matter, am I?* . . . But men had the greater freedom, to
look at a woman and think of things other than blood and battle, and
the repercussions of them. A woman must be circumspect, and chaste,
disdaining such crudities, while a man could look and think without
hiding so much of himself.

It was easier, Dair felt, to divorce such thoughts from a mind when
that mind was taken up with other curiosities. A woman was bound by
convention in all things, and not the least of them the knowledge of
such necessities as names.

Looking at Cat Campbell, Dair wished it otherwise; that for one moment in time they might set aside such things as enmity and heritage to
think of themselves instead.

She leaned against the shieling with head tipped back, eyes closed,
folded arms in crimson sleeves all atangle in pale plaid, as if she were
chilled and sought the warmth of wool—or hugged herself against unexpected incursions in her spirit.

He knew what such things were. It was easier to deny them than to
give in to them, the impulses that lured a man or woman into looking
aslant at things instead of meeting them frontwise. If one looked aslant
at a thing, the certainties of life became *un*certainties, such as the need
for enmity between Campbells and MacDonalds.

He had looked aslant. He was certain no longer of anything but that
he had tangled himself in a skein-knot too complex to undo . . . and
that it was far easier to ignore what he wanted to explore, lest he lose
himself altogether in an issue too volatile, too impossible to ponder.

But Dair knew very well that even impossibilities found ways of being
pondered despite a man's wishes. It was the curse of imagination that
lent a Scot the magic to make the songs and sagas, giving life to voice
and pipes; to create of unreality the potential for something more.

He hesitated briefly, then walked on until he paused before the shieling, before the woman there. He had only to put out a hand and
touch her sleeve, but he would do no such thing. She would revile him
for it, and he would, seeing her afresh—and despite resolution—be
hard-pressed to touch no more than cloth.

Her vein-blued lids were fringed with fine, red-gold lashes less vivid
than her hair. He was loath to disturb her, but did because he must;
when he spoke her name quietly from so near she jumped like a star-

tled hare. He saw an awakening in her face akin to his own regrets, and regretted hers more: a brief, fleeting innocence banished by comprehension, by the realization of who he was, of who *she* was, and how the truths in their nakedness were more painful than kind-meant lies.

There were no secrets in the honesty of the bones underlying duplicitous flesh; she hardened, as he watched, like mortar under the sun.

"Come inside." He spoke more harshly than intended; but harshness diverted truth, and truth he could not afford. "There will be rain again; will you drown yourself outside merely to spite Robbie?"

She, being Campbell, desired to refuse a MacDonald; he saw it clearly, and grieved. But a quick glance at decaying skies told her he spoke no falsehood. Cat stared at him a moment from the mortared mask of her face —*is she expecting a chisel?*— then turned away abruptly and preceded him into the shieling as he pulled aside the curtain.

Inside, Robbie Stewart prowled restlessly like a Scottish wildcat, ill content to bide his time. "Well?" he asked abruptly, swinging to face them. "Well, Alasdair Og, what becomes of our moonlight ride?"

There was little desire in Dair for conversation. He raised a plaid-draped shoulder in a passive half-shrug; his mind was not on cattle. "We could go back." Robbie said nothing, waiting. There was more he should say; he said what he could. "And return later."

It was something, it was enough, though Stewart's expression was baleful. " 'Tis not how *I* entertain, sending my guests hither and thither like a clutch of day-old chicks."

The image was so inconsequential that Dair laughed aloud, relieved to fasten his mind on something entirely innocuous. "Day-old chicks, indeed! I doubt Glenlyon would call us so . . . and as for entertaining, have you no' had a bonnie ride?"

Robbie scowled, though his eyes flicked momentarily to Cat consideringly, as if he intended to make a crude comment. But he didn't, being more disposed to growl at Dair. "If I wanted to ride the glen, I could have stayed home in Appin."

Cat's muted tone was nonetheless ironic. "In your stolen castle."

Caught by surprise, Stewart nearly gaped. He swung toward her, plaid flaring, astonishment remolding his features. The expression was so alien to his features that Dair, equally startled by Cat's declaration, paid less attention to her than to his astounded friend. He laughed aloud at Robbie. " 'Twas a blow you didna expect!"

Robbie ignored him altogether. "Stolen?" Then, more strongly, "Stolen! 'Tis no such thing, you muddleheaded bizzem! Castle Stalker belongs to the Stewarts!"

Glenlyon's daughter smiled. Dair felt his own mouth mimicking its irony. *Give her a dirk, this lass—she's a match for the man—*

"Oh, no, I think not," Cat countered lightly. Then, with a deliberate pause, "Dinna you ken your history?"

"Dinna I *ken*—"Stewart cut off his response abruptly, color rising in his face. He was not a remarkably handsome man, was Robbie, but there was a ruthlessness in manner, eyes, and mouth that attracted certain women as much as legacy and reputation.

Dair's amusement dissipated. *Cat isna a woman for that—*

As if sensing that thought, Robbie Stewart tucked ruthlessness away. He could be charming when he chose; he knew how to lure women. Dair had seen them answer such summons avidly.

"Tutor me, lass," Stewart invited. "Tell me my history."

Dair saw contempt show itself briefly in her eyes, then she dismissed it as if understanding emotions might become weapons turned upon herself. Evenly she said, "Castle Stalker is a Campbell castle."

"Was," Robbie retorted; Dair was surprised she got that much of him.

Cat shook her head. "More than eighty years ago an Appin Stewart traded it to a Campbell for an eight-oared boat. A *boat*, man! 'Twas a silly thing to do, but 'twas done . . . except the Appin Stewarts refused to honor the bargain."

Unexpectedly, Robbie grinned. "Wouldna you?"

Cat scowled. " 'Twas a *bargain*—"

" 'Twas nonsense," Robbie said firmly. "They were in their cups, the both of them . . . and the Stewart no' called Silly-Headed for naught." He chewed thoughtfully at his cheek, then bestowed upon her yet again his bright-eyed grin. "Would ye care to come and see it, the castle you claim as Campbell?"

Cat's face was tense and white. "My father is the drukken man. D'ye think *I'm* in my cups, to be so *baothaire* as that?"

Robbie's smile was diminished under an abrupt, focused intensity that was nearly tangible. Dair, being male and not impervious to similar needs—who had felt his own urges as they sat talking on the hillside—knew what it was, realized what it portended. Cat, wholly innocent, clearly did not; she gazed warily at Stewart with no comprehension of such things as male desire and the sometimes overwhelming impulse to satisfy it immediately with few preliminaries, without explanation.

Stewart said, "I think you're a bonnie lass." And he put out his hand to touch her, as he had done before.

It shifted abruptly from baiting to stalking. Dair tensed, poised to move, but Cat brought up the hand clasping the *sgian dhu* he had returned to her. Even as Robbie reached, Stewart blood was renewed on the blade. *"Christ—"*

Her words were spoken quietly over Robbie's blurted protest. "Dinna touch me, Stewart."

Dair waited. Robbie was unpredictable; even he did not know what Stewart might do. He knew only that Cat would not thank *him* for fighting her battles—and that he would, despite her wishes, despite Robbie's intent, prevent the young heir of Appin from harming Glenlyon's daughter.

'Twill set us at odds . . . It would do more than that; it invited dissolution of the sometimes turbulent bond they shared, but Dair could see no other alternative. He would not risk Cat Campbell now, not even to Robert Stewart. He had in youth and manhood, despite her ignorance, despite her blatant resentment, committed too much of himself.

But the bond yet held, and with no need to break it; Robbie swore and sucked a finger, assessed her anger briefly, then turned from her entirely and cast a murderous scowl at Dair. "Have you lost your *wits*, man, leaving her a knife? 'Tis *twice* she's cut me, now!"

The tension snapped like morning ice beneath a dirk handle. Dair, relaxing, could not suppress a smile. "I thought she might require it, knowing you so well."

"Aye, well . . ." Stewart's black scowl faded. He was high-humored again, if rueful. "No' so much blood lost that I'll die of it. And worth it, I'll swear, to see the lass color up."

The lass duly colored up, which infuriated her as much as amused Robbie. She looked instead at Dair. "What will you do with me and my men?"

"Send you home," he answered. "We came for cows, no' you."

Robbie's sandy brows arched up. "And will we take her up to Glenlyon's door, where he can hang us before midday?"

"I wasna going home." Cat hesitated as they looked at her, startled, then explained more fully. "I was bound for Kilchurn Castle. And if you'll give me leave, I'll be on my way again."

Dair's attention focused abruptly. "Kilchurn . . . Breadalbane's there, they say. What d'ye have to do with Grey John?"

Cat's chin rose. " 'Tis a Campbell concern."

"Campbell concerns are often *MacDonald* concerns—"

"—*and* Stewart," Robbie interjected.

"—and therefore of interest to me." Dair did not so much as glance at Robbie; he wanted truth from Cat. "Why would Glenlyon send his daughter to Breadalbane?"

Cat offered no answer. It was Robbie who fashioned one. "He's sons, has the earl . . ." His slow smile filled his face, lighting up his eyes.

"Which are you meant for? The heir, likely; Duncan's as yet unwed
. . ." Robbie's tone was thoughtful. "Breadalbane hates his heir." As
Cat stared, he shrugged. " 'Tis well-known, lass . . . Duncan Campbell
is no' the son he wants to inherit his titles; he'd prefer the second
son—though he, I think, is wed." Again the negligent shrug, but a
glint in shrewd eyes belied the laziness of the tone. "There was talk of
my sister Jean wedding wi' Duncan Campbell a year ago . . ." He slid a
bright glance at Dair. "Was there no'?"

Dair, who did not at this moment desire to think of Jean, remembered it vividly; they had both of them, he and Jean, protested vigorously to Robbie, who had enjoyed the incident.

He baits both of us now, even as he did Jean and me . . . Yet he answered
with a careless shrug; he would give no satisfaction.

The Stewart's grin widened. " 'Tis no' so bad a match, when all is
said and done; Stewarts and Campbells have wed before." His look on
Cat was openly suggestive. "But my Jean would have naught of him,
being a bold, brave Stewart—*and* being disposed to take no man for
husband who might yet be disinherited." The glint in his eyes made it
quite clear he understood how mercenary the words sounded; but Dair
knew Robert Stewart was not a man much troubled by what others
thought. "Being disposed *instead* to have a MacDonald in her bed"—
he cast a glance at Dair—"where titles are less important than the
wielding of the sword."

The vulgarity burned crimson in Cat's cheeks. But it was not at Robbie she looked, nor at Dair she could; she fixed her eyes instead on the
brooch of his plaid. "Well then," she said, "will you be letting us go
on?"

Dair was less compelled to answer than to contemplate possibilities.
A wholly inexplicable intransigence left him indisposed to consider
seeing her wed to any man, one of Breadalbane's sons or no. He had
not risked Robbie's wrath for this . . . *And Duncan Campbell is not the
man for her, either. Christ, everyone knows his own father despises him; what
marriage would that be?*

It was folly, such thinking. He thought it nonetheless, moved by a
hostile belligerence alien to his nature. "Is it true?"

His brooch lost its fascination; Cat met his condemnation with equal
belligerence. "And if I said no? Would you let me go the sooner?"

He scowled at her even as she scowled back. "I would not."

"Then aye, 'tis true." Color moved in her face beneath the pale surface of flesh, like a curl of newborn wavelet breaking free of wind-
kissed loch. "I'm not worth so much, aye?—to keep me from one or
the other."

Robbie snickered. Dair knew what he thought; a man like Robert

Stewart might ask payment in something other than coin and would measure her worth by that. He would not look at Robbie to see collusion there; Stewart would expect a crude witticism, or even implied agreement.

Dair looked straight at Cat and shook his head. "I said it before: we came for cows, not you."

"Then release us."

Stewart sighed and folded his arms across a plaid-slashed chest. "Lassie, lassie, have ye no wits? My name isna *Baothaire,* so you willna call *me* Silly-Headed . . . if we let you and your braw laddies go, they'll be setting about dirking us the first moment we look away." He cast a bright glance at Dair. "Though the entertainment 'twould make the ride worthwhile."

Dair ignored Robbie. "We'll send you down the glen," he told Cat with a glance at Una. "You and your woman and two Campbell men— the rest will bide here a wee bit."

Robbie nodded. "Until we have what we've come for."

Cat was astonished. "You dinna mean to steal the cows *now!*"

Dair frowned as he saw Robbie's grin expand; such risk would garnish the task. "We'd do best heading home to Glencoe."

"No," Robbie said. "No, no, not yet, not empty-handed, to face the ridicule of MacIain." Thoughtfully he sucked again at the cuts Cat had inflicted. "We came for cows and we'll take them, even now." He grinned, eyes alight. " 'Twill sit in Glenlyon's throat like a clot of soured cream—d'ye think he'll choke of it? Christ, his body'll keep forever, soaked so much in usquabae from the inside out; if you dinna bury him, we'll no' forget his pawkie face!"

Dair stripped the knife from Cat's hand before she could so much as raise it. His grasp was tight on her wrist, squeezing the bones together. "You will not," he said mildly.

She twisted, testing, then stopped. She stood quite still and fixed him with bright, angry eyes. "You'd do the same," she told him, between set teeth. "In my place, Alasdair Og, you'd be doing the same!"

Dair had never believed the simple use of his name could incite him to anger. But she wielded it now as a weapon, when he had presented it ten years before as a gift to a young girl. "I would," he agreed tightly. "But there are two of you—here, this moment—to our twelve . . . I think the odds are in our favor."

Robbie snorted. "If she's as bad as her father at wagering, she'd not know what odds to play."

Dair saw the outraged tears and looked away from them so she need not count him again among those who ridiculed. "Four men," he said.

"They'll see you safely down the glen, while we go about our business."

"I'll get them back," Cat promised. "Every Campbell cow."

The heir of Appin laughed. "I'd like it verra much to see you try!"

Dair named four of his men. He told them to take Cat and her woman and two of the Campbell men with them as far as Balloch, where they were to turn back; Balloch was Campbell-inhabited, and they'd be hard-pressed to win free if Cat's men raised an alarm.

And then he took Cat out of the shieling, into the damp dawn of the day, and escorted her to her garron. A MacDonald saddled it for her; Dair lifted her up. It required effort wholly unexpected to take his hands away. "They'll see you safe."

"I *was* safe," she said. " 'Tis you who means me harm."

"Cat—" But Dair dismissed protest, banishing the desire to make her think kindly of him. He gave her truth instead and let her think what she would. "I mean you no harm. If I did, it would have happened."

Scorn was plain. "With you and Appin taking turns?"

The flesh of his face felt stretched over stone and very near to splitting on the sharpness of it. "Robbie is Robbie," he said with a mouth too stiff to shape the words easily. "I am Dair MacDonald. Never confuse us."

Cat laughed. The sound was ugly, comprised of something akin to shame, leavened by bitterness. "You bed with Stewart's sister, you ride with him lifting cows . . . how could I be *confused?* You're one and the same, I think; you've shown me no differences."

That stirred him at last to strike back if only to assuage his own guilt, the fears that he and Stewart were indeed too much alike. Before she could say more he jerked up her hem and jammed the knife back into the sheath strapped to her stockinged leg. "If you mean to carry one, learn when and where to use it. Otherwise you'll do naught but arm the enemy." He yanked the skirts back down.

"Which fact you've learned, I've no doubt, from all the brave battles you've fought. 'Tis a change, aye?—stealing cows instead of lives?"

He thought of Jean again, of the knife she made of her words to bleed him bit by bit. But her blade was honed of frustration, of an absence of comprehension; he could not explain the words that lay in his heart, and Jean in her ignorance could not speak them for him. Instead she cut at the canker, thinking to give him relief, and cut into his heart instead.

Jean would not understand. Cat Campbell would. "I was at Killiecrankie."

It was enough, he knew, for her—and then more, far more than enough. The words proved his manhood if not his potency, but he remembered too late even as she recoiled that Glenlyon's daughter knew very well by its aftermath who had been at Killiecrankie.

Her mouth warped briefly even as he tried to explain. " 'Twas a brave battle, that . . . and braver still when MacDonalds stripped Glen Lyon of everything—including our pride." Her hands gripped the reins, white-knuckled and trembling. "People died," she told him, "inside as well as out. Tell me again, *MacDonald,* how I should feel safe with you."

Governor Hill, when told of the royal commission given the Earl of Breadalbane to treat with the clans, was first astounded, secondly disbelieving, lastly infuriated. He himself worked to bring peace to the Highlands, going among the people with candor in his mouth as well as honest kindness, and had been justly treated by them in return. He held hopes that his efforts would be repaid by renewed willingness to swear oath to King William as opposed to supporting James, and while Breadalbane's proposal was much the same, Hill could not but complain that much of his own work was undone, or at least appropriated by a man who himself was a Highlander, and whose true interests in the outcome could be discerned by no one.

He did not consider himself a petty or malicious man, but his patience was ended at last. Clearly a man with no more than the interests of Scotland at heart would not be heard without proofs of duplicity where other men worked, and so he set about interviewing friendly clanspeople who had been given warranties to attend the meeting at Achallader but weeks away. It was Breadalbane he examined through the earl's own promises to give silver to the clans, and it was Breadalbane whom Hill knew to be playing a dangerous game.

The governor had his information from such chiefs as Ewan Cameron of Lochiel, less disposed to hear from the Campbell earl, and was explicitly told that the preeminent MacDonald of Glengarry would spend his time raiding Ross instead of listening to Breadalbane's lies.

And yet the lies might be believed. Silver meant much to clans who in winter found living difficult. John Hill knew it entirely possible that even those who disparaged Breadalbane would nonetheless meet with him at Achallader; there was nothing to be lost in going, and perhaps much to be gained.

To the governor in Fort William there was little to be gained, and everything to be lost. He was caught between a Dutch king advised by a Lowland Scot who despised Highlanders, and a Highland-born Campbell earl who had a trunk full of coats from which he might choose a color, depending on circumstances.

Hill capped his inkhorn, set his quill aside. *Someone will suffer. Someone must suffer.* He put his papers into order, aligning tattered edges. *There will be an example made of those who are innocent, or wholly inconsequential, to prove that Highland power is negligible when compared to that of a combined Parliamant, and a king who brooks no rebellion.*

On the track toward Balloch, Cat pulled up her garron, waiting as the four mounted MacDonalds dispatched to escort her gathered close enough to hem in the Campbell gillies on foot, Angus and Ewan, and for Una to come up beside her. She lowered her eyes in embarrassment not entirely unfeigned; given another course, she would prefer it to this one. But these were men; it was the only certainty.

"You'll wait," she said curtly. " 'Tis for a woman to tend."

They did not ask; they knew. She saw glances exchanged, the small language of the bodies: squinted eyes, a twitch of the mouth, hunched shoulders; one man looked across the turf to the stone-crowned rise with a twisted tree atop it breaking free of granite cleft. A small measure of modesty for a woman riding with men.

"There," one said, while the others kept wary eyes on Angus and Ewan, whose cheeks burned crimson for their laird's daughter.

It wasn't shame, Cat decided, but the natural needs of a body. They'd think nothing of it, being men and more capable of unencumbered relief; but she required more shielding, more forbearance. More time.

Una's expression was frozen into disbelief. *Does she mean me to hold it all the way to Kilchurn?* Cat smothered a laugh and busied herself with unhooking a foot from a stirrup. "Una—you'll come." It was necessary she come.

Una came, clambering down from her garron to assist Cat with her needs. Cat paid little mind to the broken ground and knurled turf, heading straight toward the tree-split, rocky outcrop. The terrain was as she'd prayed: behind the outcrop and tree was a hollow, and beyond it a rill that sloped into a slantwise depression running back the way they had come.

She glanced behind anxiously and was pleased to see the Mac-Donalds had all dismounted, tending their own needs. "Una—hurry!" The woman muttered of undecorous haste; Cat climbed over the outcrop and dropped to the earth, flattening belly down. "Listen then, Una—you'll go back in a moment and ask for linen."

"Linen!"

"Say I have none!" Cat hissed. "Say my courses have come on early, and I am desperate . . . say a shirt will do—"

"*Catriona Campbell*—"

"They will debate about it at some length; they will none of them want to give up a shirt for *that*—"

"D'ye think I'll ask such of them?" Una was mortified. "Catriona, we've our own linen—"

"But we need *theirs.*" Cat glared at her. "Have you wits, Una? If we're to stop our cattle from being stolen, we must act now."

Una clamped her mouth closed repressively. "I'll no' speak to men—*MacDonalds!*—of such things."

Cat transfixed her with a baleful stare. "You will," she said clearly. "You will do whatever I tell you to do, Una; d'ye hear me? You canna stop me. You can help me."

"I'll no' *speak* of—"

"You will go and ask them for linen. 'Twill be Angus who offers his, to save me shame—*think*, Una!—and you will refuse him that, he being Campbell, and then it will be for one of the MacDonalds to do—"

"Better a *Campbell* shirt—"

"—and by the time you've got a shirt and come back to me with it, I'll be gone."

That shut Una's mouth again. "Gone?"

"On my way; 'tis what this mummery is for."

"You canna walk all the way to Chesthill!"

Lord Christ, but the woman's a fool; and what does it say of my mother, who kept Una by her? "I dinna *need* to walk all the way to Chesthill. They've left horses at the shieling, you ken, wi' the men yet being held. I'll no' trouble them over that—I've enough wit to ken I'm outmatched, there—I only want a horse. We're no' so far from the shielings, Una—and despite your wishes, I'm no soft woman, am I? D'ye think I canna do this?"

Una stared at her in such dismay and horror that Cat wanted to swear at her. But that would stir Una to further declamation, and she had no time.

"Then stay," Cat hissed. "They'll come to see no matter . . . I only meant to gain the time you'd win me, but I see 'tis more important to you not to speak of such to MacDonalds than save *the laird's own cattle* from Glencoe-men."

As expected, Una surrendered to the reminder of whose cattle were at risk and whose daughter she served. She turned stiffly and began to pick her way slowly toward the clustered men.

Cat sighed. *Praise God for the woman's loyalty, if not her wits . . .* Taking care to keep her head down, she edged deeper into the hollow and turned toward the rill. —*not so far . . . and not so much to risk to thwart MacDonalds!*

Especially Dair MacDonald.

Four

*W*hen Glenlyon, met on the road by a clutch of tacksmen and gillies mounted on heaving garrons, was told his cattle were threatened, he was slow to comprehend a message he might otherwise answer at once because of the messenger: his disheveled daughter, tunic skirt kilted up for ease of riding which perforce exposed a long stockinged leg on either side of the horse. Her smaller woman's plaid, the arisaid, was torn loose from its breast-brooch and hung down from her belt in folds and tangled coils; her braid was wrung free of its bindings by the forcefulness of her riding.

She had, she said, called at each bothy and cottage on the ride back to Chesthill, gathering such men as were willing to fight for Glen Lyon's cows; the implication, even from her, was that they would not be so willing to fight for Glen Lyon's laird.

It hurt very badly, that comment. Glenlyon glared at her and at those she brought with her.

Cat bestrode the garron with no thought to her appearance or to what others might think, shaking back tumbled, wind-wracked hair with an impatient toss of her head. "You'll go," she said, short-winded, before he could speak. "*At once . . .* they'll be after those closest to Rannoch Moor, I'm thinking—wanting to come no nearer . . ."

"Cat."

"—they will catch up what they can and sweep on, not wanting to waste time . . ."

"Cat—"

"—there are twelve altogether, but he divided them—two left at the shieling, though they may be gone by now; and four to escort us to Balloch—" She drew breath hastily. "—That leaves only six for the cows—"

"Catriona—good *Christ* . . . will you get down from that horse?"

Startled by his tone, she stared at him blankly. "Get down? Would you have me walk, then?"

"I'd have you *down!*" he shouted. "Where is Una? Why are you unattended?"

The wind of her ride had painted bloody roses in her cheeks. Now the flowers faded, leaving her corpse white and too bright in the eyes from something other than shock or sorrow. He knew that expression.

"The *cows,*" Cat said succinctly. "They'll have them if you tarry."

"Pull down your skirts," he commanded. "There isna a woman among us, and you come here like a—like a *whore.*"

Cat recoiled. He heard a stirring among the men as they shifted their eyes and attention elsewhere, resettling reins, plaids, stirrup leathers, avoiding any commitment to what was said between a father and his daughter; but he was aware of disapproval. It was palpable. They give his daughter more respect than he.

"I *came* here to warn you of cattle thieves," Cat declared tightly. "Will you go?"

—*She's more a laird than I . . .* And that hurt the worst of all, that men once sworn to him could believe a woman more fit than he, a mature man who had led into battle other men, when all Cat had ever led were her own personal rebellions for those small, insignificant issues as only she believed important. She had always been headstrong and impossible to train. He saw now what it earned him, his kindness, his affection, his laxity; time she *was* married, if only so another man had the training of her.

He scowled. "Where is Una? What have you done with her?"

"*I've* done naught with Una, and I doubt they have, either; with her grim face and sour mouth, there's not much for a man to go soft about—"

"Cat!"

"—so likely they've left Una and Angus and Ewan there in the road whilst they ride back to their thieving compatriots, *who are meanwhile lifting our cattle—*"

"Attend your clothing," he said curtly. "We will see about the cows—"

"Then go—"

"—while you return to Chesthill—"

"Will you *go?*"

"—for I willna have my daughter seen so by men." He straightened his spine, thrust up his chin, and glanced at the men who accompanied him to Stirling, and those men Cat had brought. "We've enough; they willna take our cows."

"God in Heaven, man, they'll be back in *Glencoe* before you so much as turn your horse!" she cried. "Does it matter more that my legs are covered than to retrieve what few cows we've managed to buy with pitiful little silver?"

It was a weapon, her tongue, and well honed; he scowled at her, knowing with each word she ate away his authority, divested him of whatever dignity he yet retained; knowing too she meant none of *that:* she only wanted the cows.

He swung his horse toward Rannoch. "We'll bring back our cows, if they've lifted them already; mayhap a MacDonald as well."

"And a Stewart," she muttered blackly.

"Go home, Cat."

"D'ye see?—I'm going. I'm *going!*"

And she was, at last, trying without much success to unhook kilted tunic skirts and pull folds of linen and wool down over her knees. It was preposterous behavior; but then he never expected anything of Cat save such. *I've ruined her. Una warned me after Helen died . . . but now 'tis too late.*

Yet as he watched her straight spine recede Glenlyon could not suppress a spurt of pride, for all it was somewhat tarnished by guilt. Once, he would not have cared what they saw of Cat, save to despair of what their thoughts might be; she was too tall, too thin, too boyish. They would have seen naught but knobbed knees and pale flesh splotched here and there with variegated bruises. And while he supposed beneath the knitted stockings she might *still* boast a collection of bruises, there was not a man among them who would not catch his breath at the sight of Cat Campbell but half-clad and wind-wracked, fiercely proud as a warrior woman out of ancient sagas.

Once, he would have hidden her for fear of ridicule. Now he desired her hidden for what she might inspire in a man less than circumspect where the laird's daughter was concerned.

Worth something after all, aye? And would undoubtedly prove her mettle as Breadalbane's daughter-in-law.

"Catriona, Countess Breadalbane," he murmured, and at last gave the order for his tail and Cat's clutch to set about retrieving what Mac-Donalds desired to steal.

Cat watched them go, her father and his men. She had long ago learned there was a line between truth and falsehood, and how to walk it without falling off so as to land on either side. Her father had ordered her back to Chesthill because he would not have her *'seen so by men.'* To her father, clearly, it was enough to keep her there; to Cat, equally clearly, it was not. It was enough only to suggest that she go, not stay, and that in order *not* to stay she need only change her clothing so she would not quite so closely resemble what her father called a whore, an observation which suggested to her that he knew what one looked like even if she did not. It was, Cat decided, fair indication he had kept company with such women, which left her all the more determined that she better than he was fit to circumscribe her behavior.

So Cat rode back to Chesthill, where she took off her belted tunic with its crimson, silver-plated sleeves, shed the arisaid, put on instead breeks borrowed from her father, and a shirt she had hemmed for him—*badly!*—but kept for herself; pinned a more voluminous plaid slantwise across chest and shoulder; belted on a dirk; and went back out of the house to mount the garron again. Winded, it could not offer much, but there was no other to ride. And she might have time to catch her father again, before he caught MacDonalds.

Rannoch Moor was a rumpled swath of land between Glen Lyon and Glencoe, made treacherous by bogs. Stunted trees dotted the moor, which yet boasted only winter finery, thick clumps of heather still dull from a duller season, plus overgrowth of bracken knit together by sienna gold carpets of grass. Come summer the blooming heather would set the moor afire, but for now it was a stony wasteland of bogs, of spindle-limbed, twisted trees, and the dead vegetation that would in spring come vigorously back to life. There were signs of it already in acid greens and olives, and the first promise of flowers, but Dair found it grimly predictable as he and the others drove the cattle from Campbell lands closer to MacDonald.

Robbie had complained there were not enough, and that Dair was too conservative by limiting them to a small herd closest to Rannoch rather than going deeper to the heart of Glen Lyon, but Dair knew better; by venturing so close to Chesthill and other townships such as those inhabited by the laird's sons, they risked too much. It was enough, he felt, to gather what cows they could on the edge of Glenlyon's lands, and drive them back to safety without alarming the Campbell inhabitants. If they got far enough into Rannoch without being discovered, they stood a fair chance even in the daylight of getting completely clear.

"We are but *six,*" Dair said when Robbie came up beside him to complain of it again.

Stewart scowled. "Doesna take much more than one or two to drive so few as this—they're *cows,* not men!—but I came to say the others will be here soon, and we'll be more than six."

"We can come back, Robbie. Another time."

"But we're here *now*—seems easier to me to gather the cattle now, than ride all the way back again."

"Seems easier to *me* to get home wi' what we've got—" A flash of steel in sunlight caught Dair's eye and broke him off mid-sentence. "—*Christ—ROBBIE—*"

It was sudden, so sudden, and proof of his concerns, but that no longer mattered. What mattered was survival as the heather clumps and hip-high bracken erupted with men clad in the deep green and black colors the Campbells favored, a'glint now with steel as they drew dirks. It was a fact all Highlanders knew that the duller tartans, despite their distinct patterns, hid a man better than solid colors.

" '*Creag ab Sgairbh!* ' " Robbie cried, wheeling his mount.

Dair did not waste breath on war cries. They were six, only six, with the others yet distant from them, and perhaps killed already. His concern was not to rouse, but to escape the trap. MacDonalds and Stewarts were scattered among the cattle, tending recalcitrant stirks, and of no use as a combined force. It was the Campbells who were to be reckoned with as a united threat.

"Chruachan!" someone shouted, and Dair realized grimly Campbells had more leisure to shout war cries meant to fire the blood; likely it was MacDonald and Stewart blood that would be spilled cold on the ground.

He reined his garron viciously, jerking it away from a man who came up from the ground with steel in his hand. But the man did not strike at human flesh, only at equine: a swipe of the dirk down low hamstrung the garron and made it into a three-legged beast.

Dair had no time for thinking, only for reacting; and yet he could not but wonder who had given alarm, who had known, who had been able to gather so many men as to offer such opposition. Raids were rapid sweeps, not pitched battles; yet there were men enough here to inhabit several townships.

His horse staggered, fighting to maintain balance. Campbells swarmed and clung to the reins, cut at a second hamstring, then pulled the butchered garron down even as Dair attempted to kick free of stirrups.

—too many— And so there were. Within minutes he was down with the quivering horse atop one leg. He cursed, twisted, snatched at his dirk; was grabbed by multiple hands. They stripped him of the dirk and dragged him free of the struggling garron even as it rolled, saving him a shattered leg; now he lay sprawled with rocks jammed into his spine, skull smacking turf-clad soil, legs and arms pinned. A dirk point teased his throat as a squatting Campbell slowly set his knee into heaving, vulnerable belly. "Dinna move," the man suggested.

There were shouts around him and the restless milling of unsettled cattle. Dust drifted, churned up by hooves. He heard the murmuring of men, the whuffing of winded garrons, and then a muffled outcry.

—Robbie— Dair tensed; the dirk bit into flesh, drawing blood, even as the knee insinuated itself more closely against his belly.

"Dinna kill them," someone said. "The laird will want to say what to do wi' them."

"Then he has three in place o' four; Malcolm's is dead already."

—Christ, dinna let it be Robbie—

"Where *is* the laird—?"

"Coming," another said.

Dair stared up at the man who held the dirk against his throat. Neither young nor old, nondescript of feature, with lank brown hair and browner eyes. When he grinned down at his captive he bared a broken eyetooth. "MacDonald? Or Stewart? We heard the Stewart war cry. Which are ye?"

Dair held his silence, tasting grit and blood in his mouth and the bitterness of comprehension: he would die unwed with no sons to his name, and MacIain and his wife left with only John.

"Aye, well, it doesna matter," the Campbell said off-handedly. "You'll die easy enough be you Stewart or MacDonald . . . and here is the laird now, come to pass judgment."

The knee eased. A man came close, peering down at Dair. "We've three?—aye, well, no' so many as I'd hoped."

"Four," someone said diffidently. "But one is dead of a dirk."

"Well, let it be . . . we've three necks for the rope." He had aged poorly since Dair had seen him a decade before, but was incontestably Robert Campbell. His eyes were set in a perpetual squint; the loose skin beneath his eyes sagged into sallow bags; and the once-firm jaw bore jowls. "They are the Gallows Herd; a tree will serve well enough for a Campbell gallows."

—*He doesna remember me* . . . It seemed inconceivable that a man might hang another without knowing whom he hanged. *This is Cat's father* . . .

He looked for something of her in the man, but found nothing there to suggest it. Dair supposed once Glenlyon had been a handsome man—it was said of him, though ten years before he had already looked hard used—but drink had ruined him. He was nothing more now than an aging, weak-willed man, but one who nonetheless now had the authority to sentence MacIain's son to death.

"Have we a proper tree?" Glenlyon asked.

"There," someone said. "Up the knowe."

"Good." Glenlyon turned away to look at the indicated hill with its lone tree. "Hang them from it. Then bind the bodies onto their garrons and send them home to MacIain. 'Twill be message enough, as concerns Campbell cattle."

—*He doesna ken who I am* . . . But Dair supposed it did not matter. He was cattle thief, reiver, be he Stewart or MacDonald; Glenlyon would take retribution from any man caught driving cattle off Campbell lands.

It was quickly done. Dair was flopped over onto his belly even against his will, face ground into rock-strewn track as they bound his hands behind him. Then he was dragged up.

"You'll mount," a Campbell said.

It was all too fast, too fast—

"Heave him up," another ordered.

They trapped his arms. Hands were on his legs, lifting him by the knees; he was tossed down across the saddle like a new-killed red deer. *—not so soon . . . not so swiftly—* Hands pushed and pulled, yanking him frontwise into the saddle. *—will you give me no time—?*

It was not his own garron, now hamstrung and due to die, but the one he recognized as belonging to Hugh MacDonald, a cousin. *Where is—?* Even as they pulled his legs down, one on either side, he searched for Hugh—and found him in the heather across a cluster of stones, with a dirk slash in his throat and the blood flowing into his eyes.

They turned Dair's horse to face the makeshift gallows: a noosed rope thrown over a tree limb. It was indeed a proper tree, not so twisted as the others, and therefore tall enough to accommodate a mounted man and support his struggling weight when the garron was slapped away.

Two others were in like circumstances: one of Robbie's Stewarts, whom Dair knew in passing, and a second MacDonald, Walter, who was kin by marriage to Dair's mother's sister.

Robert Stewart was absent. *—one man dead, they said, and that man being Hugh . . .* Then Robbie had escaped. Of the six of them, Robbie and another had escaped, while Hugh MacDonald was already dead, and three more bound for hanging.

Glenlyon stood by the tree, one foot set up on a stone. He gave the order, and the Stewart's garron was brought forward.

Dair supposed, as they set the rope around the Stewart's neck and slapped the garron away, that it was good Robbie had survived. He was violently traditional, and would see to it that proper songs were sung of them all.

Dair did not flinch as the Stewart's cry was cut off abruptly when he dropped against the rope. A good hanging, then, with his neck quickly broken; better than choking slowly.

Then Walter, much younger than Dair, who stared wide-eyed at his laird's son as the Campbells pulled down the dead Stewart and tied him onto a garron.

Walter's horse was led under the tree. The rope was settled around his neck and snugged tight. "Alasdair—?"

He knew what Walter required: explanation, absolution, a word from his laird's son to make it easier. But such things were hard come by when Walter's death would be his own in but a moment.

"Alasdair—"

Dair unclenched his jaws. He stared fixedly at Glenlyon until the laird looked at him, and then he offered Walter all he could: *"Fraoch Eilean."* When Glenlyon's eyes narrowed, he spoke again in words the

Campbell laird knew very well: *"Per mare per terras."* The MacDonald
clan slogan: *'By sea and by land.'* "Now you'll ken," Dair said.

"Wait—" Walter began, but the garron was slapped away as if in
repudiation of MacDonald war cry and slogan. This death was not so
easy. As Walter kicked in protest, gagging against the rope, Dair felt
the sweat running icy down his flesh.

—dinna dishonor MacIain, or your mother—

When Walter hung slackly, Campbells took him down.

—dinna dishonor John—

They tied the body to the garron and sent it on its way.

—dinna dishonor Glencoe—

They took up the reins to Dair's horse and led it under the tree.

—Christ, Alasdair Og . . . dinna dishonor YOURSELF—

The bite of the rope was harsh as they set it around his neck.

Cat saw the cows first. And then she saw the granite-crowned hill
with its single tree as a scepter, Campbells gathered there like subjects
before a king, and the man atop the horse with a rope around his neck.

—oh, no, no—

This was not what she had envisioned, not at all, none of it, not the
dying, the death; she had envisioned none of it because she had
thought no further than *catching* the MacDonalds; than keeping them
from stealing more Campbell cows.

"Wait!" That much she got out at last, aloud where a man might
hear; but they did not hear, or did not heed. The horse was driven
away and the bound man was jerked free of the saddle to dangle, kicking frenziedly, until he choked to death.

Another horse waited. Another man waited. That man, that Mac-
Donald, she knew.

A violent shudder shook her. Cat dug heels into her garron's side,
urging it through milling cattle. Her eyes were fixed on the dangling,
now-slack body. "No, no—*wait*—"

They took the body down, brought the quivering horse back, and
slung the dead man across the saddle, where they tied his body and
sent his garron off again with shouts and crude witticisms.

—wait you— She wished she had a claymore to use as goad, driving
the cattle from her path. All she had were feet and lungs, and she used
both frantically, cursing, shouting, kicking, pushing cows aside by forcing the garron through them.

She stared now at Dair, waiting on his horse. "Hold!" she cried.

Atop the hill with its hanging tree the Campbells led him forth.

"Hold!"

They set the rope around his neck.

"CHRUACHAN!"

That they heard. As she reached the outer perimeter of the gathered Campbells, faces turned toward her. She saw men she knew well, and men she knew very little. She saw her father with one foot set upon a stone as if he watched in idleness, resting a leg. She saw Dair Mac-Donald with his hands tied behind him, and the rope around his neck.

"No!" Cat cried. "Hold—"

Glenlyon put up his hand as he had before to signal the hanging commenced.

"Dinna—" Cat shouted, "—dinna *do* it!"

She was through at last; men were easier to part than cows. She broke free of them and halted atop the hill, staring in shock at the dirty, blood-smeared face of Dair MacDonald, turned to her now but partially obscured by the rough hemp rope knotted beneath one ear.

—I did this . . . He was white, very white, very stark except where he was bloody, except where a smear of dirt darkened a cheekbone. The brown eyes were black and bleak and empty altogether of the light she had witnessed before, the amber-hued whisky-warmth she looked for now and did not find, while knowing why she could not; the eyes were instead wholly transfixed by the moment, by the rope, by the quivering of the horse he rode unwillingly, and which would, if it moved too far, yet carry him to his death.

Cat looked straight at the Campbell who held the garron's reins. Explicitly she said, "Dinna let go."

"Cat." It was her father.

"Dinna let *go!*"

This time the Campbell nodded.

Glenlyon took his foot from the stone. "Cat, what have you come for? I sent you home."

She again looked at Dair and saw Robbie Campbell instead, dead Robbie, her brother, her MacDonald-murdered brother. She saw the pallor again; the frozen, rigid, blood-sullied features; the exquisite stillness of his limbs, his skull, lest something happen to harm him, or to kill him. It was Robbie come again, dead Robbie Campbell, who had died not of enmity but of a meaningless scuffle intended only to contain him. It was her dirk, her borrowed dirk, that had had the killing of him.

And her alarm that had brought the Campbells here, where Dair MacDonald, captured, would be hanged for his name as much as for his crime.

"No," she said.

"This is for men," Glenlyon told her. "Go back home, Cat."

She could not look away from Robbie's face, the face that was also Dair's. "*I* killed him."

There. It was said, was admitted, was declared before them all, who believed the laird's son murdered by Glencoe MacDonalds.

—I did that . . . now I do this—

Below the hill, cattle milled and began to scatter, grazing in indolence alien to the men who gathered to kill. There was silence save for the cattle, an intense, tangible silence. The faces stared back at her, waiting; she had asked them to wait, and they waited. Now it was for her to explain her purpose here, where men killed men in a common retribution never questioned among Highlanders.

For her to explain why they should not kill a MacDonald who had, in all likelihood, killed a Campbell. Or two. *As we have killed MacDonalds.*

He had asked it himself: '*Have you forgotten the times Campbells came a'raiding to Glencoe?*' Her brothers had done so. They had intended to do so the night Robbie died, and they had *done* so four years later, when she had tried very much to keep them home; they had gone a'raiding to Glencoe and brought home cattle. Some of them Campbell cows, she did not doubt, but as many perhaps MacDonald.

There was no guilt in the world between them save it was not equally shared, as well as blame. For that hard truth, that reality, if for no other reason she could not freely admit, she would prevent his execution.

"We owe him something," Cat said, and saw Campbell eyes narrow; what was owed a MacDonald but the death awaiting him now? "We owe him for kindness," she told them. "We owe him for an honor none of us will admit, but me; it was me he aided, when another meant me harm." She looked at her father's dissolute face. "It was me, aye? . . . *I* killed Robbie. I took your old dirk—they were going, the lads, and wouldna have me with them because I was a lass . . . so I followed. I took your dirk and *followed*—and Robbie was caught, and me, and the MacDonalds held him, and it was *my fault* he died because he fell upon the dirk." She was shaking, and cold, and crying. "They didna mean him to die. But he tried to twist free, and fell—and they fell *on* him, and scuffled—and the dirk was there, *my* dirk—"

"Cat." Glenlyon's face was wasted. "Cat, stop this—"

"—*my* dirk he fell on, he *fell*—and they ran, all of them ran; they kent what would happen, what would be said . . . and it was: MacDonalds killed Robbie Campbell, the laird's own heir—but it wasna, it *wasna* MacDonalds—it was me . . . it was me . . ." She caught back a sob before it broke her entirely. "We owe him something, this MacDonald . . . of all of them, he has never intended us anything but fairness and honor. I will swear it. Give me a Bible, a relic . . . I will swear it." She looked at Dair as the pain broke in her chest, and the wild grief welled up for a brother who was dead and another man who would die. "Dinna hang *him.*"

Glenlyon put hands to his face and rubbed it all out of shape. The flesh was much abused, sallowed and ruined from drink; the eyes dull and watery; the hair lank and graying. He was an old man to her, made older by her words, who looked at her now with such an emptiness of spirit she feared what was in his mind. It was possible, she supposed, he would still blame MacDonalds—and one of the Gallows Herd yet present and in an attitude that cried out for hanging. They need only send forth the horse.

She opened her mouth to tell Glenlyon who Dair was, thinking it might mean something; and shut it immediately. It would mean too much. One laird's son was dead. Glenlyon, in his grief, his shock, might decide it worth doing to kill MacIain's son, so the Glencoe laird would understand the anguish.

"I have told you," she said rustily, "so you willna kill him."

Glenlyon's dulled eyes were bleak and glistening. "Would you have told me ever? Ever?"

From atop her garron, Cat looked down on him and shivered. "I told God," she answered. "I kent He would punish me for it, one day. I didna see the sense in punishing you with it."

"Me!"

"I thought 'twas easier for you to believe MacDonalds did it. You hated them already. I didna want—" It was hard, harder by far than anticipated, all those times; and now was here at last. "I didna want you to hate me."

"MacDonalds *did* do it!"

"They didna mean it. I saw it. I saw it then . . . I see it now whenever I summon it up." Cat looked at Dair's white, stone-battered face. A trickle of blood bathed his throat; she could see the dirk cut and the vulnerable flesh beneath. " 'Tis easy to blame them, any of them, even for such things as Campbells are responsible. Well, I willna see this man hanged . . . he of them all has done what he could to give back what was taken."

"Give back!" her father cried. " 'Twas MacDonalds who stripped Glen Lyon after Killiecrankie!"

"And this MacDonald who gave me back my mother's kettle!" She looked again at Glenlyon, knowing he saw the tears in her eyes; tears for a MacDonald? Or for her mother? "Not so much, a kettle—but more than we would have had."

"A kettle." A vast disgust was in the words: such as a kettle meant nothing to Glenlyon, who valued in place of pots and pans usquabae and dice.

"I've little enough of my mother," Cat said unsteadily. " 'Tis the only thing left of her, now."

It enraged him. "Oh, aye? Is it? Then what have you of me? What have you of *me*? Christ, Cat—'twas *my loins* that sired you; you forget it often enough!"

She stared at him, transfixed by the sudden eruption of anger and anguish. "Of you—?"

"Of me! Have you anything? Or are you too ashamed to claim it?"

Humiliated, she glanced sidelong at the Campbells, thinking of dignity long banished, now destroyed again. "Father—"

"They ken what I am!" he said. "Christ, Cat, you've cut at me so many times I've no more blood to shed. You come to tell me Mac-Donalds and Stewarts have lifted our cattle, then draw your dirk again—the one in your mouth!—to bleed me of dignity. But now when you're faced with the truth, with what comes of cattle-lifting, you play the woman with me and appeal for his life!"

She retreated from his attack. "Because—"

"Because you say he's been kind to you. Well, he hasna been kind to me." Glenlyon drew his claymore. " 'Tis time you learned what responsibility means, Cat. You canna use it this way and that, according to your whims. There *is* only one way—"

"No—*no*—"She threw herself from the garron. "No, Glenlyon . . . *NO*—" She tripped and fell, landing painfully on hands and knees. "Father—*dinna do it*—"

He turned from her to the garron with its MacDonald burden. Glenlyon brought the flat of the sword down across the broad rump—

"NO—"

—watched the man jerked free of his mount—

"—Oh Christ . . ." —*oh God, oh God, no*—"

—then sliced through the rope cleanly. "There." He turned on his daughter as Dair dropped heavily from the parted rope. "Hanged, but not dead. Should serve both sides, I'm thinking." He stared out at his Campbells. "Those of you going with me to Stirling had best prepare; we've a ways yet to march. The rest of you who came for cows, drive them back home. We're done here this day."

Cat knelt on the ground beside the sprawled body. Loose hair dragged in the dirt, was caught beneath her knees. "Father—"

"You'd best get yourself to Kilchurn," he told her. "Breadalbane willna wait forever."

Trembling, she sat back onto her heels, pressing bleeding palms into the tartan fabric of her breeks. *"Why?"*

"Why that? Or why this?" Glenlyon's face warped briefly, then solidified. "Because you shame me, lass. 'Tis time you learned you canna have your own way always." He jerked his head at her garron. "Mount your horse, Cat. You'll come with us until the road splits."

"But—" She looked at Dair, who lay on his side with his arms yet tied behind him. He breathed; she could see the heaving of his chest, the puff of dirt dusting from beneath his warped and gaping mouth with each noisy exhalation. "But what of—"

"Mount your horse. He's breath yet, aye? The walk will restore his spirits."

Cat considered rebellion. *If I say no, you canna make me.* But she looked at the man again, the man her father had hanged, and offered nothing at all. She would not risk him again.

She got to her feet and went to the garron, gathering dangling reins. She wanted very much to protest, to insist upon leaving a horse, but did not. She had won him his life; she refused to win him his death.

Cat mounted her horse. As the Campbells set themselves the task of gathering and driving the cattle back to proper lands, she fell in beside her father and did not look back again.

Dair lay for a very long time sprawled upon the ground, lest a man change his mind and decide, on his way home, to kill a MacDonald. Perhaps three were not enough, two MacDonalds and one Stewart: three men dead for wanting Campbell cows.

Perhaps more than that; they had left two at the shieling and four with Cat. Perhaps nine dead. And no cows brought home to make the price worth it; but then he was not certain a handful of cows was worth a single man, unwilling as he was to count the others.

He thought of Killicrankie, of Dundee's proud words and Dundee's common death, killed by a musket ball that snooved beneath jacket skirts. He thought of the men he had killed in the name of King James; but as much in the name of MacDonald superiority, his ears filled with the skirling of pipes ranting "March of the MacDonalds." War was war: men died on both sides, and whichever side claimed more alive at the end of the day, or whichever side did not run away by the end of the day, won the battle.

But this. This was not war. This was not battle. This was not done for king.

This was done for clan, but as much for young men too bound by day-to-day, seeking release in risk and activity from mundane concerns. When there was not war, there were raids to be made. It was done all over Scotland, above the Lowland line; to feed the clan, to increase the herds, to tend one's responsibilities.

His now was to live, and to make his way home to Glencoe.

The trembling, the weakness, the gasping had lasted a long time.

The Campbells were gone with their cattle. The dust had settled. Such sounds as were normal, bird and wind and vermin, had come back to the hilltop where a length of rope, gently waving, yet depended from the tree. Where MacIain's second son, with blood in his mouth, at last made shift to rise up onto his knees, so he might view once more the world he had believed taken from him.

He rolled forward, then gathered legs beneath buttocks. A heave brought him up, lifting shoulders from the ground, raising a torso and balancing it firmly atop bent legs. He spat out blood and grit, aware of the cut he himself had made with teeth in the flesh of his mouth, wanting very badly not to cry out as Walter had and dishonor his clan.

From there to knees, buttocks brushing heels, sword-severed noose flapping against his chest, and then finally to feet, lurching awkwardly with no arms to balance, no flesh and bone counterweight. But upright at last, standing at last, and viewing at last the remains of Glen Lyon Campbells: a distant glint of steel, the dust raised of reclaimed cattle.

Dair blinked dry eyes. He was glad Cat had gone.

When he was certain his legs could be trusted, he walked down from the hill. The muscles of his thighs trembled. He took short steps at first, thinking through each one— —*one, and one, and one*— —and when the trembling at last lessened he lengthened his strides. —*one— two—three—*

He stopped walking only when he reached the body on the rocks: Hugh MacDonald, a cousin, bled dry of life. It pooled sullenly in a mud-bloodied puddle, giving drink to thirsty grass.

He could not close the eyes. His hands were bound behind him.

"*Fraoch Eilean,*" he rasped as the wind blew down the moor.

Then he turned himself westward and began to walk home.

Emptiness. Empty house, empty heart. Chesthill was, in her father's absence, more a travesty than when he was present, lost in whisky haze. Cat had often believed it empty even in his presence because there was so little of him save his desire for drink, but he had all of a sudden become another man, and one with more power than to which she had long been accustomed, weighing out her chances of escaping punishment.

He had struck her rarely; the last time she recalled such punishment had been before Breadalbane, when the earl had come to shout of her father's folly in selling off Glen Lyon. This time, despite her hatred of it and the furious tears it would bring, she wished he *had* struck her. Then she could hate him for something identifiable, for his humiliation of *her*, instead of detesting him for what he had done to Dair Mac-Donald.

She had not been permitted to stay. She had not been allowed to explain to a dead man yet alive why she had told the truth of Robbie's death after so many years, when she had feasted on it so long to give fuel to the hatred.

There were other reasons. There were always other reasons; she was Campbell, he MacDonald.

Cat stood in the front room of the house. The door behind was open, admitting sunlight, admitting air, while *she* admitted it was time she took up responsibility for such things as she owed to others, even as her father had ordered her to do.

He had said it plainly: ' *'Tis time you learned what responsibility means. You canna use it this way and that, according to your whims.'*

But she *had* taken responsibility. For her brother's death, and for Dair MacDonald's life. And Glenlyon punished her for it.

"Damn you," she said. "For that, if for naught else; you did it because I *embarrassed* you; me, a Campbell, pleading for a MacDonald."

In that terrifying moment when she believed Dair would die, she too had died the little death that came to every daughter, every child, who was suddenly adult enough to see the child in the parent, to admit her father was no more wise for his age than she was ignorant for her youth. That death of innocence was multiplied one hundredfold by the other more painful deaths: love for her father, pride in her name, unwavering resolution that no matter what the reason, there was always justification in what a Campbell did in retribution for MacDonald crimes.

Dair MacDonald still lived. She supposed they would make songs of it, one day: the man Glenlyon hanged. But she and half a hundred others, and Dair, and Glenlyon, knew the truth: her father had cut the rope in punishment, not clemency; he wanted everyone to know at whose behest a MacDonald survived.

It was a strong man, and a brave one, who permitted his direst enemy to survive so that *in* that survival the enemy's final courage was diminished by the greater courage of another. Robert Campbell, Laird of Glen Lyon, at whom others laughed, had restored much of his name, much of his reputation, with the single slice of a sword.

He has made himself a man again. In his daughter's name.

Campbell the laughingstock, Glenlyon the drukken man was no threat but to himself. Campbell the hero, Glenlyon the brave laird was a man others would praise, would follow, and such praise as they would offer would empower her father with the will and ability to commit such acts as he deemed necessary in the ordering of his life.

In the ordering of mine. She wanted to grieve for the loss of her freedom, but all Cat could do was cry from relief, from the recollection that her father, for whatever reason, had seen fit to sever the rope.

Punishment, such as it was, was pain she could bear.

Dair did not at first credit the hand on him. One hand only; the other held the reins to a garron, though the man was afoot. "Dair—oh good *Christ*—" The hand stopped him with pressure, urging him to halt. He halted. The garron was freed; both hands grasped the noose and loosened it, then lifted it over his head.

Dair began to shake.

"Dinna fret, dinna greet—" Robbie Stewart dropped the rope, drew his dirk, cut through the bindings. Dair's arms were freed at last, flopping to his sides. "Aye, I ken—I ken what you're feeling . . . Wait. Wait."

He turned abruptly and went away. Dair heard low-voiced murmurings as Stewart spoke to another man, then the sound of receding hooves.

"Better, then," Robbie said. "Only me to see it; aye, Dair, I ken . . . there's no shame in it."

He knelt down suddenly because he could not stand, could not keep himself from shaking. Shoulders ached as he drew slack arms forward, crossing wrist over wrist as he pressed them against his belly. Stone bit into his knees. A spasm cramped his belly, then spread insidiously into thighs to rob the muscles of strength.

He bent over rigidly, biting deeply into his lip. He felt the blood rise, tasted it in his mouth; tasted the bitter tang of fear once repressed and now free of it, free in safety to make itself known, to govern the body of even the strongest man, and rob him of self-respect as he gave way to the knowledge that he had been *hanged*—

To relief that he had survived, and was found by a friend.

"I ken," Robbie said rustily. "Battle is fair, is clean . . . a man faces that death with fear, but he hears the pipes, and the war cries, and he kens he isna alone. He overcomes it in the rising of the blood. But this—*this* . . ." He let go a noisy breath. "This is not so fair, not so clean—and it doesna shame a man to be glad of it, and to weep . . ." Robbie's hand was on his shoulder, pressing fingers into flesh as he gripped rigid muscle. "I think no less of you for doing what I've done," Stewart said, "and of what I'll do again, I dinna doubt; and what I *would* do, me, were I in your place."

It was not the words so much as the tone. He was foal, pup, kitten, answering the voice of a man who understood what it was to be so afraid, to be so relieved, to comprehend the uncounted complexities of new life beginning on the death of the old.

He spat out blood. He pressed his palms against the ground and thrust himself upward, so he stood again as a man and looked upon the world Glenlyon had given him back.

Not Glenlyon. His daughter.

Dair looked at the garron. His body seized into stillness, into the abject inability to mount. It was too soon, too sudden, too like; it had been a horse that carried him willingly to death, though a sword had kept him from it.

"Aye," Robbie said, and sent his garron westward with a slap on its rump. "I favor a walk myself on a day like this day."

Five

*T*he Earl of Breadalbane never spent time in Kilchurn's kitchens, but his eldest son did, and frequently, swilling ale with turnspits and trading gossip with the cooks.

It was a habit that displeased Breadalbane, but did not surprise him particularly in view of Duncan's propensity for questionable companionships; at least the kitchen was his own, and the servants as well. It was better, he decided as he made his way to the kitchens, that Duncan waste time under his father's roof than waste it in a tavern.

Breadalbane's heir, sitting at the massive slab of wood used for preparing feasts, with ale at his elbow and meat pie half-consumed, was not pleased to see his father. The earl was equally displeased by Duncan's malignant attitude as he overfilled his mouth with food: a certain sullenness in the sallow face and an enmity in the eyes that reminded the earl of his own father— *God rest his pawkie soul!* —who had rarely understood the needs of the world as his son did; now the grandson showed a remarkable aptitude for his grandfather's lack of insight.

The cooks and kitchen staff were nonplussed by the earl's presence. He sent them away, knowing dinner might suffer, but there were things he considered far more important than the flavor of his meat.

"She is here," Breadalbane said without preamble. "She is currently in the chamber assigned to her; I wanted to make certain you would treat her as befits my heir before permitting you to meet."

"Why?" Duncan asked around a mouthful of meat and crust. "Do you believe I might belittle her, or express my wish to wed another woman?''

"I do . . . and you would."

Duncan's swollen smile was neither amused nor friendly. "So I would." He picked up his ale and drank lustily.

The earl knew very well his son sought to put him off; well, it would take more than poor manners. "Her father may be a man worth little respect, but she deserves something of the Breadalbane courtesy—"

Duncan smacked down his mug, slopping its contents over the rim. "Courtesy! From you?"

"From you." The earl toured the kitchens, absently marking how much flour was used for bread; how substantial his salt supply; how the cooks hoarded spices. "I dinna ken what you may have promised Marjorie Campbell of Lawers, but you'd best *un*promise it; she is not whom you shall wed. I've my own reasons for it, good reasons, which you no doubt will decry, but 'tis done. And I believe it might be a good match, Duncan . . . I saw her but two years ago—or was it three?—when I went to Glen Lyon. She's spirit of her own, so you will thank me for that. She isna a lump of suet."

Duncan tore at his bread. "And is she fair? Or d'ye give me a plain woman to settle other debts, when I may have my own?"

"I've never lied to you, Duncan, and I'll not begin now: no, she isna fair. No man would name her so."

"Ah." Duncan's sallow face displayed its tendency to splotch as angry color fed flesh. "Why not marry her yourself, aye? You've your own reasons, you said; good reasons, you said. You're not belike to die any day soon, I'll warrant—why foist her off on me? And I daresay were John not wed already you'd marry *him* to her . . . or would you no' give him a woman who isna fair? Does he deserve better?"

"He does," the earl declared, continuing his inspection, "for his courtesy if naught else; have I raised you to speak so?"

"I learned it of necessity; I am your son, aye?—and not entirely witless. I ken when defense is needed." Duncan tucked bread into his mouth, chewed vigorously, then shrugged. "Well, there's naught I can say, is there? 'Tis decided. All that is left is for us to meet: Breadalbane's heir, whom he would change for another, and the drukken man's plain daughter." He paused to swallow elaborately. "Have you told her of me, then? Have you warned her of my habits?"

Breadalbane sniffed at the bubbling contents of a pot hung over the hearth. "I havena seen her yet. I've business to attend; I'll send her to you."

"Without warning her first?" Duncan laughed, washing bread down with ale. "Shall we suit, then, the two of us?—both of us unloved?"

Breadalbane sighed. "She isna unloved, unless you intend to deny it to her."

"To her? No." Duncan's mouth twisted. "Only to you."

It was a craggy, upthrust heap of granite tall as a man, in breadth as wide as ten standing shoulder to shoulder. Uncounted crevices divided it vertically in rough precision, striations eaten into its flanks by time, by wind, by rain. In winter it was gray on gray, leavened only with a crop of sere, sienna-colored grass and ocherous lichen, but in spring it boasted a viridescent wealth of new life where fertile stone pockets caught soil and seed.

Legend claimed the huge rock in the center of the glen had been sacred to druids. Dair did not know. He knew only that it was a place of silence, of solitude, where a man might think without interruption as he perched upon rocky rib.

The flat-crowned, uppermost surface of the stone was heavily pitted, carved into large, jagged depressions which caught and held rain puddles and blown soil; other areas more dominant jutted sharply above the depressions, so that a man walking the spine of the rock must watch where he put his feet lest he be brought down. While the formation was not nearly so high as the Pap of Glencoe, overlooking the glen, nor so treacherous as the Devil's Staircase between the glen and Rannoch Moor, its hard shoulders were nonetheless equally unforgiving.

He stood for a long time atop the rock, letting the wind blow in his face. He tasted the dampness of Loch Linnhe from the western end, and the nearby River Coe flowing the length of the fertile valley cradled amidst the mountains, smelled the earthy richness of spring, the thicker fug of peat-smoke, a drift of roasting venison. He welcomed the touch of the wind, glorying in its buffet until his memory likened its caress to Jean Stewart's, and then he sat down all at once on the edge of the massy granite and let the pines surrounding it screen him from the wind.

When John came up from his house, Dair was unsurprised; his brother understood him better than most. He watched John stride up the glen by the drove-road, kilt hem swinging, Young Sandy in one arm; then he cut across to the rock itself. John did not climb up its back side but stood at its foot on the pebble-strewn verge below. The rock's crown was not so high that John had to tip his skull back very far, nor to shout. "Jean is at the house."

Silent, Dair watched the nephew named for him as he plucked at his father's plaid brooch. Young Sandy would be MacIain himself one day, the fourteenth of the name; between him and the present laird lay John MacDonald.

"She said she'd come to speak wi' Eiblin," John explained, rescuing his brooch and the wool beneath the massive tang. "Eiblin elbowed and eyebrowed me to the door. Since 'tis not so often I'm thrown out of my own house, I thought I would ask you why."

Dair sighed, using a twig to draw idle designs in the damp earth caught in a stony pocket. "Eiblin will tell you later. She tells you everything."

"She is my wife; 'tis required. You would ken it if you were married." John set down his son into the verdant grass and handed him a stick. "But why should I wait for my wife to tell me tonight, when my brother can do it now?"

" 'Tis your house, John. You dinna need to let the woman direct you in it."

"*There* speaks a man who isna wed!"

Dair grimaced. Then he looked at his brother. One end of his mouth hooked wryly. "You're nearly as white-headed as MacIain."

"And like to be whiter before you tell me the truth." John paused. "Is it Jean?"

"Christ." Dair sighed. "You'd best come up, John. No sense in a man standing when he can sit."

"Aye, well—I wouldna ask it of him if he wasna ready for company."

"I said for you to come up."

John bent over his son. "I'll be up there"—he gestured at the crown—"so dinna set a course for the river, or I'll fly down and scoop you up again."

Young Sandy was at present much taken with his stick and the resultant excavations in grass and dark soil. He seemed disinclined to wander, so John walked around to the hindmost end of the rock and climbed up the series of sloping steps God had seen fit to shape. He picked his way across the uneven surface and stood beside Dair, looking across the verdant vista. " 'Tis the best place in the glen for a signal fire. Every house can see it."

"Could you see me?"

"I kent you'd be here. Didna need to see you." John found a benevolent perch beside his brother and sat down, arranging the folds of his kilt. " 'Tis woman's talk, that. I'm better here." He reached into his scrip and pulled out a flat, leather-wrapped flask. He pulled the stopper, raised it briefly: "*Slàinte.*" He drank, then held it out.

Dair accepted it. "*Slàinte.*" Whisky burned down his throat.

For a long time they shared a companionable silence, asking nothing of one another; theirs was a close relationship built on trust as well as affection, and neither saw sense in rushing the other before his time.

But my time will come, aye? Dair picked pebbles from a depression near his knee and tossed them away one by one, aiming at a tree well beyond his nephew. "You said something to me at Killiecrankie, before the pipes began."

John tipped back his head and squinted into the sky. "You recall it better than I, whatever it was I said. I was somewhat taken up by the wait before the battle."

"You said battle makes a man think of his wife, think of bairns."

"It takes most that way. But 'tisn't a *rule.*"

Dair dug a thumbnail into a minute crevice in unforgiving stone. "When they put the rope over my head—"

He broke off; his throat tautened painfully. He felt the rope again on his neck, felt its touch, its bite; felt the saddle move beneath him, and the garron; felt the stirrups jerked free; the weightlessness of his fall; the jerk of the knot as it snapped past his ear, bringing blood from burned flesh; but the ear was nothing, nothing at all . . .

It was the rope—

—the noose—

—the tautness that shut off breath—

—shut off voice—

—shut off thought . . .

—save for the knowledge he left no one in the world to live beyond his generation.

For a long moment he said nothing more because he could not find the words, only the feelings, and those were too private, too powerful. He took comfort in John's quiet presence, knowing his brother would never require him to speak of something he could not. And yet Dair knew he must, if he were to heal the inner wound even as the flesh of his neck restored itself.

"When they set the rope around my neck and Glenlyon raised his hand, I thought of MacIain, and you, and Glencoe, and my mother. I thought of the bairns I would never sire. But not once, not *once,* did I think of Jean." The thumbnail snapped. He looked at John. "Should a man who survives wed a woman he doesna think of as he prepares to die?"

It had been years since Duncan stirred Breadalbane to anger, and he did not do so now. The earl dealt with him as he always dealt with him: he gave him orders, knowing very well Duncan would obey them because he always obeyed them. He was a contentious sort, but one lacking the initiative that might make him truly troublesome. He did not have the ballocks to defy his father in anything save words.

Words were a weapon the earl understood, and he was far better at wielding them than his heir would ever be. "Go out to the garden, Duncan—I'll send Glenlyon's lass to you there. You'd best be civil to her; she'll be coming to Achallader with us."

"Achallader! When?"

"A matter of weeks. We've business wi' the clans."

"Achallader's naught but a ruin!"

"Aye, it is; we'll sleep under plaids like Highlanders, with naught for our roof but the sky." Breadalbane smiled. "You are a Highlander still, you ken, albeit you spend your time in taverns with Lowlanders and Sassenachs."

"They are better company than what you might wish for me."

"Only because you are *my* son. Have you no eyes, Duncan, nor ears? They promise you things because you will be Breadalbane one day; dinna put such trust in their mouths."

"While you go to the clans?" Duncan shook his head and set down his ale. "You're William's man, Father—they'll no' listen to you."

"They'll listen. There is silver in it for them."

But he did not speak of what else would be in the oath, for Duncan's mouth was too loose. Breadalbane understood very well the choice left for the lairds. If they did not swear, no matter the reason, the weather, they would be dead within the year. William, at Stair's behest, gave them only six months.

"They are Jacobites," Duncan persevered. "They'll no' listen to *you.*"

"One day they will. Today. Tomorrow . . . who can say?" Breadalbane smiled. "Come with me to Achallader and learn a thing or two. 'Twill be you who deals with them when I am in my grave."

"And shall I reap what you sow?" Duncan picked up his meat-knife with economical purpose. "They would as lief dirk you as listen to your words. And they'll take your silver first, so what need of listening at all?"

"Oh, no, no. They'll listen to me first, then take my silver . . . or *agree* to take it; 'tis another thing entirely to have it sent up here from Edinburgh, or London."

Duncan was astounded. "You dinna have it yet?"

" 'Tis a fool who carries with him what Highlanders can lift." Breadalbane shook his head. "You've been too much among the Lowlanders; 'tis time you recalled your blood."

Duncan tossed down the meat-knife. It rattled on wood. "Recalled I am bred of cattle thieves, and worse?" He laughed harshly. "Black

Duncan of the Cowl. My namesake. And he was no better than any thieving Highlander; worse than most! He didna buy what he could steal—''

"A thrifty man, Black Duncan.''

"—and didna steal but by guile when he could, murder when he could not. By Christ, Father, do you follow in his footsteps?''

"My question is: do *you* follow in them?''

Duncan's mouth dropped open. "You believe I might drive out John?''

"Black Duncan did it with the brother *his* father favored.''

"John would defeat me! You ken it! He is better than I in everything—''

The earl cut him off. "Then best you remember it.''

Duncan's color ebbed. "You are what they say of you!''

"Am I?''

Duncan quoted, " *'No Government can trust him but where his private interest is in view . . .'* ''

Breadalbane scoffed. "Coffeehouse stories. 'Tis a waste of time to read the broadsheets; you canna trust what is written.''

" *'—he knows neither honor nor religion but where they are mixed with interest'*—''

"Have you memorized it, then?''

"I have. I ken 'tis true, and perhaps the only truth I'll ever have of you.'' Duncan laughed. "Gey perceptive, to capture you so well . . . there was an etching, also—''

"Enough,'' Breadalbane said. "Go out into the garden; you've your wife to meet.''

"Glenlyon's daughter?'' Duncan made a rude sound. "Then I'd better take whisky with me, or dice.''

Breadalbane recalled the defiance displayed before her father, and the blow withstood as if it were worth ten to ensure the earl would do what he could to get Glen Lyon back from Murray of Atholl. He had not, but not without effort expended; it was the Earl of Argyll who thwarted him.

Now he shook his head. "She isna her father, Duncan. Dinna forget that.''

When Cat went out to the earl's walled garden at Kilchurn, she found the door ajar in invitation. But she did not go in at once because she could not; she could only stand there caught midway like a hare about to bolt, wanting to run away but not knowing which route might offer the best escape.

It was not fair, she knew; Duncan Campbell deserved better. She supposed his father did as well, though she was less inclined to offer the earl any kindness other than was required by good manners. She recalled too clearly how Breadalbane had refused to pay off her father's debts, thereby forcing him to sell Glen Lyon, and how the earl had, despite promises, failed to overturn the sale to Murray of Atholl.

And now he suggests I marry his heir . . . Cat supposed it might be Breadalbane's way of setting things to rights after all; despite her father's penury he remained Glenlyon, and of no small repute. She was a Campbell as Duncan was, and related by blood. They could both do worse.

She was not opposed to marriage. She wanted a husband, a household, and children. She knew marriage required things, and that she would have to compromise ideals as well as behaviors; that a man suffered less than a woman in such things as compromises, because he was required to make none. She was willing to do what was necessary to make a settled life. But she had expected one day to marry a Glen Lyon Campbell, a man she knew, or an acquaintance from a neighboring glen, and now that she stood on one side of a wall, fully aware her future husband, a stranger, perhaps waited on the other, she was less inclined to meet than to walk away from him.

Cat drew in a deep, noisy breath. "Duncan Campbell," she murmured softly. "Christ—I dinna even need to change my name!"

But the rank would change, and with it her world. When his father died he would become an earl, and she a countess. The new earl would own a half dozen or more castles scattered all through Campbell country, as well as a town house in Edinburgh, and she doubted very much she would ever again see Glen Lyon.

Cat supposed many women would rejoice, but such knowledge brought her no peace. She cared no more for the rank than she did for the man, though she had never met him.

"Dinna be daft," she muttered, and stepped through the open gate.

At first she believed herself alone, but that was quickly dispelled. A man also was present, digging in the soil from which grew a profusion of tangled vines intermixed with tattered roses. To her unpracticed eye the garden was unkempt, but oddly appealing for all its disarray; it seemed unnecessary to prune back all the wildness, but that was precisely what the man was doing.

Duncan? Duncan Campbell? But she said nothing aloud. It would serve her better to see him without his knowledge, without the taut civility they would offer one another because they did not know what else there could be between them.

He knelt beside a wall, cutting vine and cane. He was not servant; his clothing made that plain, though his efforts soiled them. Cat watched

the economy of his movements, the clean precision with which he se-
lected stem or cane and cut, then pulled it from the shrubbery and set
it aside. Heaps of trimmed, discarded growth lay about the walled garden, marking his progress.

She could not speak. She could not break the silence that, once broken, would never again be the same.

Someone had spent a great deal of time designing the castle garden.
Years before cobbles had been put down in an elegant, curving walkway along the beds, but time and unchecked growth had overtaken the
walkway. Now the grass-hatched stone path was treacherous as she
made her way out into the cobbled center where a bench had been set;
shrubbery snagged her skirts with nearly every step.

Cat stopped finally and wrestled with the annoyance, plucking insidious cane and thorny vine from the linen-and-woolen weave of her
skirts. She had put on her best, a voluminous crimson-sleeved tunic of
subtle green and black sett against a field of undyed creamy ivory,
belted with green-dyed leather. The arisaid, less vivid, was fine and soft,
pinned at her breast with a heavy double brooch. The inset stone was
bulbous, ruddy amber taken from a Highland river.

As she worked free the thorns, Cat heard a murmured blurt of discovery and a rustling in the shrubbery. A moment later the man knelt
at her side, lifting from her the burden of freeing her skirts. His hands
were dirty beneath the nails, but he took great care not to soil her
skirts. The fingers were supple and quick; in a moment she was free.

He smiled up at her. " 'Tis in a frightful state, aye? I've no' been
here to tend it, so now 'twill take me days." And then he was solemn all
at once, weighing her expression; she feared he marked the nervous
tension that beset her limbs. He rose, gesturing toward the bench.
"Will you sit? I've bannocks set aside, and a wee flask of ale."

Cat accepted the invitation; her knees trembled enough to make her
grateful for the chance to sit down. As she smoothed her skirts into
order he fetched a linen-wrapped parcel and dented pewter flask. He
uncapped and cleaned the mouth of the flask, then offered it to her
along with a bannock cradled in clean napkin.

Cat managed not to gulp. "You are the earl's son, not a servant," she
said after returning the flask.

Unoffended, he grinned. "Not a servant, no, though with the state
of these clothes—well, my father would clout me upside the ear and
send me back inside to present a better face."

She broke the warm bannock in two and offered him a steaming
half. "Is the earl here?"

He accepted with thanks. "Inside. Has he no' seen ye?"

Cat shook her head. "His gillie brought word I was to come out here to meet you."

"Aye, well . . . there's much on my father's mind, what wi' the meeting at Achallader."

"Achallader?" Cat's stiffening fingers crumbled the bannock crust. "I thought Achallader was destroyed after Killiecrankie." By MacDonalds, in fact, before they came to Glencoe. *Before Dair MacDonald gave me back my mother's kettle.*

"So it was, with thanks to MacIain and others of his ilk." His tone did not disabuse her of the notion that the knowledge was bitterly felt. "But 'tis closer to the clans, and I dinna doubt he has his reasons. The earl always does." He tucked bread into his mouth. "Catriona, aye?"

Something kept her from divulging the shortened form she preferred. He was an informal man, but there was no part of her that desired, at this moment, anything *but* formality; she did not at all like the hesitance making itself more apparent with each passing moment. He seemed kind enough, well cognizant of manners and her own natural reluctance. "And you are Duncan."

"I? Och, no . . . I am John. Duncan is my brother. 'Tis he you're to wed; I've a wife already." He finished the bannock and shed crumbs deftly, then rose. "I imagine Duncan will be along; I'll just gather up my tools and let you meet without me so near."

Not Duncan . . . Not Duncan at all, but the second son, whom it was said the earl favored. *I must begin all over again!*

John Campbell collected his things and turned back, then arched dark eyebrows. "Ah, here is Duncan. 'Ware the rain; the clouds are on the march." And with that dry obliqueness—there were no clouds in the sky—he was gone, slipping out the gate.

Dair discovered the truth was not easy to share after all, for all he and his brother were so close. Dair was not proud of himself. He had gone home to Glencoe from Glenlyon's Campbell justice and said no word to Jean at all, waiting in his house; he had merely walked directly into his bedroom, knowing she would follow, and set about establishing the evidence of his survival in the most primitive of ways, as well as rectifying his lack of a child at once and without preliminaries, knowing she needed none; knowing she would understand and abet him, hungry as she was; knowing the fire that blazed between them would burn away the pain, burn away the anger, burn away the memory of a rope upon his neck, and the recollection of what had happened there on the hilltop gallows.

—*Gallows Herd indeed; I proved the truth of that!* Except he had survived.

But the fire between them was unaccountably too quickly quenched, and the seed as quickly spent, his offering received, her absolution granted; yet he was empty of spirit as well as seed, and unable to fill it again in Jean Stewart's bed.

She had been furious, seeing his neck; had raged at Glenlyon, threatening retribution. But he was empty of fear, empty of hate. And he had known, though she did not, that the fire had, in its blazing, burned itself out. There was no more fuel to consume. He had depleted it at last in the final conflagration, and he did not have the heart to search for kindling or flint.

He knew very well that one intent might be fulfilled; in a month or two Jean would tell him. But the knowledge offered no joy, no quiet triumph, no vindication, no redemption.

Dair supposed it did not matter how a child was conceived, merely that it was; but he was no longer on the gallows with a rope around his neck. He was no longer a man bought back from the devil by a woman's anguished pleas and a drunkard's private reasons, but a man who wanted far more than Jean could offer; far more than a child born merely of any woman who happened to fill his bed.

Jean had offered what she could because he had required it, because he had demanded it with no choice in it for her, thinking only of himself. He hated himself for that as much as Glenlyon for bringing him to it.

"What I want," Dair explained with difficulty, "is what MacIain and our mother have. What you and Eiblin have. I see it. I ken it. I want it for myself. But—"

John waited.

It came out in a rush, but was as definitive in its intent as in its emotion. "Jean isna the woman to give it to me."

John set his elbows against his knees and leaned forward, staring intently down at his son. A lock of thickly silvered hair lifted in the breeze, carried forward to brush against one still-dark eyebrow. " 'Tisn't the same wi' every man and woman," he said at last. "You are no' me, and Jean isna Eiblin. It doesna mean there is no ground on which to build your house."

"I am twenty-eight . . . I've built my house." Dair stared fixedly into the distant vista: a haze of green, of gold, of purple; the rich backdrop of the sky. "But all the rooms are empty even with her in them."

After a moment John sighed and shredded a scrap of pine bark in his hands. "Then it seems to me there are but two things for it. You owe her a decision."

"I ken that, aye? I dinna want to hurt her."

John tossed down the bark scraps and looked at his brother. "You are young, Alasdair, and you dinna ken women so much as you may think.''

''But—''

''Sleeping with them isna the same as living,'' John declared. ''Dinna argue it, Alasdair—you will lose. Any man in the glen wi' a wife in his house will tell you that.''

Dair sighed. ''Then I willna.''

''Good. What I am telling you is—and 'tis true—that you canna help *but* hurt her. Unless you marry her.''

''But—''

'' 'Tis true a handfast is amicably broken if both sides decide so, but will Jean do it? Will Jean pack up her pots and pans and sewing and go home meekly to Castle Stalker, wi' no harsh word for you?''

Dair knew better. ''She will not.''

''She will not. Which means you must devise a way of telling her the truth. And it *will* hurt, laddie . . . 'twill hurt a great deal.''

Dair shut his eyes. ''Oh Christ . . . Christ, John—I fought at Killie-crankie and was wounded, and nearly died a week ago from a Camp-bell rope. And do you ken, I think this will be worse?''

''Aye,'' John agreed. ''I do ken that. But when God made woman for man, he didna promise it would be easy . . . Sandy! Sandy, what did I say?—you're no' to go toward the river . . . oh, Christ—'' John pressed the flask on his brother and got up, slapping his kilt free of debris. ''Any more than He promised having *bairns* would be easy!''

Cat stayed where she was, bannock forgotten in its napkin set on the bench beside her. Her palms were suddenly damp; she spread them against her skirts and let the fabric dry them.

''Tell me,'' Duncan asked as he came into her line of vision, ''do you like him better? Everyone else does.''

It so astonished her that Cat forgot all about newborn nervousness and stared at him. ''I have barely met him!''

Duncan hitched a shoulder. It made the negligible length of his neck shorter yet. ''Doesna take anyone long. He's a bonnie lad, my brother, warm of smiles and heart. 'Tis why my father favors him; I am difficult.''

Nervousness dissipated. *This is what John meant by clouds being on the march. Not the weather, his brother!* ''Are you difficult?'' Cat assessed him rapidly and gave him tone for tone. ''Is it a natural state, or do you work at it?''

Duncan Campbell, who stood before her now, linked his hands be-hind his back. He was nothing like his younger brother, who was taller, darker, kinder, and unquestionably handsomer. ''I work at it,'' he said, "because 'tis the only thing I am good at. My father will tell you that.''

"That you work at it? Or that you *are?*''

"I am. 'Tis natural, aye?—but I will admit I practice to make my nature more annoying to him specifically; he sired me, after all, and helped make me what I am. He has only himself to blame. My mother died too young. 'Tis his crop to reap.''

"It could be a sweeter crop.''

"Not at his table.''

She eyed him askance; this kind of combat she understood very well, growing up with four brothers. "You're no' so young anymore. 'Tis time to set your own table.''

"I intend to,'' he agreed. "Indeed, I have every intention of it—or did, until he saw fit to interfere.''

"Ah.'' Instinctively Cat knew, and rejoiced. "You dinna want to marry.'' She grinned. "Well, 'tis no' so uncommon, is it? Neither do I.''

"*You* dinna matter.'' Infinite derision.

"*I* dinna?'' *You pawkie, ill-mannered lad—*

"No. I am *his* son, the Earl of Breadalbane—and a host of other titles. . . .'' He waved his hand dismissively. "You should ken it already, if you've been sent to marry me.''

"Oh aye, I ken your heritage. I've my own as well; I am a Campbell, *too.*''

The emphasis was deliberate and served to give him pause. He reassessed her. "But your father is not an earl.''

Cheerfully she said, "Naught but a wee laird, is he? Glenlyon of Glen Lyon.'' It was a desperate dignity which she knew very well he could easily disparage if he were familiar with her father's tattered reputation, but she would not yet surrender the battle.

"Aye,'' he agreed less curtly, "but you must ken 'tisn't so much as an earldom.''

Cat smiled kindly, then set an edge to it. "Not everyone wants an earldom.''

He sighed, surrendering. "I dinna.''

That was unexpected. She reconsidered his demeanor. "*You* dinna want it? Most heirs would.''

"Oh, I dinna mind the wealth. I dinna mind the power. But I do mind *him.*''

Somewhat dryly she reminded him, "He willna be here when you inherit.''

"But meanwhile he is.''

She began to understand Duncan Campbell better than he did himself; they were not unalike. "So, 'tis your way of fighting back by being rude to his guest?''

"One way." He grinned; though he never would be a handsome man, not as his brother was, with a genuine smile lighting his sallow face he was no longer so unattractive. " 'Tisn't your fault. But if I give you courtesy, you'll tell him so. I'd rather have you tell him I was rude."

"You are."

"Then I am content."

Cat picked up the flask. She felt immensely better than a matter of moments before. "Your brother left ale, and bannocks. D'ye want any?''

"I ate less than an hour ago. In the kitchens." The slight smile was smug. "And it fair set him back to find me there."

"He doesna want you in the kitchens?''

"Eating with turnspits and cooks? Och, no! I'm his *heir,* dinna ye ken? I'm to behave myself in acceptable ways." He moved abruptly and sat down beside her. He did not encroach upon her skirts, but kept such distance between them as could be managed. "Have I been rude enough? Will you carry him tales?''

Cat grinned. "If you ask it, I willna."

"Why not?''

"Because if you want me to, I'll no' do it."

His brows came down and locked. "Why not?''

"Because you ask it."

"You're a contentious bizzem!"

"In your company, I acquire your habits." She took back the flask from him. " 'Tis in no wise surprising why he favors John. *He* is courteous."

"You canna have him. He's wed."

"So he told me."

"I daresay you *could* have him—as mistress."

Cat laughed because he meant her not to, and because she was truly amused by his blatant pettiness. "I would not."

" 'Twould be easier than being wed to me."

"I daresay."

"And which willna be done anyway, have I a word to say." Color splotched his face. "That isna meant as rudeness, but the truth."

"Truth wears many coats. Some are fairer than others."

"So it does, and so they are. But this time I dinna *mean* to hurt you. 'Tis the truth, and wearing no coat at all."

"You meant to hurt me before?''

"I did." Duncan smiled. "He said you were not fair."

She was unprepared for that. It was wholly unexpected and left her without clever reply.

He gave her no time to conjure one. "And because you *are* fair, I have naught but rudeness for you."

It shocked her utterly; this kind of battle was unfamiliar. *"Why?"*

The high color ebbed slowly, leaving him sickly and sallow. "Because I am not," he said tightly. "Because I am *not* fair, and I ken it, and you ken it, and everyone else kens it; and because he has taken such pains to explain in all the ways that matter that I canna be the man he is, nor what John is."

Something from deep inside bubbled up inanely. Cat pressed a hand to her mouth to keep it from escaping the confines of her chest.

"Christ!" he cried. "Are you laughing—?" He leaped to his feet and stood before her, outraged, like a ruffled heron save its neck was short. "You are! You are! You're no better than he is, then . . . I should take you back in there myself and put you before my father and congratulate him on finding a woman so unco' much like he is!"

"Stop!" Cat cried, and when at last he held his tongue she was able to speak. "I am no' laughing at you."

"You *were* laughing—"

"Not at *you!* God in Heaven, Duncan Campbell, did he tell you naught of me?"

"He told me—"

"—that I wasna fair. Did he no'? *Did he no'?*"

His mouth was clamped together in a repressive line. "He did."

"Aye, well, he had reason." She paused. "Sit down."

After a moment he did as told.

"I dinna ken what he said, but likely 'twas true," Cat told him. "I have had names attached to me before." The pain was distant; he of all people understood what it was to be so disparaged. "But for most of my life—and certainly when last he saw me—none of the names were kind."

"In the name of Christ, woman—"

"I do ken, Duncan. I ken it gey well. You dinna need to explain. I have worn your shoes." She set the crumbled bannock remains on the napkin beside others. "But explain something else. You said it a moment ago. You said we wouldna be wed had you a word to say about it."

His profile was stark. "We would not."

"Because of the earl? D'ye say so to fash him?"

"I'll fash him whenever I may, but I say so now because I dinna want to marry you. I want to marry Marjorie."

It stunned her; she had not considered there might be another woman. "Marjorie?"

"Campbell, of course; is there another name fit for a Campbell?"

Cat thought there might be, that indeed there was, but she forbore to say it; he would not understand. His brother would not understand. His father would not understand. Neither would hers.

Neither do I. She drew in a deep breath and stared hard at the wall opposite the bench, deliberately studying the tangled vines. "I think you owe me courtesy now."

"Do I?"

Because of Marjorie he owed it, whom he wanted to wed in her place; because she was cast out before being properly wed; because she didn't want to come anyway, but came— —*and all for naught!* But none of those things would she admit. "I've come a long way; the verra least you owe me is courtesy."

"I didna invite you."

"*I* didna invite me."

After a moment, he smiled crookedly in rueful acknowledgment. "You didna."

"And they didna ask either one of us."

"They didna."

"And we are left here in the garden to sort out what we will do, while everyone else kens there is no help for it." Cat inhaled deeply. "D'ye love her?"

"I do."

"Does she ken it?"

"I've told her so."

"Ah. Then she kens there is a difficulty."

"Difficulty. Aye, a *'difficulty.'* " He was disgusted. "I'm of no mind to wed you. I want to marry Marjorie."

"Then do it, aye?"

Duncan did not answer at once. He stared blindly at the grass cropping up between cobbles worn smooth. "He is the earl."

It was a simple four-word statement, and yet in its stark simplicity lay the weight of power and truth: that no matter what they believed, no matter what they preferred, the man who put the game into play had control over its pieces.

"God in Heaven," Cat murmured. And then the irony of it struck her. "You ken, it might be worse."

Duncan, bemused, frowned at her. "How could it be worse?"

"It could be that you wanted me, while I didna want you; or it could be that I wanted you, while you didna want me." She smiled at him in an amusement no less honest for all its poignancy. "At least this way, whatever becomes of us, we both are unco' certain neither of us wants the other."

After a moment his mouth jerked in reluctant concession. "Fitting, is it no'?"

Cat frowned down at her skirts, tending the folds with every bit of attention. *'He is the earl.'* Duncan's declaration said all that was necessary. And she comprehended gey well.

She sighed and looked at him. "I suppose there are marriages built on worse things than mutual disaffection."

For the first time she witnessed the real Duncan Campbell. The mask of resentment was put aside to reveal the clean face beneath, young and impassioned and wholly honest as he struggled to say the truth without hurting her. "But I dinna *want* to marry you."

It hurt. Not because he did not want to marry her, but because he would be made to and would regret it all his life. She had spent so many years with people regretting certain aspects of her presence in the world . . . and now that two men had told her, unsolicited, that she was fair, that she was bonnie, after all the years when she was not and others told her *that,* she found it did not matter.

Neither wanted her: one could not because to do so abbrogated everything he believed in; the other loved someone else.

Cat stared hard at the wall. "Good," she said. "I dinna want to marry *you.*"

And knew as she declared them the words were wholly true, including their emphasis.

Six

*I*n his house, Dair gathered together the things he would need for the meeting at Achallader, most of them weaponry. His father was the MacIain; it would not do to offer the laird anything but the finest tail of men, fully equipped with such implements of war as they had borne at Killiecrankie and other victories, accompanying him into Campbell lands with all the pipes ranting.

Many of the men of Glencoe would go, though some could not; it was summer and the cattle were out by the shielings. MacIain's tail would be reduced accordingly, though Dair knew there was also another reason. Killiecrankie, and the loss at Dunkeld.

Glencoe-men had been killed in both battles. It was somewhat easier to think of those dead at Killiecrankie because the battle was clean and the victory glorious—save for Dundee's death—but Dunkeld had been little better than a disaster. Too many MacDonalds had been left lying dead in burning streets— —*too many of them of Glencoe.*

But those who did accompany MacIain would see to it no one doubted their zeal and loyalty. The laird would require a full complement of personal servants: the henchman who would stand behind him at meals; the *bladair,* his spokesman; the bard; the piper, Big Henderson, and his gillie; the *gillie-mhor* who would bear the laird's claymore; the *gillie-cosfluich,* who would carry him across rivers; the baggage gillie; the gillie who led his horse through treacherous terrain; and assorted *gillie-nuithes,* who would run alongside his garron.

Dair gathered up a clean shirt, freshly brushed bonnet with eagle feather and heather sprig attached, the most ornate plaid brooch he possessed, his claymore, Spanish musket, Lochaber ax, dirk, targe, sporran, *sgian dhu,* and set them out where he could dress quickly in the morning.

It was the gloaming, passing quickly into evening. He was alone— Jean was yet up the glen at his brother's house—with a peat-fire in the hearth and a single candle burning.

Illumination sparked off pewter, off copper; the detritus of his life, his two visits to France. He was neither a rich man nor a poor one, and able to set himself up with such ease of living as any woman would desire. He would never be chief, but was nonetheless a chief's son, and would be remembered for it all of his life.

The laying out of his things ordinarily took little thought, save he would be aware of the need for additional dignity at Achallader. But now he did think as he set out each item, because he could not touch brooch or bonnet without thinking of Jean Stewart, who had tended his things for weeks. She had made his house hers as well with spring flowers set out in horn cups throughout, and in the scent she wore: French perfume, brought by him from Paris, which she did not stint.

Dair frowned at the assortment set on a bench near the fire. By ignoring the issue he dishonored Jean, who deserved better, and so he stopped ignoring it and let it come into his mind unhindered, snooving like a *sgian dhu* into what he did not know to call save cowardice, an abject reluctance to address with Jean the truth of his feelings, the truth of his desire to end what they had shared, if in markedly intermittent fashion, for six years.

It would be best to tell her before he left. Then she would have time to gather up her things and go back to Castle Stalker without doing it under his eye, or where everyone in Glencoe knew the truth. There was some dignity to be preserved, and he wanted to deny her none of it; she could go home with no one the wiser until she did not return. By then there would be Breadalbane and Achallader to discuss, whatever came of it, and King James in France, whatever came of *that*, and King William in Flanders with the Master of Stair, Queen Mary in London with the Privy Council, John Hill and his garrison at Inverlochy, Thomas Livingstone and his army in the foothills . . . *And pawkie naval cannon at Fort William with gun-weighted patrol boats on Loch Linnhe—*

He was abruptly and quite unexpectedly assailed with the feeling of smallness, of insignificance; of a conviction that what he knew of his people and what he knew of Scotland was on the verge of dislocation, if not destruction. The old ways were changing, in fact had already altered; it was possible Breadalbane merely paid lip service to tradition by calling the clans to a meeting to discuss their loyalty to James, but the old ways were all Dair knew. He was a Highlander; the French in Paris had told him repeatedly he was too wild at heart for them despite his quiet manners, and that if he joined Louis's service, or even James's shoddy court, he would require taming.

Dair looked at his weaponry glinting on the bench. He thought again of Killiecrankie and Mackay's Lowland and English troops, supposedly civilized while the Highlanders were called barbarians. He heard the pipes again, heard Dundee's speech, heard his father's shout and the bard's oratory, and felt the hairs on his flesh stir, the groin-deep tingle of anticipation.

He was what he *was:* a Gael committed to Scotland, and to her Highland ways.

There were many more things of which Dair MacDonald might think while he sorted out his life, but it was Jean in his mind. He dreaded telling her the truth as he had dreaded nothing save the need to kill a man the first time he had done so.

"Christ—" he began, and then the latch rattled and the door swung open and Jean came into the house.

And he knew, as he looked at her against the gloaming beyond the door, that he would tell her nothing, nothing at all; that he *could* tell her nothing, nothing at all, because it was none of it her fault that he had fallen out of love, if indeed he had ever been *in* anything save her bed, and her body.

After, he promised himself. *When the Highlands are settled, I'll settle this with her.*

If he could.

If she would let him.

And Robbie, who would be no more pleased than his sister.

Kilchurn Castle sat on a low, stony promontory that swelled into Loch Awe. It boasted a sharp-edged, five-story keep verging on the water, while at its rear bulked a lower, rounded tower house. It was at times cut off from the land, becoming an island; at others was reached by a marshy peninsula. Behind it the time-rumpled slopes of Ben Crua-chan were ruddy umber and heather-brilliant, and a frieze of green trees crowded the land between the lower braes and gray-gilt castle.

The Earl of Breadalbane was not a man for soft words, even in his mind, and did not waste time admiring scenery. To him the most beautiful of all things was the accomplishment of a task that added luster to his name, holdings to his legacy, coin to his coffers, and status to his house. But at this moment he was caught unwary and unaware, and when he glanced out of a keep window to look upon the glassy surface of Loch Awe, well satisfied by his plans for the Achallader meeting a matter of days away, he saw the woman at water's edge and stopped thinking altogether about the clans, about the king, and his own part in Scotland's future.

Scotland's past and her present walked the water's edge. He saw the crimson of her sleeves, the glint of buttons and brooch, the brilliance of braided hair. She was not so distant that he could not mark her height, nor the way she carried herself, and he knew it was Glenlyon's daughter who, quite alone, paused and raised a hand to stare across the loch with eyes shielded against the setting sun.

In a moment she lowered her hand. Breadalbane watched her bend and strip off her shoes, setting them aside, then kilt up her skirts around her knees. She was not wearing stockings; a flash of pale leg showed, and then she waded out into the reed-spiked shallows, sending ripples across the surface.

He might otherwise be offended by her informality, by the mud and damp hem such enterprise would incur, but he was not. He smiled. In that moment she was everything that was and everything that could be: a proud, unyielding Campbell born of an ancient heritage that he hoped would bring spirit back into his own line, much as he bred a specific deerhound bitch to a specific dog to fix a temperament.

Duncan has need of such a woman to strengthen his seed. . . . And the earl was convinced Catriona Campbell might do it. She was everything her father was not in all the ways a man might count; bred to Duncan who was, despite his demeanor, a direct descendant of Black Duncan of the Cowl and might yet possess some modicum of ambition and competence, she could well produce the kind of grandsons of whom the earl could be proud. He desired to die knowing his lands were left to heirs who could properly administer them.

Behind him a deerhound stirred. The earl glanced back briefly, watching the bitch stretch, sneeze, then resettle herself near the bigger dog. He could not help but smile; she was a lovely red fawn with black ears and muzzle, very keen of intelligence. The big storm-colored dog was the finest hunter he had ever bred, and he had high hopes for their get.

He turned to the window again and saw Glenlyon's daughter was no longer entirely alone; a single figure made its way out of the castle toward the woman on the shore. Duncan himself, walking out to speak with her.

At his call she turned, holding up her skirts. She did not leave the water, nor make any indication she would, merely stood quietly in the shallows, straight as a spear or claymore with hair glowing red in the sunset, and waited for him to join her.

It was a subtle tableau few would mark, but Breadalbane was not a man who let such things pass; they might be important if one knew how to read them.

They had met. They were not strangers, nor enemies. They accepted one another's company without expectations of prescribed behavior, nor made any indication of enmity or false modesty.

Breadalbane smiled. He had seen her earlier, had spoken with her. She was in many ways the young woman he remembered, and in the most important of ways nothing at all as she had been. And she was ideal for his heir, who would surely see her worth as only a man could, even unprepossessing Duncan.

—*Twill do, aye?* She would accompany them to Achallader and see Duncan's promise as heir, and by the time they left there would be nothing left to do save escort them to a kirk.

With care Cat waded out through spiky reeds, tending her hem, then stopped as the water lapped above her ankles. It felt inexpressibly good just to stand still, to let the setting sun warm her face, its light glowing red-gold through closed eyelids.

An old tune came into her head, a snatch of childhood song.—*so bonnie, so bonnie was he . . . with white teeth a'gleaming and silver in his hair*— Cat's eyes opened wide as she stopped, shaken. She recalled the tune, recalled the words, recalled the progenitor of them—

"Catriona!"

Peace was broken, but it was respite from unexpected memories. Cat turned, saw him; smiled as he approached, content within herself. The pain of his rejection had lost its small sting; she had never expected a man to be won by her features, despite Dair MacDonald's words, any more than by her tongue, and was not disappointed that Duncan Campbell should prefer someone else to her. It simply meant she would go back home to Glen Lyon rather sooner than expected, where she would tend her father's house while he was away at Stirling—or wherever else the army might care to send him—and indulge herself in unfettered freedom, which was all she had ever wanted for as long as she could remember.

Duncan Campbell at last arrived at the water's edge. He eyed her askance, but did not reprove her.

"Come in," Cat invited, knowing he would refuse. " 'Tis cool, but no' like winter."

"I dinna think so."

She smiled to herself. "Would Marjorie come in?"

He scowled faintly. "She would think to ask me."

"How tedious. And would you give her your permission?"

"I dinna ken."

It did not surprise her. She provoked purposely. "A man who prefers the company of turnspits and cooks to those his father believes more acceptable isna put off by the thought of shedding shoes and stockings . . . aye?"

He scowled. It did not improve his features. "I didna come to argue, Catriona."

Cat grinned. "Am I being difficult? As difficult as you?"

After a moment he relaxed, offering a smile and a resolute expression less severe than he had been wont to wear. "Gey difficult; but 'tis *me*, if you'll recall, and I am master at it . . . can we speak of something else?"

She studied the reeds breaking water near her feet. "Of what, then?"

"Marjorie Campbell."

"Ah. Marjorie." Cat sloshed along the shoreline, squishing her toes into the bed of the loch. "What is there left to say?"

"I want you to meet her at Achallader."

There was an undertone of desperate declaration mixed with uncertain hope. Cat stopped sloshing and held her place, intrigued by his suggestion. "Why, Duncan? D'ye want us to be friends? D'ye expect her to like me, when I'm the woman the earl wants you to marry in her place?"

"I expect—I expect . . ." He set both hands into his hair and stripped it back from his face. "I *dinna ken* what I expect . . . only that perhaps you'll see why I love her, and why I canna love you."

It was a most peculiar hope. Cat stood very still while the water warmed on her ankles. "Does it matter?"

"John said—"

She did not let him finish. *"John* said; I thought you didna care what your brother did or said."

Duncan sighed and closed his eyes. A trickle of perspiration made its way down one temple, until he wiped it away impatiently. "John said I could say what I would to my father, but I'd no call to be rude to you."

She could not suppress the irony. "Then 'tis no surprise why they prefer him to you; he has sense, does John."

He scowled at her. "I thought you would want to marry me no matter how I was . . . that you would want to be countess. But you say no, and I think perhaps if you met Marjorie you might understand—"

"—and then I wouldna be 'difficult' when you asked the earl for a release from the agreement." She was no longer disposed to laugh, nor to provoke; he was not, she understood, so very different from her. "There is no need. I told you earlier: I dinna mean to marry you."

"But—" His perplexion was manifest. "Then what will you do?"

Cat turned slightly, gazing at the horizon as the sun slid below it. It was clear to her, abruptly, utterly clear, as if God had cracked open her skull and put a thought into it. This was opportunity if she chose to accept it. Duncan did not know it, but he held out a weapon, or offered her a key; she need only decide which one she wanted, and the manner in which she desired to use it.

A chill breathed across her flesh, until the blood beneath warmed it to burning and chased the chill away. *This is how Breadalbane treats with others . . .* and Argyll also, and any number of other men who aspired to higher places.

It was power and promise. Cat tasted it for the first time and discovered its appeal, the subtle seduction of its traps, the sweet cruelty of its potential. She understood at last. *This is what men are . . . This is how some men think.* She smiled across the loch. *'Tisn't so large a step, when the man whose back you muddy is deserving of the muck.*

Cat slanted a glance at Duncan. "You ken my father has debts . . ."

"I ken."

"You ken he is in the army now, but will still have debts; there are dice with the soldiers, and he'll no' stop now."

His tone was less certain. "I ken that."

"Then you'll ken also that your father can hardly be expected to send me on my way with no payment for my trouble; 'tis an insult you've offered, and there are costs to be paid." She turned to face him squarely, unmindful of splattering water. "I dinna want it for me. I've no need of it. But the earl has ignored Glenlyon's need for two years."

Duncan stared mutely, blind to subtlety. She understood in that moment why his father despaired of him. Her calculated approach was suddenly consumed by emotion: Breadalbane had failed her father, failed her house, failed her.

"We are Campbells, aye?—and deserving of better! He is head of the house of Glenorchy . . . and 'tis time he served those Campbells in need of his aid!"

The color departed Duncan's face. " 'Tis blackmail!"

Ice trickled down Cat's spine, though the flesh of her face burned. "I tend my house," she said tautly. "I tend my father in it. Now I tell you to tend *your* father, to tend *your* house, and put Marjorie Campbell in it."

After a lengthy moment of crackling silence, Duncan Campbell laughed. "Christ!" he cried. "You're a match for my father!"

Cat glared at him. *'Twould be easy to scoop up a handful of mud and daub his face with it!* But she let the impulse die. She had purposely set out to grasp the earl's methods; the intent was wholly successful.

"Well," she said finally, "that may be taken as insult, or also flattery; dinna tell me which—you're no' a respectable party to tell me unbiased. I suppose what matters is that we will between us sort things out so we both get what we want. If that makes me a match for the earl, then I've no cause to complain."

Duncan, sorting *that* out, eventually grinned. Cat, turning away, was pleased she could offer him such happiness at so little cost; and Glenlyon's debts paid, also.

He stood slantwise in the doorway, left shoulder set against the jamb, spine hidden beneath linen and tartan plaid, barefoot in summer warmth. Jean Stewart knew Alasdair Og well enough to understand he was not as detached as he seemed; that, in fact, he was acutely aware of the movements she made, as always, but steadfastly refused to acknowledge them.

She supposed it was not necessary that he acknowledge such movements; after six years, no matter how many respites, they knew one another's bodies as well as their thoughts, and the intentions of both.

His intention, at present, was to ignore her; hers was to seduce him from intransigence.

There was Achallader, of course; it was his excuse, offered for days. And it was not wholly untrue, because nearly every man in Glencoe prepared to accompany MacIain to Breadalbane's meeting.

He had taken some time and care laying out his things, leaving her with no task. She had looked on such duties as a private, personal thing, the tasks a woman undertook for her man, who was more often than not pleased to have her tend such things as the shining of his metal, the folding of his clothing. For years, when she was present, he had allowed her to do such things, but this time, this first time, he did them for himself.

She had been up the glen to his brother's house, spending time with Eiblin, but that was no excuse. He would have waited; he always had before. But this time he had not, and she came home from her visit to find herself with nothing to tend but his melancholy.

But there be cures for that, aye? . . . And he as much as most answered to the healing in a woman's body. But she had seen something in his eyes, an unfamiliar taint in the whisky-warmth of them, that kindled her apprehension.

He turned from her mutely to stand silhouetted in the doorway of his stone, slate-roofed house, gazing out across the glen instead of into her eyes.

Her belly knotted. For the first time in her life Jean did not know what to do. As a girl she had been pretty, and men responded; as a woman beautiful, and men responded. She did not know what they needed, save her body; they none of them, prior to Dair MacDonald, suggested there was anything more a man *might* desire.

She could not play chess. At backgammon she lost, and he preferred a challenge. She sang indifferently, had no skill upon the harp, sewed, wove, dyed, and cooked as well as any woman in the glen, if no better than most. Her skill was in her company, her wisdom in her bed; if a man desired neither, there was nothing left to offer.

By his detachment he did not insult her, but stripped her of her purpose. While some men beat their women, Jean Stewart was wholly diminished by a man's indifference to her.

She went to the bed and turned the covers back. She had set fresh herbs beneath the pillow to lend a sweeter scent. With care she took off her belt, unpinned her brooch, unwound her arisaid, then set all aside. The ankle-length tunic was loose now, unbound, and shifted against her flesh with a seductive caress. But tunic she shed also, so that she stood within his house utterly naked.

Jean unplaited her braid, then shook the loosened hair across shoulders and breasts. "Alasdair," she said.

He turned halfway. Then fully, beginning to speak, "I'll be going up the glen to MacIain's house . . ." And then let it fall into silence, heavy as a wall between them.

"I am twenty-five," she said plainly, "and as ripe tonight as ever I was. Will you deny it?"

He smiled faintly. "I am no' a blind man, aye?—and there is light to see by."

"You dinna need the light. You never have before."

But there *was* light, soft light, glinting on brooch and badge, and he did not move to extinguish it, or to kindle a new flame.

"Dair," she said.

He came then, left the doorway, but did not shut the door. He came to her and put his hands on her shoulders, her bare, French-scented shoulders, and told her she was beautiful, that even a blind man would know it.

"And one who sees?" she asked. "Alasdair Og MacDonald?"

"I see," he said, "and I am suitably humbled."

Jean laughed a little. "I dinna want *that*!"

"You always have," he told her.

She did not care to debate the issue with him. "Will you come?"

"Not now."

He had never, ever said such words to her. " 'Not now,' " she echoed. "Not now?"

"I mean to go up to MacIain's; there are plans to be discussed."

Jean lifted her chin. There were all manner of words in her mind; words meant to deny, to entice, to argue, to disparage, but she brought none of them out of her mouth. "I want you now," she said only, "as I never have before."

"Jean—"

She was as warm now in her face as she was between her thighs. "Is it old?" she asked. "Has it grown stale? D'ye want me to beg, then, to offer or invent a way we've never tried?"

"Christ, Jean—"

"Tell me," she said, "and I will do it for you. I will do it *to* you."

His hands were yet on her shoulders. He moved them now, sliding them down, not up; not up to cradle her face as he did so often, or had; but down to her elbows, clasping them slackly. " 'Tisn't that, Jean. I've things on my mind."

She put her hand on his kilt and shifted wool, grasping him skillfully, but knowing now what he would not tell her.

Desperately she said, "A man has two minds: the one in his head, the one atop his ballocks . . ." She did not know a man in all of Scotland who could remain slack at her touch; she did not know a man in the Highlands who would not harden at her glance.

—*except Dair MacDonald* . . .

He took his hands from her. "I will come back before dawn."

She watched him turn, watched him move away, watched him pause long enough to pull the door closed, so she would not share her nakedness with all of Glencoe.

Jean laughed aloud. She strode to the door and snatched it open, crossing the threshhold to stand in the dooryard where anyone with eyes might see what bounty she offered.

"*Alasdair Og!*" She thought she might yet seduce him; she had never done this before.

But he was gone, did not come back, and it was all for naught.

There is no shooting here, no shouts of fear and fury, no triumphant war cries. What has been done is done, and no one remains behind.

She runs until she trips over an obstacle just before the door. Pain steals her breath; until she finds it again she lies where she has fallen, unmindful of her sprawl.

It isn't until her senses, less startled than her thoughts, identify the obstacle as a body does she make any attempt to get up—and then it is in a lurching scramble that flings her back from the corpse.

Her fall has disturbed the snow. She sees the trews around his ankles, the bloodied nightshirt, the hair dyed crimson. Nothing remains of his face save the dull white splinter of jawbone.

Part IV

1691

One

They are hunting hounds, Cat decided, *come up to prove themselves* . . . all a'bristle with Lochaber axes, bows, muskets, and claymores, and spike-orbed targes, poking about their persons like hackles across the shoulders.

They came from all over the Highlands, leaving behind familiar dens to mark new territory with elaborate care and precision, a wary new kennel overrun with multiple pedigrees, waiting in tense anticipation for the kennel-keeper to come.

—But he is here already. . . . And so he was, Grey John Campbell of Breadalbane, walking through the rubble of split and blackened stone lying in tumbled heaps now time-dusted and grass-corroded; of the fire-ravaged masonry corners, still erect as *menhirs,* the standing stones of the Celts, left to loom stark as a skeleton's ribs on the grassy hilltop. He was smiling, always smiling, offering only serene blandishments and careful courtesy, speaking nothing of the wreckage and the insult done to Glenorchy, to Clan Campbell, to himself.

Within two days the kennel settled, having got through the first meeting, and now they gave themselves over to lesser responsibilities, recalling they were not hounds but Highlanders, and men. Pipes skirled *ceol beag,* the little music of strathspeys and reels; and *ceol meadhonach,* the jigs and airs; and more rarely the *ceol mor,* the big music, but not of marches or rants leading them into war. They had come instead for peace.

There was usquabae for drinking, dice and backgammon for wagering, chess for challenge, field games such as stone-hurling, and *camanachd,* or shinty, quick-footed sword dances, and much feasting on beef—though none asked from whose lands the cattle were driven for fear they had been lifted, and such topics as that, the earl made clear, was not what they had come for.

Cat did not know why she was there, save the earl desired his heir to know her better; and Duncan was disinclined to spend any time with her when there was Marjorie instead, who had come over from Lawers with a clutch of Campbell kin. Duncan gave Cat no warning, he was simply gone one day, lost among the forest of colorful tartan and glittering steel in place of needles and pine knots, and when she looked for him in the mass of bonneted, bare-legged men she saw those who resembled him, but none of them who *were.*

In the midst of an army of Highlanders, albeit they did not gather to fight a common enemy save their own suspicions of the kennel-keeper, Cat found herself oppressed. And so she turned away and made her way through the unkempt cornfield where horses had not grazed, or men had not trampled.

Up. Away. Apart. Where she might think in peace, and not shy from it despite the name it wore, despite the sett of its tartan, the motto in its mouth, the heather on its bonnet with the single eagle feather.

With silver in its hair, and white teeth a'gleaming.

The Earl of Breadalbane played genial host and arbiter in the midst of his gathering, turning aside the occasional hostile glance and wary stares with ease and courtesy. It was expected that the chiefs would hold him in some doubt, and by some of them in disrespect; he was, they all knew, the other half of Clan Campbell's powerful dual houses, Glenorchy and Argyll. The Earl of Argyll was William's man almost by default; Stuarts and Stuart supporters had seen to the execution of Archibald Campbell's father and grandfather, and he would have no love of them. His loyalty to William then, even politically motivated, was inviolable, and no Jacobite could trust him.

Yet it was trust he needed, if not absolute respect, and trust he asked for, knowing precisely how to phrase it to win it. For now he let them be Highlanders, revelling in the raucous companionship and friendly rivalry of other clans, often enemies, now allies in the earl's name; let them think of peace as they feasted on Campbell cattle and drank Campbell whisky; let them recall their ancestors in the words of the bards and the music of pipe and harp, ignoring the occasional lapse into *ceol mor,* the war marches, which the clan harpers would occasionally summon to stir the hearts once more.

Above all he let them be content in their names, in their blood, in the essence that made them Highlanders and subject to Highland laws: the sacred trust of hospitality that no sane man would break, under which sworn enemies might sup together despite blood drawn but moments before, and which all men understood and did not question.

It was that hospitality he offered now in the shadows of Achallader's blackened brickwork, with MacDonalds sitting amidst the destruction they had caused. He was born of Highland blood, of Highland pride, and felt his own measure of the bone-bred affinity for the past and its traditions. But he was ambitious and brilliant and knew it, knew also how to use his brilliance to further his ambitions, so he might yet be more than *of* Clan Campbell, but its head in place of Argyll, who was a man of whom it was said Scotland owed much.

Och, I am of them, but wiser, aye? . . . And he would use them as he must to change the face of Scotland.

For now the land and its future yet lay in their trust, which he could not easily win. But he knew that the greatest strength of all lay in unity, and that if he permitted them to use that unity against him as they had used it against Hugh Mackay at Killiecrankie, he would lose.

Unity perforce must serve me in another way. And to make it so he would destroy it.

Robbie Stewart grovelled in dirt. Dair, much taken with the unlikely posture, grinned mutely, arms folded against his chest; it would be well if Robbie's grovelling bespoke humility, but its genesis was a desire to brag, not to ask absolution.

He himself did not kneel or grovel but watched from above. He had been there; he knew the formations, recalled the words, remembered perfectly the outcome of the battle—even, more intimately, the pain of his wound.

But Robbie did not dwell on such things as wounds or on such men as Dair MacDonald, but on himself, his Appin Stewarts, on Dundee's strategies.

There were men who had not been at Killiecrankie for this reason or that; none would ask why, in courtesy, and no explanation was offered. But there was interest, taut and sharp, in what they had not shared, and Robbie had never been a man for hiding pride in accomplishments. The young heir of Appin had been part of the victory, and he saw no sense in saying nothing of it.

Dair scratched an eyebrow, biding his time watching Appin's heir cut lines in the turf with his dirk.

"Here," Robbie said. "Here on the braes of Craigh Eallaich—and there the Pass of Killiecrankie, over which Mackay, the muckle-gabbed moudiwort, brought his Sassenachs and Lowlanders . . ."

And something else was added to it, vulgar and uncomplimentary; the men around him laughed and suggested punishments for Mackay.

"They came down so—"

The dirk tip carved a line . . .

"—and we came down *so*—"

Another line . . .

"—and the pipes were ranting, and Dundee speaking of what we are, and who we were, and how we were Gaeldom's heirs . . ."

And more, lewdly eloquent as always, with Robbie, of no small effect if with little of absolute truth in it; Appin knew how to tell a tale in the way to hold a man.

From above, carved out neatly in dirt, Killiecrankie was much easier to bear. And convincing in the extreme of Dundee's genius, his heroism, and the courage of the clans. The knot of young men gathered around Robbie were much impressed, as they would be, though they said little more than an occasional comment or question.

A young man next to Dair chewed at his bottom lip, rapt in Robbie's tale. Dair smiled faintly; he shifted just enough that setting sun sparked off his brooch and caught the young clansman's eye, who looked from Stewart's war to a man who had been in it.

Dair's expression was assessed and found wanting. Blue eyes narrowed. "Were ye there, that ye doubt him?"

It was challenge, but only slightly belligerent; he was much taken by Robbie's tale and personal bravery, and did not think well of a man who stood beside another and smirked.

Dair was diffident. "Oh, I dinna doubt him; I *was* there. But he tells it from a Stewart eye."

That got Robbie's attention, who did not like having his listeners distracted. "Then what if from *yours?* Better than mine, d'ye say?"

"Depending on which is your clan," Dair retorted dryly.

Robbie offered his dirk hilt first. "Here, then. Instruct me, aye?— *and* them."

" 'Tis your tale, Robbie."

"Then I'll thank ye no' to interrupt it." The sulfurous glare cleared as he bent again over his carvings. "We were here, d'ye see—"

The young clansman next to Dair did not look back immediately. "And where were you?"

"With MacIain," Dair answered, "as any Glencoe-man should be."

The other grinned. *"Per mare per terras."*

The MacDonald motto . . . "Ah?"

"Keppoch."

Dair nodded. "Have you come down with Coll of the Cows?"

"I have. Though I dinna ken if 'tis worth the journey; no Campbell I ever kent offered hospitality."

Robbie's voice intruded. "Will you learn from this, young MacDonald of Keppoch, or will you listen to a man who owes me his life from Killiecrankie?"

It was impressive, as Robbie meant it to be. Every eye fixed on Dair, who sighed. "There is much to be learned from a man so brave as Stewart of Appin. You'd all do well to listen."

"I thank you." Robbie went back to drawing.

The young Keppoch MacDonald grinned privately at Dair. "Coll could teach him a thing or two."

"I dinna doubt it. But I'd best hold my silence, lest he use that dirk on my tongue."

And so he held his silence, losing interest in the recounting but disinclined to move away. His attention wandered; Robbie's voice faded into the background as Dair cast a glance across the encampment. A piper had begun the *ceol mor,* if lament in place of war rant. Another took it up. The field below the ruined castle glowed like burning water, pocked throughout with cookfires. He smelled roasting beef, and whisky, and the underlying tang of tense, active men who had met summer's warmth in linen and wool.

There were women as well, though not so many; and they stayed in clusters near the fire to tend the cooking. But his eye was caught by one who strode forthrightly out of the throng as if of a mind to escape it even as others gathered. She was very tall, long of limb, and moved more like man than woman with no compromise in her strides. Braided hair glowed brilliant as coals in the setting sun.

"Holy Christ—" Dair blurted, staring; he was cold, and hot, and rigid with memory, with shock revisited: the last time he had seen her was on a hilltop on Rannoch Moor, with a rope against his throat.

"Here, then." It was Robbie. "MacDonald—'tis your turn. I wasna the only one there, ye ken . . . you'll have your say."

But Dair was no longer interested in Killiecrankie. " 'Tis you who tells a better story, aye? . . . I'll let you go on with it."

"I canna take *all* the credit—"

"Why not? You usually do . . ." But the gibe was feeble; his mind was not on it. It was on the woman, the red-haired woman who strode so easily through the crowd and was lost; and on the flesh of his throat that burned with the memory of hemp, and a tree, and the Campbell laird with a claymore.

"I do no such thing," Robbie declared. "Have I no' said you killed your share of Mackay's men?"

But Dair did not look again at Robbie or the dirk-drawings in the dirt. He turned from those who waited and walked away into the sunset, seeking Glenlyon's daughter to thank her for his life.

If he could find her. *If she will listen* . . . If a Campbell could ever believe the words of a MacDonald, even in gratitude.

Here, perhaps she would. In the spirit of Breadalbane's peace.

Breadalbane moved among the chiefs and found them one by one, isolating them from other chiefs, from gillies and tacksmen, from rivals, from comrades, until one by one he spoke to each alone, saying what he would of his pride in his Highland birth and blood, and his desire for triumph over the Williamite forces.

And when they questioned him and claimed him William's man, as he anticipated, he denied it. He said he was a chief even as they were, and therefore responsible for his people in all the ways a chief must be. If it served his people now to keep them from battle that would only injure them, he would do so by claiming what was required . . . and if it meant misleading Stair and the Dutchman into believing him one of theirs, a Williamite at heart, when in truth he served James Stuart, well, let it be so; he was a Highlander, a Campbell, a man of their own flesh and spirit, and he would do no harm to Scotland albeit cost him his life.

To Coll MacDonald of Keppoch, who had long opposed him, the earl offered his truth from his perch atop a scarp of lichen-frosted granite. "I will ask of you no oath, as to do so would forswear the one of Dalcomera to King James, sealed in the blood of Killiecrankie, but instead a truce: peace until October. No more than that of you, Coll, and your people; is it so much?"

Coll of the Cows sat likewise, hunched upon a stump in the fir wood near to the ruins. His plaid in summer warmth was but loosely draped over arms folded tight against his chest as he considered carefully, staring hard at the ground. The sett of the tartan was black cross-hatching on a crimson field, with the faintest stripe of blue showing itself occasionally. He wore as did all of the MacDonalds, regardless of their lands, a sprig of heather in his bonnet; and also the three eagle feathers to which he, a chief, was entitled.

Keppoch was young, well-made, and strikingly handsome, but no less shrewd for his prettiness. His hand was as quick with dirk or claymore as any man's, and his pride equally prickly; Breadalbane did not placate, plead, or prevaricate, but spoke plainly instead. Coll would take his time, but he would offer answer; it was a skillful man who understood the best method was not to push a stubborn man, but to let him come to his mind of himself.

Breadalbane waited. Keppoch eventually took his attention from the ground beneath his feet and looked at the earl. His smile was edged, with a dirk behind his lips. "And what of it? What does this truce gain you?"

"Time."

"To do what?"

"To get terms of William which are favorable to such men as ourselves."

Keppoch arched dark brows. " 'Men as ourselves'? What men are we, Breadalbane?—what men are those such as *you?*"

It was not unexpected; the earl had heard it from others. "I am a Highlander, as you are. I am the warden of my people—"

"Campbells."

"Aye, Campbells; would you have me repudiate them?"

Coll laughed silently, baring strong teeth. " 'Twould come as a shock to Argyll."

Such small offenses the earl could withstand; he offered no weapon. "In my own way I have supported the Stuart cause—"

"By keeping your Campbells home from Killiecrankie?" Keppoch shrugged. "Such support as that offers little."

"I offer it now," Breadalbane said. "I have worked long and hard to gain the trust of Stair and William, and I have it. Now I intend to use it—but not in a way they might suppose."

Keppoch raked him with a scalding glance, then smiled to dispell it. He knew how to use his looks, and his smile was very bonnie. "In what way *will* you use it?"

"To aid the clans."

"Ah."

"I have been given a commission by the king himself—" Breadalbane caught himself; to the clans, *James* was king. "—by the Dutchman to offer settlement to the clans. He is at war with France. The Jacobite rebellion robs him of strength; he would do better to have Highlanders *in* his regiments than destroying them."

Keppoch grinned again. "Killiecrankie was sweet."

"And Dunkeld, after?" The earl saw the flash of anger in Mac-Donald eyes; they had all lost men in the Cameronian fires. "He has put an army into the foothills under Livingstone's command, and a garrison at Fort William at Inverlochy. There are naval cannon on the walls. There is a patrol boat with guns on Loch Linnhe. There are frigates likewise mounted tacking off the Isles. Killiecrankie, despite its glory, was an aberration, not the rule." He waited a beat as color stained, then drained from Keppoch's swarthy face. "I greet for my people. I greet for the Highlands. I have no wish to see our ways crushed under the heels of the Dutchman's rule."

"What would ye have?"

"A truce, as I said. No oath such as William might prefer. Time, so I may present our case to Stair, and to William, and make them understand that Highlanders as a force canna be overlooked, lest the war with France be lost."

"Time." MacDonald of Keppoch twisted his mobile mouth. He was a young man, much younger than Breadalbane, but Highland chiefs were bred to privation and conflict. He would not be intimidated by the king's promised strength, but neither was he blind to its presence. "Such terms as are favorable to us?"

"As favorable as can be."

"He canna have us for soldiers if we are sworn to James Stuart."

"Of course not. He honors the oaths you swore at Dalcomera, and later at Blair after Dundee died; the Dutchman isna a Scot, but he's no' blind to a man's pride." Breadalbane smiled. "He would give you time to know James's mind."

"Jamie's mind?" Coll took his arms out from under his plaid. "We've had nothing of the king for months; who is to ken what is in his mind?"

Breadalbane proceeded with care. "We might ask him."

"Who would ask him?"

"We will send emissaries to his court at Saint-Germain and ask what is in the king's mind, and what he would have his Scots do. If he released you from the oath to him, you would be free to swear another . . . And there would be an end to hostility in the Highlands."

Keppoch laughed softly. "You make it sound gey easy, aye?"

"It *is* easy, when one kens the way." Breadalbane did not trouble to hide his confidence; Keppoch would have turned him down by now if he intended to. MacDonalds were not known for patience or political wisdom, only hot tempers and intemperate wills. "Three months only, Coll . . . and if nothing comes of Saint-Germain, or William sends his soldiers against you, then you've no choice but to remain loyal to James. What harm in waiting?"

"Naught in waiting, I ken. As for after . . ." Keppoch shrugged broad shoulders. The cairngorm set in his plaid brooch glinted bloody amber in tree-filtered sunset. " 'Twill be for Jamie to say, and Willie to do."

Softly Breadalbane asked, "Will you sign a bond?"

Keppoch stilled. "A bond."

"What you have just said. Sign your name to the words. A treaty in writing."

Dark brows arched again. "You'd have it on paper?"

The earl smiled temperately, certain of his course. "William is no' a man who honors the word of a Highlander. He is ignorant, and rude."

Coll of the Cows laughed ironically. "No worse than Jamie, then, who rots in France and forgets altogether he is a Stuart. But an oath is an oath . . . aye, then. I'll sign this treaty. You'll have my name, and eight of my tacksmen."

Breadalbane rose. "I thank you for it, Coll. You are a wise man."

The wide mouth twisted again. "I am a Gael; I wouldna turn from any battle, nor look to another weapon save my claymore and my dirk.

But only a fool would believe steel might win against so much cannon." The young face hardened; Breadalbane had won a skirmish, but not the war. "Bring me your truce paper, then . . . you'll have my name on it. But—" Keppoch put out a delaying hand. "There is something more, aye? Something given in return."

Breadalbane was surprised only that it had taken this long for Keppoch to ask what he was prepared to offer; others had demanded it sooner. But Coll MacDonald was young, his suspicions as yet unseasoned. And so the earl explained it clearly, so that Coll of the Cows would hear the most powerful of inducements. It was, in its five-part simplicity, the most clever of all his plans.

"Private Articles," Breadalbane explained, and he ticked them off on his hand, so intimately acquainted with them as a man should be who wrote them.

MacDonald of Keppoch had lost his smile, and his irony. "Proof of these 'Private Articles' would get you beheaded for treason. Rumor could ruin you."

"If it were proved true that they were from me, indeed." The earl smiled. "But such things as honor demand sacrifices, and risks."

"And these are yours, aye?"

"And these are mine. Aye."

There was no more respect in Keppoch's eyes than had existed before, but a grudging acknowledgment that at least the Earl of Breadalbane knew enough to come into the Highlands with something of worth with which to bargain. Too many too often did not.

The young chief turned, plaid swinging, and strode away swiftly, making little noise in bare feet against summer turf and fir needles. Breadalbane waited until Coll of the Cows had disappeared before he permitted himself a broad, jubilant grin of sheer elation.

Coll MacDonald of Keppoch. He had the others already, save for three: Robert Stewart of Appin, MacDonald of Glengarry, and MacIain of Glencoe. Three men only, and the Highlands were his.

Breadalbane laughed. *And William's.*

Cat rescued her skirts as the hem snagged, snatching fabric off plundered cornstalks. With so much commotion behind her, so many tanglings of shouts and jests in Gaelic, she remembered her history. There was a tale told of old Achallader, before the castle was built, of an English mercenary with no Gaelic who, riding through, staked his horse for forage in the cornfield, and when discovered by the Fletchers, who held the Achallader lands, was asked his business. Having no Gaelic he could perforce offer no answer, and so after a warning to leave—in Gaelic, and thus unheeded—they killed him.

The township near the castle had also been burned after Killie-crankie. But on the brae above the ruins, swelling gently out of turf, was a green mound known as Uaigh a'Choigrich, the Grave of a Stranger, after the English soldier. It was there Cat went, climbing through rubble, skirting trees, to gaze down upon the fields which once had been carefully tended, which once grew Fletcher, then Campbell corn, yet now lay beaten down beneath the feet of a hundred Highland chieftains and their followers.

A dun-gray haze rose up from the field to drift upon the air, a smoky tapestry through which Cat counted the colors, the shining bits of pewter and iron, the glint of honest steel. It was summer and verdant with brilliant hues, all rich as new-dyed wool, none of it the brooding, blood-dark colors of winter, all brown and gray and black. At sunset the sky was gilded carnelian and salmon and orchid, tinted against the deeper violet haze of the heather-clad braes, the blazing vermilion of cloudberries, the spark of new-kindled fires leaping here and here and here.

The castle ruins stood stark against the horizon, jutting skyward from brick-strewn ground. She wondered what the chiefs and tacksmen and gillies thought to look upon the rubble, the cracked and blackened brickwork, the rigid corners still standing as sentinel to the fallen. Did they think of MacDonalds, who had plundered Campbell lands and laid waste to a Campbell castle? Did they think of Breadalbane, whose claim now was of broken brick and blackened rubble? Did they think of Killiecrankie and revel in victory, naming Achallader a symbol of Jacobite strength in the wake of Jacobite triumph?

Cat looked upon the ruins. She thought of none of those things, symbols or otherwise, but of a man instead. Of Dair MacDonald, who was, she knew, somewhere below tending his father, who had himself set fire to Achallader while his second-born son and Robert Stewart rode on to Glen Lyon.

A curl of music came up from the field below. She heard harp and the faint skirling rise of a bagpipe lament, the *ceol mor,* keening now not of war but of the brooding of the soul, of grief, of the indescribable longing of a Highlander for his past, bred so close to the barrow-graves of the Norse and the habits of the Celt.

She knew there were those who cursed the pipes, Lowlanders and Sassenachs, who lacked the blood of the Highlands, the burn-water and usquabae that ran so hot in their veins. But she was not one of them.

Another piper took up the lament. The *ceol mor* squeezed Cat's heart, winding itself around her bones until she believed they might break of the longing. There was pipe-born grief, and taut yearning, and a loneliness of spirit she could not fully acknowledge, not knowing its name, its need.

She closed her eyes. The music took her, and its promise—and then of a sudden and unexpected the fire was in *her:* the kindling of her soul, the blossoming of arousal that sent a long convulsive shiver through every portion of her flesh, so that it moved upon the bones.

She was twenty years old. She was innocent of men. She was a woman, no longer a lass; and in that moment, at last, after years of ignorance, she was aware of the tides in her body, the beating of her blood against the fragile vessels that contained it, and the heat of tingling flesh birthing dampness in private places.

As the pipe music rode fir-smoke to Uaigh a'Choigrich, high on the brae above MacDonald-razed Achallader that once was Campbell-built, Cat could not but know what it was she wanted, how badly she wanted it, and that she could not have it.

He was after all MacDonald, and she a Campbell.

The shout came from behind. "Alasdair!" He twitched as a man does, hearing his name, yet hesitated only a moment before going on; it was a common name, as he had once told Cat Campbell before her father's door.

There. She was in his mind again. *Still . . .* The first shout was closely followed by another in a voice that was too familiar, and it added the Gaelic diminutive that set him apart from his father. "Alasdair *Og!*"

He swore beneath his breath and swung around, scowling. John came up quickly, undaunted by the black expression. "What is it?" Dair asked. "Can it no' wait?"

"MacIain wants you," John answered. "And I wouldna take that face to him this moment, were I you . . . he's had better moods himself, with no need to see it in his son."

"His son is his own man, with his own moods," Dair countered curtly, then regretted it; it was none of his brother's doing, nor even his father's. "Forgive me, John—but there is a task that needs doing."

John MacDonald was disinclined to surrender the course assigned by his father. "Aye, well, I dinna doubt you'll have a chance to do it— *after.* 'Tis MacDonald business."

"So is this."

"And Campbell."

"So is this."

"Oh, aye?" John did not hide his curiosity. "Has Breadalbane come to you already, then, in hopes of winning one of MacIain's sons?"

Astounded, Dair was immediately diverted. "Does he mean to?"

"I imagine so."

Suspicion bloomed in place of shock. "Has he come to you?"

"Earlier, aye."

It was very nearly inconceivable. "To say what?"

John's tone was ineffably dry, but Dair knew the ironic glint in his eyes. "To suggest he is a friend to the Jacobite cause."

"Breadalbane? He is William's man!"

" 'Tisn't what he claims here." John shrugged in eloquent dismissal; he would conjure no explanation for a man such as the earl. "He's said naught to MacIain yet, and took care with *me* to say naught a man might construe as politics; he kens a laird's pride, in such matters as precedence, and MacIain's is fiercer than most. But he's said enough. I thought he might have asked for you."

Dair shook his head. "Breadalbane will say naught to me. I am a *second* son; he's no need to speak to me of politics and James Stuart." He glanced slantwise, and quickly, toward the trees and the brae beyond. His mind strayed from politics; she had gone in that direction. But his own curiosity roused in response to John's last comment. "What did you tell him?"

John pressed a flattened hand against his plaid. "That I was not *yet* MacIain of Glencoe—and a man, even a Campbell and an earl, would do best to ask the one who still was."

Dair grinned; he could see it, and hear his brother's dry diplomacy. "Wise man . . ." But renewed consternation replaced amusement. "Does MacIain believe he's come to me?"

John hitched a single shoulder. "I didna ask what he wanted you for. Would you, if he sent you after me?"

"I would not . . ." Dair glanced again impatiently toward the brae overlooking the encampment. " 'Tis only—"

"You'd best go, Alasdair. He'll no' wait all night."

He shut his teeth with a click. "Where, then?"

"There." John motioned with a jerk of his head toward a cluster of fires. "Back there, with Glengarry. They are none too content, either of them, with Breadalbane's topic, or the mood of the meeting. Pick your path with care."

"Why? Do they think the lairds will forswear the oath to Jamie?"

John sighed. Patiently he said, "I dinna ken what they *think,* Alasdair, other than what they've said. But if you want to ken for yourself, you might go and learn it." He glanced over a brooch-pinned shoulder, then smiled at his younger brother. *"Before* he comes here himself and clouts ye over the lug-hole for keeping him waiting, aye?"

Cat came down slowly, picking her way through the gloaming as light left the day. Below the brae fires bled one into another until the field was a lake of flame, moat to the castle ruins. She saw people before the fire: kilted men, tunic-skirted women, some wearing kerches, some wearing bonnets according to their gender, with light sparking off brooches and badges. One of them, somewhere in their midst, was Alasdair Og MacDonald.

Resolution wavered. With effort she steadied it. She had come to a decision on the Grave of a Stranger and would not shirk it no matter how difficult; he was deserving of it if for no other reason than he had survived to hear the words. But it would be hard, gey hard, to say those words to him.

She did not know his direction, but others would know where Glencoe and his sons were. She asked a man, and he told her; now there was no reason to turn from the task save cowardice, and she would not tolerate that.

Until she came near the fire and saw him there with MacIain.

Cat stopped short. She had but to raise her voice and call his name, and he would turn, would see her, would be made aware of her presence near a fire no Campbell was welcome to, especially Glenlyon's daughter.

There was too much between them, so much, a shared but separate horror of what had nearly happened on a hill on Rannoch Moor. She recalled his face, so stark and bloodless; recalled the sound of her father's blade against the horse's rump; recalled the lurch of the garron that stripped it of its rider.

And the nightmare of him hanged, legs beginning to kick.

Cat shut her eyes. When she opened them again he was there still beside the fire, poised in profile, blind to her, mute and very still, the good bones of his face shrouded on one side by darkness, the other bled white by light.

She had forgotten how very huge MacIain was, so much larger than anyone else, towering over others clustered near the fire. Riotous white hair flowed like snowmelt onto his shoulders, curling upswept moustaches shrouded his moving mouth. MacIain spoke steadily and with some vehemence; she could see the jaw working, shielded by beard, but heard no clarity in his speech, occluded by pipes and harps, that told her what he said.

Cat looked at the son. His posture was taut; his language, even in silence, spoke to her of regret, of deep concern, of a dutiful obedience to listen and hold his silence no matter what he might be thinking within the skull.

And then MacIain finished speaking. She saw the giant turn, hitching his plaid higher on a shoulder; he bent his head briefly as another spoke to him, and then they strode away on some purpose of their own. Dair was alone at the fire, and she had no more excuses.

She wished in that moment that it was a cattle raid, which would be easier to deal with. There were fewer risks attached. And then she thought of the raid that had claimed her brother, and the one that nearly claimed Dair, and no longer wished herself there when she could be here, with him.

He turned then and saw her. Firelight glinted off badge, off brooch, set a sheen across his flesh and limned the planes of his face, etching shadows into contours. He saw her and went still, even as still as she.

Around them, bagpipes mourned. She saw revealed by light, above the linen of Dair's shirt, a dark, shiny rash of rope burn as yet unhealed.

He took a single step toward her, and then another, and within three more strides he was there before her, close enough to touch. She had not fled after all.

"Cat," he said only, but a world was in the name.

More was in his eyes, she saw: a hill; a lone tree atop it bearing hemp-hung fruit . . . and her father using the claymore to drive the garron away.

He had been cut down alive after all, but in that moment he hanged. In that moment he died.

It filled her chest, her throat, and burst free of both all at once, on a rush, needing to be said, to be put between them like a dirk, a claymore, so they would understand the use of such things if not their intention. "I never believed it of him." It was a beginning, if badly begin; she had intended other words. "I never believed it, my oath on it—never believed my father such a man as that. And I am ashamed—*ashamed*—" She looked again at the hemp-scraped flesh and put a hand to her mouth, stopping it with fingers; the words she longed to say could not make their way through the tears.

Ceol mor filled the air, riding fir-smoke into night. Dark brows, indistinct in firelight, overshadowed his eyes, damping the whisky-warmth. His hair was more thickly than ever sprinkled with silver threads, shining pale and importunate in the near-black of the rest. Mute, he reached out and caught her wrist, took her hand from her mouth, then carried it to his throat and set the palm against it.

Her fingers spasmed. "Oh—*no*—"

But he did not permit a retreat. "D'ye feel it? There—beneath your hand?"

She felt much more than he meant, abruptly aware of his touch, his warmth, his maleness. Flesh vibrated faintly as he spoke. Her fingers were rigid. She had not expected this, though she supposed she should have; he would bear her no kindness for being Glenlyon's daughter, and would have devised punishments if he ever saw her again.

The skin was different beneath her hand, the hemp-torn scar pebbled with minute blemishes like a rash in healthy flesh, rubbed slick in other places. But the skin was warm, wholly alive as her own despite the rope's abuse.

In that moment it did not matter that he was MacDonald, only that he was a man she had, in her stubbornness, in prickly Campbell pride, nearly gotten killed.

"I am sorry," she said. "My oath on it: I didna think of it . . . I was angry that you meant to lift our cows after all, but I only wanted you stopped. I never *thought* . . ." Her hand trembled against his throat. "First Robbie," she said tightly. "*My* Robbie—and I couldna bear it again."

It was said, it was done, she was free of the penance. But nothing induced her, in his eyes or in his posture, in the pressure of his fingers, to take her hand away.

His eyes did not waver. "No one kens what another man can do, till 'tis asked of him," he said. "Not even that man's daughter."

He would absolve her of it, when she expected bitterness. It was too much; it hurt. "I thought . . ." Cat drew in a breath and let it out abruptly, willing the pain to go with it as well as tight-coiled tension. "I thought you would hate me."

She waited. He could say so much now, making weapons of his words. But it was due him because of her father, and owed because of her name; she did not think she could sleep again if this moment were not endured.

His palm pressed hers against the pulse of his throat. " 'Tis still beating," he said quietly, "because of you."

Its rhythm matched her own, quickening at her touch as much as hers was quickened by awareness that he did not mean to punish her for what her father had done.

Even in innocence, she knew. Something in her kindled, answering his touch; something understood the small indications of the body, the lesser ones in speech. Words between words, the implications of tone. Their language, now, was not shaped of old enmities and feuds, drowning in pipes and war cries, but was silent instead, and private, and wholly, intensely intimate.

Behind him, the fire glowed. He lifted her hand from his throat and carried it to his mouth. It was warm against her palm.

Cat shivered. "Dair," she said helplessly. "Oh no—dinna do this—" And pulled her hand away, curling her fingers against the palm to shut out the memory of his mouth.

He smiled. "Ye ken it," he murmured. " 'Tis begun, aye?—and all against our wills."

"—begun—" she echoed. "No—"

"I am somewhat more practiced than you," he said. "And somewhat older, aye?" His smile now was rueful. "And perhaps not wishing so much it might be another way."

He *was* older, and male, and understood such things. But she refused to acknowledge it. " 'Tis *finished*. Not begun." How could it be begun? There was nothing between them, nothing at all but heritage that proscribed such feelings. "I've said what I meant to say—"

"Wait you," he said. "Dinna run just yet—or stalk with your head held high." The smile did not die. "I've something for you. I meant to look for you—to find you up on the brae—but my father . . . well, wait you . . ." He reached to his sporran and undid the thong doubled around the stag-horn peg. He took something from it. It flashed in firelight, until he turned its face toward the earth. Then he set the object into her hands.

Cat did not immediately look at it. She looked instead at him, seeing kindness in his eyes, the genesis of hope; hearing diffidence in the tone, and a certain shy hesitance unexpected and oddly appealing.

"You have lost more than I can repay," he told her. "A kettle is little enough, I ken, and so is this, but—" He shrugged, a hitch of taut-held shoulders silhouetted against the fire. " 'Tis all I can offer . . . and pray you will accept it."

Now she looked at what he had put into her hands. A mirror, a small silver-backed mirror. The handle was short, much-worn; a hole was pierced through its end for a cord to be strung, so a woman might wear the mirror around her waist, dangling from her girdle. Fashion had changed; this mirror was old, of another century, and made not of Scottish hands.

She could not help herself; she was yet Campbell, and he MacDonald. "Is this plunder?"

It was a slap, if noiseless. Color burned in his face. " 'Twas my mother's," he answered eventually, "given her by my father after a visit to Paris. It was purchased. Not lifted."

She ached with shame. " 'Twas undeserved, that."

"What Robbie Stewart did to you was undeserved."

The moment eased. This she could speak of; it was easier by far to admit the truth, to herself or to him. "They why d'ye makes amends for him, when 'tis his work to do?"

The line of his mouth was level. "Because Robbie wouldna think of it."

That was blatant truth. "He would do what he did, again."

It did not please him to know the truth of his friend, but he refused to shirk the admission. "I dinna doubt it."

"And will you go to his other victims and offer reparation?"

His mouth jerked briefly. "And will you speak for another Mac-Donald with a rope around his neck?"

It shook her, that he would understand so clearly without an explanation. "God in Heaven," she said, "you cut as well as a dirk!"

"I've had some practice, aye?—we've passed words between us before." His tone gentled then. "I do it when I am afraid, you ken. Verra much as you do."

The bagpipe lament died. Leaping light from behind her painted his face in vivid chiaroscuro. His eyes were shielded in shadow except for the gleam of whites, and the reflection of flame in pupil. In that reflection she saw a man, and a tree, and a rope, and heard herself tell her father, for Dair MacDonald's life, that she and only she had been the cause of her brother's death.

In that admission she knew the truth, clean and sharp as a blade. She gave to him what she would give to no other man, because he deserved it. Because she wanted to.

But protest was not so easily overcome, nor the restive apprehension. "You are a man," she said. "What have you to fear?"

"That I *am* a man," he answered. " 'Tis always a woman's choice."

She thought of Robert Stewart. "Not always."

He thought of it too and reconsidered, offering no rebuttal; he knew it as well as she, once reminded of it. "In this there is. With me."

He wanted the truth of her. And Cat could not lie, not to him to whom she owed something, nor would she prevaricate; she understood very well—was shocked she knew it so well—what he was asking. "You want me to say it was because of you. Of *you,* and no one else. But if I do—if I do that . . . ." If she did that, he would know. He would know it all.

Though he seemed to already, far better than she. He understood even her silence, her awkwardness, which frightened her badly. "We have paid the debts of our names," he declared. "What is left is something else, something new . . . and neither Campbell nor MacDonald. Only you and me."

It verged dangerously too close on honesty unfettered by misdirection. Obscurity was easier, *dis*honesty much safer. "We owe one another naught."

His laugher was quiet, but no less telling for its softness. "Dinna lie to me, Cat."

Intimacy, and impasse. She stared at him even as he stared back, and found herself counting the silver threads in his hair—many more than there had been, when she was but a lass; marking the creases beside his eyes—carved deeper than before; the oblique slant of cheekbones, the fit of his nose to the arch of his brow, the kindness in his mouth so perfectly balanced with maleness.

Cat backed away hastily. There was no grace in her movements, only jerky, awkward retreat. It was escape, nothing more, and he could not but see it.

He did. "Why?" he asked. "Why *now?*"

"Because—" She caught her breath, then laughed. Then caught her breath again. "You dinna understand."

"Then tell me. You shared a wee bit of your heart with me ten years ago . . . can ye no' trust me now?"

"I canna." It was definitive.

"Why not?"

"Because I am no more a wee lass, and you—and you—"

He waited. Smiling. Patient beyond bearing.

She said it all at once in a tumbling rush of confession. "Because I am trying verra hard not to kiss a MacDonald!"

His words, though the name was changed, and he knew it. He remembered.

His grin, in its birth, was dazzling. "Then dinna try so hard, aye?"

"Oh *Christ,*" she said in disgust.

Dair began to laugh. In its noise was nothing of ridicule, no suggestion of unkindness, but a wild and glorious sound of realization and elation.

And then the laughter died. He held out his hand and waited.

Fingertips at first, the merest brush of flesh on flesh. But it was enough, it was always enough; there was no room for denial, no more wish for escape. She put her hand into his.

"Come with me," he said. "Come home with me to Glencoe."

The knot of men around Robert Stewart of Appin were very young, which told Breadalbane something as he returned from his meeting with Keppoch: Stewart himself was not so much older and would undoubtedly appeal to others of a similar age, who were impressionable and quick to rouse, eagerly giving ear to one of their own who shared the councils of men greater than they.

He quietly joined the clutch surrounding Stewart, making deprecating motions when a few recognized him and fell away, giving him room to see the complex drawing in the dirt. "Who is who?" Breadalbane asked diffidently as Stewart took up his dirk as if to put it away. "I wasna there, you see . . . I am interested."

It was a blatant admission no one expected from him, and therefore proved most effective. They all knew Glenorchy Campbells had stayed out of the conflict at the earl's behest, and had undoubtedly spoken derisively of cowardice and weak spines, of blood thinned with water, and Williamite politics. But to his face they offered nothing now but unpracticed masks swept clean of all save wariness, and confusion, and the curiosity of the young. He was Breadalbane, after all, and Glenorchy, and Campbell.

Stewart indicated with dirk the positions of various clans, and Dundee himself, and succinctly explained how Hugh Mackay had brought his men down through the pass into defeat.

Breadalbane watched the dirk with half an eye; his true attention was almost entirely taken up in an assessment of Robert Stewart, though he did not divulge it.

Not a fool, Robbie Stewart . . . But neither a man who understood patience, nor politics, nor the need to accommodate himself in whatever fashion he might that served his personal interests. *Pride will cost him, yet.*

When the Appin heir finished his explanation, the earl nodded avuncular approval. "Dundee was a military genius, much as his ancestor Montrose was. I dinna doubt he could hae done as much for the Highlands as Montrose, had he lived."

Stewart's mouth hooked down. "And lost *his* head, too?"

Breadalbane met the challenge with a bland smile. " 'Tis better to die on the field, in honor, than under an executioner's ax."

"Aye, well . . ." Stewart glanced around at the clutch of young clansmen; he had lost their attention. He rose and sheathed his dirk as a few drifted away toward the other fires and other tales. "So, have ye come to tell me you are Jamie's man?"

No subtlety in this one . . . The stragglers instantly departed. Breadalbane smiled again. "Will you drink whisky wi' me?" He gestured elegantly. "I've a fire back there, near the ruins, and a gillie to serve us. Or we might walk through Black Duncan's trees."

The firelight gilded Stewart's hair. He was not tall but compact, and his neck was warded either side by pronounced tendons. Linen-clad shoulders were wide beneath the diagonal swath of plaid. "I've a mind to stay here," he said, "and have you say what you will say without snooving amidst the trees." He jerked his head toward the scattered fires where lairds and clansmen gathered. "You've taken them all aside, one by one; d'ye think I'm blind to it, and why?"

"Not you. You proved your mettle there." The earl glanced pointedly down at the map drawn in dirt. "And I've a mind to ken you better."

"You ken me well enow. You ken what I am. But I dinna ken what *you* are—save a Williamite."

Breadalbane demurred, deflecting the barb easily. "I am a Scot. A Highland Scot. And I love my people."

A hint of a curl in the lip. "Enough to inflict a Dutchman upon them."

William of Orange was also a Stuart and the grandson of another, but the earl did not remind Appin's young laird-to-be; such was not the point, and he did not care to split hairs as decisively as James's reign and subsequent exile had split Scotland. "Such afflictions can be cured."

"Ah." Stewart nodded; the lip's curl was more pronounced. "Wi' Jamie's return, I dinna doubt?"

The earl did not hesitate. "He is the rightful king."

Stewart barked a disbelieving laugh. "I've no' heard you say so before!"

"A man says many things."

"So he does." Young teeth were bared in a brief, mocking grin. "And what does this man say?"

"That he would do much to restore his land."

"How?"

"By making a peace."

"How?"

"By giving her lairds such things as they require."

Softly Stewart inquired, "Such things as silver?"

As softly Breadalbane answered, "There is enough for all."

One sandy eyebrow lifted. "Even MacDonalds?"

Breadalbane permitted himself a smile. "Ask Coll of the Cows."

Robert Stewart's humor dissipated instantly. "Keppoch has agreed?"

It pleased the earl to shrug as if none of it mattered. "Earlier. Keppoch and his tacksmen." They were straight-worded now, dancing no dances; there were no swords beneath their feet, albeit honed edges under the tones. "And others. Many others."

"Glengarry."

"Not yet."

"Glencoe."

"Not yet."

The grin came back. "Not ever."

It was wholly honest, and clean as a blade. "I came to speak to Appin. Last I kent, he was a *Stewart*—not a MacDonald."

The dirk struck home. A wave of hectic color rose from the coarse-muscled throat to stain the flesh of his face. Blue eyes glittered balefully. "So is he *still* a Stewart . . . but he is welcome in Glencoe, which isna said of Campbells."

Breadalbane waited a beat. It would not do to lose his temper. "In time, the world changes. Old enmities are settled. Shall we settle ours?"

In the silence between them pipe music skirled more loudly. It was *ceol mor,* but not a battle pibroch. A lament instead, of old ways treasured, old ways altered, old ways lost.

Roughly Stewart said, "You do ken 'tis to the Earl of Argyll that Appin owes loyalty. Not to Glenorchy."

And so now only two are left . . . "This is not about loyalties within Clan Campbell, and those from older times owed of Stewart to such as I. This is not about Clan Campbell at all. This is about Scotland. There is a fort at Inverlochy with guns on the walls, and soldiers in the foothills, and a patrol boat in Loch Linnhe, and frigates off the Isles. D'ye believe we can win?"

"What *I* say is: do you?"

"I do not. But there is hope for peace. What is required, for now, is no more than a treaty, and your name upon it. No oaths sworn; I'll no' ask you to break your honor. A truce only, until such a time as James gives you leave to swear a new oath to William."

Stewart's expression was taut. "Is he a fool, our Jamie, to give over such men as might win him his throne back?"

"I would ask another question."

It provoked, as intended. "Oh, aye?"

With careful precision the earl said, "I would ask myself if *I* were a fool, to let my clan be broken in the name of an exiled king who doesna have the faintest notion of Highland ways, or Highland honor."

Indolence was banished. The compact body stiffened. "You would ask that?"

"I would. I have."

"Jamie's man wouldna."

"Jamie's man would do better to ask himself if he might profit more from peace than from war."

"Jamie's man might. So might William's."

Robert Stewart, the earl decided, was too young to know when he was beaten. By dawn, he would see it. But for now there was another whose aid might yet prove invaluable, if Breadalbane could procure it.

The earl smiled. "I thank you for your time. I'll no' press a man for what he willna give willingly."

And as he walked away he took care that his shod feet scuffed into disarray Robert Stewart's detailed map of what might be, all too plainly, the final Jacobite victory.

The flesh of his hand warmed hers. MacDonald flesh. MacDonald hand. Upon a Campbell woman.

Let it be so . . . I want it to be so.

He repeated the words. "Come with me."

She wanted it to be so. Needed it.

"Cat."

She gripped his hand. *Could I do it? Should I?*

"Come home with me to Glencoe."

And then a man came up in the darkness, firelight sparking off brooch. "Would that be your price," Breadalbane asked, "to bring MacIain to heel?"

Two

*F*rom a distance it had been innocent enough: MacIain's second son extending a hand to a woman, his expression in moon- and firelight one of taut expectancy. It was an eloquent tableau with pockets of fire gushing about them and *ceol mor* haunting the air, and one no man might misunderstand who had ever desired a woman.

Initially it meant nothing at all to Breadalbane save it was oddly if distantly touching, a reminder of his youth when he bedded a woman for his body's sake instead of the sake of his house. Until the earl realized who it was MacDonald seduced.

Anger quickly replaced startlement. Then anger dissipated into preternatural calm. *There is something to be gained of this.*

Glenlyon's daughter broke the handclasp first. She clutched against her skirts an object that flashed briefly, blindingly silver, and said nothing at all, neither in shock nor in explanation; was wise enough, or shamed enough, in this discovery, to hold her silence.

MacDonald, seduction diverted, grace dismissed, turned at once, abruptly. Color stained flesh, underscoring the symmetry of a face that was, unlike his father's, innocent of beard. His features, to the earl's eyes, were unremarkable if cleanly formed, and not so handsome as other men hailed for their appearance; nor was he as overwhelming in presence and personality as Glencoe's towering laird.

But he is at peace with his body . . . and was, the earl realized, supremely content with his place in the world. That of itself made him more than an arrant pup meant to be kicked aside by a casual foot.

Breadalbane's reassessment was rapid. He needed this lad as much as Robbie Stewart, or John MacDonald. He knew very well that by stirring argument within the sons he might well defeat the fathers.

The earl flicked a glance at his cousin's daughter. Her eyes were empty of enmity, too busy with implication. They were both of them stunned by his presence, but MacIain's youngest son mustered self-control more quickly than she.

"My father," he said plainly, "isna a *hound,* aye?—to be made to come to heel."

Breadalbane froze into stillness, but managed a bland smile. This meant something. This was significant. It made Alasdair Og more important than anticipated: he could discern the object beyond obfuscation.

"Oh, I think he is," Breadalbane said lightly, "but we are all of us hounds, ye ken, fighting over the bone some men would also call Scotland."

"Scotland," MacDonald affirmed, "but no' this woman."

The earl raised his brows. "And why not? Is she not worth it?" He looked pointedly at her. "You risk a treaty for her."

Her face was taut and white, but the eyes were not subdued. He saw her father in her—and perhaps her mother; he did not recall Helen Campbell—save her strength of will was greater.

"You willna do this," she declared. "Not to me."

He smiled, intending her to see it; she was no fool despite her parentage, but she understood nothing of politics. She comprehended only emotions, as all women did, especially those emotions the MacDonald had recently roused. She thought in terms of herself and of newfound appetites, and now of MacIain's son.

But not in terms of a country, or of the insult she does my son.

Steadily he said, "I will do it to anyone, ye ken, be he man or she a woman. 'Tis for Scotland, aye?—and I am a man who considers his country worth it." It silenced her, as expected; free of the woman, he turned again to MacDonald. "He is gey stubborn, is MacIain. He'll no' take my silver, I ken, and he'll no' take my word that what I do now is done for Scotland."

"Is it?"

"In all I do." He glanced again at Glenlyon's daughter, who lingered yet despite implied dismissal. "Go to Duncan," he told her flatly. "He is expecting you."

Flags of brilliant color suffused her face. MacDonald moved, reaching, even as she turned in rigid retreat. "Cat—"

But she was gone before he could stop her, walking straight-backed into shadow. His hand fell to his side in a futile, eloquent slackness.

"Now," Breadalbane said, "let us speak of Glencoe."

"And Campbells?" It was derisive, but clearly it required effort for MacDonald to forget Cat and speak of other things. "If you will speak of Glencoe," he said plainly, "speak *to* Glencoe."

The earl offered an inoffensive smile. "So your brother said."

"He is wise, aye?" MacDonald retorted dryly. "And *he* will be MacIain; you've no need to speak to me."

"I speak to any man who may have a say in Scotland's future."

MacDonald's answering smile was thin. "The future I would speak of is no' a country's at all, just at this moment. This particular moment."

There it was: risk after all, if on a highly personal level. He did not shirk the truth, nor attempt to underplay what the earl had witnessed. It lay between them, bright and sharp, and full of consequences.

Breadalbane did not easily lose his temper, but he thought now of the ramifications that had nothing to do with preferment and even less with politics. "She *is* bonnie, aye? . . . and as unlike her father as a woman might be. Strong where he is weak. Determined where he is malleable. Fully cognizant of her pride." He waited, sure of his course. "But more: she is a Campbell. And is wholly subject to Campbell authority. My authority, aye?"

MacDonald was, the earl thought, indistinguishable from other men save for the incongruity of prematurely graying hair—and except when he chose to be someone altogether different, even as he did now with a subtle shifting of posture, of assessment of the enemy.

Breadalbane was instantly alerted. He had seen this in dogs. Such intangibles as these set the pack leader apart from the pack.

"She is not my price," MacDonald declared, "as you would have it, aye? Because there *is* no price. Not for Scotland. Not for a woman. What I do, I will do. What my father does, he will do. Have you a thing to say of MacIain, say it *to* MacIain."

"I see the old fox bred true." He paused. "You are more eloquent than your brother."

Teeth were bared briefly. "I am not the heir, aye? It affords me latitude."

"The latitude to seduce a woman meant to wed my son?"

If MacDonald had known, he had forgotten. Ruddy color stained his face, then drained slowly away. Even his lips were white.

The earl smiled coolly. "You have lifted our cattle," he said, "with impunity much of the time, though your neck might argue it; oh aye, I heard the tale. But you will no' lift our women."

It roused a tangible anger; the self-control was no longer suppressed, nor its presence overlooked. "Is this how you court MacIain?"

"But you have made it clear I canna do it through his son." The earl paused. "I breed deerhounds. Did you ken it?"

MacDonald clearly did not, and as clearly did not know why it should matter that he did.

Breadalbane said, "The bitch I have in my kennel is meant for a better dog."

MacDonald's hand went to his dirk. "Good *Christ*, Campbell—" But the taut hand moved away again, albeit the fingers trembled; he was as angry as a man might be, as the earl had intended, but was cognizant of his place, of his name, of the name of the man who baited him, and decidedly disinclined to start a fight that would lead to a war his clan could not win. He would not risk Letters of Fire and Sword, and the breaking of MacDonalds as the MacGregors had been broken.

"There is little to lose," the earl said, "of what is left to win. Glengarry. Glencoe. How will either of you stand against a united Scotland?"

"United under William? Or James?" The fury had passed, or was better controlled; MacDonald's eyes were steady. "Or does it matter? To you."

"It matters. But it will not be under kings." The young man's presumption had angered the earl more than he knew; he offered honest emotion in place of diplomacy. "Under the Master of Stair. Under the Earl of Breadalbane."

The fine mouth curved. "The Earl of Argyll might have something to say of that, aye?"

"*He* is not here. I am. It is I who make this treaty." The earl paused delicately. "Which all the chiefs have signed, as promise of an oath, save Glengarry and Glencoe."

"Appin," MacDonald blurted, and Breadalbane knew he had won.

"Ask," he suggested, in perfect courtesy.

She sat under the light of a bloated moon, surrounded by the ruins of Achallader Castle. Time had softened the edges; grass overtook fallen bricks, lichen cloaked the cobbles, strangers had carried off anything of value so that only the bones remained. The flesh had fallen away in the aftermath of the raid. All that remained standing were three of four corners.

Her seat was a pile of brickwork, tilting slope-shouldered to one side. It was not a comfortable seat, but Cat did not want comfort; she was angry, very angry, wishing she were a man who might say what she thought, who might, in fact, challenge the man who injured her so.

—that pawkie bastard . . . that God-cursed, pawkie bastard!

She wanted very much to shout at the earl and tell him what she thought of men who used women, who relied upon a woman's presence to manipulate other men. She had seen his eyes, heard the steel beneath the tone. Within his words, ostensibly of Scotland and of loyalty to his king—whichever king it might be—was a wholly separate conversation intended mostly for Dair MacDonald with a little left over for her, enough to punish her for presumption, to remind her of her place. She was angry for herself, but angrier for Dair.

And cognizant of a loss far greater than there should be, for something just begun.

Just begun? No. Indeed, it had existed in her girlhood, in her childish dreams; in the memories of kindness, of gentleness and compassion, freely offered the enemy. In even the dismay that he had seen her as Robert Stewart presented her, sodden with mud and horse-piss, with the smell of whisky about her from that which she had spilled so she need not serve MacDonald.

Need not serve *him;* but had she known it was he, she would have served him gladly. He was deserving of that, even as MacDonald, for being honest with the lass.

And now? Loss. The ending of something not so newly begun, though perhaps it was new in *his* eyes; he was a man, and grown, and with lasses aplenty, no doubt; he had said something of that, of experience. And that experience had seen she was different that day before the shieling, when he had wanted to kiss a Campbell.

An ending, before a proper beginning. An ending to girlhood dreams and the beginning of adulthood, now stolen from her in the blade of Breadalbane's words.

Dair knew, or had once known. She had told them in the shieling, Alasdair Og and Robert Stewart: that she was on her way to Kilchurn to visit Breadalbane. It had been Stewart who pieced it together, who declared she must be meant to marry one of the earl's sons. Not John, he had said, because John was already wed. Therefore Duncan, whom Breadalbane detested despite his pedigree; but *then* it had not mattered what Dair MacDonald thought. There was nothing between them then but an enmity shaped of tradition, except what they overlooked. What they chose to overlook, because it was easier.

And overlooked it they had, choosing to do so, in spirit if not in words, though neither of them would acknowledge it to themselves or to one another.

It made a cruel sense, the ending. There was no future in it, no purpose to the madness. There could never be anything more than what their clans had sown, and the crop of acrimony was what she and Dair must reap.

I dinna want to.

There. It was said. Her loyalty declared.

Cat yet held the mirror. She raised it, turned it, looked into its glassy surface. The night behind her was dark; there was little illumination save the diffused glow of distant campfires and the moon overhead. The woman in the mirror was nothing more than a collection of blurred features leached stark and pale by tension, and the false brilliance of unshed tears.

It had not just begun, what Breadalbane ended, and was not easily reconciled. She could count the days, the years, all the meetings between them, and knew in no way did their infrequency influence significance.

She lowered the mirror and stared blindly at the encampment as tears ran down her face. "You pawkie bastard," she said. "I am *pleased* they razed your castle."

Dair wanted to go to Cat at once, to find her and tend her chancy temper as well as explain himself; he had invited her home to Glencoe without thought, without preparation, reacting to his heart and the tension of the moment. In this it was *his* thought, his will, not Jean's, who wanted him then as he came first to Castle Stalker . . . as he wanted Cat now, in the ruins of Achallader, if for different reasons. For deeper, more honest reasons as well as requirements; companionship of the spirit as well as of the body.

But he knew he must not go to Cat. Not now, not so soon after the earl's interruption. It was what Breadalbane no doubt expected, what Breadalbane probably planned for, and was therefore far too dangerous for Dair in his present mood. He did not anger easily, but the fire burned hot as Robbie Stewart's once fully kindled.

But there was yet another thing for him to discuss, and with another man. Dair set out to broach it.

He wound his way through clansmen clustered around fires in tartan-clad companionship and went directly to the Appin Stewarts. They were snugged against the slope, content to pass the evening in talk and usquabae. *Ceol mor* had at last given way to subtle music, piping down the night.

Dair came to a halt at the fire. "Did you agree?" he demanded without preliminaries; without an invitation to bide a wee with them. "Good Christ, Robbie—did you *agree?*"

Robert Stewart, sprawled inelegantly across battered turf with his head propped on a braced elbow, offered detached consternation. "You are shaking, MacDonald . . . and verra black in the face."

It took effort not to shout. And that made him shake all the more. "I dinna care *what* color my face is, and I am shaking because I'd as lief put a dirk in Breadalbane as spend another night on his land."

"Fletcher land, once," Robbie observed mildly. "A Campbell stole it from them . . . but I wouldna say *now* 'tis so much to claim; there is no more roof, or walls against the wind." He swung a boiled-leather bottle in the general direction of the castle ruins. "He's no cause to thank you, has the pawkie earl."

"To thank *MacIain,*" Dair clarified. "You and I were in Glen Lyon when they burned Achallader."

"Aye, so we were, collecting cows and other plunder." Stewart hoisted the leather bottle. "Usquabae," he explained. "By your face, you need it."

"I dinna want *whisky,*" Dair said plainly, "I want the truth of you. Did you agree to sign the treaty?"

Robbie sat up. In firelight his hair shone gold. " 'Tis a Stewart concern," he said. "I thought you were MacDonald."

Dair spared a glance for Robbie's men. They looked at him briefly, then away to the fire, to their whisky, to their comrades, avoiding his eyes entirely. He knew most of them; they had gone on raids with their laird's son, gone to war with their laird's son. They would defend his life, but they knew Dair MacDonald; they would let him say what he meant to say and keep themselves out of it.

"MacDonald," Dair said. "So I am, aye? Robbie—" He sat down abruptly, too angry to stand without taking action, and accepted the proffered whisky. With some violence he tilted the bottle to his mouth, drank much of the contents, then glared at his friend. "How could you, man? He is of two tongues, is Breadalbane, promising a thing to one man, and a second thing to another."

"I havena sworn for him yet."

Dair looked at him sharply. "He said you had."

Robbie muttered an imprecation and gestured; one of his gillies tossed over another boiled-leather bottle. " 'Tis precipitate of him— but aye, I think I will put my name to this treaty. D'ye see a way out of it?"

"Aye—dinna *do* it!"

Robbie drank deeply, then wiped a glistening smear of liquor from his upper lip. " 'Tisn't so easy as that."

Dair swallowed whisky, welcoming the burn. "No? You dinna *sign,* Robbie; that doesna seem gey hard."

Stewart eyed him assessively. "Have more. Dinna spill it, now; you're still shaking, man." He grinned in delight. " 'Twas always you telling *me* no' to be so angry . . . Christ, MacDonald, 'tis a shame we're no' in battle! You'd hew down a hundred men!"

"Fifty," Dair said darkly. "Dinna exaggerate." Then the anger boiled up again. "Christ, the bluidy Campbell . . ." He wanted badly to speak of Cat, of Breadalbane's deliberate insults, to share his rage and the true reason for it. But he did not because he knew better, even in his anger: Jean's brother would hold no sympathy for a man who was upset because of another woman. "I'm unfit for company . . ." He held the bottle out. "Here, have it back, aye?—I'll go."

"Sit," Robbie said. "What will MacIain do?"

"MacIain?" It distracted him. He relaxed muscles tensed to rise, settling back onto his buttocks. "He isna pleased by this meeting."

"Well, no, I wouldna think so," Robbie agreed mildly. "Not MacIain, aye?—he's no love of Grey John Campbell."

"Have you?" He had drunk too quickly with no food to mitigate it; the fire in his belly now threatened his head. "Has any man here cause to love Breadalbane?"

"Och, the Campbells might . . ." Robbie grinned and made a placating gesture to ward off sputtered protest. "But it isna a question of love. 'Tis survival." Humor dissipated; his expression was pensive as he set aside his bottle. "There is that fort at Inverlochy . . . and an army in the hills—"

With withering disdain, "I have eyes, ye ken, and I live in Glencoe; I've seen it for myself."

Stewart judiciously chose to overlook it. "Then ye ken what we'd face, were we to go against William's forces."

Dair raised his bottle. With deliberate derision he said, "Those are no' the words of the man who was at Killiecrankie."

Robbie brightened. "You want to *fight* me—!"

"Not you specifically. But someone, aye; you seem the most fit for it . . . and God in Heaven kens I've wanted to before! 'Tis time we learned who is the better man."

Stewart was delighted. Blue eyes kindled. "You would lose."

"I dinna think so."

"*'Fou* or sober, you'd lose."

Dair smiled with careful condescension. "I dinna think so."

" 'Tis the usquabae."

"Does it matter?"

"Och, but it lies, does usquabae . . . it convinces a man of his own superiority." Robbie laughed at him. "I'd prefer you sober. I'd want you to remember the beating I gave you."

Dair set down the bottle. His thighs tingled with tension. He trembled again, but no longer from anger. His body demanded release; if it was through a fistfight rather than lovemaking, he'd not debate the issue. "Well?"

"Tempting as it may be"—blue eyes were speculative—"no." Robbie sighed and settled back on his elbow. "We are here for the purpose of peace."

In deep disgust, Dair said, "Dinna sound so pious; you havena the makings of a priest, or a kirk minister either."

Stewart grinned briefly, but it died away. "Killiecrankie is over. 'Twas two years ago. There is a fort now, near to Glencoe—and Appin isna so far from it, either. *Think,* man; which clans would see Livingstone and his army first? Which clans would meet with Governor John Hill first?"

"Robbie—"

"Let be," Stewart said briefly. "Whatever the earl said, 'twas said of a purpose. Would you let him win? 'Twould be something of which to boast, to rouse Alasdair Og."

Dair glared at him blackly. "Will you sign, then? For Appin?"

Robbie's expression was solemn. "Before you shout at me—aye, I can see 'tis in your mind—you'd best ask your father what he intends to do. Then you may be shouting at us both."

Dair shook his head. *"He* willna sign."

"He has said so?"

"Breadalbane hasna spoken to him yet."

"He told *you* he wouldna sign."

"He told me he will hear what William's lapdog has to say; 'tis why he came, after all."

"Ah." Robbie considered it. "Then by this time tomorrow night you may be telling me how sorry you are for your words."

It provoked, as Stewart intended. "Glengarry isna so quick to agree, either, aye?"

"He told me that. The earl." Robbie frowned, taking up his bottle again. "Appin isna so large—"

"Neither is Glencoe! D'ye think that would keep MacIain from following his conscience?"

Robbie sighed. "MacIain does as MacIain wants . . . I ken that, aye?"

Dair's tone was deadly. "I never thought you were a sheep."

The Appin Stewarts stilled; this promised a fight. But Robbie, notorious for his temper, remained unprovoked. He grinned. "You are surly when you are *fou.*"

"Christ, Robbie . . ." The anger had died; his temper never lasted. In its aftermath was a certain laxity of limb he attributed to whisky. Dair sighed and let himself go slack, stretching out on cool turf. "I canna believe him. Breadalbane. I canna believe his promises." He gazed up at whisky-blurred stars. "I think MacIain is right: he is Willie's man in Edinburgh, and Jamie's in the Highlands."

Robbie laughed. "MacIain says that?"

"He does."

"Aye, well—his tongue has always been sharp as his dirk." Robbie uprooted turf idly. "What d'ye mean to do with Jean?"

It was wholly unexpected. Slackness fled, replaced once more by tension. "Jean?"

"My sister," Robbie reminded with elaborate precision. "The one you left in Glencoe."

Dair shut his eyes. There were things he meant to say, but he could say none of them. His brain was muddled with whisky, his tongue too thick; what he needed to say, the explanation he wanted to make, required clarity. Robbie Stewart was not a man another man faced full of whisky. "Naught," he said at last, knowing himself a coward.

Robbie grunted. "Aye, well . . ." He heaved himself to his feet. As Dair moved an elbow preparatory to rising, Stewart waved him back down. "No, no—dinna go. I'm only meaning to piss." He poked a toe at Dair's bottle. "Have more usquabae; your temper's improving."

Dair sat up as Robbie departed, intending to rise and go despite the invitation, but the world moved slowly around him in ways it was not meant. "No' fit," he muttered, as one of the Stewarts laughed.

Not fit at all. And Cat deserved better than a man in his cups swearing himself to her; she had seen that in her father. He would not offer the same.

Dair lay down again and draped a crooked arm across his face, shutting out the Highland moon. "Christ," he murmured, thinking of Breadalbane; of Glenlyon, and a tree, and a rope around his neck.

Thinking also of Jean, and of Glenlyon's daughter.

With cordial greetings dispersed like alms as he walked, and with only a few stops along the way to clap shoulders, grasp forearms, or to pass along a warm word, the Earl of Breadalbane moved steadily among his gathering to the fire in the lee of the hill. There he found the ragged remains of a beef haunch hanging lopsidedly on the wooden spit, and his son, but not his cousin's daughter.

He paused at the edge of light. "Where is she?"

Duncan Campbell of Breadalbane, plaid stippled shiny with dollops of grease, was perched atop stone and turf with a horn cup clasped in equally greasy hands. He smiled blandly around a mouthful of meat. "Up there."

The earl waited patiently; this was Duncan's game.

"In the ruins." Eventually Duncan swallowed and waved in casual indication toward the hill behind them. "She said she was of a mind to see the handiwork of a man who defeated you."

Breadalbane sighed inwardly. In the midst of negotiations for a new Scotland, the ill-mannered daughter of an insignificant drunkard cousin, little more now than a bonnet-laird with so much of his lands owned by Murrays, was proving more troublesome than she had any right to be. "She was to remain here. I sent her to you."

"She wasna of a mind to remain here." Duncan, redepositing grease across one cheek by scratching at a midge bite, was clearly amused by the whole matter. "She arrived, scowled at me—she has a verra fierce scowl, ye ken, near as black as yours!—then went promptly away to the castle." He glanced over his shoulder at the charred, skeletal remains looming atop the hill. "I never liked this castle. The Mac-Donalds did well by it."

Breadalbane surpressed a comment that would mark him undignified. "Was there anything *else* she said?"

"Oh, aye. She called you a pawkie bastard." Duncan grinned in unmitigated pleasure and gulped more whisky.

Now the earl was irritated. And also hungry. The remains of the beef haunch still laggardly dripping fat into a hissing and snapping fire set his belly to griping. "Where is Sandy? Has *he* gone up to the ruins?"

"Making water." Duncan wiped away grease and whisky on the back of his wrist. His linen shirtsleeve was crusted. "Does he need your permission for that, too?"

"Duncan—" But the earl contained himself. "She will come back. She has no choice."

"Och, *I* judge her a woman who will make a choice for herself even when there isna one." Duncan shifted closer to the sizzling fire; it was the cusp of August, but nights were cool. "You treat us both as fools."

"You *are* fools, the pair of you. Left to yourself, you would marry Marjorie Campbell of Lawers, who brings naught to the earldom—"

"Glenlyon's daughter does?"

"—and Catriona Campbell, left to *her*self, would sleep with a Mac-Donald." He was pleased to see that comment earned his son's attention. "Aye, a Glencoe-man; 'twas why I sent her here, to save her from dishonor."

"A MacDonald," Duncan echoed thickly. "Which MacDonald?"

"Alasdair." With his gillie not present, the earl made shift for himself. He took up a silver cup brought expressly for his use and poured it full of whisky, then knelt and drew his dirk to carve off a chunk of beef.

"MacIain?"

"No, not MacIain—Alasdair *Og*. His youngest son." Breadalbane bit into his cooling meat, absently grateful he still had most of his teeth. Other men his age were not so fortunate. "But a MacDonald all the same, and of Glencoe."

" 'The Gallows Herd,' " Duncan murmured. He was clearly astounded, which pleased the earl; it was not always a simple task to get honest emotion of his heir. "What was she doing with him?"

"Allowing herself to be seduced." Breadalbane chewed meticulously—it was why he still had teeth, he believed—then washed it down with whisky. "Naught has come of it; you need no' fear he bedded her before you."

Duncan recoiled. "I dinna *mean* to bed her!"

"You dinna?"

"I mean to bed Marjorie. And I have."

The earl dug out a meat string from his molars, studied it briefly, then flicked it into darkness. "Is she breeding?"

"I dinna ken!"

"Well, it doesna matter now. I will settle some silver on her if there's a bastard." He made himself more comfortable on a length of wool brought for the purpose of keeping his kilt unsoiled. "I'm to speak to Glencoe at dawn, and Glengarry . . . we'll be finished here by tomorrow night. Then we'll go back to Kilchurn—I'll have to go on to London, to the queen and the Privy Council, and then on to Flanders to give the king and Stair my report—and you'll wed Glenlyon's daughter."

Duncan's sullen face closed itself like a fist. "She doesna want me. I dinna want her. But even if we loved one another, you'd see to it we couldna wed."

The earl looked at him in surprise. "Why should I be so perverse as that?"

"Because."

"Because?"

"Because you *are.*"

Broken brickwork clinked. Cat looked up quickly, tucking the mirror beneath her arisaid. Irrational hope kindled abruptly; was mirrored by fear, by nervousness, by something to do with need—but all were damped immediately as she saw him. It was not Dair, could not be Dair, *would* not be Dair. Not now.

"A bonnie sight." Robert Stewart moved out of the shadow of an aborted column into lucent moonlight. "Campbell . . . and MacDonald." His tone was exquisitely ironic. He wore no bonnet; uncombed sandy hair, backlighted by distant fires and the moon overhead, glowed a pale, night-burnished gold. "Soft words, were they? In the spirit of Breadalbane's peace?" His teeth flashed briefly as he walked; Cat was put in mind of a snarl in place of a smile, especially as he had not shaved and stubble sparked gilt on his jaws. "Aye, well, I canna blame him . . . a man might choose to warm himself at a Campbell fire, was it offered in the winter."

He paused indolently, letting her think; one bare foot was propped on a broken lintel stone. The ankles, like his wrists bared by cuffs turned back, were thick with corded muscle. The purposeful pose, if less languid than he intended—he lacked the frame for insouciance— reminded her unpleasantly of her father on a hilltop with a claymore in his hand.

Damn you, you bluidy Stewart . . . She could not see why Dair valued him; could not imagine what bond they had forged, save an affinity of opposites. And perhaps that was it. Perhaps they balanced one another. She could well believe that for every good thing Dair MacDonald did, every kind thought he considered, Robert Stewart would see a way to pervert each deed and every thought into a childish humiliation.

Irony was exquisite. *—no' so different from my brothers, when it comes to it!* Except they had teased in ordinary if unpleasant fashion, had sought to humiliate her only as they did one another, if with greater effect because she was a lass and therefore subject to different whims. She believed Stewart truly looked for weakness to exploit it, meaning to destroy the spirit housing it.

Cat drew in a very deep breath, stirred as always, by him, to intense dislike and apprehension. She struggled not to show it. " 'Tis summer," she said lightly. "If *you've* come hunting a Campbell fire, you'd best look elsewhere for it."

"Because another man kindled the spark?" Stewart picked his way once more through turf-clad, tumbled stone. He was as unlike Dair as could be, in frame as well as temperament, but grace was not lacking in him. It was simply housed in a different frame. "I've been honest all my life in the appetites of the flesh . . ."

Cat held her tongue. She would give him no opportunity, no specifics he might target.

He moved steadily now, unhindered by poor footing. "But I have some understanding of a woman's sensibilities; no doubt you're wishing now I were Alasdair Og of Glencoe instead of Robert Stewart of Appin." The moon was kind to his face; by day his features were harder, and far less sanguine. "Did he tell you of Jean?—but no, he wouldna . . ." He grinned. "Few women long to hear another woman's name when they've bedding in their minds."

He stood close to her now, very close; it took immense effort not to rise. She gave him power by remaining seated, surrendering precedence in height and posture, but to stand suggested fear, and that triumph she would not offer.

"Jean," he said with careful precision. "Stewart. My sister. With whom he has shared a bed for six years." His smile had faded partway through; there was an edge now to his tone, and a glitter in his eyes. "D'ye think you're woman enough to wean him from her?"

She recalled an image etched in memory: Robert Stewart handing Dair her mother's kettle, bidding him give Jean something of Glen Lyon. But Dair had not; he had, if secretly after the others were gone, returned the kettle to her.

And gave Jean himself instead— Cat clamped her jaws shut. She knew very well what Stewart meant to do. In his own way he was as bad as Breadalbane, if for different reasons; they each of them guarded intent with whatever weapons necessary, cutting with tongue if steel were judged inappropriate. But *this* attack was ill-advised; had it not been Robert Stewart here before her, slicing with his tongue, it might have proved successful. But she knew his moods, knew his methods, knew intimately to what he would stoop. *There is no horse-piss here . . . what will you use instead?*

She wondered if Stewart knew what Breadalbane had said. Surely he had seen her with Dair at the MacDonald fire, or he would not have come here with a honed dirk in all his words and the wherewithal to use it. But she had the advantage, such as it was: the earl's efforts had already blunted Stewart's blow. It was not so much a victory when the enemy was already felled.

Before him, *because* of him—and because of Breadalbane—she was empty of grief, of rage. What was left in aftermath was a powerful desire, a calculated intent, to defeat Robert Stewart in the only kind of battle Cat knew she could win.

God grant me the wit and tongue of other women! Perhaps even of Jean herself.

Cat retrieved the silver-backed mirror from the folds of her arisaid and held it up before her face, ostensibly studying the insignificant curve of a mostly level eyebrow. "If you mean me to look to you in his absence, you might find softer words," she suggested with purposeful idleness. "And if you mean me to hate him for bedding your sister, well . . ." She shrugged, deftly tending an eyebrow. "He isna a priest, aye? I wasna expecting him to claim he was celibate."

Beyond the mirror, Stewart smiled thinly. "Och no, not Alasdair Og—*I'll* swear he is no priest. So will my sister swear it . . . she has naught better to do, waiting in Glencoe."

She lowered the mirror and appraised him. She supposed some women answered such boldness, responded to sly, insidious cruelty;

even she, who disliked him intensely, was aware of something in his posture, tightly leashed and unnamed, yet waiting impatiently for release like a hound prepared to leap.

She was put in mind abruptly of Killiecrankie, and countless cattle raids. He would make a formidable enemy— *—or a formidable ally—* —and in that instant she understood that men's thoughts worked differently, that they did not weigh others in the same balance as women did; that in fact the need itself determined a man's decision-making and response, wholly independent of emotion.

Lastly, perhaps most significantly, she realized that if he were friend—or brother—intent on guarding her, she would be grateful for it. Dangerous men, in dangerous times, had their uses.

"Were I your sister," Cat said, "I wouldna count the days of my future by the days of my past."

"Because he put out his hand to you?" Stewart glanced briefly at the hall corner near which she sat, then turned his brilliant stare back on her. "A man might look," he explained, "and a man might ask, and a man might take what is offered—only a fool wouldna!—but it doesna mean he will put the woman in his home out of his bed while he woos another into his plaid while he is out on the heather."

She knew better; she knew *him,* but her throat was so tight it ached. It took effort not to shout imprecations at him. She was sick to death of pawkie bastards and their pawkie ways. "Is there a woman in *your* plaid?"

His intensity was tangible. "Not this night. Nor in my house, when it comes to that; the last one I put out of it."

Cat let the mirror drop to her lap. Softly she asked, "Are you lonely, then?"

A glint of teeth and anticipation; a hand pressed against his plaid in the vicinity of his heart. "Gey lonely, lass."

She thought of her brothers and recalled their habits, their crude speech, their lewdness. Her own childhood mimicry of it had earned a few skelpings until she learned to hoard the knowledge away, whispering it in her mind, or muttering the insults to animals who were disinclined to regard her with proper respect.

"Aye, well . . ." She stood up, aware he watched her avidly. The brick beneath her feet gave her added inches, though with him she needed none. "Oh—" She affected surprise. "I forgot . . ." She hitched her shoulders in idle regret. "They do say a man's height is the measure of his cock—" Her eyes assessed him neatly, even as he had assessed her. "—and I dinna think after all there is enough of you for me."

The Earl of Breadalbane was content in several things, immediately and most significantly the assuagement of his hunger, and in the approaching culmination of his grand scheme. Scotland was very nearly his, if vicariously—it was William who would rule in name, if not in reality—and would be wholly his in short order. There remained only Glengarry and Glencoe to convince, a momentous task another man might count impossible, but one which he was certain he could successfully accomplish. He was not a man who accepted failure, and he had worked too long to bring this to fruition to see it falter now.

Meanwhile there was his heir, whose management should be infinitely less difficult than the clans, but which so far had proved eminently more frustrating.

Duncan, sated on whisky and beef, had collapsed against the slope into an indolence most inelegant: flat on back and buttocks with bent knees elevated and feet squarely planted. It tented his kilt skyward and left markedly visible the underside of his thighs. It was, the earl felt, a supremely undignified posture, which was undoubtedly the reason Duncan assumed it. That, or he was too *fou* to care.

He studied his son with suitable objectivity. *He is a weak-willed youth easily misled, regrettably plain in appearance, whose time is taken up by too many thoughts of how to annoy his father.* Breadalbane did not see how such a thing could come to be; he had labored assiduously to educate Duncan in the responsibilities of an earldom, but his heir remained stubbornly devoted to intransigence. The earl could not even predict how much was a natural if inappropriate contrariness—which, while annoying, was not a permanent affliction and often passed with the assumption of responsibilities—and how much was stupidity.

Equally sated if more circumspect in his habits, the earl sat back against the earth, separated from turf by the length of good wool blanket. "It has been six days," he observed, "since the Highlands as a whole came to live in Campbell lands. What have you learned of it?"

Duncan wobbled his knees back and forth in idle self-amusement. "That so many pipers together make a dreadful noise."

Breadalbane bided his time by meticulously cleaning his dirk.

Duncan was himself not so good at waiting. "That *camanachd* can be a dangerous game; I near had a leg battered into pieces by the sticks." He tapped one shin. "See the bruises?"

The earl did, but said nothing of them. He inspected the dirk blade, then slid it home into his belt.

Idleness was not Duncan's virtue. "That no one is quite certain what you get of this, nor why you should concern yourself with an oath to William if you are Jamie's man." He sat upright, striking the tented kilt as he crossed his legs beneath him. "What *do* you get of this?"

"Peace," the earl answered. "And power." He repositioned the dirk so its stag-horn handle lay in easy reach. "Tell me how."

"A lesson, is it?"

"You should have learned one. You should have learned several, but one will do—provided it is the right one." The earl did not smile. "Tell me how."

Duncan shrugged, shaking his head. "Power is easy enough; the man who offers Highland peace makes William take notice of him."

"Aye?"

"And peace is the means to win that notice."

"It is."

Duncan scowled into darkness, looking across the encampment. At distant fires men laughed and talked, trading jests and stories; the bards held sway for many. "They dinna trust me, the chiefs. I am a Campbell of Glenorchy, and Grey John's heir." He looked back squarely at his father. "You have a gey supple tongue and the wit of a fox; which king *do* you serve?"

Breadalbane did not shirk the truth. "The one who can hold Scotland."

"But that could be *either* of them, William or James."

"Aye, so it could be."

Duncan was perplexed. "The Jacobites want James, but the Sassenachs dinna. They prefer William."

It is so obvious; are you my son, truly? Or merely passed off as mine? "Then one must weigh whether the Jacobites are strong enough to win."

Duncan muttered an imprecation beneath his breath. " 'Tis the only thing that matters to you. Winning."

"Losing is cold company: one lives his life outside of politics, or one loses his head." Breadalbane did not smile. "Is this what you have learned? To question my intent? But that, I should have said, you learned long ago."

"I will reap what you sow," Duncan retorted. "Therefore it makes some difference to me what you do."

"As it makes some difference to me what *you* do." The earl's tone was deadly. "Such as desiring to marry against my wishes."

Duncan stiffened. "You canna blame me! You've had the ordering of my life in everything . . . now when I've met a woman *I* want, without depending on you, you say I canna have her. I've given in on everything else—I willna give in on this!"

Despite the inclination, Breadalbane would not shout. Instead he took solace in soft condescension. "If I rule you, 'tis because someone must. You are a fool with no wits to see that sacrifices must be made—"

"*What* sacrifices? You? You've made none; 'tis *me* who makes them all!"

"Ah," he murmured, thinking of his father's paupery and indecisiveness that had nearly ruined them all. But Duncan could not see it; he saw only what lay before him, what his father had won. A mark then of his success: that his son could not see the failure that preceded it.

"Well?" Duncan challenged. " 'Tis true. You are the Earl of Breadalbane, Lord Glenorchy, and all the other titles—you hold lands I canna count, own castles all over Scotland—"

"And how do you suppose I came by all these things?" the earl asked silkily.

Color splotched Duncan's face. "They say you stole it all, through lies and trickery."

Breadalbane had learned long before not to get angry; it weakened a man's position and damaged his dignity. "And do you believe that?"

Duncan flung out a hand to encompass the encampment. *"They* do."

"I asked you: do you?" He paused. "Or are you a blind boy led everywhere by one-eyed men who would be kings in Breadalbane's place?"

"You would," Duncan said tightly. *"You* would be king, if you thought you could keep the crown!"

The earl smiled blandly. "If it were offered to me, I would certainly accept . . . but Campbells are not kings." Not *crowned* kings, perhaps; but there were ways of ruling Scotland that did not require anointing.

"Aye, but—"

"Meanwhile, William holds the crown and James wants it back, whilst the clans desire nothing more than to be left alone in their petty Highland kingdoms so they may raid and pillage and kill one another with impunity." Breadalbane lifted a single shoulder in elegant disdain. "But the price is too high. William needs peace in the Highlands to salvage face and pride—and Highland flesh to catch musket balls and cannon scraps in place of Dutch and English."

Duncan gazed at him blankly, then swallowed back a choked laugh. "If I went to them now and told them what you said, what you truly believe—"

"They ken what I believe. They ken it gey well. But they also ken that their days of freedom are numbered; William holds the Highlands by virtue of his forts and the soldiers within them—do you think there is a chief here foolish enough to turn his back on my truce? *That* is power, Duncan . . . *that* is sacrifice: to ken what must be done no matter how much you hate it, and to do it. One time or one hundred."

Duncan sat very still. "Then none of this matters. None of it."

" 'Tis over," Breadalbane said. "They will agree to my truce, swear the Oath of Allegiance by the end of the year—or their clans will be subject to extirpation." Stair had promised it.

"Extir—"

"And every man here—every man out there"—he gestured expansively—"understands it perfectly." He smiled; it was truth, it was power, it was Duncan's future—if he understood how to grasp it. "Though they will none of them admit it."

Duncan's jaw worked awkwardly. "This is a sham, a travesty—this is done for your own amusement!"

"No; there is naught here that amuses me. Certainly not my son."

The splotches grew redder. It was all Duncan could do to force the words from his mouth. "I'll see you have it, then. *Amusement.*" He flung himself flat on the turf, tugged his plaid over his shoulder, and turned his back on his father.

"Sleep well," Breadalbane offered.

Sometime before dawn Dair awoke. He was aware that the side of his face hurt and that his right arm was trapped beneath his body. Alarums rang faintly: he was hardly in a state to defend himself with his dirk-arm dead as stone.

He rolled over, grasping his right arm and carrying it across his abdomen. For several moments he lay quietly on his back, sorting out his senses; and then he remembered.

He stared blindly at the sky and damned Breadalbane.

He was still amidst Stewarts despite his MacDonald name; Robbie had not roused him from his stupor to send him back to his own fire. Around him lay clumps of plaid-wrapped Highlanders nestled in against the turf. One man snored dreadfully, while another murmured tender words not meant for others to hear.

Dair contemplated his state. He rarely drank overmuch, and usually when he did he went to sleep before causing much trouble. But whisky wore off; he always awoke too soon for sobriety, left dulled in wits and with a powerful desire to return immediately to the kind of leaden sleep that had won him his current afflictions: a pebble-pocked, turf-chilled face, and a wholly useless arm.

Dair worked the flesh of that arm, trying to rouse its responses without encouraging the discomfort that came with such a thing. But it came to spite him, and he gritted his teeth against the tingling; to take his mind from it he sat up slowly. His head remained attached, permitting him to view the encampment.

It was false dawn, illuminated by a raft of stars. With the fires died out to coals and the moon beginning to fade, there was little diffusion of starlight. He could see very clearly. Here and there gillies sat watch for their chiefs, but nearly everyone in camp was soundly asleep.

Dair glanced at the plaid-wrapped man closest to him. He saw little enough of the face, which was pressed into wool with a tartan edge fallen across one cheek, but he knew Robbie. He was boyish in slumber, stripped of the hardness that aged him.

He worked the arm again briefly, then gave up; he was now too awake, too restless to stay, and his mind too full of thoughts. He got up quietly and resettled a sagging plaid. He made his way carefully through scattered fires and clumps of men, lifting a hand in greeting and placation to watching gillies, and came at last to the Glencoe fire.

They were no different from Appin Stewarts or any number of other clans strewn throughout the encampment: men redolent of whisky, swaddled in tartan grave wrappings, snoring gently against the turf while the travesty of Achallader stared starkly down upon them.

Dair looked at the castle. *What did MacIain think, riding up to the ruins?* It was his father, as well as others, who had raided and razed Achallader, destroying all outbuildings and the braeside township. Dair supposed then there had been jubilation at depriving Campbells yet again of possessions they had, in the MacDonald view, unfairly gained; he supposed there was something of that again when MacIain came across Rannoch Moor to the wreckage he himself had caused. It would take more than Breadalbane's summons to peace to settle the Campbell-MacDonald feud.

Dair knew there were no regrets of the burning. There were never regrets when a MacDonald took back from Campbells what Campbells had won from others by their own insidious methods. And MacIain of Glencoe would be the last man on earth who might admit there could be.

I am not MacIain . . . will never be MacIain—Dair stumbled over an object, saw it was a corked, boiled-leather bottle, and retrieved it. He sat down with care, rearranged his plaid, then uncorked the bottle. There was little whisky left; he drained what there was, then set the bottle aside. In a matter of moments the new usquabae introduced itself to old, and he felt the slackness in his body that presaged welcome sleep.

He lay down against the turf and gave himself over to it, but it proved a contrary beast after all and remained at bay in the bleak darkness of his thoughts. He was aware within himself of the regret denied—or denied by—his father, if for a different reason; aware of desperation, that he might not get what he wanted; fully aware of fear that she would refuse it herself.

The plaid-wrapped bundle beside him stirred. Hoarfrosted hair, not much grayer now than his own, poked its way above a tartan shroud. Only the brow followed and let itself be seen; John MacDonald was not prepared to surrender sleep entirely, only a moment of it. " 'Tis settled, then?"

Dair sighed. Trust his brother to know what ailed him. "I dinna ken."

"There was some talk of it, aye? If you wanted to keep it secret from others, you and the lass might have picked another place."

There had been no choice. Keeping it secret had not been in their minds, because in that moment they had lost them entirely.

Uneasiness threaded his spirit. "Did MacIain see?"

"He was with Glengarry; there was more in their mouths than Catriona Campbell and Alasdair Og." John shifted against the ground, pulling the wool away from his face. "Is this why you want to break with Jean?"

"Christ, no—I barely kent who Cat was . . . well, I kent who she *was*—" *—had known for a long time—* "—but there was naught in it then." Dair sighed; whisky lulled him into confession. "Am I a fool?"

John's laugh was a soft gust of air, and not unkind. "All men are fools when there is a woman in it."

"Do *you* think I'm a fool?" It mattered very much.

"I love my wife," John said. "I am no' the man to ask."

Dair stirred restlessly. "MacIain would skelp me."

"Not once Mother has clutched his lug-hole and set him down before her."

Dair smiled. "Och, aye . . ." He squinted into starlight. "I told her something of it."

"Mother?—aye, well . . . she would have something to say, would she no'?"

"Little enough," Dair replied. "I expected more . . . but she said I wasna ready to hear it."

"Likely because you didna ken—*then*—what you wanted." John tugged his plaid more closely around his shoulders, exiling drafts. "Do you ken now?"

Desperately. "Oh, aye," Dair answered without hesitation, with a hard edge in his tone and a perfect certainty. "I ken it verra well. But there is Breadalbane in my way."

John's tone was neutral. "Aye. And a Stewart."

Dair shut his eyes. "Two."

Three

Governor John Hill, behind the new-built walls of Fort William, within his spare officer's quarters, received the caller with courtesy. He truly admired the Highlanders, no matter the tales told of their crudity, their barbarism, and it was always a pleasure to welcome one in to share a dram and pass an hour or two while they spoke of inconsequential things in place of reality.

But reality now had come; the man was a Cameron, a dusty, wind-ruffled Cameron of little style or consequence, and clearly reluctant to spend more time with the Sassenach soldier than was required. Even whisky had small appeal.

Hill welcomed him into his tiny private sitting room as the Highlander stripped off his bonnet, signalled the door to be shut so they might be alone, and offered usquabae by its Gaelic name as he waved his visitor to a chair. But the man refused the seat as well as the liquor. Lamplight sparked dully off a mud-smeared plaid brooch, weighting draped wool at one shoulder.

"I'm no' to stay," he said diffidently, clearly ill at ease as he gripped the doffed bonnet. "I'm to tell you what my laird says I should, that you'll ken the truth of it."

Hill, in the act of pouring a dram, froze. He set down the flagon and turned, aware abruptly of apprehension: his own, as well as the Highlander's.

A lad. Fifteen? Sixteen? Tall; I took him for a man . . . But he managed a smile, and did not drink the whisky. Nor did he sit. "Are you from Ewan Cameron, then?"

The Cameron bobbed his ruddy head. His eyes were set deep in hollowed sockets, bright and wary as a fox's. The bones of his face had not yet settled into manhood, but the line of the jaw was there, stubbled rusty red as his hair. "Cameron of Lochiel, aye," the boy confirmed. "I'm to tell you the laird isna so willing to treat after all. I'm to say: look to *Iain Glas.*"

Grey John, in Gaelic. Breadalbane. Hill's fears were coming to fruition. "Aye?" he asked cautiously.

The Cameron shifted awkwardly from bare foot to bare foot, plainly wanting to leave. "I'm to say: he no longer trusts the earl to deliver as he's promised. The silver. 'Tis yet in London, the earl says, but there is a tale told of most of it carried to Edinburgh, or Kilchurn."

"They are at Achallader," Hill said, chafing inwardly. "The lairds, and their tacksmen." As much as he detested Breadalbane for stealing his idea that the Highlands might be tamed with a treaty, he could not fault the earl's attempts to find a peaceful resolution. "Do you say they will not agree to any treaty?"

A single hitch of a plaid-draped shoulder: crimson field, cross-hatched boldly by black, and a narrow white stripe. "I'm to say: Lochiel of Cameron doubts the earl, as does MacDonald of Glengarry."

"And Glencoe," Hill murmured. He drew breath. It burned in his chest till he nearly choked on it. "Will you carry word to Lochiel that I mean to hold him to his agreement? That he has given me his willingness to consider the treaty, and to withdraw that willingness now could endanger the safety of the clans?"

He realized that despite the words he sounded too conciliatory; he should *tell*, not ask. But no man achieved success by telling the Highlanders anything. One asked, one hoped. One prayed.

The young Cameron worked the worn bonnet in grimy hands. Then he stopped and looked straightly at Hill. The spark of the plaid brooch was extinguished by the light burning in his eyes. "Look to your own safety."

Another man might arrest him and clap him in irons for such insolence before the king's governor. But Hill knew better. It was not insolence. It was truth, as far as any Highlander could recognize, or speak it.

"I thank you," Hill said, "for your honesty. Will you have us-quabae?"

The Cameron demurred. "I'm to go back at once, aye? To say what *you* have said."

"Aye." Hill managed a smile. "He is a man, your laird. Worth honoring."

The boy smiled. "Aye, I ken that!"

"And I." Knowing, as he opened the door so the young Highlander might leave, that he would have to find a way to impress upon such men as Ewan Cameron of Lochiel that the only safety he and anyone else, even this lad, might know lay in respecting the soldiers housed in the fort at Inverlochy.

The argument between the Earl of Breadalbane and the Laird of Glencoe brewed very briefly, then boiled over into steam-laden virulence. Cat, who had grown up amidst the verbal and physical battles of her brothers—had, in fact, been a frequent participant—was not taken aback by the birth of the argument, its noise, or the identity of the men involved, but by its bitterness. MacIain she knew all too well as a loud, argumentative man, but Breadalbane was not. She had never seen him angry, only icily disdainful when tested by Duncan's truculence. It astonished her to hear him cast back at the giant MacDonald such words as would infuriate even a temperate man.

She wondered ironically how many wagers were won or lost in that moment, and could almost hear the coins changing hands as other men became aware of the disagreement.

It was of brief duration, even as they stood in the looming ruins of MacDonald-razed Achallader. A tall, massive Gael swathed in plaid and hostility, while the shorter, slighter man wore the suit of a Sassenach as if shamed by his Highland birth despite his Highland titles.

And perhaps that is a part of it. . . . That, and the castle, and cows, and titles, and one hundred other slights they might manufacture between them, dredging up history to fling at one another: Campbell and Mac-Donald, enemies from the beginning. Born into an enmity they could only preserve, because to do otherwise was to defy their heritage.

Is that what we do? she wondered, thinking of Dair, of a fire, and the warmth springing up between them that had nothing to do with the coals, with the flames, or even with the music rousing the blood and the bones. *Do we defy what we are, mock our heritage—*

"Well," said Duncan, coming up beside her. " 'Tis of some comfort to me to see him lose his temper. No matter the provocation, he always turned it aside."

She cast him a sidelong glance. "Which made you provoke all the more."

Duncan smiled slyly. "Which you do gey well yourself, aye?—with *me.*"

"And you deserving of it." Content with the exchange, they grinned inanely at one another; united against his father, they were in perfect accord.

But the momentary pleasure faded. With a final exchange of insults—Breadalbane's hissed, MacIain's roared—the giant turned on his heel and strode down the hill into the gathered crowd, plaid swinging, shouting for his MacDonalds to ready themselves at once to leave the foul stink of Campbell lands and lairds.

Neither Cat nor Duncan smiled now. They watched the MacDonald, head and shoulders above others, as he made his way brusquely toward the fire she and Dair had shared, albeit briefly, while discoveries were made of such things as attraction against and in spite of all that was proper in their separate worlds.

"No treaty," Duncan said on a note of satisfaction. "He'll no' have Glencoe after all, agreeing to be bought."

"Bought?" Cat echoed incredulously. "Did he think he could?"

He slanted her a look of scathing disdain. "What d'ye think he came for? To buy off all the clans so they turn their backs on Jamie, and Willie can have his war.''

She eyed MacIain's retreat uneasily; would the son echo the father's fury? "I've heard they've built that fort at Inverlochy . . . and put guns there, and soldiers. And boats on the loch.''

Duncan's mouth twisted. "He'll tell them all 'tis naught. He'll tell them all 'tis only MacIain, a pawkie cattle-lifter, and jolly them back into seeing things his way.''

"Not MacIain." She was certain.

"No," Duncan agreed without argument. "Nor likely Glengarry, I've heard. They'll no' put their names on any treaty. But the others will. Or they'd be leaving, too." He looked beyond her, beyond his father. Something bloomed in his eyes, setting color to his face. "Aye," he whispered. *"Aye*—in the confusion, who would ken?''

Cat frowned. "What?''

He was tense as a hunting hound, nearly trembling with it. "Now," he said. " 'Tis the best time, aye? While the MacDonalds gather their garrons . . .''

"Duncan—''

But he was away at once, running gracelessly across the rocky ground on some errand of his own.

A massive foot well planted kicked Dair into wakefulness. "Up!" a voice roared. "Ye shame me, aye?—asleep like a drukken man here in Campbell lands!''

Dair roused at once, if catching his breath at the shock of it, and answered the tone and the thunder as well as the foot.

"Up!" MacIain repeated, moustaches bristling as he loomed like a demon from out of folktales, eyes glittering beneath the white shelf of brows.

Behind him lurked his gillies, faces blanked by a diplomacy Dair might have appreciated had he the time to think. The giant scowled fiercely at all the MacDonalds gathering now, some waking blearily, gathering puddles of plaid, while others, alarmed, put their hands to weaponry.

"I'll no' have my MacDonalds drink another dram of his whisky, nor set tooth to his cattle, aye?—we are quit of this place! Faugh! No more of Campbell courtesy; best ye look to yon castle to ken what they're owed!''

Dair caught his breath, stung by shame at such dishevelment and unreadiness before MacIain. They were all of them gathered now, all the Glencoe-men. Bonnets were pulled on hastily over tousled locks spiky from sleep, weapons sorted out about various persons, garrons brought up in answer to the laird's gillies, who saw efficiently to the ordering of his tail and of his things.

Beside Dair, John resettled and pinned his plaid. "Breadalbane," he said simply, in eloquent explanation.

"The pawkie bastard!" MacIain spat. "No more of him, d'ye hear? I'll none o' his lies, none o' his promises, none o' his Sassenach ways." He jerked his massive head. "We're home to Glencoe, and none of this liar's oath. . . . I dinna trust the man, and I dinna trust his treaty." Fierce blue eyes fixed avidly on his youngest son. A hand cuffed smartly. "Alasdair Og! You spoke to the bastard and said none o' it to me!"

No, he had not. He had thought only of Cat and later of Robbie, not of MacIain at all.

The abused ear stung as he staggered under the blow, catching his balance gracelessly against rocky soil and the impediments of straggling plaid, but he made no protest, not to the one man who had a right to beat him bloody if he chose.

"Get on your garron," MacIain said. "We're home to Glencoe."

There was Cat—was Cat— *"Wait—"* In desperation, but the giant had turned away; was bellowing at his gillies.

John caught his arm. "Alasdair—no. Not now, aye? He's had words wi' the earl this morning, and no good come of them. Let him bide a wee . . . and if you didna say aught to him of speech with the earl, 'tis no wonder he is angry."

Dair had bitten his tongue. He tasted blood in his mouth. Anger, kindled by humiliation, flared abruptly. "Christ, but I'm no' a fool nor a bairn to be treated this way—"

"Why not?" John asked as he scooped up bonnet and bottle. "Even a drukken man kens 'tis better to go to his laird with such news as speech with Breadalbane." Then his expression softened. "Think, man. She's a Campbell . . . and the earl's kin, aye?—you'd do better to let MacIain settle before you think on her again."

"I canna ride off with no word to her!"

John's glance went beyond Dair. "You'd better," he answered succinctly, slapping the boiled-leather bottle against his brother's chest. "Or risk worse than a cuff of the man."

Awake in the dawn, and alone, Jean Stewart stared into the pallor of the day and cursed herself for her folly. Her eyes burned for staring so hard, so fixedly at distance, but she neither shut nor blinked them. She would hide behind nothing, not even the fragile shielding of her own flesh.

She was a woman who knew men, because they were, to her, the only thing in the world worth knowing. Most women she disdained, save those she was required to deal with, such as Lady Glencoe and John's wife, Eiblin. Women did not offer the same diversions as men, the same culmination to the dance, save a momentary competition that ended the moment she gave a man leave to pay his favors to her in place of anyone else. And they did pay favors, at once and fully consumed with it, forgetting immediately the other women, their lasses, whose spite and anger and bitterness Jean did not credit as anything more than impotence: they were not as she, were they, in beauty or in bed.

She did not wholly blame them. She would be jealous, also, if a woman stole her man.

But now? No woman; Jean was certain. There were signs in a man of distraction, of interest snooving elsewhere, and Dair showed none of them. What he showed was indifference, and a different man withal, someone growing apart from her. Someone very like the man he had been that day he came with Robbie to Castle Stalker, offering nothing of himself save a name, a smile, and casual courtesy, no spark in his eyes for her beyond a momentary acknowledgment that he saw the beauty, yet was not blinded by it. Thus it had been her task, her doing, to lure from him the same manner of attraction and need other men felt when they saw her.

She had won him, eventually. And kept him far longer than intended. Six years, if counted altogether, six years with one man.

To Jean, there was only one thing worth such fidelity. From him she had it in full measure, and returned it willingly; or as often began it. But there had been no oath. No declaration before witnesses. No proper handfasting, making them wed in the sight of others until there was a minister who could marry them in God's eyes.

He has not once offered, nor asked. And now he had packed his own kit. Had withstood her blandishments, the lure of her body; even the insistence of her hand, that knew how to work a man. Had turned his back on her and walked out into darkness, wanting nothing of her, clearly, save to be away.

She burned with shame, with anger. Who was he to treat her so? How dared he suggest in any fashion that she did not, could not, rouse him?

Jean stilled abruptly. She had said it to him plainly, too plainly, perhaps: twenty-five, she said, admitting her age. Was she too old for him?

Have I lost my beauty? Had she, in complacence, in neglect, damped the fire between them?

Dair owned no mirror; she had used his eyes, and those of other men, to know her appeal. But those eyes were gone, and the others of men who rode to Achallader with MacIain, and the glass she used otherwise was home at Castle Stalker.

"Lady Glencoe," she murmured. "The mirror MacIain gave her, brought back from France."

A small mirror, a lady's mirror, meant to hang from a cord around a woman's waist. It would do.

Jean Stewart got out of Dair's bed and began to dress herself. By the time the sun was up she would look into the mirror and know again if she had won, or if she had lost.

Cat stared after Duncan, then looked beyond to the hoof-churned dust clouding the air, the detritus of departure.

MacIain was leaving. And taking with him all of his men, including his youngest son.

'*Come with me,*' he had said. '*Come home with me to Glencoe.*' He had meant it. She was certain. She knew little of men save her brothers, her drunkard father and ambitious Breadalbane, but Dair MacDonald had never offered her anything save honesty and kindness.

Their enmity was banished. They had buried it between them by the fire the night before, in the skirl of *ceol mor* snooving into hearts and souls to root out the bone-bred hostility of Campbell and MacDonald—

And Robbie Stewart in the moonlight, speaking to her of his sister waiting for Dair in Glencoe.

Cat caught her breath, recollection shattered as abruptly and irreparably as her mother's mirror. That Dair had replaced.

But Robbie Stewart was there yet, laughing at her in the darkness with bare feet planted and wide shoulders thrown back, the thick column of his throat rising inviolable from summer-soiled linen.

His sister in Glencoe. And Dair inviting *her*.

Stewart had made it plain: '*A man might look, and a man might ask, and a man might take what is offered . . . but it doesna mean he will put the woman in his home out of his bed while he woos another into his plaid while he is out on the heather.*'

What did Dair mean to do? Set them at odds, her and Jean, and bed the winner? Grief rose up, and bitterness. It hurt so badly she choked. "Pawkie bastard," she said. "God-cursed, pawkie bastard." But even in her bitterness, even in her shame, Cat could not be certain which man she meant. It applied to all of them, equally: Breadalbane. Robert Stewart. And to Dair MacDonald.

Around John and Dair the tacksmen gathered, forming MacIain's tail. It was for his sons to do as well, with no protest uttered. The laird himself, incongruous on his small garron, was setting out already. It was expected everyone else of Glencoe would follow immediately. Their only loyalty lay with their laird.

Certainly not with a Campbell, be she woman or no.

It was bitterly painful. "John—"

"Dinna do it, Alasdair."

"I can catch up."

"No." John grasped his arm again and jerked him back roughly. "Christ, man, I ken what you're feeling—but would you shame him before them all? Before Breadalbane?"

"I canna just *go*—"

"If she has any sense at all, she'll ken what has happened."

She had sense, aye. And wit. And the tongue to use it. But she *was* a Campbell, and deserving of explanation lest she believe him lying to her.

A gillie brought up two garrons. John took the reins and thrust one set into Dair's hands. "Dinna be a fool," he snapped, and swung up onto his mount with a flare of kilt and plaid. "You are MacIain's son."

It was honor or indictment, depending on one's view. Bitterly Dair arranged his reins and hurled himself onto the garron's back, not caring of the disarray in plaid and kilt, nor the testiness of his head. The bottle was empty; he tossed it toward a gillie. "I'll go to Chesthill," he declared. "Into Glenlyon's lands, if 'tis what it takes."

John's mouth jerked flat. "He hanged you once," he said. "Will you give him a second chance?"

Before Dair could answer, the heir to all of Glencoe set his garron after their father. But John knew nothing of temptation, nothing of the conflict, the desperate, newborn yearning. His Eiblin was home in Glencoe. Cat Campbell was here, with the earl.

Dair slammed bare heels into the garron's ribs so hard the animal started in surprise. "Christ," he muttered viciously, "he'll have me castrated, aye?—so as not to soil his seed with the taint of Campbell blood!"

MacIain, his son knew, could spill Campbell blood. But he would not welcome it as a woman, and Breadalbane's niece, in MacDonald lands.

Cat stood at the remains of the MacDonald fire. Burned-out now, burned to ash in the daylight, as impotent as her anger. But she did not doubt buried beneath was a glimmer of ember that could be coaxed to kindle again into flame, even as her anger might flare again into grief.

'Come home with me to Glencoe.'

They were gone, the MacDonalds, vacating Achallader and the

promise of peace. Breadalbane had his treaty, though lacking two signatures.

Cat looked up. *Just* gone, the MacDonalds, so recently departed they left dust in their wake, settling now to the ground, drifting on the draft of air caused by hasty horses.

She could see naught of them save the glint of their weaponry, the colors of their tartan bleeding together into distance. And heard the piping of *ceol mor* fit to raise the spirits of men setting out to war.

A single horse, abruptly, burst free of the encampment, scattering clansmen who, in their startlement, damned the rider to hell. And then Cat saw it was not a single rider, but two on one horse; and the one riding pillion clutched the man in the saddle while her lank yellow hair tumbled down around her shoulders.

Marjorie Campbell of Lawers. And Duncan in the saddle, riding hastily after MacDonalds.

Or not *after* them, as an enemy. Nor to join them as a friend. But to appear as two tardy MacDonalds riding hard to catch up to the others.

How better a way to elope with a woman underneath the imperious nose of the man most definitively opposed?

"Oh, Duncan," Cat murmured, watching the flag of Marjorie's hair. And then she began to grin. *"Aye,"* she said, laughing, "Poke a stick in his eye for us both!"

But the laughter died away as Duncan abruptly hesitated, reining in frenziedly as a mounted MacDonald wheeled and broke free of the others. The confrontation was immediate—and as immediately dismissed. The lone MacDonald, no woman riding pillion, came at full gallop toward the ash-clotted fire. Beyond him Duncan went on with Marjorie clinging still.

She knew the eyes, the face; loved the bonnie grin, with white teeth a'gleaming.

He scalped himself of his bonnet and tossed it to her even as he reined the gape-mouthed garron to a haphazard halt. "No proper Scot goes out without his bonnet," he declared. "I'll be back for it, aye?"

And left her standing there in the dust of his delivery, clutching the hostage bonnet as he spun the garron around and galloped back again toward his father.

Home, to Glencoe.

On the thirtieth day of June in the year 1691, according to the copy John Hill read repeatedly, all save two of the lairds meeting with Breadalbane signed the Treaty of Achallader. It was but a temporary measure, the governor knew, and would not result in the lasting peace

King William desired. What it did, in fact, was give credit to Breadal-bane for bringing about the very thing Hill had argued for—but also time in which such men as the Master of Stair, who was with the king in Flanders, to prepare for rebellion.

The balance was delicate, too delicate for Scotland. In ignorance, a foreign-born king sought to use such men against those he perceived as enemy; in full knowledge, men such as Stair, as Breadalbane sought to pervert the strength, the wild and stubborn courage that defined Scotland's heart.

Hill knew he had failed. It was a matter of time before he was removed; he suspected his appointment would last only so long as Stair and Breadalbane paid lip service to peace.

Unless they expect me to carry out their depredations.

It was not a new thought. He was a disposable man with no connec-tions of any substance, no familial grace. He could die in the High-lands and no one would know—or he could kill in the Highlands, and have his name cursed forever.

He looked again at the copy of the treaty sent the day before. Simple words of complex promise, and signatures that bound souls. But only so long as such men as Coll MacDonald of Keppoch and Robert Stew-art of Appin, intemperate and arrogant both, agreed to be bound by empty promises and equally empty purses.

MacIain had sworn nothing, nor had Glengarry. And Ewan Cam-eron of Lochiel, thinking twice and thrice, had withdrawn his support.

They would honor no conditions. To them, there was no treaty. It gave them the freedom to do as they would, and would in fact create the reason for William to levy such punishment as he desired.

As he was *told* to desire, by Stair and Breadalbane.

The blow, when it came, split his lip, cracked a tooth, and set Dair's head to ringing even as he staggered. Sunlight filled his vision, too much sunlight all at once, and then the second blow landed with enough selective force to knock him off his feet. He measured his length on the ground, aware vaguely of a rock grinding into his spine, but more aware of the silence surrounding him save for his father's breathing.

He had expected it. He had known from the moment he decided to risk the hasty delivery of his bonnet what the result would be. So he did not immediately rise again but sat up slowly, blinking away the shards of blackness floating in his vision.

Dair discovered his nose was bleeding sluggishly. He spat out blood as well as a piece of tooth and chanced a glance at his father.

The imperious gesture from outstretched hand brooked no hesitation. Dair got to his feet.

"Are you contrite?" MacIain asked.

A wise man might say aye. But Dair was not so much unwise as he was honest. "I am not."

"Fool," MacIain declared and knocked him down again.

Dair might have preferred the punishment in private, but its cause was not a private matter. He had defied his father before all of the others, and thus they were entitled to witness the beating so they might understand even a laird's son was subject to punishment when he transgressed MacIain's wishes.

There was no shame in it, no humiliation. Dair might have wished it otherwise, but accepted the consequences. It was a duty to accept without question the discipline of his laird, as any other MacDonald would accept whatever the laird decreed.

He also might have wished MacIain's fists were smaller.

Dair rolled painfully onto a hip and shoulder and spat again. Whisky would clean the cuts. Time would heal them. For the moment, he had to suffer whatever his father meted out.

"Up," MacIain said.

Dair hesitated a moment, then got to his feet again. He was aware of all the eyes, but no man made a sound save beyond the clink of metal and tumbled stone as he shifted against the wind.

Beneath thick brows, MacIain's eyes glittered. "Were you a lad, I'd skelp you," he said. "I'd raise such weals on your arse you'd not sit for half a month. But you're a man grown, aye?—and you make your own decisions. Even when ye ken what the result will be."

Dair held his silence; it was expected of him. But he was supremely aware of everyone who watched, including his mother. They had come home to Glencoe from Breadalbane's Achallader folly, and the public punishment of Alasdair Og was the first order of business.

Cat herself was not the primary reason for punishment, nor was her identity. That he had left his father's tail to return, however briefly, to Breadalbane's encampment was tantamount to treason, and worth a skelping. But his behavior, if not the beating, would cause talk regardless, and word would go around that the laird's youngest son had eyes for a Campbell lass.

To Glencoe lasses, it was insult. In that lay more punishment, that he dared to waste himself on a Campbell when there were MacDonald women.

Dair grimaced. *And meanwhile a Stewart in my bed . . .* He had looked for Jean as the first blow fell. Surely she would be there. Unless she had slipped away as soon as the beating began, desiring an explanation of his own mouth instead from those of others.

He would sooner take the beating than explain the truth to Jean. And that, Dair knew, was the true punishment.

"Faugh!" MacIain, in deep disgust, turned on his heel. It was the signal; those who had gathered began to disperse, men meeting wives, lads meeting lasses, children reunited with the clansmen all come home. Even John deserted him, catching Young Sandy into his arms as he walked back with black-haired Eiblin toward the house he had built.

It left Dair, and his mother. Who waited until all were gone, then came to him in silence with linen for his face.

When he was clean, when he could manage the smile against the pain in his head, he offered it to her freely: twisted wry a little, acknowledging his folly.

"Here," she said. "There is more, aye?" And took the soiled linen, gently blotting away the last of the blood. She eyed him critically, " 'Tis stopping on its own. Will you come in, then?"

He looked beyond her to the house in which his parents lived; in which he and John had lived until building their own dwellings down the glen a way. "I'll go to Jean," he said. "I owe her an explanation."

His mother's callused hand brushed the hair back from his face. "Jean is gone, Alasdair."

The words were wholly foreign. "Gone?" Dair echoed.

Lady Glencoe's eyes—his own her legacy—were kind. "Come into the house with me, and I'll tell you why."

It gave Cat immense pleasure to explain to the earl what had become of his heir. She was not at first certain he understood a word, so concerned was he with other matters, and so she repeated the heart of the issue: Duncan Campbell was gone, and with him Marjorie.

She did not tell Breadalbane immediately upon the departure of the lovers, choosing instead to hoard the knowledge so Duncan would have opportunity to get as far from his father as possible before pursuit was levied, and when she did at last tell Breadalbane she did so collectedly, admitting no knowledge of the moment of elopement.

"And so I am shamed," she said dutifully, standing beside the fire the earl's gillie tended. What Sandy thought she did not know, but a flicker in blue eyes betrayed his private amusement.

The earl finished his task, folding and sealing several sheets of parchment, then putting them away into a leather wallet. It was the treaty, she knew, signed by the others earlier in the wake of Mac-Donald departure. Cat wondered how much of the general acquiescence came from a desire to poke a stick at MacIain, who inspired tremendous loyalty and equally marked dislike.

"Shamed," Breadalbane murmured. "But not particularly despondent, if one marks your tone." His gray eyes were opaque as he looked up at her at last. "If anything, somewhat cheerful for a woman so insulted."

Cat smiled serenely. *Let him make what he will of it.*

"Aye, well . . . he will come back sooner rather than later, when his silver runs out." He rose and tugged his English suit into order. "We'll have you wed yet. In the meantime—"

"In the meantime, let me go home," she said. "Let me tend my broken heart among people who care for me."

"And do you think I, his father and your kinsman, do not care?"

"Oh, aye," she answered promptly. "For the things—and people—you need."

The ice of his eyes thawed. There was, for the first time, a hint of humor in the shape of the earl's mouth. "You would be wasted on Duncan."

That, she knew. "Then I may go home?"

"For now," he agreed. "I must go first to London, then to the king in Flanders. But you need not despair; you will be a countess yet."

Cat laughed. "Do you think it will be so simple a thing to bring him back? He is your son; he may have grown a spine at last."

" 'Tis possible," he acceded. "And it may be that John becomes earl in his brother's place. That would not displease me."

She had known that. Everyone knew that, even Duncan. Especially Duncan.

"But you would still be a countess," Breadalbane said.

It made no sense. "John is wed already."

The humor, now, was more marked. "But I am not dead yet."

"No, but—" And then she knew. She understood at once. "I will *not!*"

For the first time in her life she saw the earl smile. "I am desolate," he said dryly, "to know I am held in such low repute. You must be the only lass in all of Scotland who would spurn my wealth."

"You," she said in shock and equal parts horror. It was all she could manage.

"I've buried three wives," he said. "I wouldna mind another."

"To bury?"

Indeed, the ice of his eyes had thawed. "*Wasted* on Duncan . . . but a worthy match for me, aye?—and one your father would welcome."

What did one say to a man so powerful, the man who ruled the Highlands? One who understood so well the working of a mind, and certainly her father's.

"It would be worth it," Breadalbane said, "to see MacDonald's face."

Illumination. *"That* is why," she blurted.

He took the cup of whisky extended by his gillie. "Among other things."

John Hill set down the quill and capped the inkhorn. His hand shook as he did so; his health yet again deteriorated. He took off the spectacles, set them aside, and rubbed at hollowed sockets to ease the tension away. So much responsibility—

The knock at the door was diffident, as if the aide suspected the governor might be asleep. But Hill had not blown out a lamp before midnight for too many evenings, and raised his voice in permission to enter.

The aide came into the light, features severe. "That Scot," he said. "I've told him to wait until morning, sir. He has the effrontery to decline."

'That Scot' could apply to anyone. "Which Scot?" Hill asked mildly.

"The boy. The Cameron boy. He says he bears a message, sir. Shall I tell him again to wait?"

Hill tensed. "Have him in at once."

"Sir." The aide saluted crisply and shut the door. A moment later he returned, gesturing the "Cameron boy" to present himself to the governor.

It was as Hill suspected: Ewan Cameron's lad, bonnet doffed and rusty hair mussed. His jaw, as before, was stubbled. Hill rose. "Come in." He gestured for the aide to leave them alone.

The boy was hollow-cheeked and gaunt. Either he grew too fast for the food he ate, or there was not enough. "I am come with a message," he said huskily. "The laird has said you're a fair man withal, despite your Sassenach ways."

It was an admission Hill found gratifying as well as surprising. "I believe we are all the same in the Lord's eyes," he said. "Sassenach and Highlander; God makes no judgment of names or birth."

"You've guns on the walls," the boy said bluntly. "And boats off the Isles."

"And soldiers in the heather, and a patrol boat on Loch Linnhe," Hill elaborated. He put out a hand to steady himself against his writing desk.

The boy saw it. "I'll sit," he said, as if understanding that Hill offered unprecedented respect by not seating himself in his presence.

"This bench will do, aye?" And hooked it over from the wall with a bare foot, though he did not sit at once.

The governor seated himself. This was nothing like the meeting they had shared but three weeks before. "How may I help you?"

"I've a message from Lochiel, though not of his making." The young man reached into his scrip and pulled forth a crumpled paper. " 'Twas sent to him, aye?—from Charles Edwards. Dundee's chaplain."

Viscount Dundee was dead two years, killed at Killiecrankie even as victory was assured. That his chaplain saw fit now to write Lochiel was indeed news, and possibly distressing in view of the fact Lochiel sent word of it to William's governor.

Hill accepted the letter as the Highlander sat down upon the bench. He did not read it immediately. "Do you know what it concerns?"

The grin was quick and fleeting, but wholly disarming. "I'm the laird's son, aye?—he does tell me what he's about."

Lochiel's *son*. There was more to the message, then, than simple courtesy. "Will you tell me?" Hill invited. It was a mark of confidence to trust the Cameron's word, rather than reading in his presence.

It satisfied. Ewan Cameron's boy smiled again, but it faded away too quickly into an unwonted severity at odds with his features. "Edwards says the promises made at Achallader mean naught. That Breadalbane intends to ruin the clans, and the lies of indemnity are part of it."

Hill drew in a shallow breath; it hurt too much to breathe deeply. "It is not indemnity," he said. "It is a truce only, an agreement lasting until October." Two months left. Only two months.

The boy agreed. "I ken that. 'Tis part of the plan, aye?"

"Then Lochiel is certain the earl plots deceit?"

"Breadalbane serves himself, no' the Highlands. The letter says the Pope has given King James silver; we would do better, my father says, to trust the word of Dundee's man than the word of Breadalbane."

It struck Hill as ironic that the Highlanders would disparage Catholics while accepting that their Stuart king was one, as well as Papist coin. But they were nothing if not realistic. It was, after all, an identical attitude that had shaped Breadalbane.

Hill looked at the crumpled letter in his hands. Idly he smoothed it, grooming the creases away. "Why does he send word to me?"

"Because you have guns on the walls and boats off the Isles," came the prompt and obvious answer. "And soldiers in the heather, and a patrol boat on Loch Linnhe."

He smiled at the boy; bald honesty. This lad and his father were not of Breadalbane's house. "Tell Lochiel I am grateful."

The laird's son rose. "He said you're a fair man, aye?—and deserving to ken the truth of what is said of Achallader.'' He nodded at the letter. "He's sent it to all, ye ken. Edwards. To all the chiefs and lairds.''

Stunned, Hill pushed to his feet. *"This* has been sent? To everyone?''

Lochiel's son nodded, perplexed by the reaction.

Hill's breath ran fast. "May God in Heaven have mercy on us all . . .'' His lips were dry; he had not drunk usquabae. "Tell your father— tell him I am grateful. And tell him also that if he has word with others, it might behoove the clans to put no trust in this letter.''

Deep-set eyes narrowed. "He was Dundee's man. His chaplain.''

It was warning, and Hill accepted it as such. "I understand,'' he said. "But if there is to be a truce, no matter the duration, there must first be trust. Whatever you think of the earl, he must be given a chance.''

He had lost the boy's respect. That was blatantly clear in the arrogant posture.

"Wait—'' Hill took a step toward the young Cameron; he did not know why it was so important the boy understand, but it was. "You must see it . . . you must understand—''

"I've brought it,'' the boy said, and turned to the door. "You must do as ye will.''

Indictment in the words. Hill tried once more. "I have no power,'' he said, "but in the orders of my king. And he is not yours.''

"I ken that,'' the Cameron declared.

Hill put a trembling hand on the boy's arm. It was stiff beneath his touch, rigid as wood. A Sassenach touched a Highlander. "If any chief acts on this letter, the treaty is nullified. And the orders I am given may not be kindly ones.'' He gripped the arm more tightly. "You serve your father,'' he said, "and I serve my king. It is duty. It is honor. *No matter what I may prefer.''*

Four

*B*readalbane likened it to a meeting of royalty, save neither of them were kings. They were merely men, and Scots, but the power of a realm was theirs. It was he who fashioned the future, he and the Master of Stair; between them they would determine who died, and who survived.

The preliminaries were over. King William had been apprised of Breadalbane's Achallader Treaty, though details were not mentioned; William, despite his ancestry, was no true Scot and understood little of them. He need be told nothing but what their efforts wrought, he and Stair, so the Dutchman could yea or nay them. Could extend his royal blessing.

Flanders, the earl felt, was no more congenial than the Highlands, with autumn approaching. But the room was warmer, as was Stair's welcome.

Sir James Dalrymple, Master of Stair, was now Secretary of Scotland and sole possessor of the position. Stair was much in favor with the king, and Breadalbane, who disliked the Lowland Scot for his pretentious manner of speaking as well as other faults, nonetheless admired him for securing a place so close to the king. While he himself labored in Scotland, Stair walked the halls of Parliament and of Kensington Palace. Just now he was in Approbaix, accompanying the king.

They sat near a mullioned window, full in the light of a fading sunset. Each held a fine Venetian glass filled with brandywine. Stair was a short man but fleshy, with small dark eyes. The preposterous wig he wore was not in proportion to his size, and gave him, Breadalbane felt, the look of an imbecile. Until one heard his words.

"We will have to give them something," Stair said quietly, swirling brandywine in his glass. "I know enough of Highlanders to be certain they will demand payment for anything approaching peace."

Breadalbane, himself Highland-born, forbore to answer.

"If we are to expect them to come forward of their own volition and accept King William as sovereign in place of James, we must promise them something." Stair looked at his visitor. "You are a Highlander. What is your suggestion of a thing they will value, and count it worth the doing?"

The earl sipped meticulously, then carried the glass away. Less robust than whisky, the liquor nonetheless warmed him. "Silver," he said succinctly, and added other conditions as Stair gestured impatience.

"Time for consideration, for travel in poor weather. And indemnities."

"Against what?"

"Past crimes," he answered easily. "The clans are riddled with thieves and murderers, and as many of them are chiefs as they are loyal tacksmen. 'Tis the lairds and chiefs we must appeal to; the others will follow them."

"Very well. Money. Time. Indemnities." Stair looked out the window. The setting sun painted his sallow face gilt and gold. "Twelve thousand pounds sterling to the landowners, thus lifting from the chiefs their need to support such men. A pardon of such things as we warrant are crimes, so no man may be hanged in his effort to sign the Oath of Allegiance. And a Proclamation of Indemnity, pardoning even the worst of the offenders, under the Great Seal of the King."

Breadalbane smiled appreciation.

"Post it at the Mercat Cross of Edinburgh, and copies in such other burghs as will be appropriate." The Secretary of Scotland tapped an idle fingernail against Venetian glass. "They shall have through the end of the year to make good their faith. They are to understand that if they fail to come forth and sign the Oath of Allegiance by the first of the new year, the pardon shall expire, and any man withholding himself shall be punished to the utmost extremity of the law." He looked blandly at the earl. "Will this be sufficient?"

It was opportunity, and Breadalbane took it. "For a wise man, aye."

After a moment of silence, Stair nodded comprehension. "*Un*wise men can be troublesome. Therefore, it may be necessary to prove to the clans the full measure of our power and the seriousness of our intent." He pursed his lips. "One must provide an example to others not as certain of the wisdom of their course."

The earl's answer was judicious, but no less telling for its diplomacy. "Surely hesitation or delay must be construed as treason, and punished accordingly."

Stair did not smile, though something of amusement glinted briefly in dark eyes. "And who among them, in your experience, is the least likely to be wise?"

The answer was obvious, and as easily declared. "MacDonalds," the earl said. "MacIain, of Glencoe."

MacIain's huge hand closed on his son's shoulder. Dair winced. "Aye," the father said, "you'd do well to recall it. I'll have you do as I say, aye?—not pleasing yourself where Breadalbane might see."

The pressure increased, then relaxed. It was a squeeze of affection, not punishment. "Aye," Dair said, "but I wasna thinking of the earl just at that moment—"

"No. That Campbell bizzem . . ." But MacIain amended it as he sat down at the table across from his son. "Lass," he said. "What is her name?"

Dair tensed. "Catriona. Cat."

"Cat." MacIain raised his silver-rimmed glass, brought from Paris years before, and downed his whisky.

He had defeated his youngest at chess but moments before and was in good humor. They inhabited the fine stone house at Carnoch companionably, with Lady Glencoe across the glen at Achtriachtan to visit her grandson, Young Sandy. It was dusk, and the lamps were lighted, lending an ocherous wash to the wood-panelled room.

"Jean was a likely lass," MacIain observed blandly, as if he moved a pawn.

Dair recognized the gambit and refused to play. Instead he poured his glass full again and drank his own usquabae.

Yet idly: "Will ye go and fetch her back?"

"I will not."

"You have before. Or she's come for you." MacIain set down his glass. " 'Tis something to have a lass like that in your bed."

"I will go to her," Dair explained with commendable mildness, "to tell her this parting is for good. I owe her that much, aye?"

"And will you tell her of the Campbell bizzem?" This time MacIain did not amend the term.

"She kens it already," Dair said, while the whisky churned in his belly. "There was a question, my mother said, of looking into a mirror . . . but I had carried it to Cat. And Jean learned of it."

"From your mother." In the awkward silence the sound of his father's inhalation was loud. "That French mirror?"

Dair flicked a wary glance at the huge man. "She gave it freely to me, when I told her the tale." He drank the remains of his whisky and set the cup down with a thump of finality. "We are much to blame for their losses."

"Whose losses? Campbell losses? Faugh!" The idle curiosity bled away from MacIain's tone. "They've lifted enough of MacDonalds over the years. Dinna spill so many tears for them, Alasdair!"

"She would spit in your face as soon as cry," Dair said plainly. "You'll no' blame her for her father's foolishness."

"I will do as I will," MacIain said softly. "As you will do as I say."

The bruises had faded, save for one upon his jaw that still smudged sickly yellow. The split lip was healed, and the broken tooth caused him no pain. But Dair recalled very well the thundering in his head after his father was done with his skelping.

"You have an heir," he said. "And *he* has an heir. What am I but another body?"

MacIain's teeth showed briefly in the thicket of beard and moustaches. "By *my* body, ye ken? Flesh of my flesh, blood of my blood, bone of my bone . . . 'tis my seed gave you life."

Dair waited tensely. He did not know what he would do until his father set him to it.

MacIain reached into his scrip and took from it a crumpled letter. He unfolded it and put it onto the table, spreading the paper flat beneath massive hands. " 'Tis from Dundee's man, Edwards. A word to the wise, ye ken?—that we are not to put trust in Breadalbane."

Dair's breath stilled.

"I dinna doubt he kens 'tis not a warning *Glencoe* is in need of, aye?—but 'tis appreciated all the same. Confirmation, Alasdair. There's no good to come of that treaty." With care and precision, he folded the paper again. "I fear mischief from no man so much as the Earl of Breadalbane."

Dair's palms were damp.

One massive hand lingered over the chess game, closed upon the queen. "You are my son," the deep voice rumbled. "Blood of my blood, bone of my bone—and you will do whatever is necessary to impede the earl's game."

Wind blew down the moor, luring hair from leather binding. Beneath Cat the garron shook its head, perplexed by what it viewed as annoying indecision; for her there was no indecision, merely patience, uncharacteristic patience, as the memory overtook her.

—*images*—

And sounds. Smells. The overwhelming fear. Her own as well as his.

Cat let it play out as the wind gusted in her face: images, sounds, and smells, the recollection of fear so great it nearly broke her soul—then at last dismounted and left the garron to wander in its idle pursuit of forage.

She was barefoot in the summer, as most Highlanders. She strode across terrain hazardous to those unaccustomed to its sly hostilities, and climbed the swelling crown to the twisted scepter atop it. Here the wind was braver, whipping at hair and skirts. Cat let it have its way as she studied the tree, marking its wracked shape and naked, barren roots upthrust from pockets of turf, knotted and twined against the soil like an ornate Celt-made brooch.

She moved beneath the tree, stood below one sturdy branch. Shut her eyes against the daylight, against the insidious sun, and imagined herself Dair MacDonald with a rope around his neck.

The rope that yet hung from the twisted branch, sliced in two by one sweep of her father's claymore.

She let wind and memory take her, lost in conjuration. For her it was not difficult; she had always been able to summon stories within her head, such as the braw and bonnie prince on his way to rescue his lass . . .

—with silver in his hair, and white teeth a'gleaming—

Her eyes sprang open. Without thought for the doing of it, with no deference to her skirts, she turned and mounted the tree, then clambered up its branches. When she could reach the knot she drew from her belt the dirk she had brought and, with grim determination, cut the rope from the branch.

It fell. From her perch above the ground, she gazed down upon it. A coil of faded hemp, half-hidden against the turf.

With less grace and nothing of dignity, she climbed down again. Her body betrayed her in womanhood; she had lost the ease of girlhood when she had no breasts, no hips. Skirts caught, tore. An ankle banged a branch. Hair caught in the twigs. But she was free at last, and jumped to the ground.

Memories crowded afresh. A body, there, spilling blood from an opened throat . . . The knot of Campbell men serving her father's interests, through which she had fought her way shouting the Campbell slogan . . . Another body, more meat on the tree, until it was taken down and replaced with another MacDonald.

No blood now . . . No bodies left to rot. From Glencoe had come MacDonalds to bear home their Campbell-killed men.

Cat sat down upon the turf. From the scrip lifted from her father's things, she took two items and placed them on the ground.

Rope. Mirror. Bonnet. All she had of him.

And the memory of his words: *'Come home with me to Glencoe.'*

Dair knew, as he rode across the hills toward the cloud-bound lands of Appin, that courage came in as many coats as cowardice, and only the man wearing one could name the proper cut. But he was not at all certain which he wore as he rode to Jean Stewart, bricked apart on the tiny island playing chatelaine to Castle Stalker, where he would go this time not to offer persuasion that they had not yet spent the spark burning in their bodies, but to explain it was truly extinguished.

"God save me," he muttered to the wind, "but I think I felt less fear as the war-pipes at Killiecrankie called us into battle!"

But that was true battle withal, for the good of Scotland and her true

Stuart king. This was a war of words he would survive battered more in spirit than in body, the more so for her bitter comprehension of its cause. He would never have lied to her, but now she would hear him speak his words with her own design in mind, a sett of false imaginings as well as false assumptions, no matter the truth of them.

Not another woman, not initially. But she would see it as such.

And if she would have of him the truth of his feelings *now*, she had indeed been supplanted by a woman. But Jean would never believe he had grown apart from her without interference, that he longed for Cat as much for her company as for her body; that he had not in fact already shared a bed with her.

Jean did not understand that the needs of the spirit compounded the needs of the body. Jean would believe her place had been usurped. Jean would believe whatever she felt she must, to reconcile rejection. *And Cat will bear the blame. . . .*

Preoccupied, Dair reined in his garron. The track wound its way through tumbled rocks, stands of trees, lush-grown heather and gorse, crossing countless burns and trickles of mountain-bred water. He swung a leg over and stepped off the sturdy pony, giving it rein to drink as he himself knelt to scoop up a handful of water.

Stone and grit bit into bare knees as he bent, and the garron pulled rein against his hand. When it whickered a greeting, Dair glanced up to see mounted men approaching. The tartan's sett, though worn by any, was the Stewart most closely associated with those bred of Appin: deep blue and rich forest green, striped alternatingly with narrow black and vivid red.

His mood plunged instantly. *Trust Robbie to come for me before I can see Jean. . . .* Dair rose, water trickling across his right palm and falling from slack fingers. Sunlight glinted off badge and brooch as the men wound through stones and burns, gleamed more dully on the sandy gold cap of Robbie's hair. He was bonnetless in the day, as if to mock Dair's gift to Cat.

The heir of Appin lifted his voice against the distance. "Did ye ken it, then? That I would be coming for you?"

But not so soon, so soon. Dair moved to the other side of the garron and stood quietly before the horse. He wore a dirk and *sgian dhu*, but wanted to use neither against Robbie. He would prefer to settle it with fists, when words would not do. And with *him*, they would not. Not ever with Robbie Stewart.

"So." Robbie reined up. With him was a tail of men nearly as impressive as a laird's, though of less ceremony. They were young and hard-faced all, with pistols tucked into kilt belts. "Are ye ready, then?"

Dair drew in a deep breath. Robbie showed no inclination to dismount; did he intend to ride him down?

"Well?" Stewart's expression was quizzical. "Has he gone lame, your garron—or d'ye mean to *walk* to Loch Linnhe?"

"Loch Linnhe?" Dair echoed blankly.

"Aye, where the boats are!" Robbie frowned. "Surely MacIain was brought word." He paused, assessing Dair's expression. "The *boat,* man! I thought ye kent what I mean!" He flung out an arm meant to suggest direction. "A supply boat is on its way up the coast of Lorn, bent on replenishing the stores at Fort William. We canna let that happen when our own people are hungry." He grinned, blue eyes alight. "And great romantic pirates we'll make, aye? Spanish pistols, Scottish dirks—they'll ken they've met their betters, those pawkie Sassenachs!"

"Pirates . . ." Dair took himself in hand. It would be gey easy to leave off responsibilities to play pirate with Robbie Stewart. "I meant to go to Jean."

Robbie frowned, then waved an illustrative hand. "Och, no, Jean's not home. She's gone off to visit some old bizzem . . . was gone when I got home from Achallader." He grinned. "Bring her back plunder, MacDonald—she'll kiss you for it!"

"When . . ." Dair began again. *I canna do this—'tis too easy. . . .* He scrubbed a hard hand through his windblown hair. *I canna DO this. . . .* "When is she expected back? Jean?"

Stewart whooped a laugh. "Good Christ, can you no' tame your cock, Alasdair Og? You'll be bedding her forbye, once we've English plunder!" The laughter died, though brows arched up. "D'ye come with us, then? 'Twill be a tale to tell, once we've won the boat."

Jean not at home.

Jean elsewhere.

Robbie did not know.

—reprieve—

Relief was overwhelming. Dair mounted his garron and sent him climbing hastily up to the higher track. He reined in by Robbie, grinning widely.

Jean was not at home . . . and for the moment, the day, perhaps so long as a week, he and her volatile brother could yet be friends, even pirates, bent upon Sassenach booty.

Dair raised eloquent brows in a mirror of Robbie's habit. "What will Breadalbane say, to have you break the treaty?"

Robbie swore virulently. "Holy Christ, man, 'tis naught to *me* what Grey John says. He's no laird of mine!"

Dair laughed. "No more is any man who stands in Appin's way when he wants to serve himself!"

"Aye, well . . ." Robbie grinned. "And who will *you* be serving?"

"MacIain," Dair declared promptly, and knew it for the truth.

Within hours Jean was forgotten. Powder and smoke burned in Dair's eyes, lingered unpleasantly in his nostrils, lent a metallic tang to his mouth. He heard shouting, swearing, muttering in Gaelic, furtive splashing in the water; wooden planks beneath his feet creaked in counterpoint to the motion of the ship as it floated without direction. It was theirs now, the *Lamb*, and all the supplies meant for Fort William would be parcelled out instead to Appin and Glencoe.

He turned toward the rail to look at the crew members gone over the side in a panicked bid for escape. It did not matter to him if they made good their attempt; it wasn't a fight to the death he was after, just provisions for Glencoe in place of Sassenach soldiers.

"Robbie—*no!*" Dair lunged and caught the outstretched arm Stewart raised, yanking it aside. "Dinna shoot, Robbie—'tis naught but plunder we've lifted, and a boat . . . if you kill anyone, we'll hang for it!"

Robbie snarled an oath and jerked his arm away, clutching the pistol. "Christ, MacDonald—" He turned hastily, leaning against the rail to steady himself as he searched again for the Englishmen. The Spanish pistol was clutched in one powder-burned hand. "There!"

The pistol came up. Dair saw from the tail of his eye the bedraggled, lake-soaked crewmen scrambling their way onto the shore from the waters of Loch Linnhe, running awkwardly in pursuit of safety. Some were bloodied, he knew, some actually wounded, but no man killed. Not yet.

"Damn you, Robbie—" This time Dair did not hold back. He struck the pistol away without regard for Robbie's hand, and was satisfied to see the weapon spinning harmlessly toward the water. Better a lost pistol than a lost life. "D'ye want to hang for this?"

"Neither to hang nor be imprisoned!" Robbie shouted back. "Have you lost your spine, MacDonald? They'll bear witness against us!"

"Have *you* lost your wits?" Dair countered. "Let them go, Robbie— by the time they've made their way to Fort William, we'll have the plunder safe home. No need to compound the crime." He glanced again shoreward and was pleased to see the Sassenachs disappear into heather and gorse. "They'll carry the tale, aye, but they dinna ken who we are."

"Scots!"

"Och, aye, Scots," Dair said in disgust, "but have you kent a Sassenach who can tell us apart? 'Tis one advantage, our names—how many MacDonalds and Stewarts are there in the Highlands?"

Robbie was breathing hard. He leaned his spine against the rail and glared at Dair, nursing a finger cut from the blow to his hand. "They'd kill us as soon as find out."

"They didna kill us here, did they?" Dair cast a quick, assessive glance over the English ship. It had not been difficult to take her with two boats of their own borrowed from Ballachulish along with some helpful MacDonalds, and a quick swarming attack that left them in possession of supply ship and her cargo. Shots fired, dirks unsheathed, a bit of blood and flesh, but no man dead of it. "We're too close to Glencoe—'tis the obvious place . . ." He looked at Robbie. "Appin."

The younger Scot was instantly diverted. His grin, behind the mask of grime, was brilliant. "You'd trust all this plunder to me?"

"Would you risk lifting from *me*?" Dair grinned back wolfishly. "I dinna think so, Robbie . . . aye, we'll sail her to Appin lands, then parcel out the plunder. The glens have need of such."

"And the pawkie bastards in the fort can starve." Robbie's anger was forgotten, as well as the wounded finger smearing blood into powder-sooted linen shirt. "Aye, we'll have her into an Appin harbor . . . will you come with us?"

Dair shook his head. "I'll go home to Glencoe—snoove back through the heather before the troops are out. . . . I'll tell MacIain what we've done. These men here from Ballachulish can carry Glencoe's share back home." He glanced shoreward. "Put me off a mile or two down the coast, aye?"

Robbie nodded absently, already lost in thought. He turned to his Stewarts and shouted orders to bring the boat around and sail her back toward Appin.

Dair nodded to himself, pleased to see Robbie so distracted. It would serve his purpose to be put ashore, where he would not, despite his words, go at once to Glencoe. Troops would likely search there first; it would be best if he were nowhere to be found, and no one in Glencoe to know his whereabouts.

So close to Glencoe, the Sassenach governor Colonel John Hill would make the obvious connection. Ignorant of Highlanders, of Highland clans and ways, he would not think of Robbie or of his Appin Stewarts.

MacDonalds would be blamed.

And to MacDonald lands the Williamite governor would send his Sassenach soldiers.

"Let him," Dair murmured. Robbie and the boat would be safe in Appin lands, and *he*, being wise, would take himself entirely elsewhere. He suppressed a grin of sheer delight and anticipation. *They will all of them, even Robbie, least expect me to go where I most want to be.*

In his private quarters, John Hill unrolled the map upon the table, arranged it, weighted it down at four corners with inkhorns and books. When he was satisfied with its placement he looked at the man who stood on the other side of the table. "If you please, Captain Fisher, show me where this incident occurred."

Captain Fisher did please. He planted a definitive forefinger on the map. "Here," he said succinctly, eyebrows locked together balefully over the flattened bridge of his misshapen nose. "Out of Ballachulish, from the smaller stem of the loch. Two boats, perhaps two dozen men. Scotch pirates, Governor. Bloody heathen savages!"

Hill nodded amicably, but forebore to correct the crude terminology. He did not entirely blame London-born, sea-reared Fisher for being so out of sorts; the man had lost his ship, his cargo; had had to swim to shore and skulk for two days through the wild Highland terrain, all the while trying desperately to avoid "heathen Scotch pirates."

In truth, Hill was no happier; Fort William badly needed the supplies now on their way elsewhere. "You are certain no one was killed?"

"No, sir, we all made it to shore safely, and all are here with me. But wounds aplenty, sir, from pistols and those bloody Highland short swords—begging your pardon, Governor."

"Dirks," Hill said absently, looking again at the map. His own finger traced a path. "From Ballachulish—here . . . to here, where the *Lamb* was . . ." he mused. "Yes, I see it—Glencoe is but miles up the glen . . . it would be an obvious target to MacIain's people, more food for their mouths and less for ours, whom they detest. . . ." Hill nodded; it made perfect sense to an old soldier, if not to an old sailor. He glanced from the map to Captain Fisher. "Did you hear any names called out?"

"MacDonald," Fisher answered promptly, "as you said. And Stewart—like their Papist king, the foolish old bastard."

"Different clan, I think," Hill said diffidently, but did not explain the details to Fisher of how Stewart became Stuart at the whimsy of a Scots—not *Scotch*—queen who spoke more French than Gaelic; how a single clan could become more than one in time, so large, so piecemeal, so scattered throughout the country.

It was a simple thing for John Hill to piece the truth together despite the paucity of evidence. He knew the map very well, and the clans who lived by its boundaries. "Think, if you please, Captain. Can you recall who was in command?"

Fisher glowered. "I don't understand their bloody heathen tongue!" he declared curtly, then mitigated it as he recalled to whom he spoke. "Sir."

"Ah, no, of course not; why should you?" Hill agreed mildly. "But I must ask you to think again, Captain Fisher . . . was there one man who spoke the 'bloody heathen tongue' more than the others? With pronounced authority?"

Fisher considered it, and nodded. "Young man, aye, sir. Sandy-haired, wearing the colored wool. Not tall, but well-made. And barefoot, like them all." He grimaced. "Bloody savages!"

Hill nodded patiently; it served nothing, with men like Fisher, to debate the truth. "Is there anyone else you recall? Another man who might have answered this one back more often than the others?" No MacDonald would take orders from a Stewart; he would command his own clanspeople.

Fisher's expression cleared. "Yes, of course, sir . . . ah, I take your meaning! Indeed, there was this young man who did most of the jabbering in the Scotch tongue, but another had as much to say. I marked him well, sir. Young face, old hair."

Hill's attention sharpened. "Graying early, was he?"

"Yes, sir. He wore no hat, sir. He was nearly gray as myself, Governor, but twenty years or more younger."

"MacDonald . . ." Hill murmured. "MacIain's son—what, John? John, I think . . . perhaps. Indeed, perhaps—the old fox's sons, they say, will be white-headed before they are forty . . ." But more telling yet: "And they've none of them signed the treaty. Nor will. *This* is their declaration, their defiance." He looked more pointedly at Fisher. "Good captain, I thank you. I believe you have solved their identities for me, if it please God." He moved the weights aside and began to reroll the map. "I do thank you, sir. You have saved me wasted effort."

Fisher was taken aback by the Hill's abrupt decisiveness. "Your pardon, Governor, sir—but what do you mean to do?"

Hill examined the parchment roll, then slid it carefully back into its leather storage tube, taking care not to tear the edges. "Catch them," he said succinctly. "I have troops, Captain Fisher, fine English troops. If it please God, I will send half of them to Glencoe and half of them to Appin." He smiled. "Despite their heathen tongue, Captain, Scottish foxes are no different than English ones. They will go to ground in territory they know best."

Her brothers had come up from their own dwellings, their own business, to tell Cat hers. That she was back from Kilchurn, back as well from Achallader where the treaty had been signed, took no time to be carried about, and soon enough her brothers came back to the house they had left years before to marry and raise their own bairns, leaving their sister to make her own life.

Until now. Until they heard of Duncan Campbell's elopement—it was a popular coffeehouse story, traded like wagers among Breadalbane's enemies—and the dishonor done their sister. Who was to have been a countess.

She had no choice but to let them in. One day Chesthill would be Jamie's, after all, when their father was dead. And so they came in, drank whisky, gathered themselves to her like kilt-clad chicks around a hen, appraised her closely— —*like a cow to be bred!*— —and muttered blackly among themselves that such treatment as she was shown by Breadalbane's son called for harsh words and dirks.

"Oh, aye," Cat said in blatant disgust. "Even the earl canna find his son . . . d'ye think you might do better?"

Jamie paced like a Highland wildcat, noiseless in bare feet. Dougal and Colin, less high-tempered than he, sat decorously in wooden chairs and drank down their father's whisky. She was mildly surprised any was left, but they had found a tun put away beneath the house. Its smoky, powerful tang put her in mind of her father, smelling always of usquabae.

Cat disdained a chair. She sat instead on the bottom step of the staircase near to the front door, where Robbie Stewart had once pressed a sword to her throat. She wore trews, of which they disapproved, but she had never put on skirts when left to her own devices. She folded up her legs and leaned her elbows upon them. "You ken gey well 'tis *your* honor besmirched," she muttered sourly. "You never cared much for mine."

Jamie stopped pacing and wheeled back, plaid swinging. "And what does the earl mean to do? 'Tis his dishonor as well . . . we are all Campbells, aye?"

"Silver might do," Dougal offered.

"Silver!" Jamie cried. " 'Tis our sister's future I'm thinking of, not having her substance bought and sold like a cow!"

"Och, save your thunder for Breadalbane; d'ye think to fool me?" Cat said wearily, shifting long legs and arms to plant elbows and buttocks into the stairs, and sprawled inelegantly. "You'd take silver for it, Jamie—you just want to make your noise so you might get more out of him."

Colin laughed briefly. "Aye, well . . . 'tis a good way to fatten our purses, Cat. Even yours."

"This is my home," she said, intending to remind them she had a right to stay in it.

Jamie interrupted. "Mine."

Cat stared, astounded, then scrambled up untidily to face him toe to toe, drawn up straight as a Lochaber ax. "And would you throw me out of it?"

"I'd sooner see you married," he retorted, moving a step away. "You need a man, Cat."

"And would you marry me off only so you can have this house?" She wanted to spit at his feet. "Just so you can move Ellen in here and spawn more bairns upon her? Well, 'tisn't your house 'till he's dead, Jamie—"

"Or until someone kills him," Dougal put in mildly. "For debts, most likely."

Colin laughed. "Or he'll put the gun to his own head!"

Cat stared at her brothers one by one. "Have you no shame?" she managed at last. "The man is our father!"

"And likely he sired us one by one in various drunken fits," Jamie said flatly. "I doubt he'd have the wherewithal, else."

"Oh, but *you* do!" she shot back. "Isna Ellen breeding again?"

Ellen was. The retort darkened Jamie's face. " 'Tis no surprise to me no man will have you . . . you'd shame him with that tongue."

"Or shrivel his cock with her spite," Dougal agreed cheerfully.

Colin grinned at her. "You'd best mind it, Cat, if you want to catch a man."

"Aye," Jamie said pointedly. "Or are we to think Duncan Campbell eloped to escape marrying you?"

"Go home," Cat told them. "I'll hear no more of your whisky-soaked wind. You are as bad as he is. Glenlyon breeds raukle fools for sons."

"There are amends," Jamie said darkly.

Cat sighed. "Then go to Flanders, aye?—and have the earl give you the silver you think you're due. Now, go home. All of you. Una isna here—I've washing to tend."

"If you were a countess," Colin declared, "you'd have more women than absent Una to do the washing for you."

Cat marched to the door and snatched it open. "I dinna want to be a countess. I dinna want untold women to do my washing for me. I dinna want anything at this particular moment save to be let alone." She swung the door so it thumped against the wall, letting the daylight in. "*Go.*"

They went, Jamie muttering of stubbornness and ingratitude for their great care and affection while Colin and Dougal, less annoyed by her mood, set horn cups into her hands as they passed through the door.

"If you're washing linens," Colin said, "you might as well wash the cups."

Cat slammed the door behind them. Angrily she set her spine against it in a vain attempt to bar further entry; if they truly wanted in, in they would come. "Pawkie bastards," she muttered. "There isna a man in the world worth a woman's time!"

She scowled at the cups. One was empty, the other nearly half-full. She would indeed have to wash them, but it was a waste of good whisky to pour it out on the ground.

—I should ken what it is my father likes so gey well! Cat lifted the cup, paused, examined its contents suspiciously, then gulped the liquor swiftly.

"Cruachan!" she gasped as the fire burned into her belly. "Och, oh Christ *Jesus* . . . 'tis no wonder a man goes screaming like the *bean sidhe* into battle—he's coals heaped up in his belly—" She coughed, pressing the back of one hand against her mouth. Her eyes watered. She caught her breath, tasting peat-smoke in her mouth along with the coals in her belly, then nearly choked in shock as a scratching sounded at the door.

She lurched off the door, spinning in place. "Which one of you doesna understand good Gaelic—?" Clutching the cups in one hand, Cat grasped the latch and yanked open the door. "I'll hear no more of your pawkie words—"

Nor would they. Nor would *he,* leaning nonchalantly slantwise in the door with one shoulder lodged against the wooden jamb. "I've lost my bonnet," he said. "Have you one I might wear?"

And Dair MacDonald smiled.

—bonnie, bonnie prince—

"Oh Christ," Cat blurted. "I canna be drunk *already*—"

He arched one brow incongruously dark beneath the silvering forelock. "Already? Have you begun on it, then?" He spied the cups in her hands. "One for each fist, aye? Well, I've kent men as prefer it that way . . . though never a lass." He grinned. "But then you have never been like other lasses."

"Och, indeed," Cat said, senses all atumble and nothing at all in her world, in her body, making any sense. "I dinna like other lasses."

The grin transmuted itself. Cider-eyes, whisky-eyes, were abruptly dark and intense. "Nor I," he said plainly.

Glenlyon's daughter said nothing as he came into her house.

MacDonald, in her house.

—bonnie lad, bonnie lad—

He shut the door on sunlight. "Cat," he said. "Come home with me to Glencoe."

She laughed at him. *Och, good Christ . . . does he think I'll say him nay?* And dropped the cups altogether to fill her hands instead with the plaid across one shoulder, with the linen of his shirt, with the thick wind-tumbled hair unhindered by missing bonnet.

—with silver in his hair, and white teeth a'gleaming—

And a fierce, wild music skirling through her body far greater even than *ceol mor,* piping the Gaels to war.

She waits impatiently as he brings up two horses. She sees the expression on his face, the tension in his body, but gives in to neither unspoken plea. And when he halts, she reaches out swiftly and takes the rein from his hand.

His expression is troubled. "What will this serve?"

Does he believe she might reconsider, given time? Or merely hopes? Grimly she says, "It serves me to see what has become of my home, and of the man I married."

He still frowns even as she mounts her horse, though he says nothing.

"You've a wife yourself," she tells him, "and two bairns. Think of them as I do this. Think of not knowing if they lived, or if they died. For the rest of your life."

He grimaces. "Not knowing might be easier."

"Oh, no. No . . ." she turns her garron toward the track that winds through Rannoch Moor.

No one can understand who has not been there. And until she goes back she will never know the truth.

She needs to know. Until she knows the truth there can be no future, only the past.

In Glencoe, she will know. If he lives. Or not.

Part V

1691

One

The floor, as the braes of Craigh Eallaich before the Battle of Killie-crankie, was a field of tartan spoor. Dair's kilt, unbelted, un-pinned, had been discarded into tangled folds, mingling with woolen trews that once had been a man's, but more recently —*and with much greater grace!*— had attired a woman instead. All such impediments as clothing lay strewn across the hardwood floor of a room Dair believed must be the Laird of Glenlyon's; the bed was large enough for two, and as they were neither of them lacking in height nor length of limb, he found it much in favor.

But far more in favor for the woman who was in it, dawn-gilded hair caught now beneath his shoulder as well as her own.

He touched a sleep-tangled, wiry coil improbably *red* against pale linens; nothing, with Cat Campbell, so restrained as sandy rose or sul-len auburn. But Cat slept on, no more self-conscious in sleep than she was awake, blatant in posture and pride.

Dair smiled drowsily, content with the day, the dawn; content within himself of what they had wrought in Glenlyon's bed. Her passion, un-schooled, had been the greater for his guidance, for his restraint and hard-won patience; she was an apt pupil and did not stint response. While Jean had been well cognizant of how to please a man and did so with consummate skill, Cat was wholly unaware and thus more honest. She was virgin and he hurt her, but the moment passed. Between the dusk and the dawn she had forgotten the pain, disdained the blood, and gave of herself freely even in awkwardness.

For her, he doubted the earth had shifted. It was more difficult for a woman, he knew, less generous with less time, and he had not been able to wait so long as he might have liked. But she, clearly, was not displeased. Once roused beyond the beginning there was pleasure in it for her, and would be more yet. They had all the time in the world to learn the ways, the movements, that most pleased them individually as well as mutually.

He shifted closer. Feet and knees aligned themselves perfectly. She was nearly as tall as he, so they fit together far better as spoons than one might expect. With his breast against her spine he could feel her steady heartbeat, and knew when her breathing changed.

She went rigidly stiff, as if astounded by his presence. Then she softened all at once and turned, grasping the hair caught beneath his shoulder to rescue her scalp. He shifted, smiling, and freed her.

She faced him now, brows level and eloquent, staring at him so critically Dair had to laugh. "Did you think I might be gone? Or naught but a dream?"

"No dream ever did *that*," she declared. "But gone—aye. 'Tis dangerous for you here."

"Why, d'ye expect your brothers to come in with dirks drawn, and claymores?" He grinned. "Aye, I saw them yesterday—had to hide myself away until they left the house. One of them had a gey black face, but the others were no' so worried."

"Jamie." Cat's generous mouth twisted. "He thinks I should be married with a house of my own so he might claim this one the sooner. As for dangerous—aye. I've a woman who stays with me."

"I heard her," Dair agreed. "Last night when she came up the stairs, but she didna look in here."

"Christ, no!" Cat said fervently. "Una would have screeched like a snared coney. . . ." She shifted against the sheets, one foot hooked with his tentatively, uncertain of her welcome but wanting it nonetheless. "This is my father's room. She'd no' come in here."

"Then we are safe," he said, trapping the ankle between his own, "from such prying eyes as a screeching coney and three pawkie brothers." He bent close, then rolled back as she jerked the covers from his hips. "Christ, Cat—what?"

She peered warily beneath the coverlet. When she lowered the bedclothes at last her eyes were stricken.

"What?" The expression disturbed him. "Cat—what is it?"

Her voice was strangled. "Dougal was right."

"Dougal?" It was preposterous. "What has he to do with anything?"

"He said I'd shrivel it, and I did!"

"Shrivel . . . och, *Christ*, Cat—"

"With spite," she explained. "Was I so spiteful?"

It was gey difficult not to whoop in laughter, until he thought of Una. Instead he had to muffle his noise against the pillow.

She was much perturbed. "Are you crying, man?"

When he could breathe again he nodded. "Oh, aye—but not from pain or sadness." He hitched himself up on an elbow and caught her hand, lacing her fingers with his. "Cat—'tis nothing like spite. I promise."

"But—" Her expression was eloquent.

Dair opened his mouth, shut it, began again. "You've seen bulls rutting, and stallions—" She nodded. "—well, you ken verra well they dinna *always* look so large."

"Well, no," Cat agreed. " 'Twould be gey difficult for a bull to walk, like that."

He caught back a laugh. "Oh, aye . . . and for a man as well."

She was dubious. "I saw Robbie—my brother Robbie—once. With Mairi. He looked verra much like a bull."

"Smaller, I should hope, for Mairi's sake!" Dair kissed one knuckle, then the back of her hand. "You didna shrivel it, Cat. Not with spite, or anything else. 'Tis only resting."

She was sly despite her innocence, tightening her grasp. "Then wake it up, aye?"

Dair grinned toothily. " 'Tis for the lass to do."

"Oh, aye? How?"

"For you," he said, "just breathe. You see?" He guided her hand beneath the coverlet, across his belly, and lower. "No' so shrivelled now . . . and if you—"

A banging on the door below drowned out his quiet suggestion. Cat jerked her hand free and sat up rigidly, yanking sheets to her shoulders. The banging repeated itself, resolved into knocking.

"Oh, Christ Jesus," she hissed, bestirring herself from bedding to search frenziedly for her clothing. "Oh Holy Mary—"

The banging continued unabated.

"Where did you put—? Oh, Christ—where is Una?" Cat knelt to the floor and began to scoop up clothing. "Is this—?—no, yours . . . *here* . . . oh good Christ—"

Dair sat upright. "Cease your swearing," he said, "and come back to bed. 'Tis your house, aye?—you've a right to answer the door when you choose."

Cat glared at him as she stuck one long leg into the trews and pulled colorful tartan over her knee. "And let Una see me come out of my father's room . . . ?" She struggled with the other leg. "Who is at the door this early?"

"Not so early as that." There was no dissuading her. Resigned, Dair bent and caught a shirt. "Here. You've got mine—" He stood, unabashed in nakedness, and put it over her head, pulling hair through. "Give me an arm, Cat—*here*—" He bent it at the elbow.

"I'll no' let you dress me like a bairn," she said crossly, thrusting an arm through the sleeve without his aid. "Oh, I shouldna had that whisky last night—I smell of it . . . ."

"—And of me, and I of you."

Her face reddened. She yanked the sleeve up so her hand was free of voluminous linen, then put the other arm through as Dair held up the empty sleeve. "My belt—"

And froze as Una's voice, outside the door, called her name.

Below, the banging continued. A man's voice shouted loudly for someone to open the door.

Una's voice was muffled by wood and distance. "Catriona—rouse yourself. I'll go down to see to the door."

"Oh," Cat gasped, "she is at *my* door . . . wait you—" And whispering urgently, "Where is my belt—?"

"Here. Dinna let your trews fall down, or they'll ken you're no lad." He grinned as she swore. "Now *I* am well acquainted with the truth of you, but strangers might not see it."

She buckled the belt over trews and shirt. Coils of brilliant hair tumbled around her shoulders. "My shawl—" she muttered, then bent and caught up the mound of wool that was his plaid and kilt. " 'Twill do, aye?"

"Cat!" But she threw a fold over her head, swirled the bulk around her body, and went out the door, leaving him with naught to wear but a saffron-dyed shirt, like a Gael going into battle. "Christ," he muttered. "I might as *well* be, aye?"

Cat checked at the top of the stairs even as Una, below, opened the front door. There was a male voice, an authoritative voice for all its courtesy. Cat drew in a deep breath, briefly rearranged the mass of Dair's plaid, and called out to Una to ask what was the matter.

Before Una could answer a man was in the house. A young man in military dress, hat tucked beneath an arm. "I am Major Duncan Forbes," he said, "from Fort William, at Inverlochy. It is my duty to locate and bring in a man wanted for piracy."

Una gasped noisily even as Cat drew herself up. "Piracy!" she said sharply, startled into genuine protest. "We are far from the water, Major . . . why d'ye think there would be such a man here?" With aplomb, she descended the stairs slowly. She was wholly aware of his puzzled appraisal; did he see the trews beneath the kilt and plaid? She had tried to hide them in a barrage of tartan, but there had been so little time. "Who are you looking for?"

"A Jacobite," he said. Then, as if aware he might well be standing in the house of a fellow Jacobite, he mitigated his tone. "A supply ship on its way to Fort William was attacked. The boat was taken, stolen, and all its cargo as well."

Cat reached the bottom step and paused. Was the accusation true? *Or some trumpery excuse because Dair fought at Killiecrankie, where the Jacobites had won?*

"And why d'ye think such a man might come here?" she asked contemptuously, playing out the role. "My father is Laird of Glenlyon— you ken him, aye?—and sworn to King William. He is even now in the

Earl of Argyll's new regiment.'' All of it perfectly true; let him read it in her eyes. ''D'ye think the laird's own daughter would hide a Jacobite pirate?''

Major Forbes inclined his head slightly. ''Indeed, I know the name. It is also known Captain Campbell is with the regiment. But that does not preclude my duty. We have intelligence that this man might have come here. I'm afraid I have orders to search this house as well as the bothies.'' His expression softened. ''There is no cause for alarm, nor any reason to fear. If you are under duress, we'll hold nothing against your denials.''

A kind man, withal, and a fool. *Good.* Cat came down the final step. ''We're hiding no man, Major Forbes, nor are we lying about it. But I canna—''

Una fell back with a shriek of alarm. *''Who is that—?''*

Cat glanced back. Dair, shadowed in dimness, stood at the head of the stairs wearing her father's trews. ''Major Forbes,'' he said evenly, smoothing his Highland accent, ''have we met?''

The soldier frowned minutely. ''No, sir, we have not. May I ask your name?''

Dair, descending, came down into the daylight, and Una drew in a breath.

'' 'Tis Alasdair—'' she began.

''—*Campbell,*'' Cat finished swiftly, not daring to look at Una. She did not know why Dair had chosen to show himself, but if she thought quickly enough, the harm would be diminished. ''He is a cousin of my father's, and we—I—'' She could not help it; her face burned with embarrassment.

Dair stood next to her now. He rested a hand familiarly on her shoulder. ''Would you have a lass speak of private matters, Major?''

''Catriona,'' Una expelled on a rush. *''Catriona Campbell—''*

Now was opportunity. Cat turned toward her. ''I couldna tell you,'' she said. ''How could I? He is not a man my father would approve—''
—indeed not!— ''—nor would my brothers. But I made up my mind to do as *I* wished, instead of letting everyone else direct my life.'' Every word true. ''Una, I am sorry—but if you could understand—''

''Understand!'' Una was horrified. ''I understand very well, Catriona—but if you think I'll permit such dishonor in your father's own house—''

''I mean to marry her,'' Dair said. ''Would you have us handfast before you? You would make proper witnesses, aye?'' His hand squeezed Cat's shoulder. ''Her brothers might be somewhat fashed about it, but the lass and I are set on one another. . . .'' His smile was charming as he looked at Una, so very, very bonnie. "Can you not find it in your heart to forgive us, Una?"

Major Forbes smiled politely. "I'm afraid that must wait. I don't believe the woman would care to forgive a Jacobite liar." He glanced briefly at Cat, then looked again at Dair even as he motioned soldiers into the house. "Sir, I must place you under arrest. You are charged with piracy, and will be taken to Fort William until transportation to the Tolbooth in Edinburgh, where you will await the king's pleasure."

"He's not a pirate!" Cat cried. "He's my kinsman, Alasdair—"

"—MacDonald," the major finished. His smile was kindly. "He may have shared your bed, but he is no kin of yours." He gestured again, and a man was brought through the door.

Robbie Stewart, in shackles. Iron chimed as he moved. His face, beneath new bruises, was white and taut. His eyes burned avidly, an intense, brilliant blue.

Another time Cat might have rejoiced to see him brought down so low as this. But this moment, in this house, she wanted very much to wish him elsewhere, away where he could not identify Alasdair Og MacDonald.

He gazed at her a moment, a very long moment, expression inscrutable. Then he looked at Dair, standing rigidly near the stair. "You dinna ask why, MacDonald. D'ye think they tortured me for it?"

Even Cat knew better than that.

Robbie's eyes were defiant as the soldiers closed on Dair. "Oh, a bit of a scuffle—I've no liking for iron, aye?—but 'twasn't so difficult for me to speak to the point when they asked which of MacIain's sons it was who went a-reiving with me." Color burned on his cheekbones. "You see, Jean had come home by then."

Dair's face blanched into alabaster. "She left of her own will."

"Oh, aye? And am I to name my sister a liar?" Robbie spat at the floor. "I dinna think so!"

"She left," Dair repeated. "She was gone when I returned."

"Driven away."

"She was not."

"Driven away by a man who would take a Campbell bizzem in his bed instead!" He glared fiercely at Cat. "D'ye think I didna see it when you gave her your bonnet? Good Christ, MacDonald, the whole encampment saw it! And not a one of my Appin men, nor any of Glencoe, who didna ken what that meant!"

"Robbie—"

But Stewart refused to listen when he could act instead. Before anyone could move to check him, he lunged forward through the soldiers and slung shackles and chain at Dair's unprotected jaw.

Dair's head snapped back. He rocked on his heels, then fell down against the stairs. His skull struck a riser with an audible crack.

"You bluidy bastard—" Cat, unshackled and much freer to move than Stewart, stiff-armed him back and back, knocking him off his stride until he fetched up against the wall. Folds of tartan fell from her shoulders. "You pawkie, bluidy bastard—"

There were men all around, soldiers in her house. Someone caught her arms and pulled her away from Robbie, who grinned and swore in vulgar admiration, bleeding from a split lip; but she heard naught of it, nothing more than noise, a roaring in her ears and light, too much light, filling up her eyes.

"Devil take you!" she cried, then pulled free of them all to go to Dair, sprawled so gracelessly, to kneel, to touch his bloodied face.

"Catriona—" Una blurted. "You'll no'—"

But the words were blocked away as hands closed on her arms again. They pulled, they nagged, they dragged her away. "Let me be—"

"Put him in irons," Forbes said. "We can tie him onto his horse."

His voice was distant, so distant.

To Robbie he said, distantly, "That was unnecessary."

"No, oh no, 'twas."

Forbes jerked his head to other soldiers. "Have Stewart taken out of here. He's served his purpose." He turned to Cat. "I told you, no lies would be held against you. No harm will come to you."

A hand stayed her when she would have moved. Instead she laughed into his face, and saw him redden. Forbes turned away.

They put shackles on Dair's wrists, locked them, then heaved him up from the floor. He was slack in unconsciousness and made no protest. Blood stained the saffron linen of his shirt. She saw a smear on the angle of the bottom step, a puddle on the floor.

Where she had stood once, in trews and shirt, confronting Robbie Stewart as he held a sword to her throat.

She could not wish upon him another fate but that he be transported to the Tolbooth and summarily hanged in Edinburgh. Save that Dair would hang with him.

The roaring yet filled her head, and the light her eyes. So much noise and light . . . she wondered if it were anger, were fear, or if something had broken inside her head even as Dair had struck his.

Robbie was gone, and Dair. They were gone, all of them gone: the soldiers, Stewart, MacDonald. Only Forbes remained.

Cat looked at him. Noise faded. The light died out of her eyes. All the weight, the pain, the paralyzing fear came up to close her throat. "Dinna do it," she said tightly. "He's already hanged once. 'Tis bad luck to hang a man twice."

There was no joy in his eyes, only duty and sympathy. "The king's pleasure," Forbes said, and took his leave.

Dair roused as they pulled him from the horse. He was aware of war being fought in his belly and the thunder of cannon booming inside his head. For a moment it was Killiecrankie come again, steel blades clashing, until his feet touched the ground. Hands were on him, but it did not matter; he sagged against the garron and felt it shift.

—och, wait—

The motion was enough. Legs collapsed and dumped him unceremoniously onto stony ground, where raw and brutal instinct rolled his body to one side, then hitched it up awkwardly on elbow and hip despite the chains— *—no' swords after all—* —as Dair lost the war. All that he had eaten, all that he had drunk, deserted his belly.

Had he been wholly conscious he would have felt humiliated before the Sassenach soldiers, but he was but barely conscious and therefore did not care a fig for what they thought of him. He did not recall ever having been so ill, so wretchedly ill, with pain crowding his skull and lodging in his jaw. He expelled what was in his belly, then fell to a cramped heaving despite its emptiness. His skull cracked open and let in all the light, the too-bright light of a day he would sooner forget.

Iron chimed as someone came to stand over him. The tone was flat, unfriendly. "They've let us stop to piss."

Dair coughed, and wished he hadn't.

Iron rang again. The man knelt next to him. "MacDonald." A hand touched his shoulder. This time the tone was friendlier. "You'll no' choke, d'ye hear?"

Scot, not Sassenach. And a familiar voice, withal.

"Dair—" Now there was sharp concern. "Christ, you willna die, aye? And rob them of their hanging?"

Robbie. Robbie Stewart. Who was wholly responsible for his straits.

The heaving died with an intemperate quiver deep in his belly. Dair remained hunched with one leg tucked beneath him, afraid to lift his forehead from the ground. His head might fall off. The jaw, he feared, already had.

"I've water," Robbie said. "Will you wash your face, man?"

He did not care the least about his face. It was all he could do to remain precariously balanced between the day and the night.

Another voice intruded. "We must go on."

Robbie, with scorching contempt: "D'ye think he'll run away if we bide a *wee* bit?"

The other voice, unruffled: "I think that as long as we remain in the heather we provide a target for such clansmen as would sooner see you both freed than put in Fort William. We must go on.''

"He is injured—'' Robbie began.

"Then tend him yourself,'' the other declared. '' 'Twas you who injured him.''

Dair, in his misery, did not know why Stewart would do other than crack his head again. Yet the hand on his shoulder remained.

"Can you sit?'' Robbie asked. "They'll haul you up again; would you give them the satisfaction?''

He would give them whatever he could manage. Dair shifted against the ground and slowly levered himself upright into a sitting position. The hand fell away with a ringing of iron links. Robbie, squatting close, eyed him critically.

Awkwardly Dair scraped a linen-clad forearm across his mouth, avoiding the heavy shackle at his wrist, then fixed his blurred vision on Robbie's bruised face. Through the pain in his jaw, he said, "Devil take you, you pawkie bastard.''

Stewart did not choose to accept the insult. "Och, as to that—he already has.'' Two-handed, he hoisted a boiled-leather bottle. "Water, not usquabae. Will ye drink?''

Upright did not suit his head. Blackness encroached. "Drink it yourself,'' he managed. "And may you choke on it—''

But any retort that might have been offered was lost in the fraying decay of Dair's consciousness.

Small trunks only, wood with leather tacked over, and tin bits at the corners for strength. Cat would take one garron and thus could not afford to pack more than two small trunks could hold.

Apart from the rest was a short length of fine-woven tartan spread out upon her bed—*her* bed, not her father's—and into the center she set three items: a sword-severed length of hempen rope, a silver French-made mirror, and a blue Highland bonnet bearing badge and eagle feather. He was a laird's son.

Una had, eventually, gone away. Cat ignored her after the first moments of argument, until Una declared her an ill-mannered, foul-mouthed bizzem, to which Cat replied, with manifest eloquence, that until Una was mistress in the laird's place she had best tend her tongue.

Cat did not like resorting to condescension, but had wearied of provocation. And it had proved successful; Una departed swiftly. But when the door below was struck open so hard it banged against the wall, Cat realized Una had merely gone, like a pawkie coward, to bring in artillery.

They were no respecters of privacy, her brothers, had no tolerance of her wishes. They thudded their way up the stairs, yanked open her door, then crowded between the jambs. The room was not so large it supported three tall men in addition to herself, but they tried regardless of it.

Jamie was furious. He spilled such offal in his words and so many all at once that she could not decipher the insults, only their intentions. When Jamie stopped swearing at her, Dougal joined in, if with less heat; Colin merely waited until both of them were done.

"Why?" he asked then. "Why a MacDonald?"

Cat found it ironic. Not '*why a man?*,' but '*why a MacDonald?*' To him she offered answer; his mildness merited it. "Because at that moment, with him in my house, in my heart, there was nothing else to do but go to bed with him. Nothing else I *wanted* but to go to bed with him." There. Frank enough. No man could mistake it, not even her brothers.

Jamie was disgusted. "I'll no' have any man say my sister is a whore—"

"Good. Dinna let him say it. Last I kent, a woman was no' a whore unless she took silver for it."

Dougal was curious. "You dinna care what they think?"

"I dinna," Cat said plainly. "Did wondering about it ever keep *you* from bedding a lass?"

" 'Tis different," Jamie declared. " 'Tis a man's right to choose a woman—"

"He chose me." She shut one of the trunks. "I dinna see the sense in explaining myself. 'Tis done."

"Where are you going?" Colin asked.

Cat set the latch. "Glencoe. I've been invited."

"Why?" Jamie, for all his noise, was desperately perplexed. "What business have you there in the midst of MacDonalds?"

Cat lifted the trunk off the bed and set it on the floor. "To tell them the truth of what's become of him."

"I dinna doubt they ken that already." His irony was weighted with contempt. "The Sassenachs went there first, aye?"

"They dinna ken the truth," she answered steadfastly. " 'Tis for me to tell them."

Dougal was incredulous. "Glenlyon's daughter in Glencoe? Are ye daft, Cat? They could hold you there and demand a trade: you for Alasdair Og!"

Cat shut the second trunk and latched it. "*You* are daft, Dougal. What value am I to the Sassenachs? We are none of us Jacobites, aye?— and the Laird of Glenlyon serves King William in Argyll's regiment."

"You have some value to us," Jamie declared sourly. "If Breadalbane's son will have despoiled baggage."

Cat laughed at him. "Breadalbane's son despoiled his own baggage," she said, "and then ran off with it. I dinna think he'll be home to consider having me."

"Cat—" As she turned toward the door with one trunk clasped in her arms, Jamie moved to obstruct her. "I canna have it."

"Because of your pawkie pride? Well, I dinna care what you can or canna have," she said. "I will do what I wish."

He did not give ground. "I'll no' have it."

Anger boiled up. "You are not the laird yet!" she cried. "Christ, Jamie, had Robbie lived you'd be naught at all, save a drukken man's second son! Let me pass."

"And Robbie *died* because of MacDonalds."

It took effort not to shout at him, to take out her frustrations on a man who would not, or could not—despite the honesty of them, the perilous power of them—comprehend her feelings.

Cat glared into his face. "Robbie died because of me. Me, Jamie! Because I lifted our father's dirk and snooved away to follow you on your cattle-lifting. Blame that! Blame yourself! Blame me for following you! But I'll no' have you blaming Dair for a thing he wasna there for!"

"And where was he?" Dougal asked. "Lifting *our* cattle, aye?"

"Or raping Campbell lands on his way home from butchering Argyll," Jamie said harshly. "He was there, aye?—with all the rest of Glencoe to watch the beheading, save for the lads who came out to lift our cows!"

"You were going to lift theirs!"

"But we didna kill anyone!"

"Stop it," Colin said, who had been quiet for too long. "Houd your gab, the pair of you. You dishonor our mother's house with such bitterness." He looked at the eldest. "Let her go, Jamie."

Dougal was clearly surprised. "Colin—what are you doing, man?"

"Let her go," Colin repeated. "Short of chaining her to the bed, you'll no' keep her here. She's enough of us in her, aye?—and naught at all of our father, who's no spine to hold him upright. You willna make her grovel, Jamie. You willna make her beg." He flicked a glance at his sister. "And even if you could, I dinna think I would let you."

Jamie was speechless. Colin took the trunk from Cat and nodded at her bed. "Fetch the rest, Cat. You willna go to Glencoe with naught but what you're wearing."

"Trews," Jamie muttered. "Dressed like a lad."

Dougal laughed. "Aye, but she proved she was no lad when she bedded a MacDonald!"

Jamie's expression was bitter. "Unless he prefers lads . . . he is a MacDonald, withal—"

"Oh, stop," Cat said wearily, wrapping up rope, and mirror, and bonnet. "Go back to your bairns and your wife, Jamie . . . surely they would do better than I to hear the droning of your pipes."

Colin waited. Cat tucked the small bundle into her belt, then hoisted the trunk from the narrow bed she would not, so long as possible, sleep in ever again.

"Dinna be a fool," Dougal said, with a note of urgency in his voice. "Oh, Cat—"

"Let her pass," Colin said.

Jamie shot him a look of pure venom. "You'll be the one to tell the tale to our father."

"So I will." Colin went out of the room, following Cat as she headed down the stairs. Where Una, taut-faced, waited at the bottom.

"Catriona—"

" 'Tis decided," Cat said. Then, more gently, "I must go, Una. But if you feel you must come to give me chaperonage—"

"I will not," Una said sharply. "You've proved yourself without honor. Nothing I do can buy it back again."

It hurt worse than expected. Cat clamped her teeth shut and went out into the dooryard.

Colin set her trunk down on the bench beside the door. "I'll fetch a garron for you. And I *will* write our father—I'll tell the tale more kindly than Jamie would."

That was true. Cat put a hand on his arm. "Colin—why?"

He smiled. "Because I've never seen you want a thing so badly as this. And you have always demanded whatever there was to have."

It made no sense. "Colin—"

"You love him," he said.

Cat's belly tautened. "As much as I am able to love anything in this world."

"Aye, well . . ." Colin shrugged awkwardly; such truth came hard to him. "You've never hoarded your passions, Cat. You share with everyone what is in your heart . . . and you've the words in your mouth, and wit enough, to make it sting! 'Tis what makes you gey hard to be with. 'Tis what angers Jamie so." He smiled crookedly, the best of all of them: a man who would permit her the freedom to be whom she needed to be. "But if *he* will have you, MacDonald or no, 'tis his to deal with."

She was not certain if that were flattery or insult, but she did not ask an explanation. She would take what was offered, gratefully, and remember him in her prayers.

Cat smiled through tears as Colin walked away. *At least one of my brothers is worth them!*

Dust rose from the parade ground as the soldiers with their prisoners rode into Fort William. It was midafternoon of the fifth day since Captain Fisher reported the attack on the *Lamb;* excellent time had been made in the apprehension of the Scots involved.

Governor Hill, accompanied by his aide, stood before the officer's quarters as the prisoners, summarily halted, were ordered off the shaggy Highland garrons dwarfed by the larger, heavier military mounts of his soldiers.

Against the uniforms and rigid discipline of Major Forbes's troops, the Scots were supremely barbaric in appearance. Bare of foot, naked of knee and leg, swathed in gaudy tartan, there was nothing about them that suggested civility. And yet Hill knew better. The lairds were not savages but often highly educated men who, Highland-born, chose to remain in their wild country, to live by the most rigorous code of all, shaped by tribal loyalty and the sacred law of hospitality despite clan rivalries that bloodied the gorse and heather. Their sons were taught the same.

And now Hill held two of them: the heir to the Appin Stewarts, and one of MacIain's cubs.

Another man might rejoice. But Hill thought it unfortunate, if providential, that imprisonment was required. He did not know of a single Scot who adapted to captivity, any more than African lions did to the Tower of London.

According to Captain Fisher's description, Hill sought out the Stewart and MacDonald. One was not difficult: Stewart was indeed a powerfully built young man despite his lack of height, and he carried himself, even in iron, with an arrogance wholly unmitigated by his circumstances. He stood planted squarely beside his garron and stared straight at Hill, a mocking smile discounting bonnetless head, heavy shackles, and the grime on his face.

The other was another matter. MacIain's son was identifiable by the signal gray in his hair, but also the grim concern on the faces of the clansmen who wore the MacDonald badge. He did not stand on his own but was supported by two soldiers. Dried blood stained the cloth of his shirt, crusted his hair, smeared one side of his face as if he had tried to tend himself, and failed. Hill recognized immediately the unfocused look in the eyes, the minute unsteadiness, the overly careful carriage of an injured head. MacDonald was conscious, but not fully cognizant of his surroundings. Or he hurt too much to care.

Forbes came forward at once, saluting smartly. He gave his report succinctly and without excess comment: Robert Stewart and certain clansmen arrested in Appin lands, as well as certain MacDonalds from near Glencoe, and Alasdair Og MacDonald.

MacIain's younger son, not the heir. Hill looked past Forbes at the dazed prisoner. Under scrutiny, MacDonald stirred in the soldiers' grasp and attempted to stand unaided. Iron chimed as he pulled himself upright. The lurid beginnings of an ugly bruise bloomed on his swollen jaw. He met Hill's gaze and raised his head, disdaining the pain of movement. But Hill saw it in the rigid mask of his battered face, the pallor of bitten lips.

Anger flared; he would not countenance unnecessary brutality. "How was that man injured, Major Forbes?"

"Sir—"

"*I did it.*" Robert Stewart took a step forward before a soldier barred his way. He checked, sent the soldier a mocking, sidelong glance, then looked Hill in the eyes. "I did it, aye?—'twas an issue twixt the two of us, and naught to do wi' you." His English was good, if accented thickly with Highland dialect. " 'Tis for Scots, no' Sassenachs. Ye wouldna understand."

Hill repressed a smile. "Do you know, young sir—do you 'ken' it?— that if the Scots just once ceased killing each other long enough to unite and meet the Sassenachs in true battle, you might very well succeed in regaining your independence. After all, Dundee did a proper job of it at Killiecrankie. A military genius; pity he was killed."

Stewart blinked his surprise. Belligerently he said, "Would your pawkie king no' accuse ye of treason for saying that?"

"My pawkie king is not present to hear it," Hill answered. "And yours, I fear, is no closer to hear what you do in his name. We are left to our own devices, sir—and to our own war." He looked back at Forbes. "Major, you will escort these prisoners to the stockade, and secure them. Put Robert Stewart and Alasdair MacDonald in one cell, the rest in another. And have the physician in; I'll not give MacIain any more cause to hate us." He was aware of MacDonald's unnatural stillness; of Stewart's start of surprise, and turned to look at them. "Gentlemen, be assured that while we await the king's pleasure in this matter, you will be treated with such hospitality as I am able to offer. I only regret it must be extended under such circumstances."

Neither young man believed him, nor the Highlanders with them. For that, Hill grieved. If the world were his to remake, he would have men trust one another.

Even Scots and Sassenachs.

Even Robert Stewart and Alasdair Og MacDonald.

Two

It was an alien land, although Cat knew its character, even knew its
names. The Big and Little Herdsman. The Devil's Staircase. Cliff of
the Feinn. The Pap of Glencoe. She had been raised on the tales of the
land, of feuds and killings, of cattle raids and field games. No Highlander was ignorant of his geography, and she no more than men.

Rannoch Moor fell behind, of the bogs and twisted trees; the memory of a hanging. Into the glen she rode, the lush and fertile valley cut
through by the River Coe, cradled by a stark and desolate beauty jeal-
ously warding secret splendors: craggy cliffs cut apart by waterfalls,
tumbling into burns that carved the softer braes into setts, like the
warp of tartan cloth; the wild, hurling power of a river halving the glen
from end to end; the upthrustings of rock bursting free of tree-clad
hills; the rills in the valley floor, the meanderings of creeks flowing
down to Loch Linnhe beyond the ferry at Ballachulish.

It was not a soft place, Glencoe, but hewn by hasty hands, then
shaped by the ages. Its strength lay in its ruggedness, its rigorous demands; its splendor in survival. It was here Dair had been born, here
Dair had been raised, here where the giant, MacIain, made a home for
his people, tending their welfare with all the cunning and strength of a
robust personality well matched to a massive body. MacIain *was*
Glencoe, his bone knit of its stone, his blood milked of its burnwater,
his pride of the cliffs and crags. And it was she, an enemy's daughter,
who would have to tell the father what had become of his son.

Cat allowed the garron to pick its way stolidly, requiring no haste.
She had departed Glen Lyon certain of her course, urged on by the
need to carry word of the truth and her own desire to go. But now she
was here, in the womb of Glencoe with the Pap overhanging, where
hatred of Campbells was bred from conception.

Her shoulders ached with fretting. It was all she could do not to halt
the horse, to turn it back, and leave. Who was she to ride in unaccom-
panied with word of the laird's son: taken by Sassenachs from the
house of a Campbell, from the bed of Glenlyon's daughter?

They none of them knew her. Only *of* her, if that; a drukken man's
lass, meant to marry Breadalbane's son. But even in that she was repu-
diated by Duncan's elopement with his Marjorie; and though she approved of it, wanting nothing of him for herself, to others it was
dishonor. A man had refused her to reject his father's wealth.

The garron plodded on. Cat shut her eyes. Sweat stung in creases and hollows, tension in breasts and groin; despite the languor of summer she felt urgency, and apprehension.

'Come home with me to Glencoe.' Well, she had come. But he was not here.

"Are ye ill?" a voice asked.

Cat's eyes snapped open. A man stood beside the track, reaching out to catch the garron's headstall. With him, clutching his kilt, was a young lad.

She snatched at reins, hastily scraped a lock of hair out of her face, tried to regain even a trace of composure. "I've come to see MacIain."

He arched a dark eyebrow beneath silvered hair. "Oh, aye? I would have said you came to see his son." He smiled to mitigate the deliberate irony. "I am John MacDonald. Alasdair's brother." He dropped a hand to clasp the crown of the boy's head. "And this wee sprat is *my* son, Young Sandy."

It escaped her mouth before she could jerk it back. "Dair said that was why he called himself that: too many men were Sandys."

"Oh, aye . . . but here he is Alasdair. Alasdair Og. Though none that I ken would mistake him for our father." His eyes, like Dair's, were brown, the bones of his face similar. His smile was his brother's, kind and very bonnie. "No one in the world would mistake anyone for MacIain. Certainly not his sons."

"He's been taken," she blurted abruptly, and wished it back badly. This was not how she had planned it. "Sassenach soldiers. They've taken him to Fort William, with Robbie Stewart."

John's smile vanished. He glanced briefly at his small son, then looked at Cat again. For all he disclaimed any portion of his father, Cat in that moment saw MacIain in his heir, a predatory stillness in brandywine eyes. "Is he injured?"

Not by Sassenachs—not yet— "He and Stewart had a scuffle."

"He and *Robbie?*" And then the surprise faded. "Ah. Aye, well . . . I kent that would come. But the Sassenachs didna harm him?"

"Not yet. But they put him in irons."

John's mouth flattened; the eyes were again predatory. "Come with me," he said quietly. "I'll take you to my father."

His father. Dair's father.

To her, the roaring giant who had frightened a lass so very badly ten years before. And who, by his thunder, by abject arrogance, had set Dair to gentling, with bonnie smile and honesty, Glenlyon's furious daughter.

There was a past between them, as well as what bound their bodies. And she would not permit MacIain to devalue any of it.

She climbed down from the garron; if MacIain's heir would walk—and *his* heir walk—so would she.

"I am Cat," she said. "Glenlyon's daughter." There. Truth. Confession. She waited for reaction, prepared, she hoped, for hostility, to keep it from hurting her.

"Oh, aye," he said matter-of-factly. "My mother had hoped to meet you."

Cat froze. Somehow, suddenly, the prospect of Dair's mother was far worse than Dair's father.

John MacDonald laughed. "She willna bite, I swear it—but will even a Campbell refuse Glencoe's hospitality?"

No Highlander would, nor would he abuse it. It was a sacred trust. Cat scowled at him. "I will not."

"Come along, then, aye?" He scooped up Young Sandy and set off with the lithe, long-legged grace she had seen in his younger brother.

Dair awoke when the door latch rattled. A moment later a soldier stepped in briefly to set a covered tray on the floor, then stepped out again without saying a word. The bolt was shot again, and the lock clanked shut.

Disorientation lasted only a moment. He knew where he was, why he was there, and who was there with him. None of the conclusions pleased him.

Two narrow barred windows permitted the sun to enter, but the day died into gloaming and the light went with it. Within half of an hour they would be swallowed wholly by darkness with neither lamp nor fir candle to pass a night grown longer and gey blacker for their captivity.

He heard the ringing of chains. Slitted eyes showed him Robbie moving to the tray, stripping back the cloth cover. Two mugs, bread, meat, and cheese. "A feast," Robbie muttered in sour derision. He squatted by the tray and cast a penetrating glance at his fellow prisoner. "Is it alive after all?"

Dair dimly recalled being brought to the cell. He also recalled, equally dimly, that he had managed to reach the pallet on the floor before losing consciousness once again. He did not recall stretching himself out upon his back with his chain-weighted arms crossed peaceably over his ribs, as if he were a corpse. He doubted very much it was Sassenach doing.

"Will it eat?" Robbie asked.

It was hungry, but it knew better. Its belly was not yet settled, and its head ached abominably. But it doubted it could chew anyway with its very swollen jaw.

Dair tongued his teeth on the side Robbie had struck with shackles and chain. *Aye, loose* . . . If he were lucky, he would keep them. He ceased examination; even the slightest pressure sent a jolt of pain through his jaw into a skull already sore. "—bastard," he murmured.

"Ah, it speaks!" Iron chimed. "D'ye want food, MacDonald?"

"Water."

Robbie brought a mug and sat down next to the pallet, legs crossed comfortably as if he hunkered around a mellow fire with pipe-song in the air. His face was dusty and bruised, his hair a wind-tangled cap of golden curls. Gilt stippled his jaw; Dair did not doubt his own, through the bruises, required a razor as well.

He hitched up on an elbow, then stilled utterly. Sweat broke out on his flesh, sheening his face. He wanted very much to release a string of vile oaths, but it hurt too much to loose the barrage with the appropriate vehemence.

"Here." Robbie brought the cup closer. "D'ye want help?"

With his free hand Dair took the mug. He was weak and shaky, but managed to hold the rim to his mouth. The water was cold; it set his teeth to aching. He wanted to gulp, but didn't; his belly's temper was chancy.

"Done?" Robbie accepted the empty mug. "D'ye want more? There's mine."

Dair managed a scowl. "You near broke my head, aye?—d'ye mean to drown me, now?"

In waning light, Robbie eyed him critically. *"You're* in poor temper."

"Christ," Dair muttered, levering himself to the pallet again. He put a filthy, rust-speckled hand to his forehead and gently massaged the flesh in an attempt to ease the ache. "D'ye expect me to forgive you? To forget? You near killed me, Robbie!"

Stewart's tone was curiously flat. "Then we each of us has something to forgive the other for."

Dair froze, then lowered his hand in a rattle of iron shackle to look at Robbie. The Stewart's expression was as colorless as his voice, and wholly eloquent in ambiguity.

"D'ye blame me?" Robbie challenged.

He wanted to. He could not. Kindling anger was snuffed on the bitter breath of acknowledgment. "No," he said finally. "I deserved it, aye?"

"You did."

Dair smiled barely; a faint twitch of his mouth in wry self-contempt. "And I'd have done the same."

"Well, then." The relief was subtle, abetted by satisfaction; the issue, for now, was settled. Robbie reached for and pulled the tray over. "D'ye want food, MacDonald?"

He tongued his swollen cheek. "Not unless you chew it for me first."

"Och, no . . . I think not. Forgiveness doesna go that far." Robbie slapped cheese and beef onto a slice of bread and began to eat. "I'd have killed you, then; I wanted to, that moment. But a clean death, aye?—and for a sound reason. Not hanging for the Sassenachs because we lifted a pawkie boat."

Robbie's perspective had always differed diametrically from his own. Despite the ache in his jaw, Dair could not repress a breathy gust of laughter. "You should have used a dirk."

"Och, well—they'd taken mine, already." He chewed meditatively. "I did feel a wee bit better when you dropped like a felled stirk—only then the lass began to skelp me, and I forgot all about you in worry for myself."

Dair opened his eyes. "*Cat* skelped you?"

"Tried. Took the Sassenach to pull her away." He gulped water from his mug. "Fitting name, aye? *Cat.* She did all but claw me."

Under the circumstances, considering the company, Dair could not think of an adequate response.

"A raukle fool," Robbie said lightly, "to trade a Stewart for a Campbell."

Dair waited tensely, but nothing more was offered. Robbie finished his meal, his water, then settled himself across the cell with his spine against the wall.

Darkness came down, and with it came a silence neither of them broke.

Lady Glencoe, Cat discovered, had bred more into her sons than MacIain. They had a portion of his height—John more than Dair—and the early graying of his hair, but there the resemblance ended. It was their mother's eyes in their heads, her elegance of feature, the quiet grace in movement.

Most of all they claimed her smile, and the warmth of her welcome. She was not a young woman, but withal a friendly one.

Cat was nonplussed. She did not see how Dair's mother could show her such kindness, despite the requirements of hospitality. There was nothing forced in her manner, no tension in her demeanor. She offered drink, food, a chair, then carried the conversation as John, still lugging Young Sandy, went out to find MacIain. But she spoke of inconsequentialities beyond determining Dair was not seriously injured, until Cat left off answering and sat in stiff silence. She was hideously aware of Lady Glencoe's studied assessment, and not for the first time wished there were less of her to assess.

"Do you have the mirror, Cat?"

It shocked her. Hastily Cat drew the tartan bundle from her belt and set it upon the table, carefully folding back the edges until the contents were displayed: rope, mirror, bonnet. She took up the mirror and held it out, trying to still the minute trembling of her hands.

Lady Glencoe smiled. "Och, Cat, I dinna want it back. I only wanted to be certain he gave it to you."

She was, for possibly the first time in her life, utterly bereft of speech.

The thought was fleeting: *Jamie would be pleased, aye?*

Desperately self-conscious, Cat took up the bonnet in place of the mirror and tended it with singular absorption, pulling the wool back into shape, grooming the eagle feather. When it was done, when she could delay no longer, she set it on the tartan and stared at the badge.

"What is the rope?" Lady Glencoe inquired.

Astonished, she met his mother's eyes—*his* eyes—and gave her honest answer. "I cut it from the tree. I couldna leave it there, you ken . . . I wouldna give my father the pleasure of seeing what he had done."

It shook the woman profoundly. She had not anticipated any such answer. Color flowed from her face, aging her instantly; the heavy white threading in faded brown hair was abruptly more pronounced, and the fit of her skin over the contours of her fine skull slackened.

Cat bit into her lip, damning herself for an overbrutal tongue. "Forgive me—"

Dair's mother reached out to catch one of Cat's hands. "There is naught *to* forgive. You are not your father, Cat—and you saved my son's life. For that alone I bless you, but there is more." She looked at the items: her French-made mirror, her son's blue bonnet, the rope a Campbell laird had used against that son. "Men dinna understand. They canna. They use the name to stir the blood, like war-pipes and a pibroch. MacDonald. Campbell. MacGregor, and Stewart. In names there is power, but also blood, and killing—and men forget too often there are more important things than how a man calls himself, or the slogan of his clan."

Cat, transfixed, stared at her.

Lady Glencoe smiled, and was suddenly young again. "He told me only what he felt, and why, when he spoke of a broken mirror . . . he could not tell me what *you* felt, and was afraid of the truth lest it be other than he desired. But now I ken it, when I see what you have carried so close to your heart. No word is required."

Cat swallowed tightly. "I am afraid. Of you. Of MacIain. Even of Dair."

His mother squeezed her hand a final time and released it. "It takes us all the same: loving a man so much it frightens you near to death, and wondering what his people think of you. And *you* have more to fash yourself over than most, aye?''

Cat nodded mutely.

"Have you a temper?"

"Och, a muckle *great* temper—" she blurted, and blushed instantly. There was noise outside the door. MacIain had arrived.

"Good," his wife declared. "You'll need it with MacIain—and I daresay with my son! For all his fine looks and bonnie words, he's as much MacIain's son as my own. They are none of them peaceable men, when pushed to it." The skin by her eyes crinkled as the door was yanked open. "Though John and Alasdair Og are less noisy about it!"

"Less noisy, is it?" MacIain inquired. "Am I to fret about the noise I make in my own house, woman?" But he did not wait for an answer. He came through the door, ducking his snowy head, and crossed to Cat in two paces. "Rise," he said. "Show yourself to me."

Her skin prickled; were she deerhound, she would hackle. It was beyond discourtesy; was everything she expected, everything she had seen and heard ten years before.

But she was no longer ten. And there was nothing in her now, any more than existed then, that would permit in silence such pawkie, high-handed treatment.

Cat pressed a palm against the table and rose with deliberate and painstaking care to her feet. "Like a bluidy cow?"

John, in the doorway, shut the door swiftly and took his son off straightaway to sit in a corner.

MacIain's eyes glittered in deep sockets. "Like a bluidy cow, a bluidy ewe, a bluidy *chick* if I ask it!" But a slight frown furrowed his brow. "You're no wee lass, aye? Tall as half the men in Glencoe!"

"I am," she agreed coolly. " 'Twould be gey difficult *now* to pick me up from the floor and dangle me in the air!"

It baffled him. "What gab is this? Pick you up? Why?"

"You did so ten years ago."

"*I* did?" White brows knitted. "Where did I do such a thing?"

"In my father's own house."

"I did no such thing, ye glaikit girl!"

"You did," put in John from the corner. "Glenlyon's lass, aye?" His smile was crooked. "I recall it myself, now I am reminded."

She was tall as half the men in Glencoe, perhaps, but MacIain still towered over her. She had never known any man so huge. "I thought you meant to drop me."

He thrust out a bearded chin in challenge. "And why would I drop a wee lass?"

Cat grinned. "Because I said you had no manners, and had come to steal our cows."

"You did!"

"I did. And indeed you had no manners—but you had not after all come to steal our cows." She paused. *"Then."*

"Then?"

"You came later."

MacIain grunted. "You've likely got Glencoe cattle out on Glen Lyon braes."

"And will you serve me meat tonight from a Campbell cow?"

"Och, and are you expecting a meal of me?"

"Lady Glencoe did offer."

His eyes narrowed as he studied her. "And did she mean to serve you supper? Or serve you to me as *my* supper?"

"Och, I am too tough," Cat retorted, enjoying herself immensely. "No softness in me, ye ken. No meek-mouthed lass to cower in the corner because MacIain roars."

Blue eyes glinted. "Such as Jean Stewart might, are you thinking?"

Humor was extinguished. She stared back at him with shocked silence in her mouth.

"Hah." MacIain glanced at his wife. Mildly, he said, "He's got himself thrown into Fort William, he and Robbie Stewart. And naught to show for it; the Sassenachs took back their supplies. And the boat."

She nodded. "I had the news of Cat."

Cat scowled at him. "Is that all you care about? Supplies and a boat, when your son is imprisoned?"

The giant grunted and hooked out a chair with his heel. As he sat down, Cat could not but wonder if the chair would break. "Sit." He waved a massive hand. "Dinna greet for him, lass—they'll no' hang him for this."

She sat. "How do you ken that?"

"Because the pawkie governor there has wanted me to speak with for more than a year." He smiled, though it was barely discernible in the depths of his beard. "I'll offer to sign his bluidy treaty."

"Offer," she echoed, reading the implication.

"Offer, aye. And he will give me my son."

"What about Stewart?"

MacIain shrugged. "He's his own father, aye?"

Cat's smile was quick, but faded as quickly. "Do you believe they'll release him for your promise, when you've no intention of signing this treaty?" She paused, struck by his expression. "You willna sign, aye? Dair says not."

The glitter died from his eyes. "What I will or willna do is for me to say. And I'll mind my own house, I thank you."

She had transgressed, but there was more in her mind than such things. Conviction. "I have the right to ask what you mean to do about him."

"And what right is that, in my house?"

His arrogance was apalling. "In your house or out of it, I will ask of his welfare! 'Tis my right, MacIain. Were it not for *me* your son would have hanged." She snatched up the rope and tossed it at him. "Ask *that,* MacIain! It has a tale to tell."

Treacherous ground. She had abrogated her responsibility to repay the hospitality in kind; defying convention, trampling tradition, would not sit well with this man.

His mouth worked briefly, then relaxed. "You go too far, lass."

She dared the truth again. "With you, one must. Else you wouldna hear me."

"There is that," John agreed, forgotten in his corner. "He is a thick-skulled old king bull, aye? Forgets to listen, forbye."

"She has more right," Lady Glencoe said quietly, "and you ken that, MacIain. You beat him bluidy for it . . . for that, and Breadalbane. Alasdair . . ." She flicked a glance at Cat. "You're a stubborn old fool, but no' a blind one, aye?"

MacIain fingered the rope's weave, examined its ends. Then put it back on the table. His gaze was steady as he looked at Cat. "Has he asked you to his house?"

"He has."

"To his bed?"

"He's already been in mine."

A flicker in blue eyes acknowledged that. "And would you leave Glen Lyon—leave the laird's house—to live in Glencoe?"

"I *have.*"

He waited, poised as a wolfhound set to bring down the game. He knew there was more. He was not a patient man, MacIain of Glencoe, but in this he would be. In this he had to be.

For his son. For his house. For the honor of his name, that she had cursed so often.

Cat laughed at him then, cognizant of commitment with but a hand-ful of words. "I'll leave a laird's house to live with a laird's son. Seems a fair trade, aye?"

MacIain leaned back in his chair. Wood and leather creaked. "The better end of it, lass, is living in my glen."

"Hah," Cat retorted.

MacIain bared his teeth. "Pour usquabae, Margaret. I'll share a dram wi' the lass."

Cat recalled the result of the first and last time she had drunk usquabae. She blushed hideously.

MacIain saw it. And smiled.

Presented with water, soap, and cloth, Dair washed, ridding his face of grime and crusted blood, his hands of rust and dirt. The bruises remained, and the stubble, but he felt somewhat clean again. Carefully he soaked some of the dried blood out of his hair, inspecting by fingertips the scabbing cut within the lump, but it was nothing that would not heal. His jaw still ached, but improved.

He tongued a molar, testing its seating. *I may keep all of my teeth after all, wi' no thanks to Robbie.* . . . But he had been wholly, if painfully, honest, despite the ache of head and jaw. He did deserve it, from Jean's brother. And he, in Robbie's place, would have done the same.

Dair set aside the damp cloth. They had left him alone to wash; as well, he knew, to think. Robbie, who had disdained such amenities—and who needed no time to think, save how to frame vulgarities—had been taken off sometime before. Dair was alone in the cell, sitting mutely with his shoulders and spine against the wall. He was aware of a greater sense of self-possession, a renewal of hope; food, drink, the means to wash himself, provided him with a scrap of dignity, a chance to recover confidence.

Dair wondered cynically if the treatment had to do with Governor Hill's personal desires to treat his prisoners well, or that he was MacIain's son, and Robbie heir to Appin.

With care he let his head settle against the wall. He drew up knees beneath his kilt and rested forearms upon them, chain dangling, then released a sigh of resignation. There was no profit in debating the intent of a Sassenach, even within his own head; John Hill was governor of Fort William, a king's man, a soldier, and wholly dedicated to the subjugation of the clans.

Instead, he would think of Cat. Cat, who had tried to skelp Robbie; Cat, who had tried to lie for him; Cat who had, despite her innocence, taught his body new things about a woman. To know the companionship of spirit as well as flesh.

Dair shut his eyes. *Christ, what if they mean to hang—*

The latch rattled. He sat upright, swore to deflect the darting lance of pain in his head, and saw the door swing open to admit Robbie Stewart. And also two soldiers, who gestured for him to come out.

Robbie still clattered with shackles. The set of his mouth and the tilt of his head was arrogance personified, as was his swagger; Dair could not help a crooked smile.

"Well," Stewart said grandly, seating himself on his thin pallet, " 'tis worth letting him mewl if only for the whisky."

Dair rose with infinite care. The soldiers made no effort to hurry him, but let him gather himself and exit without haste. The door as he stepped out was closed, bolted, locked.

From behind the heavy wood came the sound of a wandering whistle. Robbie had never been able to make behave the notes required to follow a proper tune.

Then he ceased whistling. Instead he began to bellow out in broad Scots his tuneless version of a song attributed to a Stewart who was once a king:

> *"An' we'll gang nae mair a-rovin',*
> *A-rovin' in the nicht,*
> *An' we'll gang nae mair a-rovin',*
> *Let the müne shine e'er sae bricht."*

His legs were pillars, Cat decided, holding up MacIain as Atlas held up the world. And more to the point, she thought, perhaps he *was* Atlas, for on his massive shoulders rested the weight of a clan.

He waded out into the shallows of the river, bare feet finding purchase. He did not go far, but far enough; another man might have sought a rock on which to climb from the water, but MacIain did not. He planted himself in the current, then turned and stared at her.

"Well?" He pitched his challenge over the sound of the river. "D'ye think you should be carried?"

She did not. She glared back at him and traded shore for water, picking her way with care.

They were not in the deeps. They did not truly risk themselves. But it was harsh going all the same, and only undertaken because he wanted her to fail.

Or wanted her to succeed, so he might know her worthy.

"Worthy," Cat muttered. "Like a cow, or a horse . . ."

She wore the trews she had come in two days before, and now the bottoms were soaked. Water crept up the wool toward her knees.

"Aye, test the mare's mettle—test the bitch's temperament . . ." Arms outflung, she maintained a precarious balance. "—escort her to the brink, then step back a pace or two to let her decide if she's man enough to take it. . . ."

A rock rolled. Cat hissed a curse as her foot banged against another, then clamped her mouth shut and recovered her balance. She flicked a glance at MacIain, who waited impassively. But she spied the glint in his eye. "D'ye mean to be a dam?" she called. "Or a rock to change the river?"

His teeth showed briefly. "I am a rock," he said, "and on me will the Sassenachs be broken."

She wobbled, then kept moving. "D'ye think they mind you, MacIain? One lone laird in a forgotten glen—?"

"Forgotten?—no, not Glencoe. Look around you, lass—could you forget this place?"

She did not need to look. If she never saw it again, she would remember it.

"A rock, aye," he declared. "Though some say the rocks reside between my ears."

He extended a hand. She felt it close around her own: huge, callused hand, hard as horn; a grasp that could break a man, if MacIain desired it. It closed, gripped, brought her across to stand beside him. The rush of the river, albeit quieter in the shallows, purled against her shins. Tugged at her trews, wool now sagging from the weight.

MacIain flung wide his other hand: elaborate presentation. "Glencoe," he announced, with infinite satisfaction.

She stood in the waters of the River Coe with a man bred of warriors, of the hostility of the land. And knew she was safe. That MacIain, unlike her father, would never permit harm to come to her, or dishonor, or vulgar treatment. *Unless MacIain himself metes it out.* Cat assessed him even as he assessed her. He had not broken the clasp. Neither had she.

" 'Tis a difficult thing," he said at last, "to do your will when others dinna desire you to."

Shocked by the subject, Cat held her tongue.

" 'Tis a gey difficult thing to ken what you want, and take it."

Still she said nothing.

" 'Tis even harder, forbye, to do what others will curse you for, especially a father."

When she could, Cat swallowed tightly. "I have given my father cause to curse me. He never has, to me." She stared hard at rushing water. "Because he doesna care enough."

It was his turn for silence.

She raised her voice. "You skelped Dair for loving me."

"I skelped my son for disobedience, for delay, for weakening my state before Breadalbane. It had naught to do wi' you."

She looked at him sharply. "Naught?"

"Where my son sleeps is no concern of mine."

It was a challenge now. "Not even when the bed is under a Campbell roof?"

He grinned. "Ah, but now the roof is MacDonald-made, aye? And is here in Glencoe."

Cat sighed. "So it is. And so am I. But *he* is not here."

His hand tightened on hers. "He will be."

She looked at him fiercely. "And if you dinna bring him out—"

Teeth were bared briefly. "What? Will you skelp me?"

Cat eyed his massive frame. "If I thought I could reach your lugholes, I'd box them both."

He shouted aloud. "Both?"

"One after another. Until you yelped for mercy."

He grunted. " 'Twould be gey hard to make me yelp, you ken."

"Even a giant has his weakness," Cat reminded. "The story of David and Goliath, you ken."

"And Achilles his heel."

"And Samson his hair." She eyed him critically. "You could do with a shearing yourself."

The snowmelt of his hair curled against massive shoulders. MacIain squeezed, then loosed her hand. "You'll do."

Cat snorted. "Because I'm daft enough to walk the river with you?"

"Och, no." MacIain grinned. "Because you *like* it."

From close proximity, John Hill discovered that the face beneath the graying hair was younger than anticipated. Not a lad, Alasdair MacDonald, unlike Cameron of Lochiel's son— —*closer to thirty than twenty, methinks*— —but neither a man as old as his hair painted him. The bones of his face were fine and clean, the flesh over them—despite mottled bruising and nearly a week's worth of sooty stubble—taut and youthful. Hill had seen spectacularly handsome men before and did not count this man among them, but even in shackles, even in soiled clothing and lurid bruises, he compelled the eye.

Confidence . . . But not swagger, not arrogance, such as Robert Stewart employed. A wholly different appeal, entirely unremarkable until a man looked, and marked.

Hill marked it now. He watched MacIain's younger son enter, clanking quietly of iron; watched him take a position in the center of the small, lamplit room; watched him settle himself to wait, to listen, to weigh. *Not Robert Stewart at all.* He gestured to the bench against the wall. "Please—seat yourself. Will you have usquabae?"

"I will not."

Hill paused. A soft, courteous voice, lacking the edged scorn of Stewart's. A calm, quiet voice, offering neither irony or enmity. "Sitting in my presence, drinking my whisky, does not make you mine," the governor told him. "I am quite familiar with your loyalties."

The mouth was mobile and expressive, but barely acknowledged the exquisite dryness in Hill's tone. "If it please you, Governor, you dinna sit inside my skull."

"And from the look of you, it *should* please me," the Englishman shot back, and was pleased to see the momentary lifting of eyebrows that acknowledged his retort. More equably, he said, "I am given to understand your injuries are none of my soldiers' doing. Is this the truth? I would know if you were maltreated."

"Whoever had the giving of it, aye," MacDonald answered. "But as I was in no fit state to ken what happened on the ride here, I'm no' the one to ask, aye?"

Oh, there is pride after all, and arrogance!

Hill sat down at last. He would not insist that MacDonald do so; let the man decide for himself if he, head-wounded, was capable of standing for so long, or if he, the son of a Highland laird, would deign to sit in the company of a Sassenach.

"It is not my task to punish you," the governor declared. "It is my task only to hold you until I may know the wishes of the king or queen. Nor will I belabor the obvious: that you and Robert Stewart, accompanied by Appin men and MacDonalds, what some name barbaric Highland savages, stole an English ship, and supplies meant for English soldiers."

MacDonald's face was a mask of self-restraint, impassive and unprovoked.

"And yet you killed no one, nor attempted to," Hill said. "No deaths, no serious injuries, and all the sailors were permitted to escape." He paused. With infinite clarity he said, "You kill more fellow Scots in cattle raids than you did Sassenach sailors supplying a fort you would sooner see burned as stand another day." Hill marked the impassive expression. "I admire your restraint," he said, "and I thank you for it. It may well save your lives." He suppressed a cough, then rose. In silence he walked around his table to meet the MacDonald on common ground, standing before him so they might view one another face-to-face. MacDonald was taller, but did not use the greater height to advantage in trying to impose. He simply stood, and waited.

The governor marked the dark, dried bloodstains on the collar and right shoulder of the linen shirt. He noted also the collar was torn away from MacDonald's throat, displaying the ruined flesh beneath.

John Hill knew a noose scar when he saw one. He looked more closely yet at Alasdair Og MacDonald, at the still features, the clear-eyed patience; at the tension in the shoulders despite attempts to relax.

But only now. Only now did the tension show, the attempt and its failure, as a Sassenach soldier looked fixedly, in dawning awareness, at the scar in his throat.

Scots did this . . . Hill tore his gaze from the rumpled, too-pink flesh and looked again at the still expression, the unwavering gaze. And the shame, so subtly displayed, by the minute narrowing of his eyes, the rigidity of his mouth. Iron chimed faintly; the king's governor had at last reached MacIain's son, who did not desire a Sassenach to know the truth of his shame.

Or was it courage, and luck no other might purchase? *—to hang, and survive—* A man killed once might brave it twice. Might know it, and be unafraid of such small consequences as a king's cast-off governor, sentenced to serve *—and die?—* in the land of savage barbarians.

But John Hill did not judge a man by barbarism, by savagery, unless he witnessed it. And he had not. Yet. Not here, where he was offered opportunity to bring peace to the Highlands, and was undone by Breadalbane.

"I cannot answer for you," Hill said, "because such punishment as you deserve will be named by the king, or queen . . . but I will tell you this: if MacIain does not come forward for his people and sign the Oath of Allegiance by the first day of the new year, he and all of his kin, all of his clan, will be subject to the utmost discipline as can be devised by two men who would sooner have him slain than forgiven." Hill looked into the unwavering whisky-brown stare. "Do you truly wish to have Glencoe's fate decided by such man as the Master of Stair, a Lowlander, and the Campbell Earl of Breadalbane?"

Iron sang again, softly, yet MacDonald did not move. Not so a man might see it.

"Think on it," Hill said quietly. "Think very hard. And then, should you be given your freedom, share this truth with MacIain, who is not only your father but the father of a clan. It is in his hands, now, the survival of Glencoe." He drew in a painful breath pulled deep into inflamed lungs. "I have failed. I am a laughingstock. I am but a poor jest, a name passed among coffeehouses in London and Edinburgh." Hill paused. "Scotland will survive. Scotland will always survive. But men such as MacIain, proud people such as MacDonalds, may not have the same future."

He turned. He moved quietly back to the other side of his table, pausing briefly to collect himself. He had not meant to be so bald in speech, so plain in confession; he had not been so with Robert Stewart. But it was done. It was said.

The voice was quiet, but clear. "I will drink your usquabae now."

Hill turned sharply, setting a steadying hand atop the table. And for the first time saw Alasdair Og smile.

" 'Twas honest, that," MacDonald said, "and deserving of respect."

Gratified for the honor, an odd, unexpected honor— —*they would laugh at me, in London*— —John Hill poured whisky.

Three

In the looming grandeur of Glencoe's Pap, Cat stood atop the massive pewter-hued stone thrust upward out of the earth. Beneath bare feet she could feel the ridges and pockets, the treacherous tributaries of ancient rock twisted as Celtic knotwork, rumpled and folded upon itself like a plaid beneath a brooch. To the west spread the glen; beyond it Ballachulish and its ferry, the waters of Loch Linnhe. Where Dair and Robbie Stewart had stolen a ship.

Frustration burned within her. "Too long," she said aloud.

John MacDonald, beside her, put a hand upon her shoulder. "For me as well, aye?—but MacIain kens what he is doing."

"He is letting his son rot in a Sassenach gaol," she said bitterly, "that is what he is doing. How many days is it now?" *How many days have I lived in MacIain's house, wondering about his son?*

"A fortnight," John answered, "but it feels like two months; I ken that, Cat." His hand tightened briefly, fell away. "He canna pursue it so quickly, aye?—or the governor and those he serves will ken they have won. Deliberation is called for."

Wind rustled the trees, the foliage below the rock. She smelled the glen, and freedom, verdant in summer trappings. "And meanwhile Dair is in irons."

"I am no more pleased than you," he said with infuriating mildness, "but I have learned the wisdom in letting MacIain do what he means to do. He is nearly seventy . . . no man lives so long lest he kens the means to do it."

The breeze teased her hair, lifting it from her face. A stronger buffet blew her clothing taut against her body, limned in the lattice of light and shadow. Cat shivered. She was young and newly awakened; she found it tedious to be still. She wanted to run, to leap, to fly from the rock; to share the day with the man who had taught her to live, and to love.

Yet she also felt oddly naked, stripped of everything save desperation. "You are telling me if MacIain went forward too quickly, they would assume his word has no value. That he intends to break it."

She heard his soft laugh. "You are canny enough yourself, aye? 'Tis the only way, Cat. Alasdair will understand."

"*If* they free him."

"No one was killed," John replied. "Bruises and blood, no more. They willna hang him for that."

She could not hide the upswell of bitterness. "Only send him to the Tolbooth in Edinburgh, where he may rot at the king's pleasure!"

John was silent a moment, as if the wind took away the means to answer. He set his face into it, folding his arms, and spoke very quietly. "You are afraid, aye? Of what the others think?"

Cat stared down the glen, unable to meet his eyes. "I am a Campbell." It was sufficient, she knew, unto all explanation.

"You are a guest of the laird."

"That doesna alter my name."

John laughed softly. "That might come yet, aye? Catriona Campbell . . . Cat MacDonald."

She turned to him sharply, needing to know. "Would that matter so much?"

"Not to me, no. Nor to most of us, if to any."

"But there was Jean Stewart . . ." She had spoken the name at last. She supposed it would be better discussed between women, but she was easier with men. Four brothers had taught her that. "Six years, I was told—and now supplanted by a Campbell."

" 'Tis no one's concern who shares his bed, Cat."

She smiled lopsidedly. "MacIain said the same."

With eloquent irony and an equally bonnie smile: "Then you've heard it twice, aye?—perhaps you might believe it."

Cat persisted. "But she has friends here . . . people who kent her well."

He shrugged idly, toeing a pebble from under his foot. "No one kent Jean well. She wasna disposed to having any of us so close." He sent the pebble plunging over the edge and down the stony face. "She was hidden in her thoughts. Private in her feelings."

"Except for Dair."

"Aye, well . . ." John sighed. " 'Tis over, Cat. 'Twas over before he saw you again at Achallader."

She took fire at that. "Dinna lie to make me feel better, John MacDonald!"

He laughed. The flesh by his eyes crinkled. "Och no, I am not disposed to do so . . . not even for courtesy's sake." He pulled a stray lock of hair away from his left eye. The silver now boasted strands of white, as if age promised premature solicitation. "We stood up here, he and I, discussing this very thing."

"Discussing *me?*"

"Not you by yourself, no. But how a man learns he is mistaken, and must set his life to rights," John said quietly. "He kent it already, Cat. I canna say if *he* kent 'twas you he wanted, but he didna want Jean anymore. He made that plain. And plainer still that he meant to tell her so, once he came back from Achallader."

She crossed her arms and hugged herself, face bared of hair by the wind. "I wondered how he could ask me to his home, with Jean still in it."

"In his heart, she wasna. Not anymore."

Cat smiled a little, though it hurt. "That means something, aye?— that he wasna intending for two of us to live beneath his roof."

"Or one of you in Glen Lyon, and the other in Appin?" His tone was kind. " 'Tisn't his way, Cat. 'Twas never Alasdair's way."

It welled up suddenly, with no warning. "I wouldna want to be Jean," she blurted. "Nor to be in Jean's place, going away from the house of a man I loved."

"What they had was never love."

It astonished her. "But—"

"You are young, Cat." His eyes—Dair's eyes—were warm. "I dinna mean that as insult—you are a woman grown, aye?—but there are things between men and women you canna envision. Pray God it remains that way."

She dared it. "You and Eiblin?"

"Eiblin and I kent we were meant for one another when we were wee sprats. There was never another for either of us."

And again: "But—"

"But not everyone is so, Cat. And if there is pleasure, even without love, a man may bide a wee."

"Six years," she said; it mattered.

"But not strung like a necklace, aye?—one bead after the other. As much time apart as together. *More* time apart as together."

"It matters," she told him.

"I ken that," he answered as steadily.

"And yet I think if he came home from Fort William and asked me to go, I would not. *Could* not. So how can she?"

"Because Jean is the kind of woman who doesna fight for a man. He fights for her. 'Tis how she wants it. 'Tis how she needs it." John shrugged. "But Dair has never done so, and that, you ken, is why there were six years. Because Jean could not bear that *he* might turn away. Such things were her doing. Her decision."

"That isna love," Cat declared decisively. "That is war."

Dair's brother smiled. "And she has forfeited the high ground. You hold it, now."

Cat turned, angrily blinking away unbidden, unwanted tears. "Not if he doesna come back."

The Earl of Breadalbane made deep obeisance before the Queen of England and Scotland. It was not his preference to see her on matters of state—that was for the king, save William remained in Flanders—but circumstances, wholly unexpected, required it. And so he faced her now, in London, in Kensington Palace, trying desperately to muster diplomacy as well as authority.

She motioned him to rise. She was plump of body, round of chin and shoulders, with a proud, straight nose—not humped as was her husband's—and an excessively small mouth nearly devoid of lips. Dark hair was piled up on her head in a myriad of waves and iron-wrought curls. She resembled her brother, the exiled king, and was not particularly attractive. But beauty was not her strength, nor equally her folly. Her strength, just now, was William's absence; the folly a romantic streak coupled with Scots blood. And she had, only today, decided rather incongruously to recollect it.

"Your Majesty," he began, "I have learned of your intent with regard to the Highlanders who stole the *Lamb* and her supplies near Fort William." Sweat stung in the fleshy hollows beneath his arms, soiling his finery; he wore his best London-made suit to meet with the queen. "If you will forgive my impertinence, Your Majesty—I would wish you might reconsider."

Mary sat very straight in the massive chair beneath a draped canopy, as if intimidated by her surroundings and desirous of not showing it. Near her feet was a tangle of silky, parti-color dogs, the spaniels called after her father, Charles I. The earl paid them no mind save to briefly mark their presence; they were not elegant deerhounds and thus did not matter. Not far from her chair, though a conspicuous distance away, gathered a clutch of silk-clad ladies as unremarkable as the dogs.

"Why might you wish it?" Mary asked in a thin, girlish voice.

"I believe it to be in the best interests of England if they were transported to the Tolbooth in Edinburgh, Your Majesty—"

"To wait upon the king's pleasure?" she interrupted. "Well, our royal husband has more important matters to concern himself with than rebellious young Highlanders."

"Yes, Your Majesty—but—"

"He is at war, my lord earl. The future of our country rests upon his beloved head. He need not trouble it with this, we think." The hem of her skirts was abruptly tugged away from slippered feet as one of the young spaniels caught the fabric and pulled. The queen laughed in indulgent amusement and bent down to free her skirts, making soft and wholly inefficient reprimands, to which the dogs responded with a marked lack of respect.

Breadalbane chewed the interior of his cheek. He did not know why this woman frustrated him so—he was well versed in dealing with recalcitrance—save he could not use the weapons he was most accustomed to. She was female, innocent of wit and politics, but wielded enough power with William away that she could undo his plans.

Patiently, he began anew. "Your Majesty, these Highlanders are far more than rebellious young men, but warriors—"

"We have ordered them to be set free," she told him firmly. "We have said so to the Council, and the orders have been drawn up. They shall be strictly warned, my lord earl—but one cannot truly blame Highlanders for being Highlanders." She smiled, and her lips all but disappeared. "We who are Scottish—we who are *also* Scottish!—understand the Scottish temperament."

The palms of his hands were damp. He pressed them against his coat. "They have not come forward to swear the Oath, Your Majesty. They are rebels, no more, and should be punished."

"What month is it, my lord earl?"

The incongruity startled him. "August, Your Majesty."

"We thought so." Mary's lips thinned; her eyes held a glint very nearly malicious. "Then these young men have four more months before they are required to sign the Oath." She cast a secret, sly glance at her women. "Let the young men have their adventures."

He could not conceive that she should be so blind. "But they might have killed the sailors, Your Majesty—"

"And yet they did not; we made certain of that." Dark eyes hardened. "Be certain that had they killed a single Englishman, we would have acceded to your wishes. But they did not. And we should be in great inharmoniousness of mind if we believed the negotiations for peace among the clans were jeopardized by overharsh punishment. Such things call for delicacy."

Breadalbane, who no longer believed in negotiations when he and Stair intended something far more harsh and indelicate, bit into his cheek again. This time he tasted blood.

"We shall forgive them this," she said. "As will you, my lord earl."

It was finality. Royal dismissal. Breadalbane bowed, cursing inwardly, and took his leave.

Robbie Stewart disdained stirrups. Freed of iron, he caught double handfuls of the garron's mane and swung up into the saddle. *"Quidder we'll zie,"* he said: 'Whither will ye,' in Gaelic, the Stewart motto that was, in this particular instance, wholly appropriate.

Dair knew whither. But *when* required patience; they had unlocked Robbie first on the Parade Ground before the gate, along with the Appin men and the MacDonalds. Only he remained shackled.

He wondered for a moment if Governor Hill meant to keep him. But no. Major Forbes came with the key and unlocked him with economical efficiency, then stepped away.

Dair's wrists and arms felt curiously weightless after three weeks of iron bracelets. He pressed his elbows against his side lest the Sassenachs see his discomfort.

In Gaelic still, so the soldiers would not know, Robbie said something rude about men wasting time better spent with lasses. Dair agreed mutely and moved to go to his garron, but John Hill stepped into his path.

"You have my words," the governor said. "In the Lord's name, I pray you carry them to MacIain. I would have a binding peace in the Highlands, not everlasting war."

A slight, wasted man, the years ungentle to him as well as the Highland climate. And yet the resolution in Hill's steady eyes told Dair he was not a man who said what he did not mean.

"I will carry them," Dair agreed, "but I canna say what he will do."

John Hill's unexpected smile was very faint. "Who else can predict MacIain save MacIain himself?"

Dair thought that was about as true and damning a statement as any man might make, Sassenach or no. He gifted Hill with an answering smile, then went with haste to his horse. *Best we leave Fort William before the king's wife changes her mind.*

And home, home to Glencoe. Home to red-haired Cat.

He and Robbie, followed by the others, departed at a gallop. Gaelic curses as well as dust fouled Fort William's air.

Cat sat inside Dair's house. A small house, a good house, built stout against the weather, withstanding Highland blizzards as well as Highland rain. Drystone walls, slate roof; a sound house, withal, if not as fine as Chesthill, but better by far than that: this was full of Dair MacDonald.

She feared at first it would be Jean she saw, Jean she sensed, perhaps even Jean she smelled when she went at last into the bedroom, the small cubby near the door. But there was naught of Jean after all, save a handful of dead flowers shedding powdered petals and dried leaves upon the sill.

The bed was not so wide as her father's nor so fine in its linens, but wide enough for two. Enough for a man and his woman.

Cat sat down on the very edge, hearing the faint creak of leather beneath the thin pallet. She had left the front door open so the wind might come in.

But she had not expected Lady Glencoe to come in as well.

Cat stood up hastily as Margaret MacDonald entered. In her hands was a folded bundle, which she set with quiet authority into Cat's arms. "Fresh linens," she said. "My own."

First there was shock, then embarrassment. And then a rushing wonder, that his mother could be so kind. Again and again and again.

"As you'll be staying here now, we'll have the others off." Lady Glencoe set to with swift efficiency, stripping the bed of coverlet and old linens. "I'll leave it to you to make it."

It took no time at all. And then the woman was gone, saying no more about it. Cat, who knew little of women, nonetheless understood the gift. Understood the blessing that would remain unspoken between them.

She pressed the new linens against her face, inhaling the subtle scents: wool and wood and tobacco, whisky and pressed herbs. With care she began to unfold them.

Cat was nearly finished when she heard the shouting out of doors, the distant hails by MacDonalds. She left the bed, the room, and went to the doorway, shielding her face with lifted hand against the setting sun.

Alasdair Og, they called him. Alasdair the Younger. But Cat, overcome by relief, mouthed another name—and with it a prayer of thanksgiving. Then she went out into the sun and waited for him to see her.

He did not at first. There were the others to greet, those who came running up to welcome him home, to remark over the gossip that had him nearly to Edinburgh, to wait on the king's pleasure. She saw him smile, saw him speak, saw him clasp hands and look around. And then there was MacIain, so tall amongst the others, and his mother, and his brother, and then Dair was off his garron, clutching shoulders and clasping arms.

Cat felt oddly detached. The whole world was centered on a single man, drawn unerringly to his presence. She felt it, wanted to answer it, but did not. Could not. This was not her place, unless he made it so. He owed his people more.

She saw his mother turn and push him gently. He looked. He

smiled. He left behind the others to stride barefoot and bedraggled across his sun-gilded dooryard to the woman in his door.

She marked the sooty stubble blooming slowly into beard. It made his teeth all the whiter.

—with white teeth a'gleaming—

Cat said it aloud: "—and silver in his hair . . ."

"Och, aye," he said ruefully. "D'ye mind it so much, lass?"

She did not, not at all; nor the grime, nor the stubble, nor the stink of a Sassenach cell.

He was whole, and home.

And the bed was *theirs* to lie in, no longer Jean Stewart's.

Snow scoured the Highlands, whitening the mountains and frosting the edges of pools. The land glittered with brittle ice-rime, crunching and shattering beneath feet now clad in brogues, cut hide wrapped skin out was pulled up around feet, then laced with thongs at ankles and calves. Voluminous plaids served as blankets and cloaks for the men, hoarding body heat, while blue bonnets powdered white kept heads from bitter cold. The women wore kerches, or plaids pulled over their heads, muffling wind-tender faces.

In Dair's house the pungent peat-fire burned, yet the warmth he sought and found came not of dried turf cut out of the braes but of the woman beneath the blankets, bare breasts pressed against his chest. His feet were tangled with hers, ankles laced like brogue thongs if with less flexibility; and her hair, free of encumbrances, was trapped beneath their shoulders. He was slack against her, but only because he had spent what was left of himself in the moments before.

There was little room to breathe; the covers pulled high against the cold shut out the air. Moments before they had thought little of such impediments as covers; but they cooled now, and Cat had yanked the covers up.

She was no longer a maiden, as he should know, but neither was she profligate in experience. Her desire to learn was flatteringly adamant, but there was yet embarrassment in her as she learned the needs of her own body as well as his, the complex intricacies of matching male to female in taste as well as fit. Yet she was withal a passionate woman in words as well as her needs, and was unstinting in offering all of what she could; as unstinting in confessing she wanted more even though she knew less. And so he took gently, forcing nothing; but took fiercely too, and gave, teaching her also there was nothing of etiquette in bed, no requirements of manners. Only pleasure, respect, affection, and the means to share it equally.

She was tall, and did not fit as Jean had with the crown of her head set snuggly beneath his chin. To do so required some bending of the body, and for now they were sealed: hip to hip, ankle to ankle, brow to brow. For each of them, so entangled, so enamored of touch, only a single arm was free.

Cat's was draped across his jutting shoulder, lax in satiation. Her long fingers caught briefly and gently in the tumble of hair at his neck, combing absently. His arm moved; fingers drifted against her rib cage, then glided across flesh toward the curve of hip and thigh.

Her breath was warm against his cheek. "Will it always be so?"

"What, this?" His fingers tightened purposefully against the silk of her hip.

She laughed softly; her knees hugged his. "All of it," she said, as laughter stilled into seriousness. "The days, the darkness . . . or will we use it up and have naught left?"

He knew then what she meant. Not only the joys of his bed, *their* bed, but in the days, the weeks; even the years of their lives. They had lived as one for three months only. It felt, incongruously, as if they had been together all of their lives; as if they had known one another for only this moment, and it so paramount as to eclipse all others.

Dair smiled, stroking flesh. It pleased him to feel the tautening of her body, the immediate response. "I am content as I have never been," he said. "I lived in the house of my mother and father, and knew security; and in this house, alone, and knew pride in adulthood, in being a man"—he put his hand in her hair, cupping the cap of her skull—"but never have I felt as content as I do with you in my house. With you in my heart."

Cat was silent a long moment. When she spoke, her voice was husky. "My father has a liking for spirits, you ken . . . and he was most pleased when a new keg came in from France, of the drink he calls brandywine. I have seen the need in his eyes, the need of his body . . . but he empties it, aye?—the keg of brandywine . . . and when it is empty, when he has drunk himself of it into a stupor, there is naught left for him but discontentment that there is no more. There is no more pleasure in what he *has* drunk, but in what he canna have again."

Dair did not smile. "Are you comparing yourself to brandy, Cat?"

Tartly she said, "Spirits do better with age, aye? Women dinna."

Now he did smile. "Then let me ask this of *you:* d'ye mean to leave me when I am white-headed, like MacIain?"

She expelled her breath as a brief, amused gust. "If so, I had best be saying my farewells in a fortnight, aye?"

He grinned. "A blow to the heart, that."

Cat affected injured innocence. "Would you have me lie?"

"Well," he observed judiciously, "you might be gentler about the truth."

She grunted. "I dinna see that white hair has sucked the marrow from MacIain's bones."

"Or blunted the dirk that is his tongue?" His hand stroked again from ribs to hip, to thigh. "He has regard for you."

She thought about it. "There is peace between us."

"But I have been there too, aye?—I have heard the war of words between you."

She shrugged the only shoulder she could. "I canna play chess, and I am poor at backgammon."

"So you give him words, instead."

Cat was silent a moment. Her body now was quiescent as she offered another truth. "I have never kent a man such as he is, Dair . . . there was a man in my mother's bed, as I am in yours, but he did no more than that to breed sons and a daughter. I canna say what my mother was—she died when I was but a wee sprat—but he was never a father. MacIain . . ." She sighed, tucking her head into his shoulder. "MacIain could be the father of us all, aye? Every man, woman, and child here in Glencoe."

Dair thought then of what John Hill had said upon his release: '. . . *share this truth with MacIain, who is not only your father but the father of a clan. It is in his hands, now, the survival of Glencoe.*'

"Even me," she said, following up her thought while he went elsewhere with his.

His father had yet to sign the Oath of Allegiance. In four weeks the indemnity offered, the deadline imposed, would expire.

"He is a gey strong man," Cat said. "Stronger than any I ken."

Another time Dair might have feigned offense; should she not say that of the man in her bed, rather than of his father? But his thoughts now ran toward John Hill, and the oath, and the promises made by a Dutchman who called himself King of England and Scotland.

'Will it always be so?' she had asked. Dair did not know. The world was larger than their bed, larger than Glencoe, larger even than the Highlands altogether. The world was Scotland, but also such men as Breadalbane, a Campbell; and the Master of Stair, a Lowlander; and an exiled king who as yet offered no answer to their request for information: would he release his Highland supporters from the oath sworn in his name at Dalcomera on the eve of Killiecrankie? *Or will James, living forever in France, turn his back on Scotland and the clans?*

He wanted naught to do with such thoughts, not now, not here. And so to drive them away he loosed his ankle from hers, bent a leg, hooked a knee athwart her thigh, snugged it behind a buttock. A shifting of weight, the leverage of an elbow and he was free, free to roll atop her, to pull her beneath himself; free to cover her, to seek assuagement in the comforts of her body even as she, rousing as quickly, murmured incoherently and offered admittance, offered surcease from his unanticipated upsurge of apprehension, the desperate uncertainty of what lay before them.

It was cowardice, not courage. Escape, not confrontation. Avoidance of what was truth in the falsehood of the moment: in her, he could forget. In her, there was no fear.

Cat guided him, as he had taught her. Welcomed him without hesitance. Took of him what he offered and returned it fourfold. She locked her legs around him, taking him deeper, taking him farther, delivering of him his substance, his self, so that he, overtaken, threw back his head and bared the taut cords of his throat as well as the scar upon it . . . begging in silence for her to take him deeper yet, and farther, that he might lose himself in the only way he could; that he need not think of such things as oaths to one king and an indemnity of another; that he could instead think of only the moment, of the woman, of the covenant of the spirit as well as of the body, and the conviction that what they shared would never, unlike Glenlyon's brandy keg, be emptied of its fire.

Cat laughed deeply as her nails dug into his hair and dragged his head to hers. *"Chruachan!"* she exulted.

He who was MacDonald did not know, in that moment, if he were victor or vanquished.

And did not care.

As John Hill set down the letter received so recently from the Secretary of Scotland, called the Master of Stair, parchment shook. His hands shook. The heart within his chest thumped irregularly, so violent in upheaval he feared it might cease to beat altogether.

Perhaps it would be well for him if it did. Perhaps it would offer release from this most onerous of duties, this most painful of all instructions.

He groped for reassurance, for something to mitigate. *Not an order—* Not yet. An advisory. Intelligence, acquainting him with the matter of the Highlands, the brutal, cruel, magnificently arrogant Highlands and her equally turbulent clans.

Not an order. A lesson, Stair declaimed in writing, that would be understood by all the rest of the intransigent lairds, taught by blood and fire in the language of the Highlands: extirpation. The cessation of a clan, one particular clan, so that all the others would hear, would know, would fear. And acquiesce.

William would have Scotland. William would have his Highlanders. And William would send them to fight the French king, on whose beneficence Scotland's Stuart-born monarch survived in exile.

—*let it not be so*—

But it was, it was.

—*let it be that I misread it*—

But he had not, had not.

—*let be a dreadful mistake*—

That it was, and would be.

And in desperate dialogue with himself: "There is yet time. . . ."

—*there is*—

"He may yet come forward. . . ."

—*but probably not*—

"If Buchan and Menzies return from James with his release of them, all the lairds will sign. . . ."

—*even MacIain*—

Perhaps even MacIain.

But equally—painful acknowledgment—perhaps not MacIain.

In his peat-heated, pungent room, Governor John Hill clasped his wind-chafed hands upon his crude writing table, crumpling the parchment. "Christ Jesus, I ask you—" He bent his head and pressed his brow into his bony thumbs. "—dearest Lord, I pray You in the name of your holy Son—" His eyes ached with sudden tears trapped behind tightly shut lids. "—let this not come to be!"

Cat laughed aloud, no longer cold but warm. He lay beside her, collapsed in all things, even of speech, grinning inanely into his pillow as she tried and failed to rouse him.

"Is he weary?" she inquired. "Has he struck his banner?"

He twitched as she investigated, drawing a quick breath. "Christ, Cat—"

"Has his claymore been blunted?"

Dair's laughter was strangled. "Will you have it *off* me, then?"

"I prefer it—sheathed."

"Aye, well, as do I—*Christ*"—Dair gargled as she squeezed—"but you might give me a chance to hone it again—"

" 'Tis for *me* to do, aye?"

"—deliver me . . ." he gasped.

"Och, aye?" She tugged gently. "Where am I to deliver you—? . . . or is it that you wish to be delivered *from* me?"

His reply, couched in half words and sibilants, was incoherent.

Cat laughed. It bubbled up from deep in her throat, bursting free to skirl like a war-pipe at the dawning. She was a steaming sulfur pool a'bubble with elation, so full of effervescence she thought she might fly to pieces. In an instant's flash of insight and quickening curiosity she sat up, then moved atop him. She straddled his thighs. With hair spilling all around, coiling against his flesh, she arched her spine and stretched jubilant arms into the air. *"Chruachan!"*

With markedly less exuberance, Dair offered dutiful rebuttal. *"Fraoch Eilean."*

She swooped down abruptly, setting forearms and elbows on either side of his head. Masses of hair fell around them like a brilliant copper-clad plaid. "What we have," she began, "what we share . . ."

He blinked, unfocused in close proximity. She hung over him like a falcon, swift of wing and beak, stooping on its prey. "What we share—?" he echoed.

" *'Ne obliviscaris'*. 'Tis the motto of the Campbells."

" 'Forget not'?" Dair smiled. "Och, I dinna think so. Not ever." He paused. "Not with you in my house—and with such a powerful inducement as that!"

She grasped again. "This?"

"Oh . . ." he hissed, ". . . aye . . ."

Cat laughed again, certain of her course. " *'Ne obliviscaris.'* Aye?"

But he could not answer, and in his taut, rigid silence she knew she had won a freedom far greater than ever imagined.

Four

I n Breadalbane's Kilchurn bedchamber, where he laired against the winter, parchment crackled beneath the earl's hand. He nodded once. What he read pleased him. Immeasurably. So much he felt exultation hastening a heart he believed beyond such emotion. All of the pieces, the plans, put together at last.

Achallader's razing avenged. And the brutal raid across Glenorchy as well as Glen Lyon. And all of the insults, all of the enmity; the interminable feud dating back a thousand years.

To MacDonalds of the Isles, usurpers of Scotland itself, and the very first Campbells.

So many years. So many offenses. And now the Master of Stair promised compensation. He declared it in his letter.

All of them to die.

Breadalbane rose from the edge of the bed, collected himself, then knelt beside the fir wood whelping box. A vein-fretted hand caressed the deerhound's head, tugging gently at folded ears. "A braw, bonnie lass," he crooned. "A braw, bonnie lass, aye?—and a fine litter withal."

The bitch licked his hand. The long curved tail thumped. Deep against her turgid belly, suckling vigorously, five squirming puppies thrived.

But in Glencoe what puppies were yet unborn might remain so— and MacDonald children as well.

Stair promised it. Stair had written it down in so many words. All of them to die.

"Aye," he said softly, stroking the wiry hair, "by the first of January you'll be free of these burdensome mouths, even as I soon thereafter shall be free of MacIain."

God would surely understand that it must be done if the Highlands were to survive harnessed *to* the wheel that was England, rather than fall beneath it. Glencoe was, after all, only a small holding, and her MacDonalds less significant in the vital workings of Highland politics than others of the surname.

All was in motion now. Nothing could be stopped. Stair promised it.

The Campbell earl smiled. *They shall be forgotten, MacIain and his Mac-Donalds, and the glen by the River Coe . . . and when this thing is finished no one shall recall them, or what was done to them.*

Dair stood at the foot of the great rock at the east end of the glen and looked at Cat atop it. She was barefoot, trews- and shirt-clad, swathed haphazardly in a man's plaid. Her hair, unbound and uncovered by kerch or borrowed bonnet, blew unfurled in the wind. Behind her, crowning the Pap and Devil's Staircase, clouds misted the morning.

"What are you doing?" he asked, perplexed, having just come up from his house—*their* house, and overempty—to search for her.

Cat, poised against the wind, smiled in extravagant contentment. "Looking."

"Och, well—I can see that, aye?" He glanced back over his shoulder curiously to inspect her view, though his vantage was not so paramount. He saw nothing he had not seen before. "What is it you're looking *at*?"

"Not at, aye?—*over*. The glen." She stood, arms folded beneath the plaid, at the western edge with muddy toes curled over the knurled lip of craggy granite. "Glencoe."

It baffled him. "Glencoe?"

She withdrew an arm from beneath the plaid and gestured geography. "Just over there is MacIain's winter house—there, Carnoch, through the trees . . . and John's and Eiblin's over there"—she swept the arm across the track that wound its way through the center of the glen—"and ours down a wee, behind that rib of mountain . . . and all the others scattered here and there like dice amidst the rocks and trees, or chicks too far from the hen—" Her arm dropped. "And beyond all that is Ballachulish and the ferry, and beyond that Loch Linnhe, and beyond *that* the Isles. But for the trees one might almost see them"—Cat grinned—"and Sommerled himself."

He had taught her that by the peat-fire, with whisky in horn cups and tall tales as well as true in his mouth: of bold Sommerled come down from northern lands and his brave sons, who made the Isles theirs; and of Donald himself, progenitor of them all who now lived in the glen of the River Coe, of such proud peaks and frozen waterfalls, of stony curtain-walls nearly impassable.

Dair grinned back, much admiring a view that had nothing to do with houses or trees or islands. "You could be a ship's figurehead, standing up there like that."

"Och, I would rather be a sailor than a piece of wood . . . to sail the oceans broad and see what there is to see, to travel to the far Indies for the spice and to China for the silk . . ." She glanced down at him, bright of eye and yearning, one strand of hair blown slantwise across fiercely beautiful features, the face of a warrior-queen. "You've been to France, aye? I've been nowhere."

"You've travelled farther than you ken, Cat." He made his way around the back of the rock. "Verra much farther, aye?"

Her tone was dubious. "Have I?"

He climbed the crude steps hewn by no man's hands but God's, and joined her atop the time-wracked stone. Wind unpleated his kilt, billowed in his plaid. Like her he was barefoot; with the snow melted, it was good to feel the earth beneath one's feet.

"You have." Dair stood next to her now, one hand meeting hers to grasp, to twine the fingers into his own. "Would you have said ten years ago that you might stand here one day with me?"

So close, she was warm, and warded him from wind. "Ten years ago MacDonalds were lifting Glen Lyon cattle," she explained with marked irony. "So no, I dinna think I would have said anything of the sort."

He laughed. "Trust you to remind me of that!"

"Aye, well, 'tis true. And I swore then to hate you."

"Hate *me!*"

"For lifting the cattle."

"I wasna there, Cat!"

She looked at him sharply. "You were. They said so."

"Who said so?"

"My brothers!"

He affected elaborate comprehension. "Oh, aye, well—*they* wouldna be lying, would they? And were they there, to ken whether I was?"

"No, but—" Cat stopped. She was silent a moment, mouth twisted awry. He felt her body stiffen. "Bloody bastards," she muttered, between tight-shut teeth. "Bloody, cursed liars!"

"Aye, well, brothers are, forbye. Sometimes."

"They *wanted* me to hate you! They kent how I felt—" She broke it off abruptly, face aflame.

This was worth investigating. "Aye?" he prodded. "And what was it they kent you felt?" No answer. "Cat?"

Mutinous, she was silent.

Dair laughed and slung an arm around her neck, pulling her closer still. "You'll no' be hiding something from me, aye?"

Cat worked her mouth, considering something. Then sighed and laughed ruefully, glancing sidelong at him and away. "That day you came, with MacIain. To see my father. About MacGregors, aye?"

"I recall."

"You were kind to me."

He smiled. "It isna my practice to be rude to a wee lass."

Cat flashed him a scorching sidelong glance. "Wee lass . . . I was never a *wee* lass! And not so much a lass at all, to hear my brothers tell it." She heaved a noisy sigh of aged aggravation, then dismissed them from her world. "You spoke to me as if you understood what it was to be overlooked, as MacIain overlooked me."

He was preposterously comfortable with his arm crooked around her shoulders, hand dangling slackly. "Because I kent it myself. I told you, aye?—I was a runtling, myself, and only a second son. 'Twas John would be MacIain one day in our father's place."

Cat's abrupt smile was brilliant. "I remember you said until your hair began to silver, you feared you were a changeling." She put up a hand and touched it, threading affectionate fingers through it. "No one would question it now."

He laughed. "My mother never did. A woman kens her own, she said. But dinna turn the subject. How was it you felt, that your brothers lied to you?"

She left off untangling his hair and let the arm slip to his waist beneath his plaid, settling there with finality. "I told you. You were kind to me. And you were a bluidy MacDonald from bluidy Glencoe, and I couldna help but wonder if you were a monster." She laughed softly. "You were gey remarkable, aye?—a monster, a MacDonald, but kind to a plain-faced lass."

"Ah," he said, as joyous laughter bubbled up from deep inside; he had never felt this with Jean, and marvelled at it. "A great romantic hero, aye?—like in *Roman de la Rose* or *Chanson de Roland.*"

Cat's mouth twisted wryly, and then she smiled. "But I was only an overfanciful lass—I learned the truth of you."

"But I wasna on that raid," he protested.

"Not *that* one, perhaps . . . but others, aye?" She flashed him an arch glance. "There was a misty morning in a Glen Lyon shieling—and you wi' Robbie Stewart."

He sought bitterness in her tone and found none. It was teasing, no more, warmly intimate, as if she had let go all the bitterness of the past, the dirks drawn between them, between Glen Lyon and Glencoe.

Overwhelmed, he caught her up in a sudden, inelegant embrace. "Christ, Cat—" He buried his face in her hair, holding her tightly, so tightly. The wind beat about them, snooving through the trees to tangle tartan plaids. *"Dinna ever leave me . . ."*

Her grip was as strong, and the breath warm against his scarred neck. " 'Tis my home," she said simply. And then, as if comprehending what he could not say, the fear he would not admit, offered him what he most wanted of her. *"This* is my home. Glencoe."

Governor Hill stared at the young Cameron come to carry him a message. He clutched the arms of his chair so tightly his knuckles ached. "James has *released* the clans from the oath sworn at Dalcomera!"

Lochiel's son would be a handsome man. His face was expressive. "He has that, aye."

Relief was overwhelming. Though still seated, Hill collapsed in upon himself, hearing the chair creak beneath him. "Praise God for His wisdom," he murmured breathily, then pulled himself to his feet. Elation lent renewed strength. "Will you have usquabae?"

The young Cameron declined. "We have but six days before the amnesty expires," he said. "My father says we had best go to Campbell of Ardkinglas to set our names to the parchment."

Indeed, time is running out. . . . But Hill believed it no longer mattered, nor Stair's hatred of the Highlanders; that such commitment by Ewan Cameron of Lochiel on the heels of James's release of them would go far to convince other clans this was the right decision.

Except perhaps for one old laird. "Glencoe," he blurted.

Lochiel's son hitched a plaid-swathed shoulder. "We've heard naught of MacIain."

Elation burned to ash. It was imperative that MacIain sign. *If he comes forward within the week, there need not be a beginning of Stair's brutal plan, but if he does not—*

Hill thought back to the conversations he had had with MacIain's son, Alasdair Og. He had seemed a fair young man, an intelligent young man, and Hill hoped the laird's second son had told his father of the governor's words regarding the likelihood of danger if he did not come forward. But there were no guarantees.

If MacIain has not heard, and continues to refuse to sign because he mistakenly believes James has not released his Highlanders . . . "I shall have to send word," Hill declared with finality.

The Cameron's eyes sharpened. His was tense as a hunting hound. "You would do that?"

Hill barked a brief, humorless laugh. "In the name of Heaven, young man, of course I would! If sending a Sassenach soldier into Glencoe would save a single life, I would do it. And carrying word to MacIain could save more than a single life, Scottish *and* English."

After a taut moment, the Cameron smiled. "I will ask my father if I may go myself."

"You owe nothing to MacDonalds," Hill said in surprise.

"And you owe less, aye?" He tugged on his bonnet. "I willna drink your usquabae, Governor . . . time grows short, aye?" There was a pronounced glint in his eye. "My father is a man who covets another's attention . . . coming so near to expiry will cause them all to talk."

Hill watched the door shut behind the young Highlander. It was pride that governed Lochiel and men such as he. If he could be seen to acquiesce only after James's release, only at the cusp of expiration, he would be remarked a man who did as he must in the name of clan and country, not as a fearful weakling who gave in to Sassenachs.

Aloud, because once spoken it carried more weight, he proclaimed, "Lochiel's son will go to MacIain, and Glencoe will be saved."

The Earl of Breadalbane walked beside the winter-crisp shores of Loch Awe, near brown and brittle reeds, watching deerhounds gambol. The bitch was free of the pups now and much relieved, though they still yearned after her; her milk had dried and she no longer tolerated importunate mouths. The five long-tailed, ribby puppies trailed after her as she walked ahead of her master, making shift to control impudent legs as yet too long and angulated for their narrow bodies.

Five healthy puppies. The four bitches especially he treasured, for

from them would come future litters. One day, with care, he would
have produced a line of deerhounds unequalled by any other.

The puppies made hard going of it; at six weeks they were independent enough to be adventurous, to test their way in the world, but in-
fancy-awkward and prone to discover trouble. And they did so now
along the rocky shore, tangling themselves in rocks and reeds and icy
snowmelt until all of them were soaked. And so the earl whistled the
bitch to his side and started back for the castle; they came at once, all
five—as expected with their damn departing—and as hastily as they
might, yelping and straggling and lalloping across the muddy turf.

The bitter cold had faded, but it was still winter withal and the puppies young. In the courtyard Breadalbane took up burlap sacking and,
with much effort and no little protest of winter-wracked joints, knelt to
dry the puppies.

It was messy work and as equally unappreciated by the squirming
subjects. He might have left it to the gamekeeper to tend the puppies,
but the earl took pleasure of it. Kilchurn was his world, inviolate of
such things as judgment by others, and he spent much time catching
and drying the puppies, gently insistent. One by one, struggling and
squawking, each leggy, fuzzy deerhound sprat was warmed in the earl's
burlap-filled hands, until all were set free again, dry, to roll against the
flagstones in frenzied disgust, or to leap upon one another in mock
ferocity.

He rose at last, if slowly, and tossed damp sacking aside. His efforts
had disordered his clothing, but he was disinclined to care. And then
Sandy came with a letter in his hand, saying a courier had arrived from
Edinburgh.

Breadalbane broke the seal and unfolded the parchment. He read
swiftly, then again, less swiftly. And crumpled the letter in one muddied hand full of damp and dog hair. "London," he said succinctly.
"At once."

Sandy departed with alacrity to make preparations. His master
delayed a moment to gaze at his puppies, but saw nothing at all of
dogs. And even when the bitch came up and set her head beneath his
hand, pressing a shoulder against his leg, he was not moved to pet her.

"One week," the earl said bitterly. "One week only before the year
is out, before the scheme can be set in motion, my compensation rendered—and now James releases them!"

But he calmed himself with effort. All was not lost. He need not
panic. One week in the Highlands, with winter yet settled in, could
equal a month on the road. And the reprieve would be undone, and
MacDonalds would die after all.

Grey John Campbell glared up at the clear skies. *"Snow,"* he ordered succinctly, as if he were God to command it.

Cat, sensitized by now to MacIain's moods, sat quietly near the fire in MacIain's house as Ewan Cameron's son related the news. The hilarity of the evening at Carnoch, begun after supper as first John and then Dair battled their father at chess and were badly beaten in flamboyant displays of MacIain's skill, faded now into stunned silence.

Lady Glencoe, pouring wine for Cat and herself, set the flagon on the table, task unfinished. Dair, who had knelt to tend the glowing peat-fire behind Cat's stool, stood up. No one spoke, not even Young Sandy, who slumped against his father's side as sleep overcame him. It prevented John from doing anything other than stare at the Cameron who brought such news.

Eiblin MacDonald, within weeks of delivering John's second child, cupped rigid hands over the mound of her belly. She looked expectantly at MacIain. So did they all, now, turning as one, while MacIain himself, masked against expression, set down beside the chessboard the pawn he held.

"I thank you for your news," he said calmly. "Will ye drink usquabae?"

The Cameron accepted with a bob of his ruddy head. He was clearly nervous—MacIain was infamous—but just as clearly proud of his heritage; he was also the son of a laird, even as Dair and John. His father was of equal standing as Glencoe himself.

But Cat could not help a faint smile; no man in the world, laird or no, was equal to MacIain in anything but title.

For some time the Cameron was hosted according to Highland tradition, given food, drink, and welcome. He declined the offer of a bed within the laird's own house, explaining his father and his gillies awaited his return near the ferry at Ballachulish by the road to Inveraray, where they would meet with Ardkinglas.

In Campbell lands was Inveraray, and the sheriff himself a Campbell. Cat looked again at MacIain. He had welcomed a Campbell into his house, but that was withal a minor thing when compared to swearing an oath.

With friendly words exchanged and good whisky drunk, the Cameron departed. Only MacDonalds now, save for Cat Campbell. She thought perhaps she should leave. But Dair, standing behind her, put a hand on her shoulder and held her there.

MacIain knocked back his whisky, then set the glass down upon the table with an audible sound. "So," he said.

No one spoke. Young Sandy stirred against his father's side, murmured briefly, then slumped back into sleep as his mother, seated nearby, leaned to smooth tousled hair. The Parisian clock on the mantel ticked loudly.

Cat was glad of Dair's hand on her shoulder. She wanted badly to look up into his face, to judge his expression, but she could not turn away from MacIain. He had spellbound them all.

John was heir, and thus perhaps the bravest. "If we are released from the oath we swore to James at Dalcomera, we are free to swear another."

MacIain grunted. "I heard the lad, aye?"

Silence again, and the ticking of the clock. Cat wanted to scream.

John continued. "The proclamation was plain. If we dinna sign by the end of the year, we will be punished."

"Och, I recall it," MacIain said. " '. . . to the utmost extremity of the law.' " He poured more whisky. "I am neither deaf nor blind, John, to not ken what we face."

Soft but pointed reprimand. Cat, who had only experienced the bombast, felt this was infinitely more dangerous. The expression on John's face confirmed it.

From behind her, Dair spoke quietly. "You have the warning I carried from Governor Hill at Inverlochy."

"I do, aye." MacIain sipped slowly, savoring the liquor. "You did tell me, Alasdair."

"For all he is a Sassenach, he strikes me as a fair man. A truthful man."

"So you said, aye. Twice over."

"Six days," John said.

In candlelight, the white mane glowed. "Neither deaf nor blind, aye?—nor unable to count."

"What will you do?" Cat asked, because no one else had. Because she thought no one else would.

MacIain's eyes burned into her own. "What would *you* do?"

It took her by surprise. "I? But—I am not a laird—"

"Does it make a difference?"

"Of course it does! If I am responsible for only myself, I might decide one thing . . . but if I had a clan to protect, I might decide another."

Teeth showed briefly in a feral smile, then hid themselves away in the nest of his beard and moustaches. "And yet you have the temerity to ask me what I will do, here and now, when there are many things to be considered, no' the least of them the people—*my* people, aye?— who depend upon me." He swept the room with a level glance. "All of you ask it. I see it in your faces."

Cat could not recall a single instance when her father had said so much as MacIain about tending his people. Glenlyon was also a laird, and yet he commanded nothing save dice, very badly, and whisky very well. *What would I do, were I laird of Glencoe?* She was only a laird's daughter. She had no responsibilities save those she created.

MacIain grunted. "This game is done." He broke up the hard-won positions and moved the chess pieces back into position for a fresh gambit. "A new one has begun."

Eiblin MacDonald looked at her husband, who looked in turn with studied consideration at his sleeping son. Lady Glencoe's hands were folded in her lap, her face composed, but Cat saw the line of tension in her shoulders. And Dair, still standing between the fire and Cat, released a quiet breath that was, by its lengthiness, a statement of itself.

Cat waited. She had said what she could, and knew no more now than she had before the Cameron had arrived. But the world had changed completely, and their lives with it. *'Twill be for him to decide what becomes of us all* . . . And she knew in that moment she would have no other man save the aging, giant MacDonald make such a decision. He was a harsh man, a stubborn old fox, but he loved his people. She trusted his conviction more than she did her own.

He looked at them all one by one, then rose and strode to the door. He pulled it open and turned. To his sons he said, "Take your women home."

Abject dismissal. Cat stiffened, shocked.

MacIain saw it and looked directly at her. "Take your women home," he repeated, "and leave me to my own." Beyond the door, beyond MacIain, snow fell out of the darkness. The respite was over; winter had returned.

Cat, chilled, rose as Dair moved to stand beside her. *But it could be no more bitter than the winter in his eyes.*

John Hill started violently as the door to his quarters was flung open. A man stood upon the threshold. In guttering light before him, with snow-scoured darkness behind, he might have been a hero out of the tales of Celtic bards, a giant Norseman come up alive from the barrow-grave dripping of earth and damp. But John Hill saw immediately the damp was melting snow, and there was no earth at all upon him. Only a mask of implacable stone in place of a man's face.

He wore wool, leather, and steel. He glinted with it in candlelight, a hard, martial glitter born of pistols, dirk, and sword. And all wrapped up in tartan, head now bared of bonnet, so that melting droplets of snow formed diamonds in white hair and a shawl across his shoulders.

"MacIain," Hill said, because there was no doubt.

"Governor," MacIain returned in a quiet rumble.

Behind him, snow fell steadily. An unrelenting storm had piled banks against the buildings, formed a second if softer defense for the palisaded walls. That MacIain had made his way through from Glencoe was a remarkable feat—until one looked at the man and judged the spirit in him, the unwavering determination. He simply could not fail, in himself or for his people. His pride would not permit it.

MacIain filled the doorway. He would dwarf the governor's spartan room. But it was the only shelter Hill had to offer worthy of his guest. "Come in. Will you have whisky, or wine?"

The giant's eyes glittered. His jaw worked a moment; his beard dripped water that beaded on his plaid, rolled across the leather of his silver-buckled baldric. He was withal a warrior, a Gael from other times, as massive in arrogance as in bone. "I have come to swear the oath," he said at last, and softly, more softly than Hill expected. "Will you administer it, that I may have King William's indemnity?"

In the moment before shock, in the instant prior to painful protest, John Hill marked the bitter conviction in aged eyes, the honed edge of rumbling voice, the knowledge that what Glencoe did ran counter to his wishes. And yet he had come.

—And very nearly too late . . . "No," Hill blurted, forsaking diplomacy in the magnitude of his surprise. "Oh no, don't you see? *I* cannot accept your signature. *I* cannot extend the indemnity of the king. It is to Ardkinglas you must go, in Inveraray."

"I have come," MacIain declared, brooking no further protest.

It washed up from out of the darkness, filling his soul with sick dread. *Stair shall have his scheme after all—* "Oh, no—MacIain, I beg you . . . I can do nothing for you." He went on swiftly despite the narrowing of distrustful eyes. "You must go to Inveraray, to the Sheriff of Argyll. Ardkinglas will accept your signature, not I."

The old face hardened until Hill believed it might shatter. "You refuse?"

"But I *must!*" Hill cried. "It is not my duty . . . it is for Ardkinglas to administer the oath. You know that, MacIain—it was stated in the proclamation. It is to the sheriffs the lairds must go."

The giant Highlander dripped snowmelt onto the floor. A gust of wind blew snow into the room, threatening even glass-warded lamps; and yet Hill could see no way to have the door shut, with Glencoe still in it. "I have read it," MacIain said at last. "But *you* are a soldier, aye?— and no' a bluidy Campbell."

It was rough flattery, and wholly comprehensible to Colonel John Hill, who had spent his life in the military serving England; he understood very well how a fellow warrior would view such meticulous service, enemy or no. It was honor of itself, despite the name of its king. He was no politician, no nobleman, merely a soldier. And it was to that soldier MacIain now appealed, a Sassenach who was, nonetheless, not a Campbell man.

Speechless, Hill looked upon the old man who was Scotland incarnate, bred of her bones and blood, of the stone and bogs and burnwater. His eyes had seen a multitude of sins, his hands had committed them, and yet he came to sign an oath that would forever mark him the Dutchman's man instead of Jacobite. Glencoe's capitulation was the death of rebellion.

And yet Hill could find no joy in it, nor relief. Only a great and growing fear. *He does not know what Stair has planned for him—and I cannot confide it—* "You must go," he said desperately. "You must go on to Inveraray. Tarry no longer here!"

The granite mask that was MacIain's face began, barely, to crack. "I canna," he said. " 'Twould take me longer than I have, before the year is done."

And so it would. The weather by itself would delay him beyond a day, and there was no more time than that.

One day, no more . . . He had come, had MacIain; Glencoe had come at last. It was the price of survival, the end of a brutal plan, and yet it might be too late.

"Wait—" Hill blurted. He turned at once to his writing table and took up dry quill. Quickly he inked it, pulled a rumpled parchment close, and began to scribble. "I will ask Ardkinglas to receive you as a lost sheep . . ."

It was done in haste, with swift explanation: a mistake, no more, and due forgiveness; surely Ardkinglas could administer the oath despite the tardiness . . . *'he has been with me, yet slipped some days out of ignorance, but it is good to bring in a lost sheep at any time, and will be an advantage to render the King's government easy.'* Hill sanded, folded, and sealed the letter. He held it out to MacIain. "Now I must hasten you away."

The old fox was not hastened. He took the sealed letter with deliberation, put it inside his battered buff-colored coat, and tugged on his bonnet once more. The tarnished silver of his clan crest glinted dully.

"God go with you," Hill said as MacIain turned and went out the door, bending his head beneath a lintel built for a common man.

The governor latched the door and turned away, back toward his bed. Relief warmed him in the snow-dusted room. *Ardkinglas is a good man, albeit he is Campbell. Glencoe is safe after all.*

Cat slid down toward sleep. She did not want to let go; the bed was empty of Dair, who had gone outside to speak with John after his

314 ～ Jennifer Roberson

brother came to wake him, but it was warm beneath the covers and she was lured by its seduction. Only when the door opened again and Dair came in did she turn her back on blandishments to rouse to full alertness.

He latched the door and came into the cubby, unwinding his plaid. Snow dusted his hair; he was, for the moment, his father, save his face was incongruously young.

It struck her afresh, the knowledge and the wonder: *This man is mine* . . . She marked anew the scar against his ribs that had come from a Sassenach blade, and the hemp-track around his neck. The flesh that was not scarred pimpled from chill. "Come in with me." Cat peeled back the covers. "I'll lift the ice from your bones."

"You could lift more than ice, were I not so frozen." The wind had chafed his face. As he got in beside her, muttering of the storm, she gritted her teeth and wrapped his bare feet in her own.

"—warm," he murmured. His hair was damp as he tucked his head against her own. " 'Twas a message from MacIain. He has been sent on to Inveraray, to Ardkinglas."

Cat, winding her limbs around his to warm him, shivered, then stilled. The words were simple enough, but the tone, for all his care, divulged concern. " 'Tis a bad storm," she said, "and a long way to Inveraray. Couldna he sign the oath at Fort William?"

"John says no, that Malcolm told him they had to go on. But the governor gave MacIain a letter to explain away his delay." He pulled a strand of her hair out of his face. " 'Twill take him a day or two to reach Inveraray, but John Hill has spoken for him."

He warmed but slowly. Cat pressed herself more tightly against him. Inveraray was a Campbell town, and in it once, many years before, MacIain had been imprisoned. Uneasily she asked, "What happens when he arrives?"

Dair shrugged: the barest twitch of one shoulder. "He swears himself and Glencoe in service to King William."

Such simple words, explaining equally simple actions. But two years before with the pipes wailing of war they had all of them sworn for James on the eve of Killiecrankie. It was not, Cat knew, as casual an undertaking as Dair suggested.

—not when one looks into their hearts.

She knew his now, better than she knew her own, as well as his courage. And what he would not admit, what he could not confess, were his own thoughts and feelings. If he feared for his father, he said nothing of it. But she had greater latitude than MacIain's son. She feared for a MacDonald gone deep into Campbell country, where he had no support at all save the strength of his own will.

But it was MacIain's will withal. She doubted even Ardkinglas, reputed a decent man, would attempt to break it. Breadalbane, a Campbell earl, and all of the other Williamites had their victory in Glencoe's capitulation. They would, she prayed for the sake of the man beside her, be gracious in that knowledge.

Quietly she asked, "What does the oath mean?" *To us?* she meant, but could not voice that selfishness.

He stirred, shifting closer. "No more nor less than it meant when Jamie's name was attached." His tone hardened. "But he isna a Scot, is William."

It mattered. It would always matter. England had usurped so much of what once was Scotland's. Even her kings, transmuted later to Sassenach ways. Rumor said neither James nor his daughter, William's wife, could speak a word of Gaelic.

Cat stroked a chilled MacDonald shoulder, coveting the flesh. "King's man," she murmured.

Dair, muffled against her, made an odd sound. "Aye, well—*that* hasna changed. Only the name of the king."

Cat supposed so. And she also supposed that if it bought them peace, the oath was worth it. Others might disagree but MacIain, plainly, had not.

Nor had Dair, nor John. The women had not been asked. *Unless he spoke of it to his wife after sending the rest of us home.* That, she knew, was likely. Margaret MacDonald, styled Lady Glencoe, was not a stupid woman, nor MacIain a fool to ignore her canny counsel.

Cat stared into the darkness, wondering what her father had said of her upon receipt of Colin's letter with news that she had gone to Dair, to Glencoe, to live among MacDonalds; wondering too what he would say to know that at last Glencoe and Glenlyon, after so many years as enemies, served the same interests.

With the wind in his face, billowing kilt and plaid, and the smell of water in his nose—imminent snow, damp wool, the pungency of peat—Dair stood beside his brother near Gleann an Fiodh, the Valley of the Wood, hard by Invercoe. He was, as John was, wholly aware of men at their backs, but more aware yet of the men who stood before them, glinting of English steel in muskets, pikes, and swords.

Dair examined them closely, learning their weaponry so he might know how to stop it; but he was not certain he could. The flintlock muskets the soldiers bore were superior to the matchlocks used at Killiecrankie, as well as the new device that allowed the dagger-bladed bayonets to be attached beneath the musket barrel so the gun could still be discharged, unlike the barrel plugs used two years before. The men also carried spear-headed pikes, scabbarded short swords known as hangers, and cartridge boxes on their belts. Soldiers all they were, clad in scarlet, black, yellow, and gray, with buckles on their shoes and uneasy eyes in their heads.

Twenty MacDonalds, no more, ranged across the track behind Dair and John from the edge of the brae to the shore of the loch. They were badly outnumbered and none of them bore weapons; MacIain had seen to that. He had announced to one and all that, in the name of Governor Hill's guarantee and the cause of peace, they were to put away the weapons of war as required by the oath. And so they had, but cleverly, hiding them in peat-stacks or beneath cairns upon the braes; yet no man among them was not suspicious of the soldiers, nor wished he had targe and claymore, or even a Lochaber ax.

"Holy Christ," Dair muttered. "Are we to accept these as friends? I've seen enemies wearing fewer weapons."

"We are at peace with 'these,' " John rebuked without heat. "He signed the oath, did MacIain; we've naught to fear of these men."

Dair snorted derision. "Aye, well . . . I trust you dinna mind if I hold them in some doubt. For all we ken they fought us at Killiecrankie."

"Then they should fear *us*, aye?" John's smile did not last. "Come, Alasdair—they've sent a man forward. Let us see what he has to say."

His body would not move. "I dinna like it, John."

"Nor I. But the oath is sworn; they havena come to harm us, when we serve their Sassenach king." Straight-backed, high of head, John MacDonald strode forward.

Dair followed after a moment's hesitation. The storm at last had died away and the weather warmed again, but he trusted it no more than the many-hued soldiers drawn up in disciplined files, filling the muddy track that cut along the lochside.

A young uniformed man waited for them, standing stiffly before the others. Papers fluttered in his hand, worried by the wind. "I am Lieutenant John Lindsay," he said, "of the King's Foot, the Earl of Argyll's regiment. These are our orders."

Lindsay held them out but John forbore to accept them. Quietly he asked, "Have you come as friends, or as enemies?"

The young officer's face stiffened. "As friends, by God! Sir, on my honor, no harm is intended MacIain or his people. But we have orders, and by his oath he must abide by them. As you shall see if you read them."

This time John accepted the papers. He made short work of them even in the wind, his face expressionless. Dair, standing next to him, could make no judgment of his brother's thoughts.

"Two companies," John said finally, "to be quartered in Glencoe. For what purpose?"

Lindsay was clearly nervous, but acquitted himself well in declaration. "There are yet rebellious clans in defiance of the Oath of Allegiance. The indemnity is lifted. But Fort William is full; it is ordered that the folk of Glencoe quarter us here, only until such a time as the weather lifts and we may set about our business. A week, perhaps two . . . no more than that. We hope it is no hardship."

It would be. "And that business?" John inquired.

"Punishment of those Scots such as Glengarry who yet defy the oath," Lindsay answered promptly. He hesitated, glanced at Dair, then looked to John again. "There is no room at the fort."

A man came forward then, clearly an officer in crimson coat and steel gorget, and as clearly a Scot with plaid thrown back from his shoulders. He glanced sidelong at his young and earnest lieutenant, then spoke forcefully in Gaelic. "Will you have us in?" he asked. "I willna depend upon the orders—what are they save the words of a Sassenach and written by English-speakers?—" With elegant disdain. "—but upon your goodwill and generosity according to the law of hospitality that binds us all, and that all of us do honor, who were born of the Highlands."

It was a crisp, calculated appeal that was also brutally honest, and clearly designed for their benefit—or perhaps for the benefit of the MacDonalds ranged behind, listening distrustfully like hackled hounds. Dair looked at the man indifferently at first, cynical in his thoughts, then stared fixedly in sharp astonishment. And found himself made mute, frozen to his marrow.

The man was much changed. Older, more haggard, very pink of face, with lank, yellowed gray hair and red-rimmed eyes, now an officer in the Earl of Argyll's regiment clad in martial finery, but his identity— and his title—was unmistakable.

Christ Jesus—

And Dair abruptly no longer stood in MacDonald lands so near the loch and the braes but in lands held by a Campbell, on a windswept, rugged moor beside a time-wracked tree, mounted on a garron with noose around his neck, with rope upon his wrists, with prayers between clenched teeth—

—and the sound in his ears of the flat of this man's sword brought down without hesitation upon a shaggy rump to send the horse away.

This man, this Campbell: *Glenlyon*—who stood before them now in service to the king, asking hospitality of them. Knowing Highland honor and the bindings it bore, and how they must respond.

Dair swore feelingly with vulgar vehemence. He felt young Lieutenant Lindsay's shocked stare, was aware of John's sharp concern, sensed the rapt tension in the Glencoe-men behind him—but could not look away from the dissipated features of Robert Campbell.

Glenlyon smiled warmly, with no evident suggestion of rancor. "Alasdair Og," he chided, as if to a son, "would I mean you harm with my daughter in Glencoe?"

Wind rustles trees. There is no peat-smoke upon the air, no smell of cooking meat, no odor of frying fish. No odor at all save of trees, of sap, of turf. Nothing at all of people.

The glen remains, girdled by cliffs and peaks, cut through by the river, but no one lives in it despite fertility. The valley is empty of habitation, save for its natural game. Empty of MacDonalds.

She rides unerringly to the house, ignoring the ruins of others. And there she finds identical destruction as well as similar methods: charred timber and broken stone shattered by the heat, collapsed roof slates. Wind has scoured the ruins free of ash, so that only the stark timbers remain thrusting impudently skyward, fallen into a tangle like a handful of dropped kindling.

Nothing remains to mark human habitation. No scrap of cloth, no pewter plate, no perfume brought from France. Only the detritus of massacre, of fire and plunder, and the flowers of late spring breaking up through blackened soil.

Part VI

1692

One

$\mathcal{G}$lenlyon discovered his daughter was nothing as he recalled—not the Catriona of old, not the child, the lass, not even the burgeoning beauty, but a grown woman of fierce, luminous will and a full understanding of how to employ its power in any circumstance.

Nor did she spare it now as he came up to the house MacIain's son had indicated, when asked for direction. Glenlyon had seen the shuttered expression in Alasdair Og's brown eyes, the stilling of his body, the tension in his mouth, but he had given direction politely enough and Glenlyon had taken it.

Now he paused before that house, marked the woman in its door. *By God, I bred this . . . no one else may claim it!*

She did not trouble to hide her shock, or the inflexible contempt of her tone. "Why are you here?"

Glenlyon forced a laugh. "Have you no better welcome for your father?"

Her expression did not change, nor her question. "Why are you here?"

He drew himself up very straight of spine, summoning what small measure of dignity he could still occasionally lay claim to. "Duty," he announced succinctly. "We're to be quartered here until the weather lifts, and then we'll be about punishing men like Glengarry, who scorn the king's generosity." And then, with blatant disdain—mostly hoping he might shake her out of such edged self-possession, "D'ye think I've come to take back a woman who's exiled herself from my house?"

Clearly she was unshaken despite his attempt; her wide mouth twitched briefly, as if she found the word ironically amusing. "Aye, exiled; and I've a better home now."

"Not a better *house.*"

"But mine."

"Och, aye? I thought 'twas MacDonald-built."

"And Campbell-inhabited."

"So." The initial skirmish was done. "I see he hasna softened your tongue."

"Did you think he would?"

"I hoped." That startled her. He smiled indulgently and reset his wind-billowed plaid, adjusted the steel gorget at his throat. *Let her see what I have become in the king's own army . . . a man to be respected.*

She lifted quizzical brows. "I wouldna have said that was your first thought, my tongue, on getting Colin's letter."

" 'Twasn't," he agreed. "My first thought was verra much as you might expect."

Now she was amused. And satisfied. Glenlyon was not certain if either set well with him. But he was adamantly curious.

"Did you do it to fash me?" It would be like her. Exactly like her. And thus he found it convenient to recall her mother had bred her as well, so he need not blame himself.

She laughed aloud, a glorious, unfettered sound that rang through the trees. "I did it without a thought for you at all!"

And he knew then he had lost her entirely. *No more the lass, my Cat* . . . Nor any more wholly his daughter. The surrender of her maidenhead troubled him not in the least, but with that shedding of virginity had come a new resoluteness, a fierce self-confidence that pierced him like a claymore.

She had always defied him, even from girlhood, depending on steely stubborness and a quick, agile tongue, but now she was collected, confident, much less driven, as if she, now an adult, assessed and knew his weaknesses, named them, accepted them—and dismissed them out of hand as wholly unimportant. He no longer mattered enough to make her angry.

And that made *him* angry. "Have you no hospitality to offer me? MacIain does, and has."

"Then accept it," she suggested.

Somehow she reduced him. Diminished him. In martial glitter and glory, in command of two companies of the king's own soldiers, he was as nothing before her, a dissolute, empty man, wholly deflated of worth as a cast-off bagpipe of air; a feckless, weak-spined man who had wagered away all of Glen Lyon's fortunes save a single house, and that house she had left to live with the enemy's son.

She castrated him, did his daughter, with no more than her contempt, a clear comprehension of what and who he was despite his best efforts to be something—and some*one*—more.

Glenlyon felt a painful quiver deep inside. "Have you no whisky?"

Winter was in her mouth. "Fetch it for yourself."

Astonished, he watched her walk away; watched her walk by him and down along the track snooving through the glen, winding up to tiny clustered settlements scattered along the river, such as MacIain's Carnoch, or Inverrigan and Achnacone. Her stride was long and unhurried, steady and unflagging, taking her away from him until he saw no more.

Diminished. Dismissed. Not worth another thought. *Castrated*— His belly cramped. The house lay before him, offering empty welcome. But he accepted it nonetheless despite its cold comforts. He wanted the whisky, to wash away the bitterness left by an ungrateful daughter.

He was Robert Campbell, fifth Laird of Glenlyon. He would give himself welcome unto his daughter's household if she would not do it for him, nor the man who bedded her, whom he himself had hanged on Rannoch Moor less than a year before.

Glenlyon drew himself up and walked into the house. Such things no longer mattered. MacIain had offered the hospitality of Glencoe, and such trust was inviolable.

Cat had no destination save to be away. She could not bear another instant in his company, nor spare a moment to listen to pawkie excuses. He was as he had always been, but less as well as more: less because he was so much the same and that not much of a man; more because now she understood his flaws, the singular weaknesses that made him, in her eyes, far worse than merely a weak man but also a worthless father.

She walked with unerring aim *away*, going nowhere, until she found herself near the massive rock at the elbow of the river beneath the looming Pap. She halted, transfixed by the stony splendor so much older and stronger than she.

Helplessness overwhelmed her. "If there is whisky in hell, he will surely drink it dry!"

"Cat."

She knew the voice, loved the voice, but it eased nothing of her fury. She did not even turn but glared balefully at the rock. "I hate that man. I *despise* him."

He came up beside her but did not touch her. It was enough to have him so close. "You dinna."

"I do."

"You love him, Cat."

It burst from her painfully, like a harp string wound too tightly breaking abruptly from its peg. "Love *that?*"

He let a moment go by before he answered. "You want him to be perfect because he is your father. Were he just another man, you wouldna care, aye?—but he is more than that. He sired you, he is in you, he helped to shape you. And you want him to be perfect so he doesna reflect on you."

In her silence she heard the wind slicing through the trees. Angry tears welled up. "How can you ken that? You've no cause to feel the same."

"No cause?" He smiled as she glanced at him. "I have a father, aye?"

It was preposterous. "But—he is MacIain."

"And no' so perfect himself." He touched her then, moved behind her and settled hands upon her shoulders. He began to gentle them, working the tension away. "You have grown up all at once, aye? It takes a man so, and some women . . . one day you dinna back down but stand your ground—not because you mean to fash the other, nor to spite him, but because you must. Because in that moment you realize you believe wholeheartedly in what you feel, and you willna allow the other to demean or diminish it. It doesna matter so much what the other thinks of you, but what *you* think of you. And if it pleases you, what the other thinks or says no longer carries weight. It doesna hurt anymore."

She stared very hard at the massive stone. "Then I am not grown-up."

He leaned his cheek against the crown of her head, looping both arms around her shoulders from behind. She felt his body against her own. "Och, aye. If it hurts, 'tis because you realize you're no more the child. You are the adult now, and 'tis for adults to make the bairns feel better. So, you are doubly taxed: you want him to make *you* feel better, because he is your father and 'tis what fathers do; and you want to make *him* feel better, because he is in many ways the bairn himself, desiring succor from you. And you ken it. And it hurts."

She pulled free and swung to face him. "He *hanged* you!"

Dair nodded as his hands fell to his sides. "But he isna my father. I am free to hate him."

"But you willna allow me the same favor!"

"Och, if you wish to hate him because he hanged me, I willna say you nay." The smile came but passed quickly, and never reached his eyes. "But that is a reason, aye? You canna hate a man merely because he is weak."

"Why not?"

"Not everyone can be as you are."

Cat made a rude sound. "The world will thank me for that!"

"The strong should never despise the weak. Cat—" Abruptly he caught her and held her tightly, hooking an arm around her shoulders as she pressed herself against him. "I ken it, I ken it . . . it hurts deep inside, aye? You want him to be everything you believe a father should be, but he is only a man . . . a weak man, forbye, and overfond of his whisky—but not a *bad* man."

She clung to him tightly. "He hanged you." It was the only thing she had on which to peg her anger; he diminished all the rest.

"I was on his land to lift his cows, *and* I was a bluidy MacDonald, one of the Gallows Herd. No doubt there are a dozen men who would care to do the same."

And so he diminished that, too. She laughed briefly and painfully into the folds of his plaid, feeling the hard cold edge of his brooch against her chin. "Dinna say that."

" 'Tis true. We've lifted our share of cattle from other men's braes, and raided their homes. We are none of us so perfect, aye?—and I hope your father doesna drink *all* the whisky in hell, or there will be none left for us."

The worst had passed. Cat drew away, smiled into his face, then turned and tucked herself in next to his body. "I thought he would order me home."

"And are you disappointed that he didna?"

She thought about that. "A little," she confessed after a moment. "I thought he would, and he didna—and so I thought he didna care. And that made me angrier."

" 'Tis easier to fight a true enemy than a man who doesna care," Dair agreed. "Takes all the fire out of your belly, and you're left to deal with the coals. 'Tis unpleasant, forbye."

Cat sighed. After the anger, the outburst, she felt weary and listless. "So, I am grown up at last?"

"In all the ways of a woman . . . as well *I* should ken." He held her tightly and stared at the rock as she had moments before, as if he could not bear to look at her. "Do you want to go back to Glen Lyon?"

It shocked her. "I do not!"

Now he did look at her. "Then why greet over it? You have made your choice, aye?"

"Women greet," Cat retorted. "We greet, because men give us reason."

"Ah. 'Tis my fault, now." In all seriousness.

"Often."

"Oh, aye. I ken that. Now." In equal and elaborate seriousness.

Cat scowled at him suspiciously. "Dinna poke a stick at me, Alasdair Og."

His teeth shone whitely. "And here I was thinking you were fond of my stick . . ."

She lurched away and struck him with a fist. "Dinna be rude! 'Tis daylight!"

"Ah. Well, then, I will save it for tonight."

Cat begged to differ, and did so. "Tonight you and John will sit up in

MacIain's house swilling whisky with my father, and dicing, and playing backgammon and chess, and telling blithe lies and half-true tales, wrestling one another with naught but words—*as men do*—and by the time you come to bed you will have naught on your mind save sleep."

He was laughing. "Will you wager on that?"

"I will not," she said. "But my father will. He wagers on everything."

"Ah, Cat." He pulled her close and planted a kiss on her forehead. "Dinna fash yourself over him. He is what he is, aye?—but you will go verra much farther."

"Och, aye? Glencoe isna so far, you ken."

"From Glen Lyon?" Dair laughed. "Oh, my Cat, think again on that. 'Tisn't measured in miles, the distance you've travelled, but in years and years, all the way back to Sommerled, and the Lords of the Isles."

"MacDonalds," she said sourly. "Aye, well, I didna come to Glencoe to sleep with history. I came to sleep with you."

Dair glanced up assessively. "Clouds come in," he said. "And if we shut the door and dinna light the lamp, 'twill seem like night within. Then my rudeness willna matter."

"And will you swear to me MacIain willna send for you at the worst possible moment?"

Dair sighed. "Aye, well . . . I didna say he was perfect, did I? 'Twas you."

Cat thought it over. "Then I've changed my mind about him."

"I thought you might."

"But we could try. . . ."

"I thought we might."

Cat scowled at him. "Houd your gab, MacDonald. Dinna look so smug."

He laughed at her. "I am as you have made me."

"*Och*, no . . . I willna take blame for that!"

He bent his head against hers. "But you *will* take blame for what is beneath my kilt."

Cat blushed fiery red. She could not help it. It was new, all of it new, and she did not as yet know how to deal with it. She had no ready response.

Dair did. "Come with me," he said. "Come home with me to my house."

In his spare officer's quarters at Fort William, Governor Hill slowly and painfully got down on swollen knees beside his writing table. There he prayed for a substantial time, attempting to reconcile his faith with his duty, his orders with his conscience. He had spent his life in service to the Crown, and now once again he was called upon to answer without dereliction, without delay. He supposed even this prayer might be construed as delay, but he judged it necessary. He judged it *required,* if he were to die a good and committed Christian secure in the conviction his soul would lodge in Heaven.

He spoke nothing aloud, knowing God heard him even within his heart. And he felt it meet, for he wanted God to know how painful this duty was, how excrutiating this service. He had written letters. He had made promises. He had believed those with greater power might also have the decency to understand the plight of an old Highland fox who found it difficult to reconcile his personal pride with the needs of his people.

I failed. . . . He had believed so implicitly in fairness that he had given short shrift to the exigencies of the times, the politics of the moment: men such as Breadalbane, men such as Stair, did not desire MacIain to be forgiven so much as an hour. And he had been late by six days.

Had I been stronger in my persuasion . . . He had tried so very hard in so many begging letters, relying on his superiors to give credence to a soldier who spent his time in the Highlands instead of in council chambers.

They want to have them killed in spite of oaths and honor. . . . And so they would be killed to present an example, to pleasure men in London who served interests Hill suspected were other than the king's.

But the king was not excluded from culpability. Hill had seen the order with its bold, scrawled signature at head and foot. He had protested the order despite the royal seal, but Stair had dismissed that final plea in his most recent letter, and now Hill knelt on the stony floor of a tiny room and knew it was ended. There would be no more appeals.

'You cannot receive further directions . . .' Stair had written. And also the damning words: *'Be secret and sudden . . . be quick . . .'*

He had sworn his own oaths and kept them, had never broken one. He was a soldier. He was an officer. Let no man ever say he did not accept his duty and the responsibilities of his rank.

Other words rang in his head, those sworn by him when James had given up his throne to keep England whole. He spoke them aloud again for the first time since. " 'I will be a true, faithful, and obedient soldier, in every way performing my best endeavors for Their Majesties' service, obeying such orders and submitting to all such rules and articles of war as are, or shall be established by Their Majesties. So help me God!' "

The room was cold but perspiration stippled his flesh. With effort Hill drew himself to his feet and sat down in his chair. He took up his quill, inked it, pulled a fresh sheet of parchment, and began to write the orders for his Deputy Governor, Lieutenant Colonel John Hamilton.

"You are with four hundred of my regiment, and the four hundred of my Lord Argyll's regiment, under the command of Major Duncanson, to march straight to Glencoe, and there put in due execution the orders you have received from the commander in chief."

He sanded it. Folded it. Sealed it. Set it aside for his aide.

It was done. But he was not Pilate. He would not wash his hands.

The knobby, hooked *camanachd* stick wielded by a Campbell soldier swung out and snared Dair's right ankle. Momentum caught and carried him through his rudely arrested motion, so that he had to twist awkwardly to avoid falling badly. Men had broken bones playing shinty; he refused to be one.

But landing hurt regardless. He ended up in a tangle of limbs and sticks, including his own, aware of pain blooming in his ankle. Around him he heard laughter, vulgar jests, the harsh teasing of MacDonalds who, under bonds of hospitality, did not take it amiss that a Campbell had hooked down one of their own, not even their laird's son. It was an active, sometimes brutal game that brought each man to a single level determined solely by skill.

Dair levered himself up on elbows, cursing mildly. He untangled the sticks and tossed his opponent's away to be recovered almost at once, then sat up to reconnoiter the stony, treacherous field as well as himself. The game had moved on, as expected, and he was left to look after his own bones . . . save for his brother, who, grinning broadly, came striding across to peer down at him.

John reached out with his stick and tapped Dair's thigh as a prospective buyer might prod a suspect shoulder on a horse. "Aye, well—d'ye mean to sit there all day, or come back and prove yourself?"

Dair scowled. "You might offer me a hand up."

"And are you a weakling, then, to need it?"

No, he was not—especially not with Campbells in the glen. Dair got himself up, gritting teeth against the pain, and tested his ankle. It was whole, but more than a little tender.

John made a dismissive sound with his tongue. "A wee sprat like you had best go sit wi' the women, aye?—and leave the game to men."

Dair responded with a succinct and vulgar expletive. Laughing, John took himself off to rejoin the game, while his brother limped from the area serving as a field. He went to look for Cat and found her pouring whisky into cups for whoever came by to wet a throat hoarse from shouting.

He saw the glint in her eye as he limped up. "I see you've done no better at *camanachd* than you did at tossing the caber."

Tossing the massive wooden log had resulted in splinters in his forearms, and a sore back. One misstep had overbalanced the caber, and the better part of courage had been to let it fall aslant rather than backward over his shoulder. MacIain, watching with Glenlyon and other officers, had not at all been impressed.

Dair scowled blackly. "Dinna ye ken a man's woman is to tend his hurts, not wound him additionally?"

"Here." Cat thrust a cup into his hands. "Whisky will do better than my tongue, aye?" She smiled widely. "And what is next? Will you heave the stone?" Bright eyes glinted. "Or is that likely to land upon your head and dash your brains out?"

He downed half the whisky in a single gulp, then pressed a sleeve against his mouth. "Christ, Cat, I should send you out there to try it. Then you wouldna be so free with your insults."

She shrugged. "I learned them from my brothers."

Likely she had. And equally likely they had given her no quarter. Mollified, he said, "I did win at archery."

Cat's brows arched suggestively. "You always have been good with a shaft."

Dair, in mid-swallow, was taken with a coughing fit that nearly choked him. By the time he regained control his eyes were streaming with tears.

"More?" Grinning, Cat held out another cup when he could breathe again.

He glared at the proffered whisky. "Christ, woman—so you can choke me again? I dinna think so!"

A clansman came by and accepted the cup in his place. A hearty slap of meaty palm on Dair's shoulder nearly staggered him; by the time he ground out a curse the grinning MacDonald was gone.

Cat came around the table and put a hand on his arm. "Come along, then . . . they can help themselves to whisky. We'll go find us a wee spot of ground to sit upon while you recover your pride."

He allowed her to lead him not far from the table, up a rise to a place beneath a small copse of fir. Behind it and other trees, down the knowe and in a rocky channel, ran the River Coe, swollen and singing with snowmelt; the weather, turning mild earlier in the week, mimicked a spring that was not due for a month or more.

Dair sat down and set his spine against a trunk. Cat settled beside him, pulling from bundled plaid a crust of bread and hunk of cheese. She split both as best she could and offered half to him.

He had shed his plaid in order to play *camanachd*. Now, in shirt-sleeves, kilt, with bare feet bruised and muddy, Dair relaxed against the tree and chewed meditatively. The days in winter were short; within two hours the gloaming would settle in, and everyone would retire to dwellings to drink, and sing of heroes. In his father's house Glenlyon would be guested for supper, eating beef and drinking whisky, and wagering on cards while Big Henderson played his pipes before the peat-fire, filling the laird's house with sound.

There was pipe music now as well, winding up from the land below, and women singing waulking songs as they cooked more beef. Wind rippled his billowing sleeves and ruffled graying hair; it promised snow perhaps by dawn, turgid with moisture. Low clouds from over the loch crowded the mountains like chicks around a hen.

Dair gazed down upon the playing field, looking idly for John. For now most of the soldiers of Argyll's regiments enjoyed the generous hospitality of the MacDonalds, though as always there was a watch. Duty would beckon them soon; for now they waited, eating the meat of their hosts. It was an oddly companionable time in which many old slights were forgotten.

But not all of them. " 'Tis a hard thing," Dair said idly, "to be civil to a man who hanged you."

She glanced at him sharply, then away. "I dinna invite him, Dair. He arrives."

"Every morning?"

She shrugged, picking her bread to pieces. "He might go elsewhere. He doesna." She stared fiercely in the direction of the game below on the field. Shouting, laughter, and curses drifted up to them, breaking through the keening of pipes, and singing. "Would you have me go elsewhere so he will? I could stay with John and Eiblin."

He reached out and caught a stiff hand. "I want you with me."

She destroyed the bread. "I wish he *would* go. I wish all of them would go. I wish they would leave us alone."

"They canna stay much longer, or the blizzards will begin and they'll be here through the season." He squeezed her hand, released it. "Though Glengarry, they say, has come forward after all and agreed to swear the oath."

She turned to him. "Then they need not punish him! They can go somewhere else and plague another clan."

He smiled lazily. "There speaks a MacDonald."

She colored. "There speaks a woman who wants naught to do with her father, or to feed so many soldiers."

"Aye, well—they will move on soon. In a day or two, perhaps." He waved at a cloud of midges buzzing close to an ear. "In a day or two we'll be free."

She shifted closer and leaned her head against his shoulder. "I would as soon he went away and never came back again."

He grinned. *"There* speaks a dutiful, loving daughter!"

" 'Tis the truth, for all it isna bonnie." She sighed. "I have not much in me for duty."

"But for loving, aye." He slung an arm around her shoulder. " 'Tis no' so bad a thing, I'm thinking, to look down upon a clutch of MacDonalds and Campbells sharing whisky and beef and games, with no more violence of it than a curse or a sour glance. No dirkings, no fist-fights, no insults. Perhaps MacIain should have sworn to William and Mary a year ago."

"You dinna mean *that.*"

"Well, no . . ." He smiled. "Perhaps not." A year ago MacIain would never have allowed the thought to be thought, let alone carried out, nor would his son have had it in his head.

She sat very still against him. "A year ago I could not have put cre-dence to this—to *any* of this: Campbells and MacDonalds in Glencoe with no blood spilled . . . or MacIain's son and Glenlyon's daughter sharing a bed."

A year ago the woman in his bed had been a Stewart, and he had not known such contentment.

Conviction blossomed instantly. "Cat." He straightened abruptly and turned to her, unmindful of sore muscles and bruises. "Cat, will you handfast with me?"

It ambushed her utterly. "Handfast?"

"You and me. We'll stand before witnesses and swear we wish to marry, and when we find a kirk—or a minister finds us—we'll do it with Scripture, aye?" It caught fire within him. "Cat, say you will! What bet-ter time to do it than now, with Campbells and MacDonalds in ac-cord?"

She stared at him. And then her eyes filled with tears.

It shook him. "Cat—?"

She laughed, then pressed both hands against her cheeks to wipe the tears away. "Oh, I never thought of it . . . I never *thought* . . ."

He waited tensely. He saw in her face and eyes all manner of thoughts, but none of them could he put name to. So quickly they came and went, leaving nothing behind but tears and tentative laugh-ter.

She drew in a huge breath and let it out all at once. "I never thought anyone would want me."

Such plain, simple words, and so eloquent a declaration. In that mo-ment he shared all the pain, all the insecurities of an awkward lass made to believe she was worthless to any man but a feckless father who preferred whisky and wagers to pride in himself and his daughter.

He reached out and caught her hand, fingered it gently, then carried her hand to his mouth and kissed her palm. *"I* want you," he said.

This time when she cried he knew it was for joy.

Replete with food, smoky whisky, and pleasant company, the Laird of Glenlyon leaned back in the best chair his host had to offer, stretching out his spine. MacDonald of Inverrigan, his wife, and seven children feasted him like a king. Weary of soldier's diet, even of the better food served officers, Glenlyon felt at home again, and respected—for all he was a Campbell in the glen of his enemies.

A wind had come up in late afternoon after the field games, carrying with it snow-laden storm clouds from Ardgour across Loch Linnhe. Glenlyon knew an incipient blizzard when he smelled one, and realized by dawn a man in Inverrigan, looking down the glen, would be hard-pressed to see MacIain's house at Carnoch, or even the smaller settlements of Achnacone and Achtriachtan.

Glencoe was not a single village but a valley-length scattering of dwelling clusters strewn from near the Devil's Staircase to the ferry at Ballachulish. All were MacDonalds and all of Glencoe, but to distinguish among them the tacksmen took on various place names. And so his host was Inverrigan, though the laird was down a bit at Carnoch a shouted greeting away and his sons farther yet, with John and his wife and son at Achtriachtan.

The room was smoky with peat and sputtering lamp oil, ocher and agate in shadows with glints off copper and silver, the dull patina of aged pewter. It was late; within the hour the overtired children would be put to bed, and he and his host as well as additional guests would sit up until dawn playing cards and backgammon. Inverrigan won frequently, but Glenlyon was not made a pauper. The MacDonald took his duties as host seriously, for all his larders were being emptied by the hour.

And blizzards coming on . . . Glenlyon knew it would be difficult for the people of Glencoe to replenish their depleted food supply before the snows locked them inside their dwellings, but there was nothing for it. The orders had been explicit: Argyll's regiments, under Captain Robert Campbell's command, were to wait for additional orders before they could leave, and until such time the MacDonalds, their laird having sworn the oath, had no choice but to host them properly.

At the table with him were MacIain's sons. The eldest, John, Glenlyon had found friendly enough, quiet of manner yet clever, but there was a honed edge to Alasdair Og's brittle courtesy. And Glenlyon supposed he did not blame him; the hemp scar on MacDonald's throat was a daily reminder of a certain discourtesy extended by the man who sat across from him now, and with whose daughter he had, but hours before, formally announced a handfasting. It was a Highland marriage without benefit of kirk or minister, but as legal withal as any according to Scottish law. And so he had lost his daughter to Glencoe forever, while his sons bred bairns in Glen Lyon.

Even now Alasdair Og was clearly impatient as he set the cards to rights before dealing them out. Glenlyon smiled; it was not a way a man might choose to spend part of his first night of marriage, but an invitation extended from his new father-in-law kept him bound to Inverrigan for a while. Glenlyon wondered how explicit MacIain's orders had been to his sons to treat the Campbell captain with utmost courtesy.

The old fox willna let a word be spoken against his hospitality— A knocking came at the door. As the latch was undone from outside a soldier entered, shaking a skein of snow from his scarlet coat sleeves.

Inverrigan, laying more peat on the fire, grunted. "Blizzard commencing, aye?"

The new arrival ignored him. "Captain Thomas Drummond," he announced, eyeing MacIain's sons with startled disfavor. Then he looked at Glenlyon. "Captain Campbell, sir, I have your orders from Major Duncanson."

Inverrigan turned to his wife. "Bairns to bed," he said. " 'Tis men's business."

Drummond took the folded and sealed order from the heavy cuff of his glove and handed it with crisp precision to Glenlyon. He waited in stiff silence.

Glenlyon broke the seal, unfolded the parchment and read rapidly in fitful lamplight, scanning the heavily inked lines. He got no farther than the first sentence beyond the salutation before his heart thumped erratically and the breath stilled in his chest.

"You are hereby ordered to fall upon the rebels, the MacDonalds, of Glencoe, and to put all to the sword under seventy."

The words blurred. Surely Inverrigan, from the fire, could hear the thundering of his heart.

"You are to have special care that the old fox and his sons do on no account escape your hands."

It was painful to breathe. Glenlyon wet dry lips. With great effort he read the rest of the orders calmly, allowing no expression other then bland expectation mold his features; when he was done he refolded the paper more tightly yet and put it inside his coat, taking great care that it was tucked away securely.

One of the younger children began to shriek petulant defiance as

Inverrigan's wife ushered them all into another room. The piercing sound caught everyone's attention but Drummond's, who waited beside the door with one gloved hand on his sword hilt.

Glenlyon looked into that pockmarked, emotionless face. Drummond knew what the order was.

"You are to secure all avenues that no man escape."

Glenlyon took up his pewter cup and downed the remaining whisky. By the time he finished MacIain's sons were looking at him expectantly, waiting explanation.

"This is by the king's special command, for the good and safety of the country, that these miscreants be cut off root and branch."

"I fear our game must end," Glenlyon declared regretfully. "We are to march at dawn, and must spend the rest of the night preparing. But now you will have your burden lifted, aye?—for no more will you be required to feed Campbell mouths." He managed a smile as he pushed his chair back and rose. "If you will forgive me, I will step outside and have a word with Captain Drummond."

Drummond opened the door immediately and went out into blowing snow. The storm had only begun; the ground yet showed dark patches of hardening mud.

Glenlyon followed, tucking his head down inside his high collar. They did not halt just outside the house but walked several paces away, into the wind, where words might be exchanged without another man hearing.

"What has been done?" Glenlyon asked as his officer of the watch came up.

Drummond's mouth was drawn into a flat, taut line. "Word has been sent to all of the detachments. The officers are aware. There is no need for the private soldiers to know until the hour your order is given."

My order . . . It was to be his responsibility, his duty, to order the slaughter of every MacDonald in Glencoe. At five o'clock in the morning, mere hours from this moment.

Wind whipped his exhalation away. Cold snow nearly choked him; or was it cold fear?

"See that this be put in execution without feud or favour, else you may expect to be treated as not true to the King's government, nor a man fit to carry a commission in the king's service."

"Sir," Drummond said, "MacIain's sons are still inside."

He was to have special care that the old fox's sons did not escape his hands. On no account.

"Sir," Drummond said; as captain of a grenadier company he was senior in rank, but made no move to assume command.

God help me, I am to order the deaths of folk who have hosted me—
"Sir—"

A slash of watery lamplight briefly illuminated falling snow. Inverrigan's door opened to admit two men to the night, wearing bonnets and tartan plaids. The house behind them bulked blocky and black against the luminous snow.

MacIain's sons, whom Captain Robert Campbell was—*'on no account'*—to permit to escape.

He heard the betraying hiss of sword being pulled an inch or two from its scabbard. Drummond.

"Wait you," Glenlyon said sharply. "Give me time."

John MacDonald came toward them, then veered away as if recalling they spoke of military matters that did not concern him. "Aye, well," he called above the wind, "we're to bed, Glenlyon. We thank you for your game."

Glenlyon turned sharply; Alasdair Og meant to go the other way, down the glen below Carnoch where MacIain slept.

"Wait!" He heard Drummond's gritted oath beneath his breath, but paid it no mind. "Alasdair Og, I am to depart in the morning. Would you allow a father a private time with his daughter?"

The second figure wavered. John swung back, calling, "Come to the house. Share a dram wi' me before you go down to Cat."

Glenlyon held his breath. If Alasdair Og insisted on going home
... *But I must see Cat alone!* "I willna be long," he said diffidently. "We havena always been close, my daughter and me, but I would like to say good-bye." He managed a deprecating smile he hoped was visible in the falling snow. It thickened, though as yet a man could see. It was not true blizzard yet. "A fool for a father, I am, but she's wed now, and I would give her my blessing."

It was enough. With a bob of his head MacIain's youngest son went with his brother, and left Glenlyon to a parental duty far more vital than he could ever have dreamed.

"Sir?" Drummond yet again.

Glenlyon glared at him. "I have until five of the clock, Captain, which gives me some little time to speak with my daughter."

The implication was plain. Drummond's face froze. "You can say naught to her! If word were carried to MacIain, or to his sons—"

"D'ye think I dinna ken that?" Fury boiled up. "Good Christ, man, surely the king wouldna ask me to leave my daughter in danger! Nor would you, I suspect, if you thought I might report it!" He turned before the other could answer to his officer of the watch, waiting in patient silence as the snow crusted on his shoulders. "You and Captain Drummond are to go at once inside this house, where you will bind and gag Inverrigan, his wife, and all of their bairns. At once." He raked Drummond with a contemptuous glance. "Will that meet with your approval, Captain?"

With equal disdain Drummond answered, "I believe it will, Captain."

Glenlyon swore, then swung on his heel and began to walk down the glen to the house his daughter shared with a man he would order murdered in less than six hours.

Two

Newly handfasted, Cat was at first indulgent of her husband's tardiness, then annoyed by it. He had told her explicitly he would not be gone long; in fact, he had not wanted to go at all, but his father had impressed upon both his sons—and even his new daughter-in-law—with explicit and crude clarity that it was *his* desire they give good welcome to Glenlyon. Cat, kin to both men now—and wise already to that tone of voice—could neither protest nor fault the suggestion.

Now, alone in the house, she dared. *But he might have been more understanding, might MacIain!*

And yet she was not certain the old laird had not known precisely what he did; he had grinned broadly at his younger son's unspoken dismay and cuffed him smartly on one side of the head, then sent him off with his brother. Cat, bereft of husband, took herself away to wait in the house that was no longer his, but theirs.

Time passed at first because she spent it cleaning the house. That she had done it but three days before meant nothing; now they were handfasted. It was her duty. Her responsibility. She would make the house new again, despite its age. The child she had been would begin anew beneath the slate shingles that formed the roof of adulthood.

Cat, scrubbing at the heavy table, caught herself in mid-whistle. She froze for a moment, then laughed aloud. "You pawkie bizzem!" she exclaimed. "Will you look at yourself, tending house like a wife—and without Una to insist!"

Una who was, she assumed, still back in Chesthill minding her father's house. *Far better than I would* . . . Cat laughed again and returned to scrubbing the tabletop with a damp cloth. Forcefully. "And I'll be stitching his shirts, forbye, and mending his plaid, and asking if his meat is cooked to his taste, and would he like a wee dram more in his cup? . . . oh *aye*, 'tis a fair revenge, this! Una would be gey glad of it, too!''

With the table clean, she was done. Cat washed in a ewer and hung the soiled cloth near the stove to dry, then wandered to the door. She lingered there a moment, trying to decide if Dair would be annoyed or pleased if he came home to find her waiting outside in the cold for him, then gritted a curse between clenched teeth and jerked the door open.

Let him laugh if he will— She blinked. Snow. The storm the day had promised was here. And Dair nowhere in sight.

Cat slammed shut the door and collapsed against it as if to lock it with her weight, spine pressed against wood as she crossed her arms and scowled into the shadowed room. She had blown out all but one of the lamps, and now her fraying temper began to match the darkness.

Into the silence she announced, "My father has corrupted him. Already!''

Could she live with another man who wasted himself on drink and dicing?

Cat ground her teeth. "I should have your head off with a Lochaber ax, or even a claymore—but you've buried all of them beneath the peat-stacks!'' She laughed ruefully. "Perhaps 'tis as well, aye?—if only so your wife doesna make it so you'll never be a father.''

But no, she thought that unlikely. There were benefits to man left whole, even one who demeaned himself with her father's company.

Irritation quickened anew. Cat straightened and strode toward the cubby. "Well, I willna wait for you. Come in when you will—I will be asleep.''

But she wasn't. Even stripped of clothing and clad in soft wool nightshift, burrowed beneath covers, she could not sleep. In four months' time she had become dependent on his presence to fall asleep.

Cat flung herself over onto a hip and mauled the pillow with rigid fingers. "Christ, is it so old already? Am I naught to him after all, even though he swore so tenderly—just today!—to love me all my days?''

But a man could love a woman and still desire dice. Or chess. Or whisky.

Or cards with her father.

Inspiration stilled her. What would a man think if his newly handfasted wife came looking for him in the night, fierce as a Gael of old? Trew-clad, hair stuffed under a bonnet, dirk thrust through her belt . . . would he laugh? Be ashamed? Embarrassed? Or pleased enough even before others to know she cared so much?

"Och, good Christ . . ." Cat tore the covers back. Inactivity was the worst enemy she knew, when all her senses clamored at her to go. He could not blame her for being true to herself, could he?—when he himself had explained that was a part of adulthood?

Trews. Saffron shirt. A cropped-down jacket. A battered cast-off bonnet. And brogues against the snow . . . no more bare feet, with blizzards coming in.

Dressed, Cat snatched up a lengthy plaid and began to wind it around her torso as she went through to the front room. Even as she tucked in a crumpled, fraying end she reached out to the door latch and tugged it open awkwardly.

She fell back at once, startled. Her father stood before the door, fist upraised to knock.

His face was curiously slack as he looked upon her, and the blue eyes in reddened rims were blackened by the darkness. It was a ghastly smile he gifted her. "Catriona . . ."

"You," she said flatly, and realized almost at once it was not the warmest of welcomes. But surely he would understand. "Is Dair with you?"

He gestured emptily. "He is with John. He will be down presently." He swallowed tautly. "May I have a word wi' you?"

She stepped aside then, recalling her courtesy. He came in stiffly, snow clustered on shoulders and head, and she offered at once to get him whisky.

"None, I thank you." He lingered aimlessly near the door.

"None?" Cat echoed, astounded.

It pinched him; she saw that. The flinch was minute but visible, and made her wish she might have framed another response. But—Glenlyon refusing whisky?

His face was strained. "You willna thank me for what I've come to say. I'll no' put whisky on the table for you to fling at me."

And she knew then why he had come without Dair. Why he had come in the darkness without an official military escort. Why he had come without a bonnet, and dripped snow onto her floor.

"I will not," Cat said. No more. More was unnecessary.

A harsh laugh issued from his throat. "Oh, aye, I kent you would say so. No need to ask it, aye?—but I will." His eyes shifted from hers to the room, inspected it blindly, then locked again onto her own. "Will you come back to Chesthill?"

She wanted to shout at him. Instead she heard a still, cool voice answering him. "My place is here, with him."

"*MacDonald!*" Glenlyon cried, and in its broken raggedness she heard a desperate despair.

"Aye," she said. "I am."

"No, no—you dinna understand . . . oh, Cat—" He bit down on his lower lip. His hands trembled as he lifted them to his face, to grope awkwardly at melting snow dripping fitfully from his eyebrows. "Catriona, I would have you come home with me."

"With *you*?"

"When I may go," he amended. "I am given leave to go in the morning. My orders have come." His eyes glistened wetly in the lamplight. "Will you come with me now, and leave with me in the morning?"

Oddly, she wanted to cry; he would never understand her. "Is your honor so pawkie," she said, "that you would have me break my own at a word from a man who has done naught but waste himself and his fortune on foolhardy pleasures?"

And then anger spilled away, carrying contempt with it. What she said was cruel, but she did not mean it to be. Not now. It was truth. It was no more nor less than a declaration of freedom, of conviction. Of adulthood.

"You have given me a home," she told him, "and kept me fed and clothed, and brought me up as well as you could . . . I ken that. And you have done as best as you saw fit to replace what has been lost, to repair what has been broken . . ." She smiled at the wasted, weeping man, wondering what he had been before drink and dice had taken him. "But I am grown now, and I have made my home elsewhere. I have a husband, aye?"

His jaw worked. She saw the tremble in sagging jowls, the bruising in soft fleshy pockets beneath his reddened, smoke-shot eyes. He was withal a ruined man, a travesty of a soldier, and not so much of a laird that she was moved to respect him. But he was her father.

"Dair isna wrong after all," she said. "I do love you. I always will."

He turned then, nearly tripping in awkwardness, and jerked open the door. He went out into the darkness in a lurching, ungainly stagger, though he did not run, and strode stiffly away from her, uniform tarnished a bloodied crimson by his desertion of laggard lamplight.

Behind him, wetting her floor, snow fell, and tears. Cat closed the door.

In his brother's peat-warmed house, Dair set down the horn cup upon the oak trestle table in the center of the room. "Enough," he declared. "More, and I willna be able to find my way home."

John slouched comfortably across from him in a chair, with legs outstretched and hands clasped over his stomach, and smiled sleepily. "You could stay here the night and go back in the morning."

"Good *Christ*, man, have you no wits—?" And then Dair grinned

342 ~ Jennifer Roberson

self-consciously as John's soft laughter betrayed the jest. "Och, aye
. . . you've had your laugh, I ken. But d'ye blame me?"

John snickered, pulling an eyelid out of shape as he rubbed a smoke-
reddened eye. "I've my own wife waiting, aye?"

It was Dair's turn to snicker. "Aye, well—you'll get naught but com-
plaints from *her,* so close to her time. Two weeks?"

"Three, we think." John shrugged. "Who can say?—the bairn will
come when 'tis ready."

Dair pushed back on his stool. " 'Tis time I saw to my own
woman"—he grinned to think of Cat as wife instead of lover—"and
the begetting of more MacDonalds."

"Dinna work so hard at it," John advised. "The bairns have a way of
appearing whether you're ready or no."

Dair laughed. "Well, Glenlyon's had enough time with her, aye?—
I'm to bed. He can spend his hours drenching his wits wi' usquabae if
he chooses . . . and Inverrigan can lose sleep keeping him company, as
a good host does—" He caught himself in a jaw-cracking yawn that
warped his words. "—but 'tis not *my* duty, aye?—he isna my guest."

"Be glad of that," John suggested, "or your new-wed wife would be
too shy to greet your soldier."

Dair snickered again, moving to the door. He tugged on his bonnet
and resettled his plaid, folding it high around bare neck. He unlatched
and opened the door, looking over his shoulder at his brother. "We
won the battle at Killiecrankie. My soldier's invincible, aye?"

"But a wee sprat," John retorted derisively, "and yet unproven in
getting bairns."

"Well, I *did* say I would make some—" Dair broke off and turned
sharply toward the darkness. "John—d'ye hear?"

John got up from his chair and came across the room. Together they
looked out into the storm and saw snow falling slantwise in the wind; a
blaze here and there of fitful pine knots, flaring like torches; a glint of
flame off metal.

"Shouting," John said, pulling the door open more widely despite
the storm. Behind them, lamp flame guttered.

Uneasily, Dair squinted through the blowing snow. "Soldiers—with
swords out, and muskets."

"Aye, well . . ." John's frown cleared. "Glenlyon did say there was
much to do to march out in the morning. 'Tis a few hours yet until
dawn, but I imagine it takes time to roust out so many men half-drunk
on MacDonald whisky."

Dair shivered. "I dinna like it, John."

John left the door and gathered up plaid and bonnet, swathing him-

self as his brother had done. "We'll go to Inverrigan and see Glenlyon."

Dair opened his mouth to say it wasn't necessary, but his nerves were
stretched taut. He would not find peace if he did not know. "Aye," he
said instead. "D'ye mean to tell Eiblin?"

"No, I'll let her sleep, forbye. The bairn makes it hard, so big and
active." Teeth flashed in a quick, self-satisfied smile as he pulled the
door shut. "Another lad, she says."

Dair grunted. "Save a lad for me, aye?"

"You're not man enough to make one."

"Give over!"

John, laughing, slapped his shoulder. "Aye, well—you're out of
charity because your wife's waiting below . . . come on, then, we'll go
up to Inverrigan and finish this business, aye?"

In Inverrigan's house, under Captain Thomas Drummond's disdainful eye, Glenlyon made shift to set about murder. With him were his
officers and sergeants, priming muskets, honing blades, affixing the
dagger-bladed bayonets to the underside of the barrels so a man might
stab simultaneously as he fired; a decided improvement over plugs that
prevented discharging of the weapon.

Throughout the room drifted a malodorous fug of smoke—peat
brought in from out of doors was damp and did not burn well immediately—the tang of priming powder, the astringency of nervous perspiration and tense anticipation. He had spoken quietly to them all but
moments before, reassuring them of their task. It was to be a military
exercise, not bestial brutality, and Glenlyon would have it said his orders were executed with a minimum of confusion. Best the Mac-
Donalds be shot in their beds, if possible; or the men killed in their
houses, whisky-weary and unarmed under the oath MacIain had sworn
at Inveraray.

The inhabitants now were all of Argyll's regiment; the MacDonalds
of Inverrigan, all nine—including the children—were bound and
gagged in the bedroom beyond a narrow door blocked by a cowhide
curtain. No protest could be made, no warning cried. Red-coated men
worked quickly and quietly, preparing for duty.

From outside there came shouts of strident inquiry and authoritative answer. Every man in the room stilled. Even as Drummond moved
to unlatch the door it was pushed open, and MacIain's tall sons came
out of the storm into the room, shawled and capped in snow-crusted
plaids and bonnets.

Not now . . . Glenlyon looked an order at Drummond, who stood
behind the MacDonalds with bayonet in one tense hand and musket in

the other. But to MacIain's sons he offered only lifted brows and polite inquiry.

John MacDonald, to his father's guest, had been only a quiet, friendly man; now Glenlyon saw a hint of that father in his posture and presence. The eyes, taking in the shine of lamplight on musket barrels and the industry of powder-stained hands, hardened. "There are soldiers," he said, "all over the glen. I would know why."

Glenlyon nodded matter-of-fact agreement. "With my men quartered up and down the glen from Achtriachtan to Ballachulish 'tis necessary to muster them here, and 'twill take some time in the storm. We are to march at dawn, as I said to you before, and go for Glengarry."

"Glengarry *signed* the oath," Alasdair Og said sharply. "Why must you go for him?"

It was not required for Glenlyon to affect surprise; if that were so, he had not been informed. "Word has not come," he replied truthfully, and knew they could not suspect a lie; he was a poor cardplayer because he was easy to read. "My orders stand, and they say we must march at dawn."

He waited. They were hackled like hounds, stiff with unease and expectation, and very alike in taut, suspicious expressions as they assessed the room and the inhabitants of it, glowing of crimson broadcloth in fitful amber lamplight, with a glib sheen glinting from newly shined steel. Neither claimed the overwhelming height and substance of MacIain, but they did not lack for wit or cleverness.

How many of my cows have they lifted? How much of my plate and plenishings?

Thus goaded, Glenlyon pulled himself to his feet. "D'ye think we mean you some ill? Is that why you have come? You suspect ill-doing because we are Campbells?" He laughed harshly, jerking his head in the younger son's direction even as he stared challenge at the eldest. "If such were my orders, d'ye think I'd give no warning to my daughter and your brother, her husband?"

It was enough. He saw so at once, and breathed again. He might have prated of honor, of offense given by such suspicion, but he had struck the proper note. *No man would see his daughter put in such danger—* Inside, his belly clenched. *But it isna my wish . . .* And it served to say so, it served very well.

Visibly, both MacDonalds relaxed. The eldest smiled a little in evident relief and stepped forward, offering his hand. "I wish you well on your morning march, then. We'll trouble you no more."

As they stepped outside into the storm, Drummond shut the door with a rattle. His eyes were furious, though he kept it from his face.

"They are to die," he said. "It was expressly stated in the order. The old fox's cubs are to be killed."

Glenlyon sat down again. "Och, aye," he said, "but the killing isna to commence before five o'clock—and I willna be precipitate in what the king has ordered." He met Drummond's angry glare. Strangely, he no longer felt tentative or fearful. He had been a soldier once; he had even won a battle for his cousin Breadalbane. He could be so—and do so—again, and this time for a king. "There will be blood this day enough," he said evenly. "Can you not wait a few more hours?"

Drummond's jaw was a bent blade beneath pockmarked flesh. "Then I will have the signal fire lighted atop that great rock, if it so please you, Captain."

Glenlyon laughed softly. "Lowland fool," he said, "dinna ye ken the Highlands? That fire willna kindle—or will die before the dawn."

Drummond opened the door. "If it please you, Captain, I will see to it."

In disgust, Glenlyon bade him go. Then he looked at the officers and sergeants, waiting until he had undivided attention. Then he issued his personal orders quietly, with explicit clarity. "You will tell your men that Alasdair Og is to die," he said, "but his wife is my daughter, and I will kill any man myself—officer or no—who harms her in any way." He paused, marking their rigid attention. *"Aye?"* After only a moment he received quiet and quick assent. "Good." He fingered his sword, resting atop the table in its polished scabbard. "At five o'clock, we begin. There will be no avenue of escape—Major Duncanson's men and others of this regiment will block the pass over the Devil's Staircase and the ferry at Ballachulish."

He slid the blade partway out of the scabbard and tested its edge. *The blood and bone will dull it.*

Glenlyon looked at the others. The wording of the order was burned into his brain. "Put all to the sword under seventy, and do not on any account allow MacIain and his sons to escape."

Cat roused as Dair climbed out of bed. He was careful not to disturb her, but she felt the cold snoove beneath blankets and murmured sleepily, tugging them more tightly around her body. She assumed he meant to use the nightcrock, but instead she heard sounds of him pulling on clothing.

It was still dark, not even close to dawn. She rolled over and peered through the gloom; only the glow of the peat-fire and a single lone night-candle illuminated the house. She saw him affixing plaid to shoulder and bending to lace up brogues. Cat raised herself on one elbow. "Where are you going?"

He turned in the dimness. His expression was troubled. "Canna sleep."

She smiled and dropped the covers down to bare one shoulder. "We could find ways to make you weary so you *would* sleep, aye?"

He answered her smile with his own, but it fell away too quickly. "I am not easy in my mind. Will you forgive me?—I mean to go back to Inverrigan's."

Her shoulder pimpled with cold. Cat raised the covers again, looping blankets over her shoulder. "You said my father was mustering the soldiers."

"Aye, well . . ." He shrugged, checking the knots of brogue laces. "I'll do better to see it myself."

She tried not to sound plaintive, merely casually curious. "When will you come back?"

He came to the bed, smiling. "Soon as may be, I promise you. And then we can set about putting me to sleep." She stretched to kiss him as he bent down, and then he pulled on his bonnet and went out of the house.

It was emptier at night. When he was gone in the day she found duties to keep her busy, but at night before he came home from dicing with her father or speaking with other officers she found the emptiness of the house excruciating. It disturbed her at first that she would be so dependent on him after spending no many years depending only on herself, but she reconciled it with the knowledge he cared as much for her as she for him, and thus it was equal loneliness when one was without the other.

She tried to sleep, but sleep was banished. Even the warm impression of his body against the linens faded with his absence, and after some time Cat at last gave up. *I'll sit before the fire . . . mull some brandywine. . . .* And drink some, too, waiting for his return.

She crawled out from beneath the covers and caught up a crumpled plaid, pulling the tartan around her shoulders, over tangled hair. There were warm, woolen slippers for her blue-veined feet; she put them on with gratitude for Dair's handiwork, for she abhorred a floor in winter.

Cat went into the front room, settling the plaid more comfortably. Dair's departure had allowed a drift of blown snow into the house. She saw the damp spot, the crystals melting against the pegged hardwood floor, and smiled ruefully to think of his warm, vibrant presence reduced to so little but wet tracery on scarred wood. Then she forgot it altogether; she heard shouting from out-of-doors, and a distant, muffled cracking that sounded again and again.

The latch rattled. Cat took a step toward it, reaching out a hand, and then the door was thrown open to admit riotous images:

—*blowing snow become blizzard*—

—*men clustered in her dooryard, engulfing the stone stoop outside*—

—*red-coated soldiers with muskets and swords, and snow piling up on their shoulders*—

Their mouths and noses were masked by cloth, but there were powder burns under avid eyes, darkening the flesh so the whites stood out like beacons.

The man in the doorway raised his musket; from underneath the barrel glinted a wicked bayonet. "Campbell?" he asked sharply.

There were questions in her mind but her mouth formed only one. "What are you doing here?"

"Woman—are you a Campbell?"

Incongruous irritation . . . "MacDonald," Cat declared. Because, now, she was.

He levelled the gun and shot her.

The storm had thickened to blizzard, snow blown slantwise as well as into dervish flurries. The track beneath Dair's brogues was deep with drifts, so that he slipped and struggled. He hunched against the wind with his plaid drawn up for warmth. He had put on trews in place of kilt and was grateful for it; all Highlanders were inured to ordinary winter, but it was nearly false dawn and the blizzard was bitter cold. Wool wrapping his legs afforded additional defense against the keening wind.

He was nearly to Carnoch when he heard a storm-dulled, muffled cracking, like a limb broken beneath a foot. It was not his own; he walked on beaten track covered with layers of snow. Dair halted, senses sharpening. He heard nothing but wailing wind.

He shivered. It was one long grue that ran the length of his spine into his limbs. *I dinna like this.* The night was still. A man should be inside. *I should be home with Cat*— Snow gathered on lashes. Dair dashed them away quickly; he had no time for such irritants. *I dinna LIKE this*—

Instincts overruled thought. He turned and stepped off the track altogether, snooving into trees. It was not thickly wooded in Glencoe, but there was enough for shelter and some defense. He paused once to catch himself against a huge fir coated on one side by a cloak of snow and ice, then went on.

The wood took him to the side of his father's house instead of to the front, as the track did. At the edge Dair hesitated. Through the flurries he saw flashes of flame, heard the cracking again, and knew it was musket fire.

—MacIain—

MacIain's house. His mother's house.

Shouting filled his ears, and a woman's shrill screaming. From the dwellings near the laird's house came the sound of musket fire, no longer occluded by wind and distance.

He knew his mother's screams.

Dair ran. Snow fouled his footing but he did not hesitate. One hand closed on the dirk thrust through his belt, but he did not draw it. He could fall in treacherous weather and stab himself instead of an enemy. *—or lose the dirk altogether—*

More shots. More shouts. More screaming. All throughout the glen he saw flashes of flame, heard the reports of gunshots.

He did not break into the open and make himself a target. He went instead around the back of the house along the edge of the wood, until he could see the front of the house, the door—

—and the broken hinges . . . the dull smolder of fire in one of the windows . . . the shine of flame on musket barrels and honed bayonets, the glint of light on sword blades—

—his mother was screaming—

They dragged her from the house, the men in crimson broadcloth, shouting and laughing and jesting. They tore her bloodied nightshirt from her so that she was naked and shivering, and even against her pleas they stripped the rings from her hands. When two would not come off, not even sliding in blood, one man gnawed them free of her swollen knuckles.

The war cry echoed, the one all MacDonalds hated most virulently. *"Chruachan!"* cried the Campbells.

Up and down the glen; no more was stealth needed. Glencoe was overrun.

Cat came to abruptly; one moment she was lost, the next found, and alive. She knew that instantly—and equally quickly that she dared not move lest they suspect the truth.

Wind and snow howled into the room. The door stood open, then . . . she gritted her teeth against a shudder. A dead person would not shiver, nor would dead teeth chatter.

She lay sprawled facedown, one arm trapped her. The left one was free, slung out away from her body . . . had she twisted, then, in falling? Had the musket ball knocked her around?

Musket ball. Cat bit into her lip. The soldier had *shot* her.

—where is Dair—?

Oh Christ. Where was Dair?

He had asked if she were Campbell.

'MacDonald,' she had said.

MacDonald—and he had shot her.

—where is Dair—?

Dead already? She lay on the cold, hard floor, naked now of slippers, wet with blood and fear, and tried to hear indications the soldiers were gone, or present.

Campbell soldiers.

A shiver overtook her. *—Campbells are killing MacDonalds—*

The door banged in wind. The noise of it filled her head.

If she moved, they would kill her.

If they were here.

The lamp had blown out. Only the peat-fire lent her light, and the subtle glow of luminous snow.

Blood soaked her nightshirt, but she did not feel pain. Snow drifted onto her feet, but she did not feel the cold.

—Dair?—

The door banged again.

Dead people did not cry.

Cat bit her lip till it bled. She knew it did not matter; they would believe that from the musket.

—am I dying—?

All of Glencoe was dying.

Naked, bloodied, now bereft of her rings, Lady Glencoe was forgotten utterly as soldiers plunged into the house that sheltered the laird, her husband. Dair pressed himself up from his crouch near the trees and ran across the dooryard.

He caught his mother in his arms, deadening himself to the opaque horror in her eyes, the blank, blinding eyes above a bloodied mask. "Huish," he said, "say naught—" He touched her mouth a moment to underscore his order, then hastily stripped the plaid from his body. "Here—we must go . . . here, Mother—" He shrouded her quickly, awkwardly; she made no effort to aid him. "Come wi' me—we'll go up the brae . . . Mother . . ." He guided her through the storm, through the deepening drifts. She was naked save for his plaid, and her feet were bare.

"Alasdair," she said.

"No, Mother—say naught—"

"Alasdair?"

She did not mean him. Dair knew that. "Come with me, aye—? We'll go up the brae behind the house—"

"Alasdair!"

"Mother, no . . . mind your tongue, aye?" He did not think anyone might hear her—her voice was thin and trembling—but he dared not take the chance. "Come along, aye?—we'll go away from the house—"

She struggled then in his arms. "They shot him," she said. "They shot him in the back . . ."

"Mother—"

"—in the back . . . when he bent to put on his trews—"

"Mother, huish—there will be time—"

"—in the *back* . . . did they think he was a coward?"

"Come with me, aye—up through here—"

"Could they not have allowed him to put on his trews?"

His face was cold and wet. The wind froze his tears. "Mother, huish—"

"Alasdair—"

He stopped then, as they reached the trees behind the house, and took her into his arms. Against his body her own trembled violently. Dair said things to her as a father to a bairn, trying to soothe the grief, the knowledge of what she had seen.

His father shot in the back. As he bent to put on his trews.

"—Sweet Jesus—" Dair said brokenly, then lifted his mother up into his arms. "We'll go up Meall Mor," he said. "We'll find shelter in the caves . . ."

His father dead. And what of Cat?

His mother was neither large nor heavy, but the snow fouled his feet. Dair staggered, biting into a lip as he caught his balance. He would not let her fall; would not permit himself to falter.

—MacIain dead . . . and Cat—?

He heard shouting again, and screaming. The crack of musket fire, flame spitting into the night.

—MacIain, John, Cat—

The world was snow and flame.

Cat did not know how long she had lain sprawled on the floor, but her body was stiff and cold. She supposed any man might take her for dead. But there was no man anymore, nor men; the soldiers had gone. She was certain of it now.

She lay on her right arm. She attempted to move it, to withdraw it from under her body so she might use both arms to brace herself. Where her hand touched fabric it was wet, wet and cold—

—the soldier shot me—

But she wasn't dead. He had shot, but failed to kill her.

She was afraid to move, but she must. There was Dair to find, Dair who was gone, Dair who had felt uneasy, Dair who had *known* some-how—who had wanted to go to Inverrigan's to see her father.

Cat's body spasmed. It brought pain, brought shivering, brought the truth of her wound. And it was blood she felt in her nightshift, blood she felt in her hand.

—my father—

Who had command of the soldiers. Campbells, all of them.

"Campbell?" the soldier had asked her.

He had come, her father had come, to send her back to Chesthill.

Even her jaw hurt. "Bluidy bastard," she whispered, barely moving her mouth. "Oh Christ, you murdering bastard—"

He had known. Her father.

"MacDonald," she had said—and the soldier shot her.

Weak, drukken man . . . weak, drukken coward. . . .

Glenlyon had *known.*

Cat ground her teeth together, locked her jaw, drew in her left arm and pressed her hand against the hardwood to push herself over onto her right side.

She smelled blood. Her right hand was full of it, clutching sodden nightshirt. Pain blossomed throughout her rib cage. Awkwardly, Cat plucked the heavy fabric away from her side, trying to pull the wool up along her body so she could see herself.

She could not. She could pull the nightshirt no higher than her left hip. She would have to sit up.

Wind banged the door against the wall. Startled, Cat looked up from the bloodied fabric, expecting to see a soldier— *—he will finish the task—* —but no one was there. The wind howled through the room and brought snow with it, so that Cat shivered again despite her prefer-ences.

Pain stabbed. Cat caught her breath on a hissing inhalation that did as much as the shiver to set her ribs afire. She held the breath as long as she could, then slowly let it out. "—move," she muttered. "If they havena plundered the house, they'll be back . . ."

They would kill her if they came. She would rather do it herself then permit a soldier to. And they would kill her out of hand, even as she tried to tell them who she was: she was shot already, and bloody, and only a fool would believe her; likely they would claim she was lying to save her skin.

"—aye, well, I *would*—" Cat took a breath, shut her eyes, pushed herself from the floor into a sitting position.

The world around her reeled. She kept herself from falling by brac-ing both hands against the floor. The right one slipped in blood, but held her upright.

Sweat bathed her flesh. In the wind she shivered, and pain broke out afresh.

She needed to know. She could not delay. There was Dair to find.

Cat hitched her hips up from the floor and tugged on the nightshirt. She pulled it free of her weight, bunched up around her buttocks; she took another breath and worked her arms down inside the sleeves until she was free of them, tented by the nightshirt hanging around her neck. It was loose now, unconfined; she reached up over her shoulders and caught the wool, wadding it as she gathered it from top to bottom. When she could, she pulled it over her head.

Naked, in pain, she shivered. Snow blew across her feet. Her pale skin showed the blue-green veins that Dair so often traced, and the spill of drying blood from the left side of her rib cage.

Trembling, Cat touched it. And found there was no hole.

Crusted blood, yes, and powder burns, bits of torn wool and a shallow gash scored in flesh, but there was no hole.

"Och," she said in brittle disgust, " 'tis no' so bad, aye?—dinna waste any more time . . ."

Relief was palpable; she would not die of this. But Dair might die. Dair might be dead.

Naked and shivering, Cat worked herself to her feet. Shock had receded; she knew the wound now, knew it would not kill, knew it was only sore and torn and bloody. That she could mend. This she could bear.

Meanwhile, there was clothing to put on and weapons to gather.

"Chruachan," she muttered out of girlhood habit, thinking of the enemy and what she desired to do—then bit into her tongue in brutal acknowledgment.

Campbells had done this. Campbells were killing MacDonalds.

"MacDonald," she had said. MacDonald she would be.

Cat bared her teeth. *"Fraoch Eilean."*

Three

*A*t Inverrigan, Glenlyon himself supervised the executions of his host, plus all the men who served him. They were dragged from out of the house, thrown down on dung heaps, and shot. Other Mac-Donalds were stabbed by bayonets or hacked to death by swords in the hands of Campbell soldiers.

The blizzard was fitful now, snow swirling so thickly a man could not see his hand, or sucked up by eddies of air that parted the blinding curtains and permitted visibility. It was enough for a man to see that other men died, as well as women and children.

He supervised the destruction of Inverrigan's household until a soldier brought him a torn and bloodied paper from Inverrigan's pocket. Glenlyon took it with distaste, scanned it, and saw that the letter was from Fort William's governor, Colonel John Hill, swearing that so long as the oath was taken no MacDonald would be killed or molested, nor his plenishings taken from him.

Glenlyon shivered. Here was a promise from a man with authority . . . yet surely Hill had been a party to the plan. Some of the companies come down to block the passes were from Fort William, sent by Hill's command.

In his gloved hand, the paper grew damp and tore. Pieces fluttered away. Glenlyon turned and looked at the house behind him, where he had been hosted in fine fashion according to the laws of Highland hospitality.

What I do has been ordered. He blinked snow from his eyes. *I have been ordered to do this.* And yet Governor Hill himself had but recently promised them safety. *I was ordered.* Who was he to question? A captain in Argyll's regiment, to be instructed what to do. It was duty.

Eight men killed, among them Inverrigan, and now a ninth pulled out of the house by ungentle soldiers.

He thought again of Hill's letter. "Hold!" Glenlyon shouted as they made to drag the MacDonald to the dung heap.

They held at his order and waited, eyes slitted against the storm, but gripping the frightened MacDonald with no thought to letting him go.

Captain Thomas Drummond, who had personally brought the order that set the killing in motion, came out of the house behind them. His pockmarked, powder-burned face stood out in rough relief against the white of the storm. "Why is he still alive?" he shouted. "What of our orders? Kill him!"

The men looked to Glenlyon, who found no words in his mouth.

With a grimace of contempt, Drummond pulled one of his pistols and shot the young man in the head. "All of them!" he shouted. "All of them are to die!"

All dead now but the child, the lad, who came crying through the storm to throw himself at Glenlyon, clutching his legs. He was perhaps twelve, and begging to be saved. He would go, he said, go anywhere with Campbells if they would allow him to live.

Drummond himself yanked the boy away and hurled him at a soldier. "Shoot him! Now!"

Glenlyon flinched as the shot rang out.

Drummond turned on him. "Are you a man," he asked angrily, "or are you a coward? These are our orders, man—they are to be obeyed to the fullest! Anything less is treason!"

Anything less would result in the destruction of what small world Glenlyon had left. The orders to him had been specific in their language: ". . . *else you may expect to be treated as not true to the king's government, nor a man fit to carry a commission in the king's service.*"

All were dead here. But Inverrigan was not the man, nor any of his sons, considered most important.

"MacIain," Glenlyon said. "MacIain and his sons." He met Drummond's eyes. "Carnoch is down the glen."

Drummond's teeth were white in the scarred field of his face. "Carnoch," he agreed.

Above the braes were corries and rough caves hewn out of stone in the palisades of the mountains. Dair carried his mother upward, away from the floor of the valley, struggling for unseen footing buried beneath snow. The terrain was not kind to a man who could neither see nor feel it, and less kind yet to a naked, plaid-wrapped woman sixty years old.

—*cold, so cold* . . . clad only in shirt and trews, but his mother was colder yet. She needed a fire, she needed clothing, she needed blankets, and he had none to give her. Only of his strength, and that was none so inexhaustible under such conditions.

He slipped, recovered, slipped again, and fell finally to one knee. Cursing breathlessly, he struggled to rise again and bring her up from the snow.

"Alasdair," she said.

Not Alasdair Og.

"Alasdair—?"

She had never called him MacIain, the man she had married, but by his Christian name.

"Stop," she said. And then, "Alasdair *Og!*"

He stopped. Cold air sawed in his chest as he tried to catch his breath.

"Alasdair Og, I willna have you spend yourself this way—"

She was his mother again. He managed a choked laugh. "Och, well, I'm spent already, aye?—too late to say me nay."

She struggled to pull the plaid more closely around her. "Where is John?"

"—dinna ken—" He coughed, leaned over, spat into the snow.

"You must find John."

"Mother—" He coughed again, spat again. "Mother, I mean to take you up to the corries—"

"I ken that," she said, "but you must find your brother."

"One task at a time—"

"Alasdair! You must find your brother!"

She had meant him after all. Her Alasdair was dead, Alasdair Mac-Donald, also called MacIain.

Alasdair Og felt the winter in his lungs and fought to expel it. And when he saw her shiver again he hastily tugged his shirt off over his head and grasped one of her arms to guide it through the sleeve. "Here—"

"Alasdair—" She struggled briefly. "You'll die of the cold!"

"Aye, well—look to yourself." She was chilled and in shock, too weak to defeat him. He unwound the plaid, then wrapped it again around her over the shirt. From his head he pulled his bonnet and put it on hers, tugging it down in an attempt to cover her ears, to shield her scalp. It was not enough, never enough, not in such snow and wind, but he had nothing else to give her. "We must go up, Mother—"

"Find your brother, Alasdair."

Her implacability was frustrating. With effort he kept his voice down, so it would not carry on the wind. They were through the trees and midway up the braes, in all likelihood safe from the Campbells down below, but he dared not take the chance.

"We will go up," he said. "I will search for John after I have you out of this storm."

She shut her hand around his wrist. He felt her broken nails dig in, felt the swollen raggedness of her fingers where soldiers had bitten rings from her. "Find him," she commanded. "He is MacIain now."

He knew then what she did, what she intended. The old laird was dead, the towering man who had ruled an entire clan with the force of his personality, the power of his presence. There were people in Glencoe who had never known another laird save Alasdair Mac-Donald. In the midst of grief and terror, Lady Glencoe—who was no longer Lady Glencoe—thought of her kinfolk.

MacIain was dead. John was now MacIain.

"I canna go," he said. "I willna leave you here."

Her hand clutched more tightly. "In the name of your father—"

"I will not." He clasped both narrow shoulders and turned her upward, guiding once again, refusing to let her fall. If he kept moving, if he took her higher, if he fastened his thoughts on her, he would not feel the cold.

Cat wound bandaging around her ribs, using a portion of her nightshift. Then she put on shirt and trews; lacing the brogues was troublesome as the exertion hurt her wound, but she could not go out barefoot. When she finished tying the knots she clutched the bedframe until the sweat dried on her body, then took up one of Dair's older plaids and wrapped it around her body. She belted it, thrust a dirk through the leather, then braided and tucked her hair up into the bonnet she had worn to leave Glen Lyon.

Could she do it, she would take a claymore. But Dair had hidden away such weapons as claymore, ax, and pistols, acceding to the order from MacIain. It was compromise; they had not given over the weaponry to the soldiers in Fort William as commanded, but had instead gifted them with old, rusted blades. The rest they had buried in the peat-stacks or beneath stone cairns on the braes.

And all now were buried beneath snow as well. There were no landmarks Cat might use, did she know where Dair had put them.

Dressing had taken time, and in that time she had worked out enough of the plan to be sickened by it. Governor Hill had written MacIain and others that Glencoe would be safe if the oath were sworn. Breadalbane had promised it. Her father had sworn when he was welcomed in Glencoe that they went to punish Glengarry; Glencoe was safe, he said, because MacIain had signed the oath. And all the weapons elsewhere. For thirteen days peace had reigned between Campbells and MacDonalds in the name of hospitality, in celebration of the oath that freed Glencoe from the threat of retribution.

"—lambs to the slaughter," she murmured. "All the oaths for naught . . ." She left the cubby and went into the room where the door yet stood open, yet banged against the wall. She left it as it was and went out into the storm.

Snow swirled, parted, thinned. The blizzard hung low in the glen, but as Dair and his mother climbed higher there was less snow. Visibility improved, but the wind was bitter cold. Even through shirt and plaid he felt the convulsing of her body.

She fell then, despite his best efforts to save her. He knelt at once, cradling her, bringing her up from the snow. In his arms she was tiny, diminished somehow, as if the death of his father had sucked the substance from her. Her flesh was so thin he felt the bones beneath it.

In falling she lost his bonnet. He saw it skid away across the snow-laden ground, tumbled by the wind. In moments it was gone.

Gray-brown hair blew around her: a thin, ghostly shroud that hid her face one moment, bared it the next. Blood still smeared her face. Dair caught up a handful of snow and dampened the stains, using the end of the plaid to wipe away the thin crusts.

"Stop it." Again she held his wrist. "I bore you twenty-nine years ago, and John two before that. I am not a bairn, aye?—and you willna treat me so."

"Mother—"

"You will leave me here and go down the brae to find your brother."

He used his body to break the wind around her. In the pocket of shielding the force of the blizzard faded, and he saw the fragile bones cutting through the thin flesh of her face. Above the wind- and age-honed blade of her nose her eyes were clear of grief. She was wholly focused on her eldest son, who now was MacIain.

He would go down, then. He would leave her after all. But he would not look for John. —*blankets . . . I will fetch blankets and clothing from the house*— If Carnoch yet stood. But he doubted it was gone; in the snow fire would burn fitfully, and would require many hours to consume stone and wood.

"Aye," he said, "but not here. There is a rib of stone but five paces away—I'll take you there for the windbreak."

The magnitude of her relief nearly broke him. She nodded; it was enough. For now, it was enough.

Cat knew not to take the track. Instead she went through the trees, relying on memory to find her way. It was to Carnoch she meant to go first, then on to Inverrigan. MacIain was at Carnoch, and Lady Glencoe, and all the strength of the glen. MacIain could tell her where Dair was, what there was to do; she was a stranger in the glen and knew naught of its defenses, the habits of its people when danger came upon them.

The wound was stiff and sore, rubbed raw by the bandaging despite her care. There was naught she could do for it save ignore the discomfort; it was not a hole, and there was no musket ball hiding within her flesh. She would do well to recall there were others in worse straits. She had heard the dull crack of musketry, the shouts, and the screaming. She did not doubt there were MacDonalds dead; what profit in it to waste time on a powder burn and scrape?

In good weather, Carnoch was close. In bad, the distance trebled. Cold snooved into her lungs and took residence there, shortening her breath, until Cat had to stop and spit out the ache and phlegm. Coughing tore through her body and set her side aflame.

In the cold she sweated, and tears ran from her face to freeze against her cheeks. Cursing, Cat pulled herself upright again and went on, setting one fist over the stag-horn handle of the dirk.

At the edge of the wood she halted. Carnoch bulked before her, an indistinct mass in the swirling snow and smoke. Soldiers had set the house afire, but as yet it merely smoldered sullenly, unable to burn unfettered. If the snow died it would catch; in the wind it would become a Beltaine fire in the hollow of the valley.

Cat cursed the storm. The haphazardness of the snowfall, eddied by the wind, hampered visibility. One moment she saw clearly, the next she was blind.

If the house is on fire, everyone must be dead— She cut off the thought at once. Not MacIain. Not Lady Glencoe. A few of their retainers, perhaps, but not those who counted, who could deter her father's madness.

Her thoughts bent in another direction. She knew where the house was. The snow could shield her. What she could not see others might not also; the storm could serve her if she used it wisely.

There was no shooting here, no shouts of fear and fury, no triumphant Campbell war cries. What had been done was done, and no one remained behind. Cat drew in a deep breath rudely shortened by the stabbing of her side, and began to run.

She ran until she tripped over an obstacle just before the door. Pain stole her breath; until she found it again she lay where she had fallen, unmindful of her sprawl. It wasn't until her senses, less startled than her thoughts, identified the obstacle as a body did she make any attempt to get up—and then it was in a lurching scramble that flung her back from the body.

Her fall had disturbed the snow. She saw the trews around his ankles, the bloodied nightshirt, the white hair dyed crimson. She knew him by his size, by the hugeness of his body; there was no face to see. Nothing remained of his features save the dull white splinter of jawbone.

The wail came up in her throat, was snatched away on the wind.

Glenlyon, Drummond, and others went down the glen to Carnoch. Around them sang the snow, keened the pipe-song of the storm, broken from time to time by the barking of dogs, by shots, by fading cries and screams cut off into silence. At five of the clock the execution had begun; an hour later much of the work was done, though soldiers still found pockets of MacDonalds, or set fire to their houses.

Other soldiers came up to ask orders as Glenlyon went down to Carnoch. Drummond spoke for him, usurping authority, and said that when every MacDonald was dead they were to plunder and burn the houses, then gather and drive the stock from winter pasturage so they might profit from that which MacDonalds had stolen first.

Glenlyon himself had suffered depredations. The raid after Killiecrankie had stripped him of what little remained to him after selling so much for debts; this was fair, this was just, this was repayment for all his pain.

Carnoch came into sight. The house had not yet burned, but its people were killed, or escaped. There were no lighted lamps, no movement within the door, no MacDonalds to defend it.

"Wait—" Drummond's hand was on his arm, holding him back. "There is someone . . ."

The curtain of snow parted. A figure before the door, crouched beside a body dragged out of the house, looked up and saw him.

"Glenlyon!" the figure shouted, and began to run across the snow.

Beside him, muttering of MacDonalds, Drummond drew his pistol.

Climbing down the brae was more difficult than climbing up, for now the storm hindered progress, trying to force him up again. Dair fought his way through drifts, battered by the wind, and struggled to remain upright. He was numb now, no longer shivering, his chest coated with wind-crusted snow. If he still had ears he could not feel them, but they heard the keening cry of the storm running in and over the stones, the humps and hollows, winding through the trees.

He fixed his concentration on one task: to get down to the house and find clothing and blankets—if any still remained—then make his way back to his mother. But other thoughts intruded. Many thoughts intruded. The one foremost in his mind could not be avoided, though he placated it with truth: she was Glenlyon's daughter. He would not harm his daughter. No man, even a fool— —*even a drukken, pawkie bastard!*— —would have his daughter murdered.

Glenlyon had gone to Cat. He had asked Dair to give him time to speak alone with her before he took his leave. And Dair had done so, and when he had gone home Cat was there to greet him, saying nothing of her father save he had come and he had gone.

A man would not kill his daughter, nor suffer her to be killed.

Of them all, Cat was safest. Cat would not be harmed.

His father was dead. His mother would die if he did not fetch her clothing, bury her with blankets. He fought his way down to the wood and through it, stumbling at last to fall at the tree line behind the door-yard.

Motion. A floundering in snow. Dair turned, alarmed, and snatched his dirk from his belt. His impression was of a plaid-swathed, bonneted man shrouded in snow—and then he saw the avid eyes: his own.

"—Christ," he croaked. "John—"

Hands were on him. "Are ye unharmed? Alasdair—?"

He nodded wordlessly, struggling to thrust the dirk back through his belt. "You—?"

"Aye—aye! And Eiblin as well; I've taken her and Young Sandy up the mountain to shelter in the corries . . . there are men with her, some wounded, and women—" John paused. "Alasdair?"

"Mother," Dair managed. "Up the brae near the caves—I've come for blankets, John . . . she has naught but my shirt and plaid—they stripped her of everything and turned her out of the house. . . ."

John's expression warped into despair and outrage. "Bluidy bastards! Oh, Christ—" But he let it go; his hands tightened on Dair's bare arms. "You're ice, man! Come on to the house, then—we'll fetch blankets for us all. . . ."

They skirted the tree line, skulking like beasts. A few more paces, then the dooryard . . . they need only get across it and into the house.

And by MacIain's body.

"He's dead," Dair blurted. "You are MacIain now."

John turned toward him, face hard and still. He opened his mouth to speak; but Dair looked past him, beyond the corner of the house, and saw the figure before the door, beside the body, as it rose and shouted Glenlyon's name.

He knew her better clothed as a lad than as a woman. *"Cat—"*

Pistol flame blossomed from ten paces away. It briefly illuminated a pockmarked, powder-burned face, a shine of white teeth, and then the report cracked.

John clutched his arms and hurled him to the ground, smothering him in snow. But Dair knew better. Dair knew the truth.

"Not me—" He gagged on snow, struggling futilely. "Christ—it isna *me*—"

It wasn't. It was Cat.

Too late, Glenlyon flung Drummond aside. "No—*no*—" Soldiers came up around them, bayonets glinting dully on musket barrels. He smelled the acrid tang of powder, tasted it in his mouth, felt the smack of metal on glove as he smashed the pistol from Drummond's hand.

He left him then, left them all, and ran, staggered, stumbled. He cursed Drummond for his accuracy, for his eyesight, for his attention to duty, all commendable things in the midst of battle, but not when it threatened a man's daughter.

The impact had hurled her backward. She lay broken against the snow, bonnet fallen aside, so that red hair spilled free of wool. Like blood, it wet the snow, and at first he could not tell which was blood and which was hair.

"Catriona—?" He knelt, trembling, and peeled a fold of plaid away from her face. It was warm beneath his knees, warm and wet . . . it was not hair after all. Drummond's aim was true.

He gathered her in his arms, cradling her head in the crook of an elbow. Soldiers came up to see; Drummond as well, who primed his pistol once more.

Glenlyon heard a hoarse cry. At first he thought it was his own, but Drummond snapped out an order. Four soldiers fired. The reports from so close momentarily deafened Glenlyon; he flinched and cradled his daughter, shielding her from further atrocity. Discharged powder stank, burning in his nostrils.

"All of them," Drummond said crisply. "All of them are to die. Even the women, so they will breed no more pawkie thieves."

Drummond had left the house when Glenlyon put to his officers the task of not harming his daughter. Drummond had not heard the order. Drummond had not been at Glencoe for thirteen days to know Glenlyon's daughter.

"This woman—" Glenlyon said. "This woman is a Campbell."

Drummond was shocked. *"Here?"*

"She handfasted with Alasdair Og, MacIain's youngest son."

The pocked face twisted. "Then she deserved to die."

Glenlyon's laughter was a harsh blurt of sound. "She is my daughter," he said, "and you had best pray she lives, or I will have you shot for disobeying my orders."

"Disobeying—!"

"No one was to harm her." He looked up at the soldiers. "Were you given the order?"

All of them nodded, avoiding Drummond's eyes.

"I heard naught of it!"

"Everyone kent it," Glenlyon declared. "Everyone." He stood up then, lifting Cat into his arms. She was not a small woman, had not been small for years; but in that moment she was a bairn again, a red-haired, helpless infant too blind to see the day, bloodied not by birth but by a man's folly.

———

Frantic, Dair threw his brother from him and stumbled to hands and knees, then pressed himself upright. His shout had done nothing, nothing at all; she fell beneath the shot without word of protest.

"Alasdair—" John caught at him again. "Alasdair—*no*—"

His arm was trapped, hindered by another. Dair swung around furiously, facing his brother as he tried to jerk free. "—Christ—let me *go*—"

"Alasdair, dinna do this—"

He knocked John back a step. "Dinna stop me—" He heard a shout. Heard the reports. Felt the impact in his thigh: a sharp rap, a burst within his leg, and then a dull snap. His leg gave out of a sudden and he fell against his brother.

"Oh Christ—*Alasdair*..."

Hands clutched at his arms, dragging him upright. But he fell again, sagging. His right leg was deadwood, useless below the hip. "—Cat..." he murmured.

"Alasdair—can ye stand?"

He could not. He tried, but could not.

"They'll come for us... Alasdair, can ye walk?"

And then the pain at last came in, snooving from out of the darkness. His body knotted with it in one unflagging convulsion.

He buried his face in the snow so they would not hear his cry.

"Alasdair—" The grasp tightened, flipped him about, then arms came around his chest.

John dragged him a single pace. Then the storm within his body proved more powerful than the blizzard. It provided welcome sanctuary; if he died he would never know it.

Most of the dwellings in Glencoe were on fire, undeterred by snow. Glenlyon carried his daughter into Inverrigan's house, as yet unrazed, and placed her in the senior tacksman's bed. Inverrigan would not mind; he was dead, and all of his men with him.

Glenlyon settled his daughter atop the bed and set about determining how badly she was injured. She bled from the wound in her left shoulder, but no major vessels had been broken by the musket ball, and the ball itself, fired from so close, had gone directly through the meat. Glenlyon had fought before and tended such things; the entrance wound was no larger than a silver penny, and the exit smaller yet. So long as he could clean the wound of powder grains and wadding scraps and keep it free of corruption, he believed she would live. *If she chooses to...*

The thought unnerved him. Hastily he tore back the plaid, the cut-down jacket, the oversize shirt, reddening at the intimacy as his hands brushed unbound breasts, and found bandaging. Blood spotted the wool in a fitful pattern; he stripped the bandages from her and saw the scorched welt along her ribs, crusted and burned black at the edges from powder residue.

"Och, Cat . . . oh my lass—" Tears filled his eyes. In the aftermath of the killing he now had time to think, to acknowledge what had come upon them all, even himself, who was required to order such undertakings. And now his daughter suffered.

And would suffer more for the loss of MacIain's son.

As yet there were no reports of the old fox's cubs. That MacIain himself was dead all of Glenlyon's men knew; the death of the man so many revered or hated with equal ferocity was not a thing to remain unspoken. But no word yet had come of MacIain's sons, and Glenlyon felt tension knotting his belly. Their deaths had been ordered as explicitly as their father's; if he failed in that, he failed in all.

And yet here was his daughter who loved one of those sons, who handfasted with one of those sons, and who defied a father's wishes that she leave one of those sons. And now it brought her to this.

An aide came in. Glenlyon called for water, for such washing soap as there was, and for whisky. He had drunk plenty before his host's fire; surely some remained. He would drink his share now to dull the tension and worry, force Cat to drink as well, then pour a goodly amount through the wound itself.

She would scream, he knew, and would as likely cry. But there was no more he could do; and certainly nothing at all to ease her grief beyond keeping her insensible on whisky.

He knew that well enough. It was his only refuge.

Glenlyon looked down upon her pale, smudged face. She had matured since he had seen her last, losing the transience of youth to a new and fixed adulthood. She had always been hard in her angles, shaped as much of temperament and determination as of unsubtle bones, but now there was no mistaking the maturity of her face, the fit of flesh over skull. She was not what all men would clamor after, being overbold in features and coloring—and her propensity for opinion—but for a man who loved the blood and bones of Scotland, whose spirit answered her history and the ballads of the bards, Catriona Campbell was as much bred up of legend as any man might be.

Glenlyon wet wind-cracked lips. "He must be dead," he said gently. "He must be dead, my lass—even if he lives." For her father's sake as well as her own; he knew her too well. If she believed MacIain's son alive, she would never give up hoping they might be reunited.

He stroked away from a blue-veined eyelid a strand of burnished hair. "He is dead, my lass . . . but you are alive, aye?—and we will find a way to make you forget this day."

Dair was borne down by soldiers, buried beneath the soldiers, with cruel hands that used him brutally, throwing him down against cold stone with no shirt nor plaid to warm him, no pillow for his head but the knobbed and icy stone. They pinned him down and held him, disdaining his struggles with hissed invectives and commands to keep him still, condemning him to pain and futility. He fought them until in his struggles he bit into his lip, and blood ran down his chin.

They would put iron upon him again . . . they would set his wrists into iron and march him to Fort William—

"Alasdair—where is she?"

He murmured something, broken words of refusal.

"Alasdair—d'ye hear me? Where did you leave our mother?"

He recalled snow, so much snow, and the wailing of the wind, keening *ceol mor* as if it went to war.

"D'ye recall a landmark, Alasdair—something we might ken to find where you left her?"

They demanded information. He would give them none.

"Alasdair—"

His lips skinned back from his teeth and he spat out the worst epithets Gaelic afforded him.

"—no water," someone said.

And "—snow," said another.

Then the voice that knew his name: "We've no fire with which to melt it . . . and we dare not set one had we the makings. The soldiers would see it."

He twisted his head away from the hand, spitting out blood in a spray that dampened his chest. It was a warm spray, incredibly warm; his flesh was all of ice against the icy stone.

"I fear the bone is broken," someone said.

"Oh, aye—I heard the crack . . . and the ball still in there—see it?" Someone else fingered his thigh, spreading torn trew. "—this wee lump here on the side, beneath the flesh . . ."

"—cut it out."

"Aye, but when? We've others to tend . . . and he willna die just yet." A hand clasped his arm. "Alasdair, we'll tend you, I promise—but can you tell me where you left her?"

He shivered against the stone. The hands were less heavy, less cruel. There was no iron after all; he heard no ring, no chime. No scrape of key in lock.

A woman's voice rose then, frightened and strained; fell away again.

Women were here . . . had they all been brought to Fort William?

Yet another voice, and urgent. "John—you had best come."

"—Eiblin?" The voice faded as if a head were turned. "Oh Christ—the bairn . . ." The tone was raw as it came back to full strength. "Dinna stop asking him. We must ken where she is."

"He canna hear us," someone said.

"How d'ye ken that, Murdo? Has he told you so?" But the voice was hoarse and weary for all it attempted irony; it took itself away.

"MacIain," someone murmured softly.

Around him there was silence. And then the shifting of bodies. "He hasna claimed it yet."

"What claim? 'Tis his. He is Laird of Glencoe."

Light came into his head along with memory. His eyes at last had opened; he stared up from his bed of stone to the low rock roof overhead, the knurled and jagged ribbing of the caves above Glencoe.

"Cat," he said. And then, urgently, "—*Mother*—" He lunged up from the stone in brief, overwhelming panic, thrusting elbows beneath for shoring—

—and the pain, like a beast, took precedence, demanding submission of him.

He was down on his back already, his belly bared to the jaws. "—Mother—"

"Where?" someone asked sharply. "Where is Lady Glencoe?"

There was a woman's voice crying out, and a man's attempting to soothe her.

"—Lady Glencoe?"

Lady Glencoe. His mother. "—brae—" he gasped. "Below—"

"*Where?*"

"—rib . . . windbreak—" Jaws opened wide to swallow him whole. Elbows collapsed. He gave over to the beast as the flame in his head guttered out.

Cat roused to flame burning a hole into her flesh. The pain was intense, eating away her shoulder. Would it also eat her bones?

She struggled against it, struggled against the hands. Fire bloomed afresh and she screamed then, crying out against it. Hands were upon her, pressing her into softness, holding her in place so the fire might consume her.

"Aye, lass, I ken . . . och, Mary in Heaven—"

Tears spilled out of her eyes despite her self-contempt. Was she so weak—? Aye, in this she was, this excruciating fire.

They had set fire to Glencoe, and now they burned her.

She cried out a protest, struggling again against the hands, trying to

escape the flame as well as her captors. She spoke of soldiery, and muskets, and bloody, pawkie Campbells . . . and of murder as well, and a
father's attempt to send her away so she might survive what Mac-
Donalds could not.

"Catriona—och, Christ . . ." Something was thrust between her lips,
rattling against her teeth. Another hand clamped roughly on her jaw,
squeezing tightly. "Swallow—*swallow*—"

She swallowed. She choked.

"More."

She spat out as much as she drank. Her neck was wet with it, reeking
of liquor.

Whisky. Her father.

Cat opened her eyes. Above her hung a face, a ruin of a face cur-
tained by lank, fading hair, and a pair of smoke-stained, weak blue eyes
corroded by dampness and fear.

"—bastard . . ." she said, forcing it past clamped teeth. "D'ye think
I will say naught of what you have done?"

"Orders," he said helplessly.

"What man—" —*oh God, she hurt*— "—what man would order another to murder MacDonalds—?"

"The king," her father answered.

Her shoulder was eaten away. He had poured fire through it.
"—king?"

"The king."

"I canna believe that!"

"Aye, Cat. 'Twas ordered. All of them to die."

The room collapsed around her, became nothing but his face.
"Where is Dair?"

He was mute.

"Where is Dair?"

Still he said nothing.

"I'll not believe it. Where *is*—" The hand closed upon her jaws
again and forced her mouth open as the flask again was pressed between her teeth. "I willna—" But he poured relentlessly until she had
no choice but to swallow or to choke.

If she choked, she died, and there would be no one left to tell the
truth of MacIain, shot through the spine and the back of his skull so
that naught was left of his face.

"Drink," he said.

She drank.

Like a horse annoyed by a deerfly fastened to his neck, Dair could
not stay still. He twitched against the stone, scraped sore elbows, dug a

heel into a hollow. He could not stay still. The deerfly burdened his thigh. He could not stay *still*—

"John," someone said.

He heard murmuring; a woman's anguished sobbing. Then the susurration of fabric against stone, and the settling of a body. He could feel its closeness so near his frenzied thigh. If only he could *move* to banish the deerfly—

"Alasdair—can you hear me?"

He heard. He twitched, rolled his head, felt stone beneath his skull, cold, hard stone, harsh pillow for a man. He moved his hand, freed it from numbness, and snooved fingers across his trews. He would slap the biting beastie—

"No, Alasdair . . ." A hand captured his and held it still. "Let be. Let be."

He writhed from captivity, fighting to free his hand. If he could kill the deerfly—

Another hand touched him, parted the tartan trew. A palm touched his thigh. "Warm . . . och, dear God . . ." The hand moved from thigh to brow. A soft Gaelic curse hissed in the darkness.

"Usquabae," someone said, "to burn away the wound fever."

The hand left his brow. "Have you a flask, then? Has any of us a flask?" The voice was hard-pressed to remain steady. "We've naught, Murdo. Naught but what we wear. And until we are certain the soldiers are gone, we dare not leave this cave."

A child wailed briefly; was comforted by a woman.

"MacIain—"

"My name is John."

"—dead—" Dair murmured.

A hand touched his shoulder. "Are you awake, Alasdair?"

He was. He opened his eyes and saw the face of his brother, who refused their father's title. "Mother—?"

The bones of John's face might cut his flesh.

It was incomprehensible. "Where is—? I left her up the brae . . . below the caves—" But he was *in* a cave. "Below, then . . . near a rib—"

"Alasdair." John's expression was ghastly. "We found her, aye, earlier . . . and brought her here. But—she died, Alasdair."

"John—" He caught a fold of John's shirt and twisted it. "—she is dead?"

"She is dead, Alasdair."

He tugged at the shirt. "But you found her!"

"We found her, aye . . . but she was too weak for the storm. Too much wind, and snow—and grief . . ." John's hand closed over his. "You did try, Alasdair. You tried gey hard."

"She was *alive*—"

"Alasdair . . ." John freed his shirt. "She is gone."

"—she was alive—" The hand flopped to the stone. "She needed blankets . . . I went down for blankets. . . ."

"Houd your gab," John said gently. "There is no profit in railing at yourself. 'Twas the storm, Alasdair—'twas too difficult for her."

"If I had *found* them . . . if I had found them and brought them to her—" And then memory came back again: snow and storm, a father's sprawled body—and a pistol discharged in the darkness. "Och Christ—*Cat*—"

"Let be, Alasdair—stay *still*, now, aye?—you've a musket ball in your leg, and the bone is broken."

He did not care about himself. "She fell—John, she *fell*—" He remembered it so clearly, recalled his cry, the shot, the hindrance of his brother keeping him from running to her. "I thought she would be *safe*—she is a Campbell, not a MacDonald—"

A woman's voice: Eiblin's. Asking for her husband.

John clasped Dair's shoulder briefly. "We can do naught yet, Alasdair, but when we can go down—when we are certain they have gone—we will go down and bury the dead."

Bury the dead. His father. His mother. And Cat?

John left him to tend his wife. Despite the bite of the deerfly that was musket ball and broken bone, Dair turned his face to the wall and in silence wept for the dead.

After his daughter fell at last into a restless sleep that was whisky-whelped stupor as much as swoon, Glenlyon left Inverrigan's house and went out into the dooryard. It was midmorning, the day as yet swathed by wreaths of thin clouds that might thicken again into blizzard, but the storm had died and Glencoe now was a field of pristine white, scarred incongruously by the still-burning rubble of razed dwellings, now naught but fallen timbers and heat-cracked stone, and snow-crusted, bloody puddles near slain MacDonalds. Timber beams yet blazed in dwellings still unconsumed, and smoke choked the glen.

Drummond was there, and Lieutenant Lindsay, who claimed he had killed MacIain. A few gathered, powder-soiled and bloodstained, while others as yet still searched for survivors to dispatch, or for oddments that might have escaped plundering.

Glenlyon frowned. "Where are the others?"

Drummond's pocked face was very still. "Others, sir?"

"Duncanson's troops. We were not to be at this alone." In no way alone; there were to be more troops. And yet there were not enough now to make up so many. "Have so many of us died?"

"No, sir." Drummond's eyes were wary. "Only three, Captain."

It was perplexing. "Then where are the others? They were to assist us. Duncanson's men!"

"Sir." Drummond drew himself up. "Sir, we are as you see us. No others have come."

Alone. He was alone in this. In the midst of the killing frenzy he had forgotten all but the doing, all but the order; yet there had been promises that he would be assisted. Duncanson's men.

But they were not here. They had not come. *He* was solely responsible.

"MacIain is dead," he declared; that much he had accomplished.

Drummond nodded.

"And his sons?"

Now Drummond smiled. It was not a comforting smile. "No report, sir. The bodies are being inspected in hopes they may be found."

No report. They might have survived.

It was abject failure. The orders had been explicit.

"Find them!" Glenlyon shouted, and the echo rang in the glen.

Drunk on whisky, drunk on pain, Cat lay slackly in the bed and tried to connect the pieces of memory, of knowledge and awareness. It was far more difficult than anticipated, for all was edged in a faint burnished glow, as if everything burned. She could account for no reason it should be so, but it was so, and even her murmurings of protest did not banish it.

In counterpoint to the shattered fragments was a faint, unflagging moaning, as if a piper played the drone without benefit of the chanter. There was no melody, no soaring *ceol mor,* only the endless drone, low-pitched and relentless.

A hand touched her brow, smoothing back hair that hurt her sensitive flesh. Another hand slipped beneath her skull and lifted it, balancing it so precariously; she drank then because she was to drink, and because if she did not, the liquid would be poured across her face and neck. She knew how to drink. She did not desire to be wet, to reek of usquabae.

She drank. As she drank the droning halted, and silence was a blessing. She had not realized how much the noise hurt her ears, filling her head with restlessness.

"—mean to keep her drunk for a week or more?"

"If I must."

"She will rouse, Glenlyon."

"So she will, aye."

"You cannot keep her here."

"I mean to take her to Chesthill. 'Tis home."

No. Not Chesthill. She had left Chesthill.

"—no, Cat . . . let be. Let be."

She licked whisky-painted lips. "—Glencoe . . . *home*—"

"Do you see?" a voice asked.

"I will take her home."

"And keep her drunk forever?"

"What we did was under orders, Captain Drummond."

"Oh, aye. And if there were no survivors to tell the tale of it, 'twould be naught to trouble us. But there *are* survivors, Captain Campbell . . . and they will tell the tale."

"To whom?" the other asked. "To men of other clans?—aye, well, let them! No one will speak against us for fear we will do the same to them."

Silence. Cat stirred, murmured. The droning began again.

There was a sound of disgust. "Can you not keep her silenced?"

"Captain Drummond, if you dinna care for her noise, you might well go elsewhere."

"There are no other houses left standing. Nor will this one be once we leave it." A pause. "We had best march within the hour, Captain."

"Then I give you a duty, Captain Drummond—have a litter prepared, and a detail of men to carry it. I will take my daughter home."

"Duncanson will not like this."

"Aye, well, Duncanson wasna here when he said he would be. He's naught to say about how I tend my kinfolk."

There was a pause. Then Drummond said, tightly, "I thought she was a man."

"Woman or man, you would have shot anyway, aye?" The tone was bitter. "See to the litter and detail."

Cat's eyes flickered open. She saw her father's face, and the face of another: a pockmarked man whose expression was baleful. But she did not know him, and her eyes closed again.

Sound. Someone withdrew. The fingers were on her brow again, stroking back her hair. "Aye, Cat, I'll take you home. You'll be in your own good bed again by nightfall."

His throat burned. It was razed by flame as a house was, his house; all the houses in the glen. That much he knew, even from within, where no one else existed save himself. Glencoe had been set afire by flame and blood, so much blood . . . and now he suffered it as well, flame and blood corroding his flesh and spirit. He twitched, then jerked against it, feeling the bite of stone into his skull.

Hands came upon him then, hands with iron. The chime of chain was lost in the murmuring of voices, the taut tone of orders given; and they chained him, chained his wrists to the floor; stretched his arms over his head and knelt upon them. Then iron upon his ankles, even as he tried to jerk away.

"—dinna let him move—"

"—he is half-dead, but still fighting . . ."

"Aye, well, so would I fight—he's no sense in his head, forbye."

"Sense enough," someone said tautly. "Sense enough to ken he doesna want to be imprisoned."

"Aye, well, we've no choice—hold him, now . . . I've to cut that wee lump of lead out—and then you must turn him onto his face so I may pour usquabae into the wound where the ball went in."

He felt the knife then, biting into flesh. He stiffened, hissing in shocked outrage, then expelled all the air in a rush that deflated his chest.

"—aye, not so hard . . . Alasdair, you're free of the musket ball, aye?—turn him *now*—"

They turned him then, flopping him over and into such pain that he cried out. The wee lump of lead was naught, naught at all compared to this.

Fire. It pierced the underside of his thigh, then took up residence. He cried out again, though it was muffled against stone; he scraped his cheek and jaw, trying to find air that he might breathe again.

"—dinna bandage it, Murdo—it must drain to banish the poison. Now, over again—*aye*—"

He shouted with outrage, in protest of such torture.

"—och, aye, I ken it, Alasdair—*Murdo!* The wood, aye—and now the wrappings . . ."

They put sticks on either side of his right leg, then began to wrap it. Around and around, jostling the offended bone mercilessly.

He came to then fully, in shock and fury, and saw the faces gathered, all taut and pale in the gloom. One wild look gave him his brother and a handful of other MacDonalds, among them Murdo, one of his father's gillies.

His father was dead.

There was no iron on him, only flesh. Hands. They pressed him down against the stone floor of the cave. "John—" he said breathlessly. "—Mother—"

John's face was grim as he worked. He offered no answer.

And then he knew again the truth, heard again the voice telling him the truth: Lady Glencoe was dead.

"Here." Murdo leaned down. "We've usquabae, now, Alasdair Og."

How had they come by whisky? "Where—?" But he was too weak, too ill to ask more.

Murdo smiled faintly. "I snooved down a bit ago. The soldiers are leaving. I found a flask fallen away—'tisn't MacDonald whisky, forbye, but whisky . . . here. A swallow or two remains. Will ye drink?"

He would. He did. But it did nothing to slake the thirst. "Water—"

John tied off the knots. "We'll send a man down to the river when we can, Alasdair."

Dair's jaws ached from the clenching of his teeth. "How many—?"

"How many dead?—or how many alive?" John grimaced. "I canna say, Alasdair. We've a dozen of us here. Alive. Two dead."

One of them their mother.

"Who else—?"

John's face was a rigid mask of restrained grief. "The bairn was born early."

"*Eiblin's* bairn?"

"Aye." John made a futile gesture. "The cord was wrapped around its neck. It didna survive."

"Oh—Christ . . ." Bound in wood and wool, the leg now was stiff. He could not move it, could not search for a position more comfortable than the one he inhabited, sprawled against cold stone.

"Here." John pressed something against his palm.

Dair shut his hand upon it, feeling a pelletlike thing, small and hard. He lifted it into the air so he might look upon it, and saw the misshapen lump of lead. Once it had been round, a perfectly round musket ball, but it had struck thick bone in his leg and no longer retained its shape.

The thought was ironic—*nor does the bone. . . .*

Cat, too, had been shot.

Irony spilled away. He shut his eyes. The hand, clutching the ball, flopped back down aross his chest. Easier, he thought, to let the darkness take him again . . . but it would not. This time it was inflexible.

He lay bound by wood and wool, sweating in pain, unremitting in recollection, while a woman cried softly of a bairn born dead.

So many dead. Too many.

Even Glenlyon's daughter.

Letter after painstaking letter, page after page, nib ground harshly into the parchment so that the ink spreads. Very black letters that even a man with failing vision might read.

She does not sign her name. She is a woman; who will care for a woman's grief? Better to let them believe it is a man who writes, a man in extremity, whose world has been destroyed.

She reinks the nib, then writes at the bottom of the parchment: "MAC-DONALD OF GLENCOE."

She has no strength to sand it. She lets it sit, lets it dry, while she waits in the chair and tries to regain her strength.

When she can, when the ink is dry on all the pages, she folds the packet and uses wax to seal it closed. There are men who will carry it to Edinburgh . . . it will reach its destination.

"There," she murmurs. "Let them ken the truth."

Part VII

1692

One

Cat remembered little of the journey from Glencoe to Glen Lyon, save it hurt desperately and she was sick so much of the time from fever and too much whisky that most of it was naught but a blur, albeit edged with the lurid red-gold flames she could not get out of her head.

Her litter bearers had not been pleased by the duty, soldiers wholly appalled by the order to carry Glenlyon's daughter all the way to Chesthill by way of ice-rimed Rannoch Moor. Though the blizzard had stopped and even the snows were momentarily banished, the journey had been difficult, made worse by the moaning of their burden and its frequent need to vomit. She recalled something of their disgust, their bitten-off mutters and sibilant oaths as she spewed liquor-soaked biscuit over the edge of the litter.

Now she was able to wish she might have pointed out they should have been grateful she missed their feet, but they were gone, and she was no longer in the litter but in her old bed at Chesthill, the narrow creaking bed in her tiny room, and such things as vomiting were no longer an issue. Una fed her porridge in place of usquabae, and she kept it in her belly.

She could not count the days. She had lost too many of them to fever. But that had broken at last, giving her body peace, and her mind too much time to conjure memories of what had happened before Drummond shot her.

Cat yearned to hate him for it, but she could not. Had she been untouched because she was Glenlyon's daughter, it would have been far worse. At least this way she suffered the same wounds and losses as other innocents, and no man need say she escaped hardship because she was a Campbell. She knew the truths far better than anyone else, the brutalities rendered unto everyone regardless of age, despite gender, levied only because they were Glencoe MacDonalds. And she was one as well.

She wanted to die at first, but realized that when she had wit enough to wish it, she would not. The wound was painful but healing, the fever broken; she was in no danger. She was spared, while others were not.

How many others—?

She stared blindly up at the roof. She recalled deaths, the dying; recalled MacIain's body and ruined face; recalled the shooting, the shouts, the screams, the barking, the shrieking—and the flames, always the flames, consuming the flesh of Glencoe, blistering away the skin to display the bones beneath before consuming those as well, altering timber to blackened, smoking rubble like a pile of discarded splinters thrown down with hoof-scattered stones.

—so much snow and wind . . . And pockets of livid flame blazing throughout the valley from the icy Devil's Staircase to the wind-whipped loch itself, one flame copulating with another until they reproduced an endless family of burning bairns, vicious children leaping from dwelling to dwelling. So *much* flame.

So much death.

She recalled little after Drummond's shot, but much beforehand, and in detail: her father's visit to Dair's house, speaking of his wish that she would leave Glencoe and go home.

And his wasted face, the desperation in his eyes, the pleading in his tone.

He knew what he would do. He knew. And ordered it.

Drummond she could not hate. Glenlyon she would.

From the sentry walk of the fort, John Hill gazed out on the milling cluster of cattle, sheep, and goats kept near the burial yard. He thought the location perversely meet; the livestock had been driven up ten days before from Glencoe, plundered from dead MacDonalds by Argyll's Campbell soldiers under Glenlyon's command.

It was his responsibility now to dispose of the livestock, to parcel them out fairly for slaughtering so his soldiers might eat, and to sell some to the Lowlanders who cherished Highland beef. But he had no heart for it.

Wearily, Hill shut his eyes. Despite the lowing of cattle intermixed with the bleating of sheep and goats, he detached himself from the present and conjured the past, recalling the image of the huge old laird come to him but weeks before, willing to swear the oath that would free his people from royal reprisal.

So many oaths made and broken. . . . Including Hill's own oath by letter to MacIain afterward that Glencoe would be safe now that he had signed. And yet MacIain was dead, and too many of the very people he intended to keep safe by swearing allegiance to William.

"Governor Hill, sir."

His eyes snapped open, banished recollection. He turned to his aide, nodding permission for his report.

"There is a Highlander come down, sir. He claims he is a chief's son and wishes to swear the oath at once. He is ill, and has had himself carried here by stretcher."

Hill tensed. Reports claimed both of MacIain's sons had escaped; his visitor could even be John MacDonald, now Laird of Glencoe in his father's place. The oath would be required of him also, now that he was MacIain.

If the new MacIain should come— With as much alacrity as was circumspect, Hill had himself escorted to his small quarters.

Before the door waited a clutch of Highlanders with wary eyes and the tense posture of those who expected hardship. Hill's expectation grew; if John MacDonald came down and swore the oath, all survivors would be free of the king's order. There would be no more killing.

He greeted them absently, saw startled glances, then went by them and through the door. Other Highlanders waited within, guarding the man they had brought to Fort William on a stretcher.

With a prayer of thanks, Hill made his way through the men and then stopped short.

He was no longer on a stretcher but sat in Hill's own chair, as it was the sturdiest in the room. He was thin, hollow-eyed, clearly ill. But even illness did not disguise the insolent glitter of his eyes, or the ironic hook of his mouth.

"You are not John MacDonald," Hill blurted.

The mouth broadened. "I am not. But you ken who I am, aye?— 'twas I who was guested in your finest cell."

Not John MacDonald. Not even Alasdair Og.

Robert Stewart of Appin.

Stewart shifted in the chair and winced faintly, as if his very bones ached, then smiled again. "Did you expect John MacDonald?"

"I hoped," Hill admitted honestly and without hesitation. "I have no wish to see any more of Glencoe harmed."

"Och, well, you've done enough harm, aye?" The stubbled jaw, despite its fever-thinned flesh, remained firm. "We all ken what was done . . . only a muckle-headed fool would believe such a tale might remain secret."

"Is he alive?—John MacDonald? And his brother?"

Stewart raised a shoulder in a slight hitch. "I canna say."

"Will not say," Hill corrected. He supposed he could not blame him. "I did not welcome those orders, Stewart. I would as soon it had never happened—and I would as soon MacIain's heir came down and agreed to swear the oath anew. He is laird now."

"And would like to remain alive so he might *be* laird," Stewart said softly. "Does a hound beaten near to death come back to the hand wi' the stick?"

"If he does not," Hill answered as softly, "I cannot say what might be levied as punishment."

"Punishment?" Sandy brows arched up. "Glencoe has been burned to the ground, aye?—and even now *you* hold the livestock that once pastured near the houses. 'Tis a glen of sorrows, an empty place of blood and broken stone, of charred timber and burial cairns—is there anything *left* to punish?"

Hill was aware of movement behind him, a subtle tense shifting among the men who waited for Robert Stewart. No one spoke; he heard no metallic scrape of drawn dirk, but knew there was no need. They as much as he understood the repercussions of Sassenach wishes disobeyed.

He looked Stewart in the eye. "What there is left to punish should remain *un*punished—so long as I am given good and sufficient reason to stay my hand."

"Aye, well . . ." Stewart's defiant insolence faded, replaced with a pallor offset by the high color in his cheeks and an overbright glitter in his eyes. "Well, I am somewhat aware of that, Governor Hill—and so I have come down to offer Appin's oath."

"From your sickbed."

"Och, aye . . . I've no wish to be Glencoed."

Hill felt the muscles of his face tauten. Already they had made a word of the killings, replete with implicit threat. "Then I shall be pleased to accept your offer, Stewart, but I will give to you such answer as I gave MacIain: you must swear the oath before Ardkinglas in Inveraray."

"I kent that," Stewart said, "but 'twasn't *his* soldiers who snooved their way under MacDonald roofs and killed them, aye?"

Hill supposed he deserved such rebuke as that. "Then I shall write you a pass, so no detachment that you may meet can detain you."

Stewart smiled again, though it faded. "D'ye mind if I wait in your chair while you write it? I'm gey indisposed to move."

Hill inked quill and pulled parchment, laboring to write clearly despite his awkward position at the writing table. He was very aware of Stewart watching every mark he made on the paper; did he wonder if Hill wrote lies and sentenced him to death? Surely no Highlander would trust him now, not even Ewan Cameron of Lochiel, who had sent his heir so often.

Trust was banished. Threat stood in its place.

Hill set down the quill, sanded the paper, then folded and sealed it. He offered it to Stewart, who accepted it in an overwarm, trembling hand.

"I am sorry," Hill said. "I know that you and Alasdair Og were friends."

Stewart stilled. "Once."

"Despite such orders as called for his death, I hope he survived."

"Aye, well . . . for myself, I dinna care." Stewart flashed a hollow echo of his usually charming, impudent smile. "I have a personal reason for hoping the Campbells killed him." He handed the paper over to one of his Highlanders, then thrust his spine against the back of Hill's chair, clutching the armrests. His mouth was hard as stone. "Will you stay and watch a sick man be carried forth like a dead one? It may prove gey amusing to a Sassenach."

But Hill, who had heard too many reports of dead Highlanders, did not care to see such. He turned on his heel and left.

Dair was propped against the cold bones of the cave wall, his own bones wary of such posture as the one he chose, spine set rigidly against ancient, unworked stone, but he paid the protests of his body little mind. It had been favored too long, his body, given too much latitude in the ordering of his life; time now for him to set aside illness, weakness, and pain and look to the present in order to shape the future, despite the grief of the past.

He was no longer so naked; he wore now the blood-blackened shirt of a dead man and his scorched, crusted plaid, for they had buried Lady Glencoe in her youngest son's shirt and plaid. His broken leg was for the moment settled in its awkward splints.

Dair smiled at his brother. He knew the expression, the stubborn set of the jaw. "You must, John. Surely you can see 'tis the only way."

John MacDonald was unconvinced. He stood in the center of the cave and glowered down at his brother. "D'ye think I could do such a thing?"

"You must," Dair repeated. "I canna travel yet myself, but you canna wait for that."

"This is foolishness, Alasdair—"

"You canna *stay* here, John, as you well ken. 'Tis too dangerous. The soldiers will come back. Would you have what few folk remain to us treated as the others were?"

It was a telling if painful argument, and he would use it as he had to. There was no choice. He appreciated John's loyalty, his wish to remain with his brother, but it was senseless to jeopardize the others.

"We have no food," Dair said evenly, "save what we can catch. The stores are burned, the livestock driven away to fill the bellies of Sassanachs and Lowlanders, even Argyll murderers. But there are caves in Appin as well, and men there who will aid you as they may. 'Twill be gey difficult, but not so impossible as what you propose in wishing to stay here."

John's voice cracked. "This is our home, Alasdair!"

"Our home is burned," he answered. "Our home is naught but a burial yard, now . . . too many MacDonald bones lie beneath the cairns." Including their mother's, their father's, and his brother's still-born daughter's, who might, God willing, one day be interred on the sacred isle of Eilean Munde. "You have Eiblin and Young Sandy, and the others to lead. You are MacIain, now. Lead them from here, John. Take them over the mountains to Appin, and make a clan out of what is left of our father's loins."

The others waited in the shadows, holding silence. John was MacIain, John was laird. They would do as he would have them do.

But Dair was not a man who refused an argument with any man, even his father for all that man might clout him over the lug-hole; and his father was dead now anyway, and John stood in his place. With John he could argue, and win. With John he need fear no clout, especially now. And he would weave strong fabric of the yarn of his injury.

"If you stay here, you will die," Dair said quietly. "You will die of hardship, or you will be killed by soldiers."

John's pale face was shadowed by dark stubble thickening to beard. "We will take you with us."

Dair laughed. " 'Twill be difficult enough for a two-legged man to make his way to Appin . . . you have women and children, John. No one can carry me so far."

"You canna stay here, Alasdair!"

"Not alone, no," Dair agreed. "Leave me Murdo. Let him serve one of the old laird's sons as he served his father, aye?—and when I am healed enough, we shall come to Appin."

Murdo stepped forward from the shadows. He was a man of middling height and frame, fined down now by grief and hardship. Tousled dark hair was flecked with gray, for he was not a young man, though not as old as his laird had been. His eyes were a clear, unclouded blue, piercing beneath heavy brows. Like all of them he had forgone shaving, and the beginnings of a thick beard shrouded half of his face.

" 'Tis for you to say," Murdo declared, "as you are laird now. But you would do better to go, John. Alasdair Og and I will come along smartly when the leg is whole again."

John wheeled, turning his back on them. He stood rigidly in the cave, the rocky ceiling looming over his head. Dair could read his spine well enough. He did not require John's face.

Dinna be a fool, John . . . not for me. He shifted a tiny amount and caught his breath on a muffled hiss; he dared not let John know how much he hurt, or his brother would surely never agree to go.

Even as the sweat dried on his face, John swung back. "Aye!" he shouted. "Aye, we shall go. But I dinna like it, Alasdair! D'ye hear me?"

"Och, aye," Dair said mildly. "And any soldiers below, as well."

John swore viciously, then caught himself. Women and children were well within earshot, waiting in the shadows. "Verra well. But come you to Appin as soon as may be." He fixed Murdo with a sulfurous glare. "See to it he does!"

Murdo bobbed his head in a nod sufficient to acquiesence. Dair waited until John turned away to set about preparing the others. Then he shut his eyes. —*Robbie will give them aid.*

And they need not live in fear that each day might be their last.

Despite Una's protests, Cat made her way down the stairs to her father's writing table, and there took up parchment, quill, and ink. It was a laborious procedure; she could not as yet use her left arm without significant pain, and if she did cause herself pain, she would be unable to write. And so with great effort she relied only upon her right arm and hand to do the work.

The stairs had tired her more than expected. She sat a moment in the hard chair, closing her eyes against dizziness, then opened them again and slowly began to write. She had never been known for her letters; now she was worse than ever, sorely troubled by pain and weakness.

"I will do this," she said aloud, grimly. "I will, aye?" If she did not, no one else would. And she would not have falsehood spread. "I will do this."

Letter after painstaking letter, page after page, nib ground harshly into the parchment so that the ink spread. Very black letters that even a man with failing vision might read.

Cat did not sign her name. She was a woman; who would care about a woman's grief? Better to let them believe it was a man who wrote, a man in extremity, whose world had been destroyed.

She reinked the nib, then wrote at the bottom of the parchment: "*MacDonald of Glencoe.*"

She had no strength to sand it. She let it sit, let it dry, while she waited in the chair and tried to regather her strength. When she could, when the ink was dry on all the pages, she folded the packet haphazardly and used wax to seal it closed. There were men who would carry it for her to Edinburgh, Campbells who served her father. It would reach its destination.

"There," she murmured. "Let them ken the truth of Glenlyon's bravery."

———————

Glenlyon's breath ran short in his chest. How could they stare at him so? How could they mutter and murmur of him? How dared they suggest he deserved disgrace?

The Royal Coffeehouse by Parliament Close had been a comfortable retreat before when he had visited Edinburgh, but of a sudden it was inhospitable. Before, he had been treated with the respect due a laird, but now they stared at him, now they murmured of him, now they pointed him out with hard glances and unsubtle stares as the butcher of Glencoe.

'Tisn't fair! He had followed orders. He had served the king. He had done as he was told.

He wanted whisky, not coffee. A dish of chocolate sat on the table before him, untouched. His hands, thrust beneath the table, trembled across his abdomen as he linked them tightly. It was difficult to breathe, to maintain the appearance of an officer at leisure, awaiting his orders to sail for Flanders and King William's forces on the Continent.

News of the killings had come at last to Edinburgh; had made its way south to London. There was no secret of it anymore, no privacy in his doings and the doings of his soldiers. What should have been touted as a discretionary action taken to suppress rebellion, to force peace among Highland clans, was now viewed with a perverse mixture of fascination and horror.

Men shot dead in their beds. Women and children, fleeing through the storm, cut down by Campbell swords.

How dared they? *Can they not understand?*

Broadsheets were left in the Royal Coffeehouse as well as in other public rooms. Little written was truthful; Glenlyon had found a crumpled copy and read it in private, appalled by the brutality the words attached to him, the merciless bloodlust ascribed to a Campbell who hated Glencoe MacDonalds.

Now he dared read nothing, not in public, lest they watch him read and remark upon his pallor, the thin, flat set of his mouth, the rigidity of his posture. And so he sat quietly at his table and did not drink his chocolate, but attempted to face down the disapproval of his peers.

No one could know who had not been there.

The stories were patently false, many of them, but there was truth as well. He did not believe the most virulent rumors truly came from a Glencoe MacDonald, but he suspected the worst. How else could there be so much fact mixed liberally with falsehood?

No one knew who had not been there.

But not all MacDonalds were dead. Glencoe was empty of Mac-

Donalds, empty also of dwellings save the charred detritus, yet some of her people survived.

How did men come by such news? How could they know what to print? And he dared not confirm any of it. It painted too black a picture.

They canna understand! He wanted whisky badly. He wanted worse to leave. But he would not. He refused to be defeated, driven away from public like a cow driven out of its pasturage.

A Campbell cow lifted from Glen Lyon and driven away to Glencoe.

He sweated. Glenlyon reached into the pocket of his coat for linen to dry himself, and felt the crackle of paper. He drew it forth, blinked to see the dark smears upon the parchment, then unfolded it.

—Duncanson's order . . . Desperation welled up in Glenlyon's chest, took lodging in his throat. Here it was. Here was proof. Here was vindication.

He rose of a sudden, shoving his chair away. The discordant scrape of wood on hard floor caught the attention of everyone in the coffee-house and stilled conversation; Glenlyon retained their attention by holding the tattered, bloodstained parchment into the air like a victory flag.

"Here it is!" he cried harshly. "Let any man who questions me read it, and understand: I am a soldier, and an officer, and I follow the king's orders!" He slapped the paper down on the table beside the dish of chocolate. "I would do it again!" he shouted. "I would dirk any man in Scotland or England, without asking cause, if the king gave me orders! So should every good subject of His Majesty!"

But they were hostile still, the faces; they none of them believed him. They chose instead to believe rumor and falsehood.

Trembling, Glenlyon rapped his fist upon the paper. "Here it is. You need only to read it to see I did my duty."

And then they began to come. Slowly at first, then swelling in numbers, all reading the words written by Duncanson in the name of King William.

Vastly satisfied, Glenlyon sat back down. They would understand. They would see he had done what any man should do who served his monarch.

In London, lamplight guttered. The Earl of Breadalbane adjusted the wick, then bent again to his labor. When he was done, he set aside the quill and sanded the paper.

Satisfied, he nodded. In careful language he had phrased a vital message to John MacDonald, now MacIain: that if he and his brother, Alasdair Og, would swear and write by their own hands that the Earl of

Breadalbane had no part in the massacre, he would use such influence
as he had to procure them full pardon and restitution.

A sound gesture, he thought, designed to mitigate the extreme political damage the failed attack had done. Mercy had its place even in a
ruthless world.

In Dair's dream she lived: a vivid, vital woman who gifted him with
her love, her passion, with her pride and defiance, altering strong men
into mere echoes of their existence. He saw her atop the great rock in
Glencoe, bright hair unfurled in the wind from off the loch, in trews
instead of skirts, and a man's bonnet on her head.

*Give her a claymore and she would wield it . . . give her a musket and she
would fire it.* Give her his substance and she would accept it, unstinting
in her vitality, in the brilliance of her spirit. He would be diminished
until she gave him strength again, the inspiration and ability to begin
anew.

He stirred, aware of an ache in his loins. He sought release, but instinctively knew there was none save the way of a young man with no
self-control. And so he let the dream go, let the memory fade, and
opened his eyes to the pallor of the cave, the hardness of a bed unin-
habited by a woman.

The intensity of his grief appalled him. It was weakness, and yet confirmation that he yet lived. There were no pipers to make a song of it,
to keen at the heavens the poignant lament of a man stripped of his
kin, of the only home he knew. There was no bard to make a saga of it,
to remind him with the discipline of words what had happened in his
life. There was no structure at all, none to guide his thoughts to a place
where he might find release, and the peace that came with such. And
no one at all to mitigate the grief save Murdo MacDonald, who himself
had lost his purpose in the murder of his laird.

The leg ached unremittingly. Dair knew little of broken bones save
they were often fatal if the flesh were torn and corruption set in. In his
case there was none because of John, who had burned him so badly
with whisky. No corruption might live against such offense, and so he
healed, but slowly. The splints and wrappings warded the leg, but
made it difficult to move. He ached in every joint from inactivity, longing to leave the cave so he might see the day; so he could walk again
and know the glen of his birth.

Murdo said he should not. Murdo considered his health, the welfare
of his leg, but also the truth that would shatter the vestiges of memory
as yet unbroken by fact.

He had seen Murdo's face the day the man came back from searching as many dwellings as he could. His hands and arms were befilthed

by ash and charring, black lines rimmed his nails, a smudge stood high on his cheekbone where the beard did not touch. His eyes were unquiet and his spirit promised grief, but he said nothing of it.

Until night fell and darkness surrounded them, softening the hard truth of a brutal daylight that knew nothing at all of tact.

"Naught," Murdo said softly.

Dair leaned against the wall. "Naught?"

"Naught."

There was water from the burns and such food as Murdo might scavenge, or catch in crude snares, or spear in the water. But he dared spare little time at any of his endeavors, lest the soldiers come to find him. MacDonalds were yet broken men and targets to others.

"You have searched all the ruins."

"The last one today. There is naught, Alasdair Og—the Campbells have plundered it all. Only scraps remain, or bits all broken. There isna even a dog."

No. They would have been killed, or, following scent, gone on to Fort William in search of food.

But *they* would not, he and Murdo; they would do neither.

"We shall make do, aye?"

Murdo's smile was fleeting. "As we have, but with less than before."

"Och, a wee bit of hardship will no' harm us, and we'll be for Appin soon enough."

The smile ghosted again. Appin was not on Murdo's mind. "He should be buried on Eilean Munde."

So he should. So should they all. "When we are free to live in Glencoe without fear of murder, we shall see to it."

Murdo nodded. He squatted upon the stone floor. "I have marked where his bones lie, so we may know them."

No one could mistake the size of MacIain's bones. But they might vanish beneath the soil, buried by turf and snows, before Glencoe was free again to tend her murdered MacDonalds.

Dair thought of Cat. *Where are her bones? How will I ken them?*

Or had her father carried them, yet fleshed, home to Glen Lyon?

Murdo turned his back. Dair heard the muffled sobs. It was easier, somehow, to know he, too, could weep in such privacy as they made.

Her shoulder ached ferociously, but Cat did not care. It was penance for her name; pain was required.

She had not saddled the garron but rode bareback instead, clad in trews, shirt, and plaid, with a bonnet on her head. The pain and effort made her flesh run with sweat, but she ignored it. She was not cold. Winter had broken at last.

She did not get far. Before she reached Rannoch two of her brothers found her. Dougal caught her rein and added it to his own while Jamie, the eldest, the cruelest, blocked her way.

"Let me go," she said tightly, willing the pain not to show.

If Jamie marked it, he did not forgive her for it. "You will come back with us to Chesthill."

" 'Tis not my home."

" 'Tis."

She thought of jerking the rein from Dougal's hand, but knew she would fail. This time. "Glencoe is my home," she declared.

Jamie smiled with quiet satisfaction. "Glencoe is no more."

Cat raised her chin. "The glen is there," she said steadily, "and houses may be rebuilt."

"By whose hands?" Jamie inquired. "No man lives who might do it."

Dougal's eyes were worried. "Come back with us, Cat. 'Tis best for us all."

"Best for *you,*" she countered bitterly. "You canna have Glenlyon's daughter in the ruins of our father's folly, aye? 'Twould no' look so bonnie."

"Naught is left," Dougal said straightly.

She challenged at once. "How d'ye ken that? Have you been there?"

"Father has," Jamie said, "and he told us what was done." His garron shifted; he reined the restive mount in. "They deserved such treatment. They were Jacobites who refused to sign the oath."

Now she was cold, cold as a claymore in winter, letting them hear her hatred. "Och, it was signed," Cat said softly. "MacIain did sign it. But they came anyway. They killed him anyway. They killed as many as they could, for no reason but the king's."

She saw it in their faces: neither believed her. Perhaps they could not, if they might; they were Glenlyon's sons.

"You will let me go," she said. "I have no place here."

"Bring her," Jamie said curtly and rode his garron past her.

Dougal held the rein. Cat had no choice, short of leaping from the garron and walking to Glencoe. *But I canna do that. Not yet.* Not until she was healed.

They led her back to Chesthill despite her protestations that she could direct her mount with no assistance. Then Dougal took the garron away. Jamie took himself.

Cat stood in the dooryard, struck by memory: a boy-faced lass warning away a MacDonald whose father was loud and harsh; overturning a cup with Campbell whisky in it, meant to succor a MacDonald coming home from Killiecrankie; standing in the doorway to welcome the same man in when he came to fetch his bonnet.

Ten years she had loved him.

"I *will* go," she said fiercely, and strode into the house.

Colin, waiting for her, said nothing as she came in. She saw the worry in his eyes, the taut lines etched into flesh, the tension in his posture.

It faded as he saw her. "Cat," he said only. Kindly.

Overwhelmed, she wavered. He caught her, held her, enclosed her in his arms. The tears were hot on her face. "I must go," she said. "There are too many tales told of that night . . . if I dinna go, I will never ken the truth."

Very quietly he said, "Even if he lives, he will not be there, Cat. Glencoe is denied to MacDonalds, lest they be killed for it."

"I must go," she repeated. "Only in Glencoe can I be certain."

"Och, Cat—"

"Glencoe will tell me," she insisted. "In Glencoe, I can be certain." *If he is dead, or lives.* But she could not speak it aloud. She dared not speak of it, lest she somehow affect the outcome.

After a long moment Colin sighed. Crushed against his chest, she felt and heard it. "Verra well," he said at last, "but only when you are well. I'll no' take a swooning woman all the way across Rannoch."

"I willna swoon!"

She heard his hollow chuckle. "You were in a swoon when you arrived."

"I was *fou* when I arrived! Christ, Colin, he poured so much whisky into my belly I feared I would drown!"

"Aye, well—our father kens no moderation. In himself or for his daughter."

Cat went rigidly still. Against his shoulder she said, "Nor in killing MacDonalds."

Two

*T*he gloaming was past and true night settled in. Glenlyon, his belly full of whisky, stumbled through the damp darkness lit intermittently by smoking torches in iron brackets. Edinburgh was a noisome city, reeking of effluvia, smoke, dampness, the turbid stench of the poor overwhelming the finer scent of the wealthy. As for himself, he was poor in coin as always, but wealthier in notoriety than any man alive.

He heard a step behind him and clutched instinctively at the pocket of his greatcoat, then laughed harshly. There was naught in his purse to steal. And so he stopped and swung about unsteadily, willing the footpad to come closer to a soldier who carried a pistol at his belt.

The footpad halted some few paces away. "I am from the Earl of Breadalbane," he said quietly. "You are bidden to meet wi' your cousin."

"Cousin, is it? I thought he had claimed I was no more his kin!"

The man gestured in dimness. "I have given you his words."

"And does *he* wish to censure me as well?" But then Glenlyon shook his head. "Och, no—he would do that where all might hear, he would . . . serves him naught to keep it quiet, aye?" He peered blearily at the man. "Will he be serving usquabae?"

The messenger did not hesitate. "And brandywine from France."

Glenlyon, mollified, grunted. And followed Breadalbane's man.

With grimy hands and black-rimmed nails, Dair tore a frayed strip of soiled linen from the dead man's shirt that now clothed his body and tied back snarled hair into a tail. It wanted cutting badly but he dared not attempt it himself, and Murdo was gone, hoping to catch a fish or two in the river.

On that thought his belly made known its temperament, growling impotently. They went hungry more often then not, depending on what small game Murdo might catch in crude snares, or the fish he managed to spear. Dair had accustomed himself to reduced rations, but no food for two days took its toll nonetheless. Murdo's luck ran bad.

He healed steadily, but the leg yet ached despite his ministrations. Each day he worked the muscles with both hands, trying to keep them supple, but he had lost weight since the massacre and the strength in his tautly bound thigh had gone. The splints aided his bone but not the rest of him, and he feared to be a cripple if the muscle wasted away.

That thought drove him more and more often to kneading his flesh, to wishing he might stand like a man again, unfettered by wood and wool.

Murdo had fashioned him a crude crutch out of a tree limb he stripped of bark so it would not bite into flesh. It was enough so that Dair might lever himself up and hobble to the mouth of the cave, or to a pocket in the back where he relieved himself. The cave now smelled of it, but he had no choice. Unlike Murdo, he could not go out and find a suitable place, but was limited by his leg to depend on the cave itself.

His mouth twisted in wry self-contempt. "I am made a beast, aye?— living in my own filth, bound to my den lest the soldiers find their prey."

And so proud Glencoe was humbled, shattered in spirit by Campbell soldiers, by a Campbell laird. MacIain killed, his wife dead, so many MacDonalds dead. Even a Campbell-born woman.

Dinna think of Cat— He shifted, then shifted again, cursing inwardly. Made awkward by the splints, it was difficult to find a comfortable position. His body ached of it, muscles trembling in spasms as if to remind him once he was a man who walked on two legs, instead of a beast bidden to slide himself across the ground when it took too much effort to stand, to balance, to hobble from the dimness of the rocky cave into the light of a spring day.

Murdo has never been gone so long. His body thrummed with tension. He could not sit still. He itched, he twitched, he bit into his lip to stave off the urge to move, the need to answer in some way his body's urgent demands.

Two days.

Murdo refused to be gone so long.

MacIain would not permit anything so puny as a broken leg to prevent *him* from doing whatever he wished to do.

No, not MacIain. *John is now MacIain.*

He could not be still, in mind or in body. Cursing, Dair reached out to the crutch and began the laborious process of rising from the floor.

Cat waited impatiently as Colin brought up two horses to the dooryard. She saw the expression on his face, the tension in his body, but gave in to neither unspoken plea. And when he stopped, she reached out swiftly and took the rein from his hand. "You need not come," she said. "I ken the way, aye?"

His jaw hardened. "I'll no' let you go without me."

"Will you not?" Cat set her teeth and placed a foot in the stirrup, then hoisted herself up. Her shoulder twinged, but save for a muttered curse she ignored it as she settled herself in the saddle, pulling folds of plaid out of the way. "Then if you mean to come, you'd best mount your horse. I willna stay here the longer so Jamie and Dougal may come out to fash me again."

Colin's expression was troubled. "What will this serve?"

Cat looked down on him. Had he believed she might reconsider, given time? Or merely hoped?

Grimly she said, "It serves me to see what has become of my home, and of the man I married."

Colin still frowned even as he mounted his garron, though he said nothing.

"You've a wife yourself," Cat told him, "and two bairns. Think of them as I do this. Think of not knowing if they lived, or if they died. For the rest of your life."

Colin grimaced. "Not knowing might be easier."

"It would not." Cat turned her garron toward the track that wound through Rannoch Moor. *And you would ken that, in my place.*

No one could understand who had not been there. And until she went back she would never know the truth.

Cat needed to know. Until she knew the truth there could be no future, only the past. In Glencoe, she would know. If he lived. Or not. *"Fraoch Eilean,"* Cat murmured, riding out of the dooryard.

Sweat poured from Dair's body. He had not expected it to be *so* difficult, to be *so* painful . . . it took effort now to breathe, to suck air into his lungs and cling to it a moment before it whooped out on a gasp of exertion, of taut, tremendous effort that drained him with every step.

Step. He did not *step*. Could not.

He could not recall now what it had been like to be whole, to stride across the glen, to nimbly avoid a *camanachd* stick looping down to trap his ankle. He could not recall the simple act of walking unhindered, of the ability to leap and run, or even to crouch.

The terrain was unkind. High above the tree line there was little ease of movement; the wild, rugged corries dug into shoulders of the peaks. Loose stone shifted as he tried to pick his way down from the cave, fouling the crutch, the splints, spilling from beneath his bare left foot so that he planted the splints abruptly to catch his balance.

Pain kindled throughout his thigh. Dair gave in to it, too weak to do otherwise; he saved himself as much as he could by twisting to the left, by taking his weight onto his left leg, and so it gave as well and spilled him there, so that his left hip was driven deep against the stone.

He lay there drenched in sweat, breathing noisily through parched throat. He dared not cry out lest there be someone to hear him, to carry tales of a hidden MacDonald, easy prey for soldiers. Instead he balled his right hand into a fist and beat it against a boulder, beat it and beat it and beat it until he felt the pain of it, the split flesh upon his knuckles. If pain lodged there, it lessened its fury elsewhere.

He pressed his hand against his mouth and bit into the heel, the flesh hard as horn from an honest man's honest work. And when at last the pain of his broken leg lessened to a point he could bear it, he swore very softly with great elaboration, recalling the crude vulgarity of the men at Killiecrankie who held fear at bay by harsh speech, who scorned the thought of falling beneath a Sassenach ball or bayonet.

"Murdo," he murmured, exhausted.

Murdo will find me—

Wind rustled trees. There was no peat-smoke upon the air, no smell of cooking meat, no odor of fish frying upon flat stones set in the fire. There was no odor at all save of trees, and sap, and turf. Nothing at all of people.

It was Glencoe. It was not. The glen remained, girdled by cliffs and peaks, cut through by the river, but no one lived in it despite fertility. The valley was empty of habitation, save for its natural game. Empty of MacDonalds.

Cat rode unerringly to the house she and Dair had shared, ignoring the ruins of others. And there she found identical destruction as well as similar methods: charred timber and broken stone shattered by the heat, collapsed roof slates. Wind had scoured the ruins free of ash, so that only the stark timbers remained poking impudently skyward, fallen into a tangle like a handful of dropped sticks.

Nothing remained to mark human habitation. No scrap of cloth, no pewter plate, no perfume brought from France. Only the detritus of massacre, of fire and plunder, and the flowers of late spring breaking up through blackened soil.

She climbed down from the garron and left it to forage. She walked across what had been the dooryard—she saw it still—and through what had been the door—she saw it still—and into the room where the soldier had shot her, believing her a MacDonald.

Because I said I was.

There was no room. There was no house. But she saw it all regardless as she stood in the midst of wreckage.

Cat closed her eyes and conjured recollection. The house was whole again, with a peat-fire on the hearth, and the wailing of the wind as it buffeted the fieldstone, teasing at slate roof tiles. She recalled her cooling bed, empty of Dair, and the cracking noise of what she knew now was distant musketry.

She let it come, piece by piece. Sound by sound. Fear by fear. Let it come, and build; let it engulf, and take; permitted herself in all the ways to relive it again: the emptiness, the fear, the growing apprehension; the shock of being shot. And going into the storm to find Dair lest he be harmed, and alone.

Remembered rage when she knew it was all her father's doing.

She was dry of tears. She was drained of grief. Nothing lived in her spirit save hatred of Glenlyon.

"Alasdair Og," she whispered. "Alasdair Og MacDonald."

"Cat."

She opened her eyes, astonished; saw her brother's face instead. "There is a dead man by the river. I wouldna take you to him, save he might be a man ye ken."

"Where?"

"By the river." He gestured direction.

Heedless of her footing, Cat ran as swiftly as possible. She was absently grateful for trews in place of skirts, for brogues in place of bare feet . . . but when she saw the body she forgot such things as clothing.

"Dair?" She hurled herself to his side. He was tattered, graying, bearded . . . facedown, she could not see him to know him. "Dair?" Colin had said "dead man." "Dinna be dead, Dair . . ." She caught great handfuls of his soiled plaid and shirt and tugged him over onto his back. "Dair—?" She stared blindly into his face, into the pale, bloodless face.

Colin came up beside her. "His neck is broken. Likely he fell here in the stones—see?" He paused as she made no answer. "Cat—d'ye ken him?"

She said nothing. She could not. She had no voice with which to speak.

"Cat—?"

At last the words came. "I ken him."

"Is it . . . is it him?"

Tentativeness. Apprehension. For his sister's sake, Colin wanted otherwise than what he feared.

That broke her. Now she could cry. Now she could grieve. " 'Tis Murdo. He was MacIain's man." She gazed blindly up at her brother. "I thought I would ken . . . I thought coming here—" All of it new again, the scab stripped ruthlessly off the wound so it might bleed afresh. "Oh Christ, I dinna ken—I *dinna ken, Colin*—"

In sudden consternation he knelt down beside her. "Och, Cat—"

She rocked back and forth, wanting to keen aloud. "I thought I would ken, if I came . . . but I dinna. *I dinna.*"

In painful comprehension, in careful compassion he reached out to her. She felt his hand touch her head, then gently cup her skull. He unweighted her, pulling her to him as he knelt there, as she did, until he pressed the side of her head against his shoulder.

Nothing now but grief, and very little breath. "I thought I would *ken* it—if he lived, or no'." And it was worse, she realized now, unspeakably worse knowing nothing after all.

"Bide a wee," he said gently, "and then I'll find a place for him and stones for his cairn."

When she could, Cat sat upright, withdrawing from Colin's shoulder. She patted his arm in gratitude, gazing blindly at dead Murdo. "Aye," she said quietly, "find stones. I'll sit wi' him here as you do it, so he need not be alone."

The Earl of Breadalbane could not suppress his disdain as his unkempt cousin stood before him. "You are *fou,*" he accused.

Glenlyon's reddened eyes gleamed balefully. "What would you have me be? 'Tis bad enough hearing the whispers when I'm sober enough to understand them. *Fou,* they are no' so loud."

They faced one another across a writing table in the earl's Edinburgh town house near Holyrood Palace. The earl set down the brimming cup he had poured and watched as Glenlyon immediately put out a trembling hand to take it.

Coolly he said, "You did as you were ordered to do."

Glenlyon tossed back the liquor, licked his lips dry of it, blotted his mouth on the soiled sleeve of his greatcoat, then stared angrily at his kinsman. "Och, aye, so I did—but they must blame someone, aye? And I was there. My boots were soiled by MacDonald blood." He looked into the empty glass, then smacked it down upon the desk top. "Did you call me here to complain I drink overmuch? Well, dinna. It has been tried before."

"I would not trouble myself with an impossible task." With economical movement, Breadalbane sat down behind his writing desk. He did not bother to point out another chair to his kinsman; let Glenlyon stand if he would. "The only hope of success we had was if all were killed. But they were not. And now the world knows." He put his hand upon a folded paper. "This is a pamphlet written by Charles Leslie, an Irishman making coin off of Scotland's private troubles. And there are broadsheets throughout the city, carried south to London."

"What of it?" Glenlyon challenged, then pressed his hand against his pocket. "I've the order here. 'Tis plain what I was to do."

"'Plain,'" Breadalbane echoed. "And plainer still your failure."

"Good Christ, I did what I could!" Glenlyon cried harshly. "I was promised aid from Hamilton, but no men arrived. I was promised aid from Duncanson, but no men arrived. Until it was too late!" His words slurred, but his anger burned away much of his drunkenness. "I was told five of the clock, and at such time did I give orders to fall upon the MacDonalds. And yet no aid came until half a day later!"

Softly Breadalbane said, "They were all of them to die."

"We killed whom we could," Glenlyon retorted. "Christ, man, the glen ran red wi' their blood from the Devil's Staircase to Loch Linnhe, and all the dwellings burned . . ." Overbright eyes glittered with sudden tears in a corpse-pale face. "You were not there to see what was done, aye?—to see those who died, the men and the women, and the bairns—"

"*All* of them were to die."

"You were not there!" Glenlyon cried, smashing his fist down so hard on the desk top the empty glass bounced on wood. "How dare you rebuke me? How *dare* you question my competence—"

"Because I must. You failed."

Glenlyon snatched up his drained glass and threw it against the panelled wall. It shattered and fell, leaving behind a sticky residue of redolent French brandy. "Pox on you!" he said harshly. "You asked the worst of me, and I gave you my best!"

The earl drew in a calming breath; it would do no good if they both lost their tempers. "And that was *my* folly, to expect success of you."

Glenlyon braced himself against the wood with both hands spread. His voice rasped in his throat. "You were not there, cousin. You canna declare it success or failure."

"But I can. And I do. I declare it abject failure." Breadalbane was not in the least intimidated by his kinsman's truculent stance. "And I fear it will undo us all."

"Undo. Undo?" Glenlyon was plainly baffled. "How d'ye mean, 'undo'?"

He kens naught of politics, this bluidy fool of a Campbell! "Only a man such as a king may survive such debacle," Breadalbane said. "There are questions already as to why this was undertaken." He tapped the crisp pamphlet beneath his hand. "Even the highest may fall, saving the king himself." Even Stair. Even himself. Especially himself, who was loved by no man.

Glenlyon grunted contempt. "Do I care?"

"You should." Breadalbane shook his head. "You are a fool, Robin. A blind, drukken fool. Your incompetence may yet touch us all."

"You would do better to ask Duncanson and Hamilton why they didna come to Glencoe until the killing was done," Glenlyon retorted thickly. "In such weather as that, we needed the aid . . . and the passes were left open. Those who escaped did so because there were not enough soldiers to catch them."

But Breadalbane did not answer. He had his own suspicions why Duncanson and Hamilton had not arrived in time. Far better to let one drunken gambler be blamed for failure than to assume any blame themselves.

It was possible that, in the bad weather, additional troops would not have made a difference. MacDonalds might have escaped regardless. As it was, only Glenlyon's command was known to have failed its duty, and only Glenlyon's command could take the blame of the people who decried such tactics.

But Glenlyon had followed orders. Those who gave them, those who devised the plan, would be blamed in the final evaluation.

"There will be trouble of this," Breadalbane said. "I have been to London. I have heard the talk. There will be trouble of this."

Glenlyon's expression was one of surly contempt.

"Bide a wee," the earl said darkly. "Bide a wee, and see."

High above the timber Dair lay sprawled in scree, drifting hazily into darkness. Hunger was but a distant goad now, hounded away by detachment, by dispassion, as if his body's pain was too adamant a guard dog to permit anything else his attention. He had tried once to rise, tried once to lever himself upright, to plant the crutch and force himself to his feet, but he was too weak, too bruised, and the guard dog unrelenting.

—*best wait for Murdo*— Murdo would tame the hound.

Easier to sleep. Easier to let go. Easier to forget what had become of MacIain's youngest son . . .

No. Of MacIain's *brother.*

Three

*T*he deerhound bitch, sitting beside the earl, thrust her sleek muzzle between his hands so he was forced to acknowledge her. And so he did, if absently, stroking the wiry hair while she rested her chin upon his thigh, all the weight of her body now transferred inexplicably into her skull so that he must hold her up, for surely she would collapse if he did not give her aid.

He took solace in the touch, eased himself in her presence. Dogs were, he knew, well cognizant of the temperament of their masters, recognized joy and sorrow, and this bitch knew him as well as he knew her.

But paces away his fine horse grazed, idly uprooting turf. Breadalbane sat upon the mound, unmindful of disrespect; despite the legend it was yet his land, and if he chose to sit upon a grave, it was his right to do so.

Uaigh a' Choigrich. The Grave of a Stranger. The poor Sassenach soldier who, having no Gaelic, was murdered by Highlanders for trespassing upon their cornfield.

The cornfield grew anew in the kinder days of summer, topknots rustling in the breeze. Before long its bounty would be harvested and carried away, to be eaten at his fancy or sold to other men. Even in Edinburgh. Even across the border between England and Scotland.

Below the brae, below the Grave of a Stranger, razed Achallader yet mocked him for its state, for MacIain's enmity. But that now was over; MacIain himself was razed even as the castle, and rumor claimed no one knew which grave was his on the isle of Eilean Munde, where Mac-Donald lairds were buried.

If he is buried . . . Even that was uncertain. That MacDonalds survived, and more than at first believed, was obvious now, and they had come down from their mountain fastness to give honor to their dead. No bodies now in Glencoe save those beneath new cairns, or carried away to the island.

So much accomplished. And so little won. Glencoe destroyed, the Gallows Herd scattered; they were broken men in hiding, living as beasts apart from civility, apart from those who knew them as something other than outlaw. The earl was fully aware the king at last offered them pardon, prevailed upon by others to give them leave to go home, but no one knew how many yet survived or where to carry word.

Breadalbane smiled grimly. "Let them rot in the caves and corries."

It tasted of wormwood in his mouth. So much accomplished, and so little won. *—and so much now at risk* . . . Glenlyon was in Flanders, serving his king in war. Stair was there as well. *He* was left behind to deal with the rumors, to turn aside the slights, to make what he could of such respect as few men offered now, contemptuous of his part in what was called travesty. Had everyone died, such things as rumor might have been controlled. But there were survivors, and those of weaker heart, hearing the tales, took the MacDonalds' part and spoke of murder under trust.

Achallader, destroyed. His career endangered. And even his kin divided; no one knew what had become of Duncan, gone away with his Marjorie.

So much lost. His second-born, John, was heir now. There was a son to inherit his work, his earldom, but what was there to bequeath save potential disaster?

Inquiry.

That was the word now in so many mouths. Inquiry was his future, and possibly his present. Political destruction; he was anathema, a leper without a blemish save in what he had designed in congress with his king, and would be publicly censured for his part in Glencoe.

Someone must pay, aye?

The old man, stroking his deerhound, gazed up at the summer sky arching over his head above the Grave of a Stranger and permitted his eyes to water. "Let me live," he said. "Give me leave to live long enough so I may repair myself."

He was Grey John Campbell, Earl of Breadalbane. He deserved that much of God.

The latch rattled. John Hill looked up, squinting, as his aide threw open the door.

A slight, gaunt figure filled but a part of the frame. Even as his aide began to announce the visitor, Hill beckoned him in. Eagerly he rose. "Have you news of John MacDonald?"

The boy slid into the room with the care of a wary cat, avoiding the uniformed aide. Hill waved dismissal and the soldier pulled shut the door; the boy relaxed only a little. From the cracked leather of his belt he took a soiled parchment.

It was, Hill discovered, his own letter to John MacDonald, but an answer was scrawled on the other side in a crabbed yet skilled hand, as if poor conditions were all that denied the flourish of trained letters.

The parchment tore. Inwardly Hill cursed, then took greater care as he flattened the paper. He held it close, scowling fiercely against the weakness of his eyes.

". . . I give you my most hearty thanks for your goodness in procuring the King his pardon and remission, the which I will most cordially embrace and will betake myself to live under His Majesty's royal protection in such a manner that the Government shall not repent or give you cause to blush for the favour you have done me and my people."

Wholly without warning, tears filled stinging eyes.

"I am this day to take my voyage to find security to your honour's contentment, and thereafter I will do myself the favour to come to your garrison and be hon-

*oured with a kiss of your hand and end my affairs, with which cordial thanks
for your courtesy never to be forgot by him who is*
    Yours most assured to obey your commands,

JOHN MACDONALD"

"Praise God," Hill croaked. "Praise God for a wise man." He lowered the paper and looked at the young MacDonald. "When will he come?"

The boy stood very straight, poised to depart as a fox to bolt. "As soon as may be. There are women and bairns with him. He is MacIain now, aye?—he must tend his folk."

Hill looked again at the young Highlander, who was a man in a lad's body, summarily robbed of his childhood by such doings as Breadalbane's, and those political creatures who believed themselves superior to Scots in general, and to Highlanders specifically.

"Have you anyone left?" he asked. "A father . . . your mother? Brothers and sisters?"

"Naught," the boy answered steadily; his grief was long spent. There was no more assuagement in it. "But now I may go home. 'Twill no' be so bad in Glencoe again."

Clearly he wanted to be gone. The governor thanked him, dismissed him, then collapsed into his chair. "Home," he said aloud, and knew that except for the army and such solace as lived in the Lord, John Hill had no home.

Dair worked himself up over the lip of the last cave. He ached with exertion but gave in to none of it; the leg was whole again, if the muscles as yet still weak, and he had walked, limped, and crutched all the way from Glencoe to the kinder lands of Appin, searching for his brother and the remainder of his clan.

Ash. Charred wood. Scrapings in the dirt. A scattered pile of bones he took for a coney's. Even a burial cairn not far from the cave. But no MacDonalds. All of them had gone.

Despair encroached. To come so far, so urgently, needing to find his people, longing to see his brother, only to know himself in hermitage again.

The splints he had cast off halfway from Glencoe, relied upon at first because of the leg's fragility in intemperate footing. But despite the pain in wasted muscle, despite the protests of new-knitted bone, he refused to give in to weakness. He limped, aye, but was whole, and had walked every step.

—*oh, good Christ*— He leaned on the crutch, overtaken by desolation. Had John feared him dead, or merely delayed? Had John trusted to Murdo to see his brother to safety? Or did John himself lie beneath the cairn of stones?

And Young Sandy now MacIain.

—gone—

Overcome, Dair shut his eyes. He had, as he healed, managed to catch small vermin to put food in his belly, to drink from running burns, but not eat so much that a man survived unscathed. Murdo was gone; had been gone for weeks. He suspected Murdo was dead. But whatever the truth of it he was made to fend for himself, or die alone in the cave below the Pap of Glencoe as his mother, too, had died, wrapped in a borrowed shirt and bloodied tartan plaid.

Outside, a stone was displaced. Thinking of his brother, thinking of his people—such as still remained—Dair swung around, wavered, cursed his awkwardness; it was the crutch that saved him from toppling headlong to the ground.

A man came out of the sunlight. Dair nearly gaped. His voice, so long unused save for occasional discussions with his troublesome leg, croaked in a dry throat. "Robbie—?"

Indeed, Robbie Stewart. "Jean is dead," he said only, and a dirk glinted in his fist.

In summer, heather blazed. Cat, unfettered by brothers, rode alone away from Chesthill, skirting the bogs of Rannoch Moor as she followed the common track cut originally by deer, if later by thieving MacDonalds intent on Campbell cows.

Una no longer mattered, nor did disparagement from men such as Jamie and Dougal; Colin said nothing of it. And so she wore trews and a man's shirt, bound about by doubled leather with a dirk thrust through it. No plaid; the day was fine. No confining bonnet either; red hair flagged free in the wind.

Cat nodded grimly. This track, this moor, this hillock with its lone and twisted sceptre atop a stony crown, from where she had cut down the rope that nearly took Dair's life.

She reined in her garron and sat silent a long moment. The tree bore no fruit, neither hemp-hung nor human; the hill bore no Campbells save the memory of footprints now blown away. Her only witness was the garron she rode, and the lone eagle soaring above.

She climbed down then and turned to the panniers fastened to the saddle. She retrieved a small wooden box and a rusted spade, then climbed the nondescript hill to the crown and the sceptre. She dug a hole, gathered stones. Then set the box in the hollow, covered it with soil, and lastly built a cairn.

It was neither kirk nor kirkyard, nor consecrated ground save what lay beneath the sky. But it would do for the bairn that died the week she came home with whisky in her belly as well as Dair's child.

So long she had waited. Una had been shocked and dismayed by Cat's wishes, but she had given in at last. In the light of a quarter moon she and Cat had dug a temporary grave near the house for the poor wee bairn, locked away in a wooden box, and dug it up again now that summer had come, now that Cat was able to say a proper farewell.

Kneeling, she placed the last of the stones atop the crude cairn. She had nothing of its father. Nothing of its clan. Nothing that had not burned on the night Glenlyon betrayed them.

Ochone.

Cat looked up at the eagle.

So many MacDonalds dead.

—ochone—

—ochone—

And now MacIain's grandchild.

"Ochone," Cat murmured.

Empty. Empty. Empty.

Overhead, the eagle shrieked.

Robbie's face was haunted, the flesh fined down so that his eyes were set in deep hollows and glittered with enmity. Sharp lines incised the shape of his mouth, had set in the flesh of his brow. Bonnetless sandy hair tangled on his neck. He wore kilt, plaid, shirt, but no shoes upon his feet.

Beyond him, down the slope, his garron nickered. Behind him the sky was a blazing, brilliant blue.

"Dead," Dair echoed hoarsely. Not Jean. No. *—not Jean also—*

On the stag-horn hilt, Robbie's fist tightened so that his knuckles shone white. "She meant to slip a bairn. She didna wish to bear it. The old bizzem gave her herbs . . ." Tears shone briefly, as briefly evaporated. "She died of it."

So many MacDonalds dead.

So many MacDonalds: father, mother, kinfolk.

A Campbell lass.

"—and now a Stewart," Dair blurted. "Och, *Christ—*" He wavered against his crutch, propping himself upright with effort. He was weary, so weary and hungry, and empty of the strength required to grieve . . . *and she deserving of it—* As much as anyone.

Stewart stared at him mutely, blue eyes black in the pallor of the cave.

Dair drew in a rasping breath. "I didna ken—I didna ken, I swear . . . och, *Robbie—*"

Briefly, Stewart bared his teeth. " 'Twasn't yours," he said flatly. "D'ye take credit for another man's labor?"

Shocked into stillness, Dair stared at him mutely.

" 'Twasn't yours," Stewart repeated. "But she went wi' the bastard because you deserted her."

"—my fault—?" He could not shirk more grief. He owed Robbie that much. And Jean. —*och, Jean*— "My fault. Aye."

Abruptly Stewart's rage deflated. His face knotted. "Oh *Christ*—" Robbie hurled down the dirk. "—Christ, I canna do it . . ." He swung then, plaid billowing, and stalked to the lip of the cave, where he stood with hands on hips and stared out into the daylight. His spine was inflexible, like a flintlock's ramrod. "She was all I had, was Jean. And twin-born!"

Dair said nothing.

"All," Robbie repeated, voice muffled. "My father naught but an invalid, laird in name—and Jean, only Jean . . ." When he swung back his face was wet. "I ken what she was. Me, in female flesh; aye, well, so she was. I let her be, because I kent what it was to be so." He scowled fiercely, painfully. "You are a man others love. I am one they fear."

Dair offered nothing. It was Robbie's confession.

"I swore to kill you, MacDonald. As she breathed her last." Stewart's smile was a rictus. "But how d'ye kill a dead man? Holy Jesus, I didna ken 'twas *you* till I saw your eyes . . . have you looked at yourself, all bearded and befilthed?"

Dair stared fixedly at the spurned dirk, unable to look away. "I havena," he said absently. "I have no mirror, aye?—and the burnwater I drink." Now at last he could look again at Robbie. He swallowed tightly. His body, having done all it could, wanted to give out. "Have you a wee bit of food?"

Stewart opened his mouth. Shut it.

Chastened, Dair gestured awkwardly. "I shouldna ask it, aye? Not of you. Not after—Jean."

"My garron," Stewart said harshly. "Would you have me butcher him for you?"

A weak laugh gusted out. "Och, no, Robbie—"

"Christ—I *should* . . ." Stewart examined him intently. The skull beneath thin flesh was more pronounced than ever. Softly he said, "I canna do it, Jean. He has suffered enough for Glencoe."

Dair blinked dazedly, clinging to his crutch.

Stewart's enmity abruptly spilled away, replaced by weariness and resignation. "John said you would come. He and the others went on. He asked me to come daily to see if you were here, so I might tell you what has become of them, and what will become of you." Blue eyes did not waver. "The king has pardoned MacDonalds. You may go home again."

"—home?" It was incomprehensible. Dair clutched at the crutch to keep from falling. "To Glencoe—?"

"Home," Robbie repeated. "John and the others have gone on to Fort William so he may wish well of Governor Hill. He has given his oath to Ardkinglas in Inveraray."

Dair's lips were cold and stiff. "My father gave his oath to Ardkinglas at Inveraray. They killed him anyway."

"Not now. No more. They'll no' do such again." Robbie's thin smile was fixed. "They have learned their lesson of it."

"*They* have learned their lesson!" Fury dulled and diminished by deprivation abruptly kindled and took fire. Dair, balancing precariously upon two trembling legs, flung the crutch against the cave wall. "What lesson have they learned save how to butcher a clan under a sacred trust? What lesson have they learned save how to kill a laird, how to kill his wife, how to hack to pieces the women and the bairns?"

Transfixed, Stewart gaped at him.

Dair sucked in a noisy breath. "*What have they learned,* Robbie, that absolves them of such things? That starving men canna fight? That people with no homes live as animals? That a woman stripped of clothing will freeze to death in a blizzard? That a woman is shot down even though she be a Campbell?" His throat was scraped raw. He did not care if it bled. "What lesson have they learned from which they take the right to pardon *innocent* people?"

Tears painted Robbie's face. He flung back his head and howled like a Gael of old, his grief and anger so loud it rang in the cave and echoed, hands knotted into fists thrust into the air.

And then he stopped the noise as abruptly as he began it and stared fiercely at Dair, new tears glittering in his eyes. "I meant to kill you. For Jean. I meant not to tell you. For *me*. So I kent you would suffer." He had bitten his lip. Blood welled in the wound. "But you have suffered enough."

Dair gazed at him blankly, exhausted by his outburst.

Bitterly, Stewart spat blood and saliva. "She isna dead, MacDonald. Glenlyon's daughter lives."

Now at last he fell. He permitted himself to fall.

"—*Christ*—"Robbie caught him, eased him to the floor. His arm was strong across Dair's shoulders, propping up his head. "Aye, well . . ." Comprehension and acknowledgment warred with loyalty to his sister. "I might wish such love for myself, one day, though it seems unlikely; I am what I have always been. But I'll no' deny it to you, even for Jean's sake." He pressed Dair's shoulder briefly. "Wait you," he said gruffly, "I'll fetch the garron here."

In great heaving gulps Dair began to breathe, to laugh, to cry. Weakness no longer mattered. Even hunger he could bear.

Glenlyon's daughter lived.

Lured by summer sunlight, Cat sat collapsed upon the wide wooden bench set against her father's house and gazed out across the dooryard. In deference to the day she had cast off shoes, rolled up trews and cuffs, and folded her legs crosswise upon the bench, slumped against the wall in a posture favored in childhood but rarely indulged when Una was present to see it.

Just now it did not matter; she was grown withal—and Una was after all too busy baking bread.

The view of the dooryard and what lay beyond—winding track, familiar hill, scant stands of fir and pine—was wholly unchanged, as was grief, the abiding loneliness. For a moment, a moment only, in the sun, she had found surcease; now it bounded back and snared her, squeezing her heart again.

—*so many rumors . . .* so much gossip traded freely, gleefully, embellished by avid mouths telling tales of the massacre and of MacDonalds escaping, including MacIain's sons.

But no one knew the truth, and no one knew to tell *her:* she was Glenlyon's daughter.

She would, she thought, go up herself to Fort William and confront the governor, who ought to know what had become of the MacDonalds.

But what if he tells me Dair is dead?

Cat shut her eyes, conjuring the memory of Dair leaving her to go to Inverrigan's in the midst of the blizzard, because he was not easy in his mind regarding the soldiers' presence. A brief kiss, a murmured promise he would be back . . . and no more did she see him again.

If he tells me Dair is dead—

The muffled snort of a garron roused her, distracting her from pain. She opened her eyes, blinked away tears, and saw the rider approaching.

She unfolded her legs and sat up straight; visitors were uncommon, and she had been bred up on Highland hospitality. It was her father who had forgotten.

From distance she marked him: an old man, thin of frame, gaunt of features, entirely white of hair. Unhindered by bonnet, tousled by wind, it flowed back from his face like spring snowmelt, though someone had crudely cut it across the back of his neck.

He turned into the dooryard. At the well he halted the horse, which stretched its neck and pulled rein in pursuit of water. The rider climbed down slowly, carefully, as an old man does; loosed the rein, drew up the bucket, let the garron drink.

At last he turned to her, paused, then began to walk across the dooryard.

Barefoot, he limped.

Thin, gaunt, white-haired. But Cat knew the eyes. Cat knew the smile.

—*bonnie, bonnie prince*—

In one taut thrust she was up from the bench.

—*Dair—oh Dair*—

Barefoot, she ran.

"—Dair—oh, Dair—"

Thin, gaunt, white-haired. Less than he had been. More than she expected.

"—*alive*—" she blurted.

"Och, aye, forbye . . ." He caught her. He held her. He crushed her against him.

No words, there were no words; no words existed in her world, in his, only the language of their feelings, and that too great, too intensely full for anything beyond the sound of their ragged breathing, the desperate clinging of their bodies.

Comprehension. Acknowledgment. Reaffirmation.

—*alive*—

Alive.

He went down, was down, and so was she, with him, down in the dirt, the turf; and he laughed even as she cried, and cried as she laughed, sharing without words what lived in their hearts and bodies, all the pent, unspent emotions. All the knowledge, all the memories, the bleak weeks of falsehoods told to them as truths: that he was dead, that she was.

Not dead. Neither.

They were tangled like puppies, limbs seeking purchase against earth, against flesh. Nearby, the garron whickered, made uneasy by their ungainly sprawl.

They tended it, that sprawl. Sat up again, but let go of no comfortable portion, nor of any part they might reach, so long as it be flesh, alive, and whole.

He was not so old after all, only aged beyond what he had been. But there was time, so much time before them to finish what they had begun, all unaware, on a dew-damp day before her father's house.

Cat leaned in, wound arms into plaid, into hollows; felt the bones beneath his flesh, the knotting of wiry tendons made pronounced by privation. But her Dair withal.

Alasdair Og MacDonald.

Whom her father had meant to murder.

She held him fiercely, setting her face into his neck. His warm, rope-scored neck.

So much done to this man.

She told him then, in words she forgot the moment she said them, of scouring guilt, of exquisite shame, of sorrow and anger and hatred. It was important that he know, important that she *said* it: how it was to house a heart burdened by so much shame, so much bitter pain. She was Glenlyon's daughter.

And that she could not blame MacDonalds if MacDonalds blamed her.

"*Why?*" he asked then, the only word of his set into the flow of her own.

And so she told him: had she not been present, had her father not used her name, there might have been no hosting, no hospitality offered. And all would yet survive.

He was not so weak that he could not threaten her breath with the force of his embrace. "No man will say so! No man alive will say so, be he MacDonald or no."

"But—"

"*No* man, Cat. I swear on my father's soul."

The great, turbulent soul housed in so huge a body that it even turned back a river when he planted himself in its current.

And now the bones of it lie on Eilean Munde.

Tears sprang into her eyes. So many words to say, so many things to confess, but something took precedence. "Ten years," she told him.

It deepened lines between his brows that had not existed before. "Ten years?"

Easier now to admit what should have been said before. "Ten years I have known you. Ten years I have loved you."

He laughed very softly. Set his head against hers. Into her hair he said, "Come home with me."

Fingers trembled as she reached up to touch his hair. All white, so white, white as MacIain's, save for a glint of gray snooving there beside his temple.

He caught her hand and carried it to his mouth, where he kissed her palm as he had kissed it once before beside a MacDonald fire in the looming ruins of Achallader, below the Grave of a Stranger.

"Och, Christ—*Dair*—"

Against her hand he laughed. But there was more in his eyes, so much more than laughter: memory, and tears. "Come home with me," he said. "Come home with me. To Glencoe."

Through her own burden of tears, Cat laughed aloud. All it wanted was a piper and the keening of *ceol mor.*

In her head she made her own: —*with white teeth a'gleaming*—
And silver in his hair.

Edinburgh

Summer

1695

S ummer, and warm, but it was not the temperature that set a sheen of sweat over John Hill's face. Before the doors of Holyrood Palace he paused to account for his appearance in the moments before he would be called to account for his actions three years preceeding.

He was as yet a colonel, as yet a governor, as yet commissioned, and wore the scarlet-and-gold uniform of his duty. He shot the cuffs of his linen shirt beneath the crimson coat, resettled the polished gorget at his throat, and nodded to the man who swung open the door of the massive palace.

Thus admitted, thus committed, Hill entered the hall. He knew what lay before him: Inquiry. King William had at long last, worn down by suspicion and questions, sanctioned an Inquiry to determine who bore the guilt for Glencoe.

I do. He accepted it. He would admit it now before the others, the Commissioners assembled to question, to weigh the answers. Titled all, powerful men, men of politics. He was but a simple man, and Englishman— —*Sassenach!*— —who loved his God and served his king . . . whoever that king might be, English or Dutch. John Hill had no power. No politics.

But John Hill had himself, as much as anyone, ruined Glencoe.

Holyrood Palace was as dark within and without, illuminated by lamplight. Beyond the antechamber lay the hall proper, where the Commissioners waited. Built against the walls, beneath ornate hammer beams, were the crowded benches.

So many gathered to hear the tragedy of Glencoe— A sound behind him, a sudden shaft of light. It fell across the antechamber, lanced through into the hall beyond.

Hill turned, blinded momentarily by the summer sunlight. He squinted, absently aware his eyesight worsened; but then he set aside such things. Others had come in, called as he was to bear witness to what had been done at five o'clock of the morning in the midst of a blinding blizzard.

Two men. Two Highlanders. Two MacDonalds.

Two tall Glencoe-men: the man who was now MacIain and his younger brother.

Not the old fox. The old fox was buried three years on Eilean Munde.

Hill drew in a breath. *Here is Scotland standing before me.* . . .

—all swathed in creamy saffron-dyed linen shirts; brooch-pinned, looping, many-hued plaids and kilts; fine-knit tartan stockings and silver-buckled brogues; *sgian dhu,* sporrans, dirks; with feather- and heather-sprigged bonnets worn slantwise on proud heads.

Both bared a moment later as, one by one, the MacDonalds removed the bonnets to clasp them in callused hands.

—*such white, white heads for men yet so young*—

The door opened again. Sunlight sparked off the silver of brooches and buckles. A woman came in behind them even as they moved apart to make room for her; one put out his hand.

Hill had met Alasdair Og. By him he knew the woman.

Her eyes were very clear, piercing as a claymore. Lamplight burnished hair. She was taller than he; nearly as tall as her husband. She examined Hill, assessed him, measured him as a man. The dim light of Holyrood Palace was gentle on her face, but the strong bones stood out as if she were carved of stone.

He drew breath and moved a single pace. He bowed before her. "Colonel John Hill," he said quietly. "Governor of Fort William."

Her tone was cool. "Have they called you to give evidence against my father?"

He did not know how to answer. She was Glenlyon's daughter, but married to a MacDonald. Such personal complexities were beyond him, and so at last he spoke the truth. "If they should ask me so, I will. But I shall give equal evidence against myself."

She laughed briefly and without mirth. "Och, I dinna care about that, aye?—I have come to hear them declare the truth of *him:* he is a murderer."

Sweat sprang out on his flesh again. Hill did what he could to mitigate the moment. "He did nothing of his own will but what he was ordered to do."

"Ordered," she echoed. "Ordered to murder MacDonalds. Oh, I ken what he was told to do. I ken how he did it. I ken *what* he did." She looked at her husband. Something passed between them, something powerful if unspoken, and then she looked back at Hill. Softly she said, "I was there, aye?"

Lamplight glittered on plaid brooch and bonnet crest as John MacDonald shifted. "For what you have done, we thank you," he said quietly. "You more than any man have done what could be done."

Absolution was painful. He could not permit it. "No," Hill said harshly, "I have done nothing. Nothing but ruin Glencoe."

"Aye, well," MacIain exchanged a glance with his brother. "We are rebuilding the houses."

"And the families?" Hill demanded. "How do you rebuild human life that has been taken?"

"You canna." Alasdair Og's voice was uninflected. "You begin anew with what is left."

"We are home," MacIain said. "We are yet in Scotland, yet in the Highlands, yet in Glencoe. We have begun anew."

Hill heard a step behind him and a diffident voice. "Colonel Hill, sir. You are called before the Commissioners."

He nodded absently but did not turn away from the Highlanders. *Not yet*— "—Begin anew," he said with clear self-contempt. "A man may hope so. Indeed, a man may. But neither does he forget."

"He doesna," MacIain agreed, forgiving nothing. "And so long as there are pipes, and bards, and poets, no man may ever forget what happened to Glencoe."

Glenlyon's daughter smiled, and this time it was unfettered. *"Ne obliviscaris."*

From beside him, less diffidence now: "Colonel Hill. *Sir.*"

He turned then and left them. He cared little enough what became of himself, called to Inquiry. He cared very much what became of them.

" 'Forget not,' " Hill murmured.

He did not see how he could.

Author's Note

$\mathcal{M}$ ost of the historical events portrayed in *Lady of the Glen*, particularly the tragic massacre itself, are documented, as are the portions of letters quoted within the text. With the exception of Cat Campbell and Jean Stewart, all of the primary people in this novel actually lived. Dair, known to history as Alasdair Og (Alexander the Younger) MacDonald, did indeed marry a Campbell of Glen Lyon, though her name was Sarah, and she was Glenlyon's *niece*, not his daughter.

The Massacre of Glencoe itself is an obscure if bloody footnote in British history, but it did succeed in forcing the Glencoe Mac-Donalds—those who survived—into obedience to William and Mary, as well as persuading such holdouts as Ewan Cameron of Lochiel, Coll MacDonald of Keppoch, and young Robert Stewart of Appin to swear the oath.

In August of 1692, six months after the slaughter, John Mac-Donald—now the MacIain—brought the survivors down out of the mountains to take an oath of allegiance to the joint sovereigns. His stubborn younger brother, Alasdair Og, held out until October.

The growing public outcry against the slaughter, though noisy, was not enough initially to force an official Inquiry into the massacre until considerable time had passed. It wasn't until June of 1695, three and one-half years after the massacre, that the Inquiry was held in Edinburgh and a full report sent to King William who, in the tradition of politicians and monarchs throughout the centuries, conveniently chose to overlook his own part in the proceedings and blamed the now-unpopular massacre on others, though he exonerated Sir John Dalrymple, Master of Stair and Secretary of Scotland; and Grey John Campbell, Earl of Breadalbane.

For some time the MacDonalds honored their oath to William and Mary. But Highlanders are Highlanders, most of them dedicated to the Jacobite cause. In the Rebellion of 1715, Alasdair Og MacDonald took a hundred swordsmen with him into battle. Thirty years later, at Culloden, John MacDonald's son led the clan into battle in the name of Prince Charles Edward Stuart.

And so in 1746 the days of the clans, the pipes, the Gaelic—as well as kilts and plaids—ended. The MacDonalds, like thousands of other

Highlanders, eventually were chased out of their glen by the Clearances and enclosure system, and the livestock that replaced their beloved cattle: sheep.

Twenty years ago, in a British History class taught at Northern Arizona University, my professor lectured about Scottish history prior to Culloden, speaking briefly of an "insignificant" little incident between Campbells and MacDonalds in 1692, a killing ordered by King William himself. It had become known as the Massacre of Glencoe, he said, and laid the foundation for a Highland hostility that exists to this day.

I believed then it would make a terrific tale, so much remarkable history commingled with the fascination of the Highlands as well as the romance of two individuals, but until I began researching the facts of the Massacre ten years ago I had no idea how much story there was to tell, nor how dramatic.

I am greatly indebted to reference works too numerous to list, but most particularly to the Penguin edition of John Prebble's outstanding and invaluable reference work *Glencoe*, a detailed, incisive, yet highly readable and evocative recounting of the events leading to the massacre, the slaughter itself, and the aftermath. If readers are interested in learning more about this debacle, I strongly urge them to seek out this fascinating book.

As both reader and writer of historical fiction, I'm very much interested in maintaining accuracy whenever possible; however, I occasionally relied on personal suppositions and interpretations, and, where necessary, significantly compressed the time frame and chronology of events to improve the story's pacing.

In March of 1985 I visited Glencoe. The valley itself is as I've described: surrounded on three sides by rugged, fall-broken mountains nearly always capped in clouds, skirted on the fourth by cold, deep Loch Linnhe, divided by the River Coe. Signal Rock, from which legend says a beacon fire was lighted to begin the massacre, stands in midglen. Sheep and cattle run free on the braes and tourists hike the mountains. But there is memory present as well, and a knowledge of tragedy.

In Glencoe today there stands a stone Celtic cross monument to the fallen MacDonalds. It is inscribed as follows:

This cross
is reverently erected
in memory of
McIan, chief of the MacDonalds
of Glencoe

*Who fell with his people
in the Massacre of Glencoe
of 13 February 1692
by his direct descendant
Ellen Burks MacDonald of Glencoe
August 1823*
THEIR MEMORY LIVETH FOREVER MORE

—*J.R.*
Chandler, AZ
1995
J. Roberson@genie.geis.com

Extermination Order

For His Majesty's Service,
To CAPTAIN ROBERT CAMPBELL OF GLENLYON

Sir,

You are hereby ordered to fall upon the rebels, the MacDonalds, of Glencoe, and put all to the sword under seventy. You are to have special care that the old fox and his sons do on no account escape your hands. You are to put in execution at five o'clock in the morning precisely, and by that time, or very shortly after it, I'll strive to be at you with a stronger party. If I do not come to you at five, you are not to tarry for me, but to fall on. This is by the king's special command, for the good and safety of the country, that these miscreants be cut off root and branch. See that this be put in execution without feud or favour, else you may expect to be treated as not true to the king's government, nor a man fit to carry a commission in the king's service. Expecting you will not fail in the fulfilling hereof as you love yourself, I subscribe these with my hand at Ballachulish Feb 12, 1692.

Robert Duncanson

Political Aftermath

The Principals:

GREY JOHN CAMPBELL, *Earl of Breadalbane*
In June of 1695, following the Inquiry, the aging earl was arrested on the charge of treason for drawing up Private Articles in agreement with the Highland chieftains at Achallader in which he promised terms he could neither offer nor authorize. Imprisoned in Edinburgh Castle until October, then released on the king's authority, he retired to Loch Tay and lived quietly, though he sympathized with the Jacobite Rising of 1715 and was nearly arrested for it despite careful maneuverings so as not to be implicated. He pleaded old age and was left alone instead, dying later in the year at the age of eighty-one.

As the Earl of Breadalbane's father detested him, so did Breadalbane detest his heir, Duncan. After Duncan eloped with Marjorie Campbell of Lawers, the earl petitioned the king to grant him the right to nominate another son as heir.

Two hundred years later descendants of Duncan and Marjorie came forward to lay claim to the disputed titles.

SIR JOHN DALRYMPLE, *Master of Stair; Secretary of Scotland*
Throughout his political life, Stair made powerful enemies. Thus it became a simple matter for these enemies to lobby for the Commissioners to pin the genesis of the now-unpopular massacre on him. But Stair, having succeeded to his late father's viscountcy, deprived his enemies of satisfaction by retiring from public life.

King William did not call for any action; in fact, he exonerated Stair by claiming that in London, so far from the Highlands, he could not have known anything of the barbarous method of execution. But William died, as did Mary, and Mary's sister Anne became queen.

In Queen Anne's reign Stair was welcomed back into public affairs, where he remained until his death in 1707.

CAPTAIN ROBERT CAMPBELL, *Laird of Glen Lyon*
In 1695, three years after the massacre, Glenlyon died a pauper in Bruges following a long illness and was later buried in an unknown grave. After departing the Highlands to fight with William in Flanders,

he never again saw Scotland. He left behind piles of debts, few possessions, and no means to pay; even his eldest son, now Laird of Glenlyon, was forced to ask his kinsman Breadalbane for money to continue. It was granted, and the children of the 'drukken man' began a long attempt to restore their name.

This task proved nearly impossible. A story is told that Glenlyon's grandson, called the Black Colonel, was ordered to carry out the execution of deserters, except that at the last moment he was to give them reprieve. As planned, the colonel pulled the reprieve from his pocket—but in so doing he dropped his handkerchief. The firing squad, responding to the customary signal, executed the men. The Campbell of Glen Lyon, seeing this, cried out it was the Curse of Glencoe.

He later resigned his commission. Unmarried, the Laird and his two childless brothers were the last of the direct line of Glenlyon Campbells.

COLONEL JOHN HILL, *Governor of Fort William*

Long a champion of the Highlanders and of Glencoe MacDonalds in particular, Colonel Hill was absolved of guilt by the Commissioners, who found that he had delayed acting on orders to kill the MacDonalds until left with no choice when identical orders were sent to his deputy governor, Lieutenant Colonel John Hamilton. Hill gave evidence against others, including Glenlyon, at the Inquiry and later returned to his duties at Fort William, where he did his best to speak on behalf of the surviving MacDonalds and other Lochaber men who were nearly broken by harsh taxes.

Governor Hill was eventually given a knighthood, but in 1698 his regiment was disbanded. He was discharged from the army at half pay, and died later in England.

ROBERT STEWART, *Heir to Appin*

Although when carried by stretcher to Fort William to swear he would take the oath, young Robert Stewart made no haste to do so. For several years after the massacre he proved an irritant to Governor Hill and his soldiers. Eventually Stewart was called to Edinburgh to explain his behavior; on the way he insulted one of Hill's captains, and in Edinburgh got into a fight with two of the city's officers. He was thrown into the Tolbooth until he swore the oath and agreed to apologize to Hill and his captain.

KING WILLIAM (III), *Formerly Prince of Orange*

William was much annoyed by the aftermath of the massacre. His war in Flanders was going badly, and his primary advisors on the Scottish problem, Stair and Breadalbane, were under fire for their part in the massacre. Highly insulted by a Parliament that demanded specific royal action, William ignored continuing requests for an Inquiry and refused to accept any written reports.

It wasn't until questions became so imperative that the king at last addressed them. William professed himself to be ignorant of the slaughter until eighteen months after it had occurred and claimed he was filled with horror by it. He pardoned all those involved save the soldiers and officers quartered on Glencoe. His wife, Queen Mary, had been so horrified she felt all those involved should be hanged, but Mary was dead.

William did nothing. He died of asthma complications in 1702.

KING JAMES (II), *Self-exiled King of England residing in France*
Despite the support of the Jacobites, James lived out the remainder of his life in France, wholly oblivious to the political repercussions of his reign and exile. He had outlived his childless brother Charles II, from whom he inherited, and his sisters, Mary and Anne, who became queens because he could not be king. His son James Francis Edward grew up in exile and was denied the throne of England; there was also a persistent rumor that this child was not James's son at all, but a serv- ingwoman's newborn smuggled into the queen's bedchamber in a warming pan.

James II died in 1701; his son, called the Old Pretender and referred to in toasts as the "king over the water," was proclaimed in Scotland as James III and briefly served as figurehead to the unsuccessful Jacobite Rebellion of 1715.

The Old Pretender sired Charles Edward Stuart, referred to as the Young Pretender, and it was this "bonnie prince" who, at the behest of Jacobites and the French, later sailed to Scotland to claim his inheri- tance.

This infamous attempt at restoring what James II had lost two gener- ations before ended disastrously on the field of Culloden in 1746, when the Highlanders were slaughtered by English troops led by George II's son, the Duke of Cumberland, later known as "Butcher" for his actions against the Scots.

> *An' we'll gang nae mair a'rovin',*
> *A-rovin' in the nicht,*
> *An' we'll gang nae mair a-rovin',*
> *Let the müne shine e'er sae bricht.*